ALL WHEEL DRIVE

Z.A. MAXFIELD

Riptide Publishing
PO Box 1537
Burnsville, NC 28714
www.riptidepublishing.com

This is a work of fiction. Names, characters, places, and incidents are either the product of the author's imagination or are used fictitiously. Any resemblance to actual persons living or dead, business establishments, events, or locales is entirely coincidental. All person(s) depicted on the cover are model(s) used for illustrative purposes only.

All Wheel Drive
Copyright © 2017 by Z.A. Maxfield

Cover art: L.C. Chase, lcchase.com/design.htm
Editor: Sarah Franz
Layout: L.C. Chase, lcchase.com/design.htm

All rights reserved. No part of this book may be reproduced or transmitted in any form or by any means, electronic or mechanical, including photocopying, recording, or by any information storage and retrieval system without the written permission of the publisher, and where permitted by law. Reviewers may quote brief passages in a review. To request permission and all other inquiries, contact Riptide Publishing at the mailing address above, at Riptidepublishing.com, or at marketing@riptidepublishing.com.

ISBN: 978-1-62649-571-5

First edition
July, 2017

Also available in ebook:
ISBN: 978-1-62649-570-8

ALL WHEEL DRIVE

Z.A. MAXFIELD

*For Marlin, always. I never knew we were so lucky until
I did the research for this.
Here's to another thirty-four years.*

Thanks to John Adamus, for all the awesome.

And for Steven Spohn. Game on.

TABLE OF CONTENTS

Chapter 1 1
Chapter 2 5
Chapter 3 9
Chapter 4 15
Chapter 5 25
Chapter 6 33
Chapter 7 35
Chapter 8 43
Chapter 9 51
Chapter 10 59
Chapter 11 67
Chapter 12 75
Chapter 13 85
Chapter 14 93
Chapter 15 101
Chapter 16 107
Chapter 17 117
Chapter 18 127
Chapter 19 135
Chapter 20 145
Chapter 21 153
Chapter 22 161
Chapter 23 169
Chapter 24 173
Chapter 25 179
Chapter 26 185

Chapter 27 193
Chapter 28 201
Chapter 29 205
Chapter 30 207
Chapter 31 211
Chapter 32 217
Chapter 33 225
Chapter 34 235
Chapter 35 239
Chapter 36 243
Chapter 37 251
Chapter 38 257
Chapter 39 267
Chapter 40 275
Chapter 41 283
Epilogue 291

CHAPTER ONE

DIEGO

The man at the door was a mess.

Diego's first look through the peephole showed a sort of monster silhouette—a weirdly shaped humanoid dragging a wheeled duffel bag.

In the porch light's acrid yellow glow, the very shape of him set off a boogeyman, stranger-danger skin-crawl. Ruthlessly, he suppressed any instinct for self-preservation and opened the door wide, but his visitor was just an ordinary man with a mass of healing facial wounds, one arm in a cast, and the haunted look of a recent combat veteran. Diego didn't recognize him, but there was nothing to be scared of. Whatever had happened to him was potentially frightening, but he was only a guy.

"Can I help you?"

"I hope so. I called about the room over the garage?"

"And I told you when you called: I'm not renting it out. I need it for storage. How did you even know—"

"I'm still hoping you'll change your mind. I grew up around here. I remember the family that used to live here, and I feel like—" The man stopped. Gathered himself. "I need a room for a little while, and if you're only using it for storage . . ."

Sorrow limned what few features Diego could guess at behind the bandages, healing abrasions, and the shiny pink newness of burns. Dude had shaved his hair on the sides but the top was long, the result being a man-bun swirl of wavy brown hair that looked greasy. How was this guy even keeping himself clean? Despair, and something infinitely worse hung around him like a toxic cloud. Hopelessness.

Diego recognized the man's helpless anxiety and anguish all too well.

"What's your name?" he asked.

"John Smith."

Irritated, Diego eyed him sourly. "I take it you ain't filling out a rental application?"

"Sure. I'll fill one out." It was hard to watch a smile crack those dry, scabbed lips, but it was a nice smile. A friendly smile. Dude wasn't using it very often, obviously. "I'm thinking of taking up fiction writing as a career anyway."

"You make it so hard to say no."

Diego started to close the door, but that soft cast shot out, and Diego didn't have it in him right then to add injury to . . . injury.

"You want to try and convince me some more?" Diego asked sarcastically. "You want to add you're also a known terrorist carrying small pox?"

"Two thousand cash a month. Six months tops. It's a room with a toilet, a sink, and a shower, right?"

"How do you know that? How'd you even get my number?"

Dude's eyes widened. Then narrowed. "Never mind how I know. My Uber driver left me, and I'll have to walk all the way to the nearest motel. Where is that, anyway?"

"Three thousand," Diego countered, "and you move whatever shit's up there down to the garage."

"Done." The dude frowned. "Wait. What's up there?"

Diego shrugged. "Stuff from my mother's place, probably. I told the company that moved me to put whatever wasn't marked for immediate use up there. And since I can't exactly fly up there to take a look around"—he thumped the wheels of his chair—"I don't give a shit. Haven't missed a thing, so whatever's up there can't be too important. You move it, hand me thirty Benjamins, and we're good."

"Yeah?"

Was that relief on his face? Diego didn't smile back. "Trial basis. For a month."

"Fine."

"Too much drinking, drugging, loud sex? Not fine. Loud parties? Not fine. No one better bother me, leave trash around, or even look at me askance. No redneck music. In fact, give me your number." He took out his phone, opened the contacts, and let his new tenant type it in. "I control all of the music around here, or you can leave right now. I can't walk up those stairs but I *can* light the place on fire from below and rebuild. If you piss me off, I'll shoot you and tell the police you frightened my permanently-seated ass, and we'll see who they blame."

"Askance? Is that a thing now?"

Oh, there it was again. That elusive spark of humor. "It's always been a thing."

"I'll be sure not to do it."

"All right, then. I'll get you a key."

"No need." Dude reached gingerly into the pocket of his leather jacket. He pulled out a fat wad of cash and a Costco card. "That lock's always been a piece of shit."

Diego took the cash, counted it out. "This is only two grand."

"I'll get you the rest tomorrow. I'm good for it."

Diego nodded, wheeled backward, and gave the door a shove to shut it. It banged in the dude's face, but that was partly the wind. Dude couldn't blame him for the wind, could he?

So. Now he had a tenant for a bit.

He could have said no.

He could have said *hell* no.

As soon as the dude got a look at his room, he'd probably come back down. If he caused any trouble, Diego could give back the money and boot his ass. If *John Smith* gave him any attitude, Diego could call the cops. But that would be a lot of bother to go through, when spending the night in a dank-ass garage apartment with no bed, no food, and a single hanging overhead lightbulb was punishment enough.

A quick look at the time told Diego he'd better call it a night. While he went through the motions getting ready for bed, the part of his brain that remembered the haunted look in his new tenant's eyes—the part of him that recognized and responded to and acknowledged the unfairness of things and the failure of good people to alleviate human suffering in the long run—listened with half an ear for the sound of boxes being shuffled around.

The man couldn't move things in his condition. He'd have to ask for help, at which point Diego planned to drive him to the nearest bed-and-waffle-buffet motel. Such a thing would probably cost less than the three grand he'd promised Diego anyway, and sure as fuck nobody'd be feeding him here.

Diego definitely did *not* think about dust or spiders or other critters. He was not imagining a room he'd never even been in but could visualize from realtor's photos—wood-paneled walls and vinyl flooring in sickly, faded shades of brown and orange and yellow. But he'd never wanted a tenant. He hadn't sent anyone but the movers up there after he'd come to Bluewater Bay. Hadn't cleaned the place. Hadn't advertised it.

It was almost a public service letting the dude get his fill of it. Returning home after a traumatic event might seem like a good thing to a guy like that. There was a lot to be said for nostalgia. But an old childhood hangout wasn't the place for someone so physically banged-up, and he'd soon realize it.

What he needed was his family. Friends. Tribe. What he was looking for was safety. Diego could tell him that safety was an illusion, but it looked like he'd already gotten the news.

Even as he grew sleepy, Diego kept an ear tuned for unusual noises.

John Smith'd be back if he couldn't get the door open. He'd knock if sleeping on the floor beat to hell like that was as fucked up as it sounded.

Diego drifted off to sleep wishing he was the type of guy to treat a man's pride like it wasn't as important as his body.

CHAPTER TWO
HEALEY

*H*ome.
Not home.

Images of playing in the front yard, of water balloons and grilling burgers and infinitely happier times, scrolled through Healey's exhaustion like a thick fog. He climbed the stairs too slowly, dragging his duffel up each step with a bang. His body felt leaden. Gravity was deliberately fucking with him. Even his heart felt hollow.

Nash isn't here, he reminded himself.

No one is here.

What you're looking for doesn't exist anymore.

Maybe it never did.

Still, he turned the key in the lock. *His* key turned silently, the same key he'd used since they'd had the official apartment dedication before he left for school. When the wooden door opened, it connected with a box, sending cardboard scudding over dusty floors.

Thud.

Scrape.

Healey flicked on the single overhead light. Closing the door behind him, he shivered. He got out his pen knife and pried away the baseboard where Nash's bed used to be.

Nash's secret stash contained an unopened fifth of Jack and a picture of the two of them, standing in front of their bikes. On the back it said, *When you're riding lead, don't spit.*

Good man. It was just like Nash to leave a present for the next guy.

"Bubba." He toasted his brother because it was only proper while he surveyed Nash's old bachelor pad.

The liquid burned his chapped lips and scorched his throat going down. He wiped his mouth with the back of his hand before capping it, then turned to look at the rest of the place. Except for the Jack, Nash was no longer here. Healey didn't know what he thought he'd find. A scent maybe. Or a feeling that spoke of being home. Of being in the last place of intersection between himself and his identical twin.

Until high school, he and Nash had always wanted the same things. Their lives, their hobbies intertwined. But Nash was physically restless, and Healey excelled in school. Nash got a garage apartment and an export auto repair shop, and Healey got a full ride to Stanford.

As far as Healey knew, neither of them regretted their choices. Except now, when Healey regretted everything.

But... regret.

Regret was as worthless as wishes. And all the prayers Healey tried went unanswered.

Seeing the new owner explained why the house sold as fast as it did. Diego Luz needed the ramps and wider doorways and lower counters they'd installed for Shelby.

But Shelby was in Spain and no part of the house belonged to them anymore.

New owner though. He was hot. And not just because he was fit. His muscle shirt wasn't too douche-y; neither were his faded, soft-as-fuck-looking denim jeans. Black Vans. His arms were ripped. New owner was very fine, and he probably knew it, not that it mattered.

A brief stab of guilt, followed by sadness, rocked him. He missed Ford—his best friend. His first serious lover.

He glanced at his messages to torture himself some more.

Email message from Ford. Subject line: *Urgent legal matters*

Heals,

We had some good times, right? I loved you. I really did. But you know it can't work with someone like me. You know that.

You're going to be named in the lawsuit. The dudes from the accident will name everyone as co-defendants: the school, my doctors, you, my parents, and everyone in my fucking life.

Our lawyers say that's normal and you shouldn't worry. My dad has offered to hire a lawyer for you, but I think you should find your own attorney as soon as possible. My dad's lawyers will throw you under the bus if they can. It's not personal with them. It's never personal.

I set this in motion and I cannot stop it. Do whatever you have to do. Sorry.

You don't know how sorry.

Ford

He and Ford'd had some good times. And so very, very many bad ones.

Most of which, if he were honest, had been entirely Ford's fault.

In freshman year, when they'd met, Ford had seemed perfect. Work hard. Play harder. Nothing was off the table when it came to having fun, as long as they advanced to the next level at school. His occasional bouts of moodiness seemed related to the amount they drank—Healey was his number one partner in crime.

After a few months of this, they decided they weren't doing themselves any favors, so Ford agreed to cut back. But as days, weeks, a whole quarter passed where Ford could barely get out of bed, Healey got worried. Ford's family grew alarmed during the holidays, because his behavior at home had changed so drastically, and then Healey'd gotten the awful call: A suicide attempt. A hospitalization. Trial and error with medications. Fine tuning.

After that, Ford's friends jumped on his "team." Healey answered to Ford's doctors, his family. He'd carried Ford's banner through senior year, been part of Ford's day-to-day support system ever since. He'd laughed with Ford. Cried with him. Held him through nights when Ford had given up hope.

They'd stumbled past the finish line together—Healey graduating with a PhD, Ford with an MBA. Along the way, Healey'd gotten so caught up in being part of the two of them, he'd lost his sense of self.

He'd lost his instinct for *survival*.

Healey and Ford's last great adventure—a quick road trip to Vegas to blow off steam after graduation—had almost cost them their lives.

He shouldn't be here.

He should be in school where he thrived.

Back in time.

Back to the beginning.

So much had happened that his brain—the one thing he could normally rely on when life hurt—couldn't even process it.

The room was a tangle of boxes and photographic equipment. What looked like wrapped canvases. He peeked, because he couldn't help himself. Colorful, abstract wooden sculptures, shrouded in old, paint-stained printed sheets, leaned against the wall like sarcophagi. It was an interesting mix of things.

Kinda creepy.

After managing to foot-push a few boxes of junk out of the way, Nash laid his duffel bag down like a pillow and fell into an exhausted, slightly loopy slumber.

CHAPTER THREE

HEALEY

The scrape of the old aluminum slider—the door from the kitchen to the patio out back—woke Healey. How weird. He could still identify the origin of every sound in the old house.

He listened, rising quietly, straining to see out the window. Low cloud cover obscured the stars and moon, made haloes of the streetlights. There was the sound of wheels on the wooden ramp from the patio to the garden, and then the grinding gears of an automatic garage door opening in the space beneath. A car started up.

What time was it?

Still fully dressed, Healey had to tease his phone out of his pants pocket to look at it.

Who the hell gets up at 3 a.m.?

Healey let his head fall back against his duffel and tried to close his eyes, but it was no use. Unless he was willing to have another sip or two off his old friend Jack, he wasn't going back to sleep. Stacks of boxes loomed over him like a miniature skyline. He could have gone anywhere. Yet here he was, contemplating cleaning out someone else's garage apartment.

And for what? Nash wasn't here. None of them were. He could feel sorry for himself just as easily in a five-star hotel. This was not his best idea ever.

He stood, shoulders and legs painfully stiff. Arm throbbing. Face itching and sore. *Ow.* Coffee would help. And there were people he could call in town without it getting back to his pop.

Oh, man. Pop.

After a decade of loneliness, Pop had found a second loving relationship. Healey was dodging the happy couple, just as he'd dodged Nash and Spencer and Shelby. Everyone he loved was happy for the first time in—maybe ever. They finally had what they deserved, and Healey wasn't about to let what happened to him destroy that.

He didn't bother trying to clean up. Hadn't thought hygiene through at all. He could use wipes to wash, was able to clean up after using the toilet, and he could manage brushing his teeth, but with an arm in a cast, he wasn't going to smell so good if he didn't come up with a better plan than "flop at Nash's old place."

He picked up a newspaper on the way to the local quick mart, where he bought the largest coffee they had and a bag of snack cakes and donuts. He got energy drinks and enough sugary junk to guarantee a cleaning frenzy and then a crash of epic proportions. He had plenty of Jack left. He could take a nice long nap.

But...

When he got back to the apartment, he prepared his tongue for the chocolatey deliciousness of a red velvet Little Debbie Snack Cake, and all it did was remind him of Ford.

Fearless Ford, who was always up for whatever prank their friends dreamed up.

And Funny Ford, who reduced everyone's stress during finals week by dressing as the Easter Bunny and sitting on a tennis ball machine, blasting rainbow-colored tennis balls out of his ass.

And Freaky Ford, who'd been Healey's first serious boyfriend. The man who'd rocked his world.

But then there was Feckless Ford, who started fights he couldn't hope to win and got his friends' asses pounded when they had to jump in to rescue him.

Frightening Ford, whose moods could swing wildly due to BPD.

And, finally, Nearly Fatal Ford, who almost got both of them killed outright, first in a high-speed car chase, and then a road rage incident.

I almost got killed.

Healey needed time.

Like Pop, he was a gentle person.

A tinkerer by nature, Healey was an engineer, a Rube Goldberg machine innovator, an absentminded ivory tower dweller.

Before the accident, he'd had a light heart and an optimistic future—nothing but possibilities. He'd wanted to get to know strangers. To help people. But now, since his near-death experience, he wondered.

Had he failed to value what he had?

Had benevolent fate turned on him?

He'd been given a glimpse into the abyss, all right, and he'd shrunk from it like the coward he knew himself to be.

So now he killed time.

He killed it and killed it and killed it, waiting with dread for whatever came next. When the hour was decent—and still reeking just a bit of Jack and unwashed sick person—he dialed the other number in Bluewater Bay he still knew by heart.

"Hello?"

That old-lady voice, Boston proper, crisp, concise, fell on him like a woolen blanket.

"Ms. U?"

"It's 6 a.m. Which one of you miscreants thinks the ass crack of dawn is a good time to call? A woman my age could die from the shock of an early-morning phone call."

"Sorry, I—"

"Don't call me until you're an actuary."

Before she could hang up, he said, "Wait, Fearless Leader."

"Healey?" She let out a gasp followed by a half sob.

"Yeah, it's me."

Of course she'd heard all about his brush with notoriety and disaster and morbid celebrity. *Stanford Students in Frightening Freeway Fracas.* He held the phone away from his ear while she wept. Waited until the snappy yanking of tissues from a box could be heard in the background along with a cat.

"I'm sorry." She blew her nose fiercely. "Oh my God. You must think I'm such a ghoul. But I heard your voice and I don't know. I saw footage of the accident on television."

"I'm okay."

"I'm not sure I really believed that until right now."

He glanced around his box-strewn squat. "I'm in Bluewater Bay."

"You are? Where?" For once someone seemed as surprised as he was by the fact.

"I'm renting Nash's garage apartment from the new owner." The tape on the nearest box was yellow. The handwriting faded. *Spring 1980.*

"Aren't you injured? Is anyone staying with you?"

"That's why I'm calling, I guess. There are things I didn't figure on, and I need help."

"You remember my house?"

"Of course." After years of Academic Decathlon and Science Olympiad and Robotics, he knew where to find Ms. Underhill. "I know your house, the lake house, and all your favorite sweet shops. I can find you."

"You come over right now."

He'd figured she'd say that. Well, he'd hoped. In all the years he'd known her, he'd never doubted her love of her students.

"Thanks, Ms. U."

"You have earned the right to call me Clara, Dr. Holly. You're my peer. Academically, you're—"

"Don't call me Dr. Holly."

He hadn't had the title long enough to answer to it. *"Dr. Holly... Are you Healey Holly? Can you hear me? Do you remember what happened? Do you know where you are?"*

He closed his eyes. "Still too weird."

"All right." Her calm acceptance of his anger shamed him.

Now he was snapping at old women. Great. "I'm sorry."

"No need for any apologies between old friends."

Warmth filled him.

"Come on over and let me get a look at you."

"What's left of me." Bitter. Bitter.

She sucked in a breath.

"No. I mean—" He kicked one of Diego Luz's mother's boxes. It rattled like glass, and he cursed. "I feel—"

He didn't know.

"What was that? Glass breaking?" She always worried about silly things.

"Stubbed my toe kicking a box." He peeled a flap back and discovered it was full of camera equipment. Lights. Reflectors. Old stuff. Well-used. "I have to move some things out of Nash's place, but—"

"You're coming over right now. I'll see you when you get here."

"Thanks, Ms. U—"

"Nah, ah, ah." He could practically hear her long bony finger wagging.

"What did I tell you about showing your work?"

"Call me Clara."

"Clara," he relented after a put-upon sigh. "Open windows, I suspect I need a shower."

He hung up.

He'd seen a television show once where a guy cut off his cast because it bugged him. Healey's arm was still in a soft cast. He could just—

"Don't think," he told himself, because even he could see it wasn't going to make anything better. "Just for today, let someone wiser think for you."

And there was no one better for that than Clara Underhill, retired mathematics teacher, Science Olympiad coach, and often-less-than-benevolent dictator. He picked up his keys and phone, and left Nash's place.

Diego drove up in a red Outlander while he was coming down the stairs. Instead of leaving, Healey waited and watched while Diego transferred himself to his wheelchair. He'd watched Shelby do the same a thousand times. She hadn't been old enough to drive when he'd left for college, but she always insisted on doing things for herself. She'd learned to transfer herself into their old Volvo and any other car she rode in by grade school.

Diego caught him watching. "Wanna get out your phone and film it?"

Healey put Diego's harsh tone down to the strain of using his upper body to pull the chair across his lap. Even a titanium sports wheelchair gets heavy.

"I wanted to say hello. Introduce myself in the daylight. I'm . . . um, Healey."

Using a piece of cloth to protect his paint job, Diego let the wheelchair's base slide to the ground and turned to get the wheels. "Fine. Then you're done."

Healey hesitated. "Did I do something especially offensive here?"

"You mean besides not taking no for an answer?"

Healey admitted he wasn't easy to say no to. When you had a stubborn, volatile twin, you learned not to let anyone get in your way.

Maybe that was one of those good news/bad news things.

Healey dug in. "Three grand to squat in a room you aren't even using doesn't sound like it'd exactly be a hardship for you."

"I hear you loud and clear, Mr. My Money Talks And My Bullshit Don't Stink." Diego continued assembling his wheelchair. He said the words like he was Mr. Chill and Healey was some rude redneck he needed to school. "When a guy comes along who thinks they can buy and sell people like me . . . it's always because they'd sell their own mothers for a buck."

"People like you?" Healey gasped. "I'm not—"

"You want to rent my place? I tell you no. You give me a fake name like we're doing some gangster shit. You figure it's about money. You think, 'What else could it possibly be about?' You ask yourself, 'What else could this man possibly want besides money?'"

Heat entirely unrelated to global warming suffused Healey's face because Diego's words felt uncomfortably true.

"Dude." Diego glared at him. "If you don't know the answer to that question, this is no longer about me."

CHAPTER FOUR

DIEGO

R ed-faced, Healey toed the ground. Good. Presumptuous asshole. "Why say yes, then?" Mr. Innocent Blue Eyes looked wounded.

"I'm not stupid." Diego shrugged. "Some dude comes along and offers you a fat wad of cash? You take it."

He turned his face away, even though he had yet to maneuver himself into his chair.

Healey snickered. "That was a damn good exit line. Too bad you're still stuck here putting your wheelchair together."

"Fuck. You." Oh, now it was on. Diego gave him his full attention. Or at least, the attention of two of his fingers.

One on each hand.

Healey said, "I apologize. You are right and I was wrong. I handled this really poorly."

"Yes. You did." Diego returned his gaze, eyes narrowed.

"What I didn't say is . . . I grew up in this house. It seemed—"

"Christ." Diego let his head fall against the headrest. *That's why the dude looks so goddamn familiar.* "You're Nash's brother."

Diego'd even met Nash when Spencer Kepler had been in town, shooting *Wolf's Landing.* Why hadn't he seen the resemblance? Everyone knew Nash was an identical twin. Diego defended his lack of observation because the resemblance was largely hidden—the dude was a scruffy mess, and instead of a buzz cut, slightly longer-on-the-top style like Nash's, this guy wore his sides shaved and the top long and silky. Past his shoulders.

Now that Diego put the whole story together, he understood. Healey had been in an accident that turned into a high-profile media event—rich, smart, white kids wreck their car and make a scene.

Who'd a thunk it? Now that Healey knew he wasn't immortal, he'd run home to lick his wounds.

But . . . maybe that wasn't fair. Back when Diego got out of the hospital, he'd have chewed off his foot to avoid the knowing looks, the shock, and the helpless pity he saw in other people's eyes.

Healey asked, "You know Nash?"

"We're acquainted. I'm with the *Wolf's Landing* production crew." Diego transferred his body to his chair, shut the car door behind him, and locked up with a lazy squeeze of the keys. "You should have said this used to be your house."

Healey flushed at the suggestion.

Diego muttered, "Right. 'Cause we wouldn't want the truth to get in the way of whatever you're up to."

"For the record"—Healey's voice was quiet—"I know there are more important things than money."

"Maybe you do and maybe you don't. The point is, you act like you think I don't know that."

"Fair enough." Healey stepped forward. "Can we start again? I'd sit or lean or squat so we're eye to eye, but you've gotta take a rain check because I'm busted to shit right now."

He moved stiffly. Painfully. Diego winced for him. "You don't belong in that upstairs room. There's no furniture. Did you sleep on the floor?"

Faint pink washed over Healey's cheeks. "It wasn't so bad."

"You can't clean yourself. You can't feed yourself."

"I can feed myself," he said with quiet resentment.

"From grocery store to food preparation to dining? Or from drive-thru to mouth?"

Eyes cast down, Healey shook his head. "I see your point, but I've got a handle on it."

Diego knew enough about traumatic life changes to spot the inertia and brittle irritability, for example, that result from depression. He could spot his own cycles and get himself out of a bad patch without help, most of the time.

Healey Holly hadn't learned any of that yet. Evidence stood before him, defiant and determined to be independent despite the fact it wasn't in his best interest. Battered but upright. Bewildered and unhappy and lost.

Diego knew exactly what Healey was feeling.

Empathy could be such a *bitch*.

"Look, you need to find another place to stay. Find people to help you. I can see why you'd ditch your family—" he put his hands up before Healey could argue "—and don't give me shit about how that's not what you're doing, because you can't bullshit an OG bullshitter like me."

"I literally *can't* go to my family." Healey glanced at the sky as if he were looking for answers written there. "Everyone has some glorious new happy thing. Everyone is—"

"No disrespect, but that's not my problem." Diego backed away. "Think this through. Here is not where you need to be. I can't even get up there if you call for help."

"I won't."

Right. You won't because you're a stubborn ass.

"And that's the other reason. I don't carry insurance against your stoic bullshit. If you won't ask for help because you'd rather die, then that makes you two times more of a problem." Diego jerked his chair around sharply. "I changed my mind. Get the fuck out of my place."

"I'll be out by this afternoon." Healey nodded solemnly before turning to go. "Thanks."

Seconds passed where the only sound was Healey's heavy footfalls on the sidewalk.

"Nah, man. Shit." Still conflicted, Diego called after him. "Don't be like that."

Healey turned around. "I'm really sorry. I've been told I'm inclined to forget other people have needs. I'm on it."

At a renewed pace, Healey took off.

Diego didn't bother calling him back. Dude had a right to sulk for a while when he lost his balance. Everybody knew that.

You could have handled that better.

Next time.

If there is one, next time I'll be more . . . hospitable.

Inside his house, Diego heated up a delivery service meal. He ate it at the table using Mami's everyday china and antique silver, chasing his mother's often-repeated admonition to eat like a civilized human being. The house was too quiet. Too large. It'd seemed perfect when he'd bought it.

He'd needed a crib he didn't have to modify too much and *bingo*, there it was.

An old place. Dated, but the price had been right. What he hadn't noticed until he'd moved in were the thousand tiny reminders that the place had been some family's home for decades. Marks on the floor from the daughter's wheelchair. Pen and pencil growth charts on the walls inside the pantry. Handprints in a newer pour of concrete. Trim chewed on by pets. Inexperienced-driver dings on the mailbox post.

By the looks of things, a lively bunch had once thrived in his house, and now one of its own had returned, but as far as Diego could tell, there was nothing in Bluewater Bay for Healey to come home to.

Poor bastard.

He took his second beer to the couch to watch the tail end of a soccer game, and while he was there, he got a call from his stepdad. Muting the TV and putting his phone on speaker, he answered.

"Hey, I caught you." Genuine pleasure backlit Cecil Luz's words. "Got a minute to talk? How are things?"

"Of course. Same old here. What's new there?"

"Your cousin Yesenia got into Berkeley!"

"I heard." Diego tugged a pillow beneath his head to get comfortable. "Tell her congrats for me."

The Luz family was massive. Diego received messages marked #FamiliaLuzNoticias from every stepsibling, distant cousin, aunt, godparent, no-longer-married-but-still-friends, or lived-next-door-once acquaintance, all grafted onto the Luz family tree by Cecil Luz.

Like the LA street gangs he preached against, lawyer Cecil Luz fostered a family culture of fierce loyalty and love.

Also like LA's notorious gangs, traffic into the Luz family only went one way.

The family motto wasn't "blood in, blood out," but you'd have to do something awful dicey for Cecil Luz to take you off the Feliz Navi-Dad(!) newsletter mailing list.

After delivering all the latest happenings, he added, "Dr. Ortiz called me over the weekend."

So.

Cecil was calling his mother's friend Rachel "Dr. Ortiz" now. Cecil was sure being cagey about his relationship with her. Like Diego didn't know they had a thing.

She'd left a message, although he'd never gotten back to her. Apparently she wasn't afraid to go up the chain of command.

"Did she say what she wanted?"

"She wants you to start on the documentary you promised to make." Cecil chided gently. *Documentary.*

More like a looping bio to play in the background when they show Mom's work.

"I'll have to go through all her things. I haven't even started on the script for the video."

"What about sending the materials for the book? Rachel's waiting. If you don't want Rachel to edit your mother's memoirs—"

"It's not that easy." Diego wished it was that easy. Why did people keep forgetting this was his *mother* they were talking about.

"It is... It can be. Your mother's papers—"

"Belong to me," Diego reminded him. "The papers, the photographs. The digital recordings. It all belongs to me."

"Diego."

Diego could almost see his stepdad. Taking off his glasses. Rubbing the bridge of his nose. Tired eyes, warm, long-suffering expression on his face, Cecil never lost the hint of a smile, even when life handed him nothing but trouble. He was one of the few truly decent people Diego had ever met.

One of the best men he knew.

"I'll be disappointed if you choose to keep her legacy to yourself, especially now that—"

"I'm not selfish," snapped Diego, artlessly.

"I never said you were. I said I'd be disappointed if you can't share her with all the other people who might also come to love her if they can get to know her."

No fair. *No fair.* "I'll think about it."

"We're not trying to take anything away from you, son. All we want is for you to think about what Gabbi would have wanted."

"Look, I was just about to put some cookies in the oven so—" Diego transferred himself to his chair to make his lie into a belated reality.

"Okay, sorry I caught you in the middle."

"No. It's no problem, I—"

"I'll catch you later this week."

"Sure." Great. Now shit was going to get awkward between them, and he couldn't bear that. "I'll think about what you said, Cecil, honest. The movers put mom's things up in the garage apartment, so I can't even get to them."

"I can fly up there anytime, son. I can help bring things down—"

"Nah, I got a guy who wants to rent the room, so I told him to put Mom's things in the garage. I can leave the car out while I go through it all."

"That'd be terrific, Diego." *Please God, don't let Cecil get emotional.* "Thank you."

"But I'll get to it when I can get to it, okay? No promises, no deadlines."

"Terrific, terrific. That means so much to us, I can't tell you." His stepfather's optimism was contagious as hell. Unfortunately, Diego'd been inoculated against it by his mother's pragmatism before Cecil came along. "That's great. Thank you. I'll let Rachel know you're working on it."

"Sure." Diego hated himself for the twinge of anger that rippled through him when his stepfather said Rachel's given name. His jealousy was ridiculous.

He was ridiculous.

His mother had been dead for two years. Plus, he was pretty sure Cecil, Rachel, and his mother had all been lovers—sometimes as a threesome, and sometimes like Noah's two-by-twos in varying combinations.

Diego had plausible deniability.

He'd never asked.

He'd never looked closely at room assignments in hotels.

For reasons of his own, he'd left them to it, and everyone had breathed a deep sigh of relief.

"Say hello for me. Tell Rachel I'll call her."

"Thanks, Diego." Perhaps he'd conveyed more than he thought, because Cecil went on. "You're a good man."

"Talk to you later."

Cecil seemed satisfied with that. "Save a cookie for me."

"Bwahaha, they're all mine." After disconnecting the call, he made his way to the kitchen.

Thanks to somebody's kid's fundraiser, he had a freezer full of premeasured cookie dough pucks, boxed by the dozen and labeled neatly. He pulled out a few of each—oatmeal, chocolate chip, and white chocolate macadamia nut—laid them out on a foil-wrapped cookie sheet, and preheated the oven.

While he waited, he got another beer.

His mother watched him from the refrigerator—or rather, he and his mother stared out at him from an old photograph, as if his past was judging his present.

He'd been about three when his mom'd set the camera down on the hood of a car, hauled him up, and pointed so he'd know where to look.

She was pretty, with dark hair over one shoulder in a long braid, but she'd always played down her looks. She'd worn men's work pants and a loose chambray shirt. Now he understood that—hiding her youthful body was safer because they'd been without meaningful protection.

In another photo, he was a big-eyed, raw-boned kid, happily sitting in a truck bed with his arm around a one-eyed dog. He didn't remember much about the dog. He'd never had a pet of his own until his mother married Cecil.

Those early years had been extra tough. He'd been passed from hand to hand, sometimes quite literally, while his mother worked, scraped by, and studied to get her degree. Art was her escape. The friends she made in her guerrilla art days were lifelong. They were all waiting for him to get off the pot. To assemble her memoirs, to show her work in galleries again. Even to make a documentary of her life, because if he didn't do it, who would?

Who could do it right, besides him?

He studied the pictures...

Sometimes they'd had a roof over their heads, sometimes a tent. She'd been a single mother, a pretty girl with no privilege and little protection, and she'd kept her head down. Life had been hardscrabble as hell. She'd had more patience than anyone he knew. More drive. More resilience. More balls.

They'd moved frequently, his mom taking whatever work she could find. They'd trusted no one person with all their secrets at once, like the characters in the wizard books he'd loved.

If later she'd made the most of her pluck and her luck, marrying a well-heeled lawyer, giving dinner parties, cajoling her friends into supporting her charities and terrifying cater-waiters, she'd earned the right.

Along the way, he'd lost the mother who'd been such a child when he was born that they'd grown up together. He'd lost his fiercest ally. His protector. His best friend.

No. That wasn't fair.

She'd widened the circle, brought others in. And she'd never left it.

Not really.

Over time, he and his mother had lost the intimacy they'd shared as outsiders living on the fringes of society, always afraid people would take advantage.

Now, he'd lost his ability to see himself apart from his beginnings. He was always an outsider.

He was doubly, triply so, since his accident.

The first dozen cookies inspired him to bake a second for the people from his photography club. That in turn inspired him to bake a batch for the guy upstairs—a sort of apology for being terse. Especially since it looked like he wouldn't have to use force to get the dude to leave.

Once the cookies were finished, he set up the coffee maker and headed for bed.

Maybe it was thinking about his mom that started the what-if game, because despite his best intentions, his brain took off on its old favorite pastime.

While his mother lived, the game had been about possibilities. *What if* I were fearless. What would I do? What if I were the smartest person in the world? What would I know?

They'd played when they had nothing.

Or maybe they'd played because they had nothing.

The only rule was that the hypothetical had to be intangible, which made it more fun anyway. No point in asking what he'd do with a million bucks. Everyone knows what they'd do with a million bucks.

But if Diego ever had to pick between the *Enterprise* and the *Millennium Falcon*, he knew exactly why he'd pick the *Falcon*, despite the fact that there's no question the *Enterprise* was a better ship.

Sometimes you went with your gut.

Now, as he engaged in the what-if game in the privacy of his room, the subject of his scrutiny was his unasked-for tenant.

Healey was good-looking and—by all accounts—brilliant. Healey was vulnerable. Until he got back on his feet, he was way off-limits, despite the loneliness Diego read in his eyes and the absolutely magnificent ass he'd checked out while Healey walked away.

Healey had to be off-limits.

But man . . . the what-if game.

What if I'd met Healey Holly in some other circumstances? What if he was just some guy who worked on the set?

What if he came on to me?

What if, what if, what if . . .

CHAPTER FIVE
HEALEY

Healey rang the doorbell. The endless clang of Westminster Chimes was loud enough to be heard through the open kitchen window.

A light breeze cooled the sweat on his upper lip.

Chronic pain management was new to him. He didn't always get the drug combinations exactly right. Therefore, when Clara Underhill opened the door, he was wiping his damp brow with an embarrassed wince.

"You are gray." His mentor's usual expression—regal indifference—faltered. For a brief second, he saw the fear, the wounded dignity, the considerable anger she couldn't hide. She ushered him inside.

At four feet eleven and three-fifths inches, Clara's diminutive, apple doll exterior hid an infinite ego, a keen mind, and a really, really sick sense of humor.

To preserve the illusion of normalcy, he spoke first. He waved his cast hand at her. "No masturbation jokes?"

"You awful boy." She led him to the living room, where she'd laid out the fixings for coffee and tea. "It's wonderful to see you, even if you're being a juvenile ass. How are you, really?"

"I'm fine." He made sure his smile matched his words, but the carnage was there for anyone to see.

"Sit," she said. "Tell me what I can do to help you."

Ms. Underhill's home was a study in natural fibers and shades of beige. She had a tabletop fountain that burbled merrily, turning a waterwheel, crystals, and a cheerful statue of the Buddha, who grinned from a place of honor amidst lush plants in a slanted grid of midafternoon sunlight.

For a mathematician, she had a surprising number of objects he'd consider superstitious. But Clara's place was still as warm and welcoming as he remembered it. The simplicity of visiting relaxed him.

He let his guard drop.

Before he knew what was happening, he'd started crying, tears only, dripping down his cheeks in two tracks to his shirt. His jeans.

She put her arms around him, and it only made things worse. He turned his face away like a dog who isn't interested in playing, one who hopes if he ignores you, you'll just move along.

"Oh." Her dismay was palpable, but he could do nothing to save the situation. "Oh, honey."

Eventually she let go, but pulled up a hard-backed chair to stay quietly by his side. Where her hug was overwhelming, her presence meant a lot to him. Eventually, he let her take his good hand between hers.

Like Goldilocks, he discovered that careful contact was exactly right.

"Th-thanks." His voice was too hoarse to talk after he'd cried himself out. "Didn't expect that to happen."

She let go of him to pour coffee, adding sugar and cream. "Do you want to talk about it?"

"No." Just the thought made him flinch.

Would she pry? Or was that relief on her face? Either way, she smiled wanly.

"Then tell me about your family? They sold the house and auto shop, didn't they?"

"I don't know if the shop sold yet." As if he hadn't lost all emotional control, he took a cup of coffee from her. He filled her in on Nash, Shelby, and Ace, who would be livid once they found out he'd left the medical facility against medical advice, and who—possibly—had no clue he'd returned to Bluewater Bay.

". . . Dad and Fjóla are awesome, but they want to drop what they're doing and hover until I'm back to normal, and that's the last thing any of us needs."

"Call them." Her sharp green eyes drilled holes in him. Her voice stayed gentle.

"I'll call them." He nodded slowly. He was so tired. She was right. He should call them.

She smiled. "Do it now."

He had his phone out before he realized he was acting like a muppet. "You still have that mind-control thing, don't you?"

"I wouldn't say that."

"Because then you'd have to kill me."

She smiled serenely.

His father answered on the fourth ring.

"About time you called me." Pop's angry voice was firmly in place.

"Because you make it so rewarding."

A sigh. "Good to hear your voice, Heals."

"You too."

So saying, Healey's world went *click* and the ground beneath his feet got pieced back together like it was made of Lego bricks. What was it about fathers, anyway? The minute he heard his pop's voice growling at him from—where were they now? New Guinea?—his heart settled happily in his chest. Bland music played in the background wherever he was.

"You left the hospital," his pop grumbled. "Nash is furious."

He deserved that. "I know."

"You left before Fjóla and I could even get on a plane. No one knew where you went. Do you know how that made me feel? Especially when I spoke to Ford's parents? I had to tell them I didn't know how to find you."

God, Ford.

Pop's tone softened. "The arraignment went without a hitch, Heals. Ford got bail."

"I know." Did his father think he'd run away from everyone's questions? "I've been interviewed too, Pop. I told the police everything."

An audible hesitation on his pop's part told Healey to brace himself.

"You should call his folks. They need to hear the whole story from you."

"No way." He couldn't do it. Wouldn't. "No way."

Pop paused a long time. Only the background music told Healey they still had a connection. "Is it because when you remember it, you relive it?"

"No." He didn't have to relieve that last evening with Ford to want to put it out of his mind. The accident had been terrifying, but Ford's behavior...

In retrospect, it was Healey's graduation that'd changed everything. Things hadn't been working between Healey and Ford for a while, but they'd agreed that stress was playing a negative role, and once Healey defended, they could kick back and enjoy things.

But while Ford had agreed with Healey's assessment, and they'd both said all the right things, Healey'd still felt uneasy. They'd been fighting a lot. Healey wanted to take a little time out after graduation. He wanted to be with his family and travel. Maybe even do some volunteer work for one of the many environmental groups he supported.

Ford had a vice presidency in his father's corporation to look forward to. He didn't have to decide what to do next. His parents were going to gift him with an expense account, a condo in the correct zip code, and a company car.

That last night, all their problems—all the ways they weren't compatible—erupted into a massive take-no-prisoners fight. They'd spent hours hashing things out. In the end, they'd agreed to end things amicably, with respect.

Healey'd felt a tingle of caution. Ford's behavior had—at times—been unpredictable, but as far as Healey knew, he'd been faithfully taking his meds.

Ford was angry, but he'd agreed.

Ford had been quiet, but not... upset. Not then, anyway.

He'd suggested they take a Vegas trip—one last mad adventure together.

Ford had acted in control. Amiable. Relaxed. Charming. Healey'd gone along, ignoring his instincts—he'd hesitated to call Ford's family for help—and things went sour. The rest was history, now.

"You were there." Pop ignored his protests. "Ford says he doesn't remember. You're the only one who can answer Ford's family's questions."

Ford's parents loved Healey, and he loved them. They'd expect him to back up anything Ford told the police about their accident.

But they were the ones building a narrative based on a lie.

"What I remember will ruin everything for Ford."

"How can that be?"

On some level, Healey knew what he *ought* to do. He ought to step up and tell the whole truth about the accident.

But how could he face either set of parents with the truth?

How could he tell them he'd ignored those crucial, crucial signs?

"Where are you?" his father asked.

Where? *I'm home. And it's not working.* "I'm in Bluewater Bay, Pop."

"Why? When you could go anywhere in the world?"

"It's home, I guess. Even now. I wanted—" Throat burning, he closed his eyes, unable to finish the sentence.

When was he going to get a handle on all this crying?

His pop took pity on him. "I'm so sorry, Heals. Me and Fjóla are wrapping things up here. We'll be home before you know it."

"No way, Pop. Don't. This obviously isn't home anymore. Let me get past the broken bones. Once the arm heals—"

"You need more than medical attention, son. Did you even find a place to stay during the tourist swarm?"

"I'm at Clara Underhill's right now." If his dad understood him to mean he was staying with Clara, the only result was the discomfort that came with a mild half-truth.

On the other hand, Clara glared at him because she wasn't a half-truth kind of person and never had been. He muted his phone to argue with her, then paused. He couldn't stay in Nash's old place.

He needed a bed, a bathtub, and some goddamn help. He needed physical therapy, and despite his distaste for talking over his problems, he probably needed emotional support too. His dad, Clara, even the dude who'd bought his dad's place could see it.

Why was he fighting this?

He couldn't do this—couldn't come back from the breakup, losing Ford, nearly dying himself—*on his own.*

Again, he felt his face crumple. He had no control over crying anymore. No shame. When emotions grew too much for him, tears simply gathered and fell.

"Oh, Healey. I'm so sorry, son." Pop's words dropped like summer rain on a graveside service.

Clara put her hand on his shoulder, and gently, she pried the phone from his hands. "Hello, Ace. I've arranged for Healey to stay at the Burnt Toast B&B for a while. Derrick is expecting him."

They spoke awhile longer, and then she left to give him some privacy while he finished up with his pop. Or rather, his father tried to reassure him, while Fjóla broke in every so often with loving platitudes.

Oh, how fervently he wished a hole would open up—the hell mouth they'd all postulated spawned Clara Underhill—to swallow him.

But alas. There was no rip in the continuum he could slip through—no convenient wormhole.

When he hung up the phone, there was only the silence and the regulator clock on the wall, a reminder that despite his inactivity, his life was wasting away, *tick, tick, tick.*

Now, too, he had the added bonus of incontrovertible proof that each second truly could be his last.

Which wasn't a problem, until he started to *think* about it.

Until he started to dwell on it.

Until he was aware of his mortality at the cellular level and it started closing in on him.

He didn't have the constitution to sit there and wait for the other shoe to drop. Sheer fucking boredom was eating away at him, along with a new perspective—*do I even have time to do anything worthwhile?*

And some new worries—*what if next time, I die and they find my body with one hand on my dick and the other up my ass?* There had to be a way to reframe his thoughts, to make the situation less distressing, but fatigue and pessimism were all Healey had to work with.

He could save more trivial problems for a day with no broken bones, at least.

"You still listening in?" Healey asked Clara.

"Yes." Without shame, Clara stepped out from where she'd been hiding, just inside the kitchen door. "Prepare to be treated to extra scrutiny until I know you're on the mend emotionally."

He nodded. "Did you really make arrangements with Derrick over at the Burnt Toast B&B?"

She nodded. "I called him. He and Gins talked things over, and they'll be happy to help."

Healey's memory was no help. "Gins?"

"Derrick's partner."

Healey stood, hating the idea of being someone's project. "I appreciate everything you're trying to do for me."

"And you despise it." Her small smile was warm and full of pity. "We all hate needing help. But you have to eat and bathe. You'll need rides to and from doctor appointments. Have you been cleared to drive?"

"I don't have my bike with me—"

"Hahah. Yeah. Okay." She took her purse and keys from the console by the door. "First things first. A bath, a bed, and a meal. Then we'll talk about how ridiculous riding a motorcycle would be in your condition—from a purely scientific standpoint."

"I ate." Even though he was pretty sure snack cakes didn't count for much with her, he had eaten. "But I could use a bath."

A soft smile battled its way onto her lips. "I didn't want to mention."

Healey picked up his jacket and opened the door to leave. It'd be just as easy to walk. That's how he'd got there, after all. He was so emotionally exploded, all he could think of was getting his rolling duffel from Diego's place. "I'll get my stuff. I can be back here in say—"

"Just a minute, mister. Jeepers, you're a hard case. I'm driving you." From behind him, she pushed the front door closed and locked it. "Come through the kitchen."

Of course, Healey followed her.

The local B&B *was* the best choice for him.

He didn't have to worry about money just then. Didn't need the hassles of cooking or cleaning. Plus, no rational person with two bum arms agrees to pay three grand and move boxes so he can sleep in a squat.

At the same time, a flash of memory—Diego's wariness, his lonely place, his smile, once he was sufficiently comfortable to offer it...

The B&B was the best choice for Healey, but it didn't do anything for his belief he wasn't the only one who needed... something.

What did they say: it takes one to know one?

Healey allowed Clara to settle him into her car, a silver Prius. She fastened his seat belt for him and smoothed the strap over his chest like a mom. It should have been weird, but it wasn't.

He stared straight ahead, listening to the *squelch-squelch* of wipers as she drove through rain-spattered streets.

A bath sounded heavenly. A bath, and a meal he didn't have to remove from protective plastic to cook.

When Clara turned on the radio, the noise startled him so hard he smacked his cheek against the window. That was going to leave another mark.

"Sorry." Inexplicably, he blinked back a fresh wash of tears.

Clara pulled up in front of Healey's—Diego's—house. She put the Prius in park, pulled a John le Carré novel from the floor behind her seat.

"Get your things. I'll wait."

CHAPTER SIX

DIEGO

Diego's tenant drove up with some lady Diego'd never met. Couldn't be his mom—the realtor'd said his dad was a widower.

Heart heavier than it ought to be, he watched as Healey put his duffel bag into the back of the Prius parked in the driveway.

Guess Healey was taking Diego's advice seriously, and moving out.

For a minute he thought that was going to be all, that Healey would get into the car and pull out of his life altogether, but instead, once his gear was stowed, Healey walked up the front steps.

Which meant he saw Diego watching him.

Smooth.

Healey waved and Diego waved back.

Watching isn't weird.

But wait—

What if Healey wasn't a decent guy? What if Healey was taking some of his mother's shit? Diego wouldn't even know. To be fair, he wouldn't really care, either. He'd stashed all his mother's things up there precisely because he didn't care.

He didn't.

But he opened the door before Healey could knock. "I take it you found a better place?"

Healey glanced behind him at the lady. "What can I say, she's willing to pay me for sex."

It took all Diego's concentration to keep from laughing at that.

After a second, Healey shook his head. "You're a tough audience, you know that?"

Yeah. Well. He did know that. But now that his unwanted tenant was safely moving on, it was probably all right to relax his guard a little. He stopped short of a smile.

"Maybe I was trying to remember how much I have in my checking account."

"Yeah?" Healey's smile fell off, replaced with an expression of pure masculine pride. "Snooze, you lose."

"Fuck off." Diego started to close the door, but Healey stopped him.

"Nah, wait. Thanks, man." He held out his hand.

Diego eyed it. "For what?"

"For letting me crash here. Not calling the cops or whatever. I was pushy."

"A'ight." Diego grinned and they shook. "I'd say anytime, but I wouldn't mean it."

"So, I'll see you around, okay?" Healey stepped back.

In spite of himself, Diego gave him a wry, squinted, come-hither look. "I wouldn't say no to a beer sometime."

"Sure." Healey lifted his chin to acknowledge the idea. After a few seconds, he must have realized it was up to him to leave. "Bye."

CHAPTER SEVEN

HEALEY

On the way back to Clara's car, Healey had an awful flashback moment. Probably some fucked-up high school memory, because that's exactly how he felt. Like he was dropping off a date, and he wasn't quite done yet. Like there was unfinished business and he—

Healey put a stop to his thoughts right there and glanced back.

For reasons entirely his own, Diego sat in the open doorway glowering at him.

He looked tired though. Healey was drawn to him, both physically and emotionally.

He approached the porch to offer, "When I'm better, I can still move your stuff if you need me to."

"Nah, you don't have to do that. But wait—" He rolled out of view and came back a couple of seconds later with a plastic-covered plate of cookies. "I baked a batch of cookies last night. Made a dozen for you."

Diego held out the peace offering.

"Thank you. That's really nice." When Healey took it, their fingers brushed, sending crackles of energy flowing between them. Healey shivered before shrugging apologetically. "Sorry again for bothering you."

"A'ight." Eyes lit with something like humor, Diego gave his neck a scratch. "In case anyone asks me, where will you be staying?"

"It's called the Burnt Toast B&B, Ms. U says." He lifted the cookies. "Thank you for these."

Diego gave him a nod. "I'll be seeing you."

A brief stab of regret flared in Healey's gut when Diego closed the door. It might have been fun getting to know him. Getting under his skin had certainly been amusing. He wished he could see if Diego's hot sly glances meant something, or if his attitude was simply adjusted too tight.

After eating one of the cookies on the way to Clara's car, he offered her one.

"Try this, it's white chocolate macadamia."

She hesitated before breaking one in half. "Looks excellent. That's the young man who bought your father's place?"

"Diego. Probably bought it for the ramps and lowered countertops, but Shelby's room was the only bedroom downstairs, and it was kind of girly."

"He'll put his own stamp on it, I'm sure."

"I guess." He scooted his seat back, unable to bear the thought of being that close to the airbags. These days, he could barely open a pop can without his anxiety ratcheting up. That would pass right? It couldn't last forever.

On the short ride to the B&B, he and Clara talked about all the things that had changed in Bluewater Bay since he'd left. Due to a relatively sunny weekend, tourists wandered the streets with printed trifold maps of Bluewater Bay clutched in their fists.

"The show can't last forever." Clara sounded hopeful.

"It's made Bluewater Bay a boom town." Before his pop got into inventing goofy gadgets, Holly's Haus of Imports kept them all fed. Ironically, when he no longer needed income from the shop, the business had picked up because of the goddamn television show. Of course, it brought all the LA types. Things had been tense until the flannel-clad denizens of Bluewater Bay saw that LA money spent like any other kind and no one had to go out in the freezing cold to get it.

"Is this B&B new? I don't remember anything called Burnt Toast back in the day."

"The name is new. It was the Bayview. Derrick inherited the business when his parents passed away." She pulled her car into the parking area designated for registering guests. It was obvious from the nearly full lot that the place was doing well.

While he was getting his duffel from the trunk, a furry tornado burst through the front door. Seconds later, a lumberjack in a pink apron ran out, chasing it.

By the time Healey got to the porch, the dude was trudging back with the dog under one arm. It snarled and tried to sink its vicious little teeth into his arm, but he stayed all smiles.

"Hey, Ms. U."

"Hello, Derrick. What a pleasure to see you again." She held out her hands for Derrick's nasty little dog. It leaped from the lumberjack's arms and turned into a kitten. "Hello, Ms. Victoria. And how are you today?"

"Every time." Derrick jammed a finger in the dog's face and growled. "I feed you. That's the last straw. Fuck off."

Healey simply waited.

"Okay, so." The big man wrapped his hand around the back of his neck.

Somebody needs a blue ox.

"All we've got is a small room on the third floor. I usually keep that one open unless we're full, because it's not real awesome. You look pretty banged up. Can you make it up a couple flights of stairs?"

"It'll be fine," Healey assured him.

Derrick's lips tilted into a faint grin. "Last guy who used that room had a broken arm too. How do you shower?"

"So far?" Healey flushed. "I'm ashamed to say I haven't."

Clara had a suggestion. "You ought to take him out back and scrub him down like a horse before you let him in your nice place."

"Ms. U," Healey whined.

"Call me Clara." She put the dog down. "I'll leave you to it. Healey. We can catch up once I know you're being properly taken care of."

"I got him, Ms. U." Derrick opened the door and the little monster dog tore inside. Holding the door open for Healey, he waited.

For a single moment, Healey felt utterly bereft. In a strange place, unable to speak the language, no memory, no map. No family to guide him. No, that wasn't fair. His family was still there. They loved him. They'd supported his every move since he was born. Plus he had the redoubtable Clara Underhill on his side.

People had built whole civilizations with less.

Nash had deliberately and selflessly given up his chance at college, at getting away from Bluewater Bay and following his own dreams for years to help take care of their sister, Shelby—all so Healey could see how far his gifts could take him. Whenever he felt low, whenever he felt like quitting—like anger and sorrow were the only things he had left—Healey reminded himself his family was there, if he'd just reach out.

They weren't *here*, though, because . . . he wasn't sure he was ready to face them.

With a last wave at Clara, he entered the bed-and-breakfast. Immediately, he was surrounded by kitsch mixed with memorabilia, along with a few modern masculine touches. *Eclectic* was too good a word for it, but it was warm and inviting. It wrung a sigh from him, almost as though he couldn't help himself. An apron like the one Derrick was wearing hung in a shadow box in pride of place.

"My mother's," Derrick murmured, while they looked at it. "They passed in a car wreck three years ago and left me this place."

"I barely remember my mother," Healey admitted.

One of Derrick's large hands fell on his shoulder. "Sorry."

He winced. "It's okay. My family's awesome."

Pop and Fjóla would no doubt show up when they could, now that they knew where he was. Insisting he was fine wasn't going to keep them away. They'd want to see for themselves.

Derrick nodded. "Sure."

"If you'll just show me my room, I'll get out of your hair and get cleaned up."

"Yeah, well." Derrick glanced toward the kitchen. "The shower in my room is probably the best one for you right now. It's bigger. Or we have a tub you could soak in. Which sounds better?"

A tall kitchen trash bag, a whole lot of duct tape, and some trial and error later, Healey flopped down on the tiny bed in his room, clean and blissfully sleepy, for a change.

He'd no sooner drifted off to sleep, than a timid knock came at the door.

"Yeah?" he called.

A scrappy-looking dude peeked in through a crack. The dog, whose name he'd learned was Victoria Beckham, burst through, widening it substantially. His visitor followed the dog to stand by Healey's feet holding a tray.

"Hungry?"

"Yeah, thanks." Tomato soup and grilled cheese sandwich. Smelled like whoever made it used real butter and sourdough bread. He was suddenly so hungry he felt inside out.

"Ginsberg." He set the tray down and busied himself with a napkin and flatware.

Healey figured that was a name. "Healey."

The smile he got was unsure. "I had a broken arm when I first got here too."

"Yeah?" He sat up, arranged the sheets so Ginsberg could put down the tray. "This level of service is totally unnecessary. I can come down for food."

"It's fine. Jim thought you might be, in his words, peckish, but it's after official breakfast."

"Jim?"

"He's our chef. Breakfast is already cleaned up, and he worried you wouldn't be up to coming down for food later. But it's fine if you want to."

"This is perfect. I could sleep for a week."

Ginsberg bit his lip. "No one will bother you if you don't want them to."

Healey glanced around the room. Filled with homey touches too old to be retro but not quite old enough to be antique, his little room was dated, but pleasant. Probably not their best, but way better than some of the student digs he'd lived in. His jaw cracked around a huge yawn. Ginsberg let out a surprisingly deep chortle he broke off with a cough.

"I'll just tell everybody you'll sleep until you're done."

Healey nodded gratefully. "Thank you." He blinked down at the sandwich. "I know what hangry is. What's hungry and exhausted?"

"Look in the mirror." Ginsberg laughed. "Come down and say hello when you're ready. Jim will want to get a good look at you."

Victoria barked, dancing around his feet.

"What?" Ginsberg reached down and picked the little dog up. "We all know Jim is your favorite. Don't rub it in. It's only because he bakes you those dog treats."

"Thanks, Ginsberg," Healey offered. "Appreciate all this."

Ginsberg hesitated at the door before he turned back. "You're very welcome."

The door closed softly between them.

Grilled cheese and tomato soup was Nash's favorite comfort food, while Healey preferred Mi Goreng fried noodles with a cooked egg on top. GCTS came in a close second. Healey let his head fall back on the pillow. He missed his twin. There were times when knowing how it would affect Nash if anything happened to him was the only thing that kept him moving forward.

Healey shook off the thought.

There weren't a lot of dark thoughts. But there were some. He'd returned to Bluewater Bay instinctively, looking to ground himself and get help.

As if thinking about Nash caused it, his phone rang.

He didn't have to check the caller ID.

"Hey, bro."

Nash's voice held anger. "I'm not even going to mention how dumb it was to leave and get on a plane just days after an accident like the one you had."

"I'm fine."

"But you're in Bluewater Bay. Which for the record, was—at the time you landed there—2,100 miles away from your *nearest* relative."

"Farther than that, cupcake. I thought you guys were in Morocco?"

"We were."

"I have news for you, Morocco is way farther than 2,100 miles from Bluewater Bay."

"It is not. Wait, I looked it up, special. Oh, crap. That's Morocco, Indiana. Whatever, man. Do you know how long it's going to take me to get home?"

"You don't—"

"Oh, don't even." Nash's raspy voice sounded as irritated as he did. "I'm already in New York. I'll be in Seattle in . . . eight hours."

"Eight? Are you walking?" Healey sat up and checked his soup. Temperature was good. Mm. Tomato and basil.

"It's called a layover, Einstein. In Salt Lake City. I hope to fuck I can get a goddamned beer there. So unless you've figured out how to fold time and space . . . ?" He paused. "I'll see you when I get there."

"I'm at a B&B. Burnt Toast."

"Derrick's place? I know it. See you there. Don't make me chase you around or when I get there, I'll break your leg too."

"Nice." *Crunch.* He lost all his table manners and started to eat while he talked. Good grilled cheese. His appetite had returned with a vengeance.

"Speaking of nice, the nurses I talked to remember you fondly. Without giving up any medical information, they all offered opinions on how hot you are."

"Wish I could say the same. I don't remember jack, except waking up and telling them I was leaving." *Ooh. Dunking.* In went the cheese triangle.

"They let you? Pop said something about an interview with the police?"

"Yeah. I did that, and I'll be subpoenaed to appear. There will be depositions later. I'll bet there's going to be a civil lawsuit."

"You don't have to worry about that now, though. What's next for you?"

"Don't know." Whenever he thought of the future, nausea made his mouth water. "Right now, I'm going to eat the last quarter of this grilled cheese sandwich, and then I'm planning to sleep."

"I'll be there soon."

"No. I'm not even—"

"Would you stay away if it was me?"

"No." He spoke through clenched teeth before disconnecting, then dropped the phone into the bedding beside him. The quilt—some handmade star pattern in rich blue shades—bore the softness of a thousand washes. Running the tips of his fingers over the stitches was profoundly soothing.

After he finished everything but the garnish, he placed the tray on the landing outside his room, simultaneously wondering if the dog was prone to wandering around by itself and whether a lick of tomato soup would be bad for a dog that size. Maybe if he left the bowl upside down? Instead, he covered it with the parsley—he didn't see a Yorkshire Terrier sneak-eating parsley.

Satisfied he could shut the world out, he placed his Do Not Disturb tag on the door, closed it, and crawled back into bed.

His last thought as he drifted off was cookies.

Wait.

He had cookies, and they were delicious.

He could eat them, if only his head didn't feel like it weighed so much.

Okay, then. Maybe later.

He'd eat them ... later.

Something woke Healey. He lifted one eyelid. Blinked. His eyes were gritty, but visibility was zero, the room mired in darkness.

How long had he been asleep? Must have been hours.

It took him a few precious seconds to remember he was at the Burnt Toast B&B.

During those few seconds, he relived the crash.

Mouth dry and heart hammering, Healey reached for the water bottle he'd left on the nightstand. Of course, he knocked it over. Water splashed into the darkness, audibly hitting the floor. Pooling on the hardwood.

Blindly, he groped for his phone, which lit up briefly before it slid out of reach.

Darkness.

Then, a slice of light from the hallway widened, and suddenly, miraculously, Nash was there, solid and strong. Healey stood on shaking legs, moving toward his twin, grabbing on to the only relief and safety he'd ever known.

Nash swept him into a full-body hug.

Into wholeness.

Into the strength that only came from family.

How had Healey imagined he could do any of this alone?

A brand-new dam burst, and Healey's heart cracked open. Sorrow he'd tried to bury rose up to confront him again.

"Ah, God." Healey tightened his good arm around Nash. He could not bear this. He wasn't letting go again. Not *ever*. "*Christ*."

"I've got you," Nash whispered. "I'm here. Everything's going to be okay. I promise."

CHAPTER EIGHT

HEALEY

Light barely cracked the darkness the following morning. Rain spattered down, throwing interesting shadows onto the wall. The droplets created patterns Healey's brain attempted to decipher. Hieroglyphics? Cuneiform? Spermatozoa?

He watched as they beaded up, smeared, and swallowed one another.

Something shifted beside him, and he remembered sharing the too-small bed with Nash.

He elbowed Nash's thick biceps. "Hey."

Still fully dressed, Nash sat up, frowning. "Jesus. What time is it?"

"Time to take a piss." Healey swung his legs over the side of the bed "Back in a sec."

He left the room to relieve himself and brush his teeth. When he got back, he found Nash sitting up in bed, digging through his backpack.

"I'm sure I put my toiletry kit in here. Is it in the suitcase? I left that in the rental car." He tossed everything aside, fell back onto the pillows, and cursed. "Fuck it. I need coffee. It's too early for anything but caffeine."

"Let's go find some." Together, they headed downstairs. In the kitchen, they found a blond man fussing over a cappuccino machine.

"At last, I meet the mysterious stranger," he purred. He stopped what he was doing to shake Healey's hand. When Nash walked in, his eyes widened comically. "Times *two*."

Healey smiled and gently disengaged. "Healey Holly. Pleasure. This is Nash."

"Jim." He splayed his hand over his heart. "My goodness. Anyone hungry? I'm up for a sandwich."

Victoria Beckham pushed her way between them unhappily. She still didn't like Healey, but she was willing to overlook his presence.

She positively hated Nash.

"Hey." Nash backed away. "Don't."

With a growl, she got a grip on the seam of his jeans. He leaped back, but she hung there like a tick, trying to tear him to pieces.

"Victoria." Jim made a grab for her.

"Get it off. Get it *off*." Nash called to Healey, aghast. "Do something, you fuck-wad."

Healey was doing something. He was laughing his *ass* off.

"Dude. It's just a dog."

"That's not a proper dog, Healey."

"Oh, snap. You talk like Spencer, now. You're hilarious."

Jim got Victoria under control while Healey poured himself a coffee from the drip machine.

Nash swatted him. "You son of a bitch."

"Sorry, man." Guilt made him hand his coffee over. "Here you go."

"Thanks for this, anyway."

Jim left the kitchen with the dog. While he was gone, Healey took the opportunity to explore. There were a ton of homey touches in the vast, communal kitchen. He studied the open shelves, which held a bunch of retro gadgets.

"I like this place." Knickknacks and vintage products and advertisements kept the eye moving. There were a few tin lunch pails that looked to be originals. Scooby-Doo. Spider-Man.

"Smells amazing, doesn't it?" Whatever Jim was baking filled the air with the scent of apples and cinnamon and vanilla.

Nash leaned against the counter with his mug. He eyed Healey. "Okay. We've got coffee. Have we got some kind of plan?"

"For the day?"

Nash nodded. "We can start there, yeah."

Jim came back into the room without Ms. Beckham. "Are either of you hungry? I could use tasters."

"Really?" Healey asked.

"Nah. I don't need anyone to tell me this is fabulous. I'm a fucking genius in the kitchen." He slinked over to a cooling rack. "But I like feeding young men."

"In that case, sure. I'm starved. Do your worst."

"Try this to start." Jim placed a small round Danish on a napkin, dusted it with powdered sugar, and handed it over. "It's quince. Fall fruit. One of my friends has a tree."

The pastry was flakey and delicious. Tart and spicy. Wholly unexpected the way Thai food could be unexpected. Sweet and ginger-hot.

Healey moaned. "Delicious."

"I told you I'm good." But Jim preened at the compliment. "I can make you a fancy coffee drink too. You want?"

"This is fine." Healey raised his mug.

Jim's smile was lazy. "Easy to please. I like that. So you—" he turned to Nash "—are Spencer Kepler-Constantine's new squeeze."

"I guess." Nash couldn't hide the blush that crept up his neck.

"I've bumped into Spencer several times. He's a delight."

"I agree."

"Did he come with?" Jim plated a couple more tarts before giving them a sprinkling of mint leaves. "Forks are in the dining room."

Nash took his happily. "Thank you. No, Spencer had other commitments and couldn't be here."

Healey took another tart. "I didn't want everyone to drop what they were doing anyway."

Nash clapped him on the back. "Good luck keeping us away. Pop and Fjóla will be here tomorrow probably. Shelby is sick about it, but she's got finals."

"I swear to God, I don't need—"

"Shut up, Bubba." Carefully, Nash looped his arm around Healey's neck. He was gentle but the move carried the threat of pain. "*We* need *you*."

"Aw. Come and have a seat." Jim led them into the nearly empty dining room.

Nash glanced around. "Where is everyone?"

"The fandom sleep off their excesses." Jim pursed his lips and held up a finger. "Shh. What happens in Wolf's Landing stays in Wolf's Landing."

Nash sat. Healey grabbed a newspaper off another table and joined him.

"I'll just go finish up breakfast," Jim tidied a table on the way to the kitchen. "I'll bring you your plates in a minute. If you want anything, just give a shout."

"Thanks." They fell into familiar patterns: Nash scrolled through the messages on his phone while Healey read the paper.

Breakfast turned out to be eggs *en cocotte* with a crumbly crust of parmesan and breadcrumbs and basil on top, slab-cut bacon, fresh fruit, and an assortment of pastries. Everything tasted like heaven.

How had he ever believed he could survive on snack cakes and canned Starbucks coffee? He brushed the last of the crumbs off his fingertips and put his paper aside.

"So."

"So." Nash spread his hands over his full belly and leaned back. "Now that you've got a roof over your head, and you're fed and caffeinated, what's next on the agenda?"

Healey resisted scrubbing his face with his hands. He had so many bruises, scrapes, and contusions it hurt. Anxiety plagued him.

"I don't feel so good," he admitted.

"We need to get you seen by a local doctor."

"Sure."

Nash took one last bite of pastry. "And Fjóla thinks you should do a sweat lodge. There's a place on Bainbridge Island. Whenever you decide to go, I'm in. Let's make an appointment."

"Okay. Um." Doctor he could see. Sweat lodge with a cast? "Maybe that can wait?"

"I'm just passing along what she said."

"You know what I really want to do?" asked Healey. "I promised this dude I'd help move some things."

Nash laughed. "Right. You're a mess and you're going to move some guy's furniture?"

"It's not furniture," Healey countered. "It's a few boxes of old camera equipment, paintings, and some wooden sculptures."

"Wait—" Nash's brows lowered. "This is the guy who bought Pop's house?"

"Yeah. He uses a chair, so until someone brings those things down, he won't even get to see them. It's his mom's things in those boxes—"

"So? Maybe that's where he wants them."

Healey made up his mind. "I have a plate that belongs to him. Let's drop it off and ask."

Nash groaned.

"What?"

"You've been in town for exactly two minutes, and you've already started an experiment?"

"A what?"

"An experiment, a project, a plan, an intervention. You just got through like, twenty-five years of school, for heaven's sake. You can take some time off to sit and be, can't you?"

"It's not like it's such a big deal is it? Moving some boxes."

"And how're you gonna do that with a broken arm?" Nash argued.

"Twin Powers! Activate." Healey fired off his most disarming grin, the one he knew his brother could never say no to because he was a sap too, and got to his feet.

"Aw. Fuck you." Nash stood. True to form, they both picked up their plates and trooped them into the kitchen for Jim.

"Oh my God. You two are just adorable, aren't you? Somebodies' mother raised them right."

Healey caught Nash's eye, and sadness passed between them. "Our pop."

"Nice," Jim said softly. "Pops are nice too."

"We're, um—"

"Gonna get out of your hair now," Nash completed Healey's thought. To Healey, he said, "Let me grab my case from the rental, and then we can get started."

"All right." Nash left him at the bottom of the stairs.

Healey took the steps up past the first floor, where some of the guests were starting their day. Jesus, had he really slept nearly twenty-four hours?

A woman came out of her room with a teenage girl, who took one look at him and squealed, "Oh my God. Are you Nash Holly?"

"Healey, Nash's brother." He held up his arms. "Nash is the cast-free, short-haired iteration of our dynamic duo."

She was so excited her face was bright red. "Huh?"

"I'm his twin."

"But you know Spencer Kepler, right?"

He nodded. "My brother's bae. But Spencer's not in town right now. I'm sorry."

"I know." The girl nodded. "They said he's in Morocco. But oh my God. I still can't believe we saw you."

Her mother wore the long-suffering look of a woman forced to listen to "Baby" for the millionth time. Or whatever the current song was.

She said, "Pleasure," as they passed each other on the stairs.

A few minutes later, Nash came into their cramped room with a navy suitcase. It had a tan strap and a red handle and it looked pricey.

"Aw, man. When did you get rich-people luggage?"

Nash shrugged. "Spencer got tired of the duct tape."

"I'll bet."

Nash waited while Healey brushed his teeth, and then the two of them headed downstairs again, out into the early-morning drizzle. Nash keyed his remote. A shiny black SUV with tinted windows came to life with a chirp. It wasn't the kind of car Nash would choose for himself—it being American, for one thing, and a gas guzzler. Plus, it was all automatic and comfortable. It appeared pretty boring to drive.

Healey guessed Spencer's assistant was responsible for the choice. "Bast hook you up with this?"

"Yeah." Nash glanced to the side before he pulled onto the road. "After the Lamborghini incident in Monte Carlo, Bast has been proactively stomping on all my fun."

"I didn't hear about that."

"That's because Spencer's PR people are worth every penny he pays them. It wasn't anything bad anyway. Just a couple of tickets. Some warnings. And a fruit stand. I bought all the fruit. We got ice and Greek yogurt and made smoothies for an entire town."

"I'm surprised Bast hasn't sent you back in a box with some air holes drilled out."

"I come back in a box, it will be because I'm dead."

Healey took a shuddering breath.

"Oh, Christ. I'm sorry. I'm such an ass."

"It's all right." He wasn't going to hold a figure of speech against his brother. But shit could get real fast. He'd learned that, and a lot of other things, in that split second when he'd believed his life was over.

Healey spent the rest of the drive fixating on the tires as they *squish*ed over the damp road. He bobbed his head with the rhythm of the wipers, wishing he could go back in time. If *only* . . .

This time he would say, "Let's stay home."

He would deliberately forget something and go back to his and Ford's apartment. He'd start another fight. Or a seduction. He'd go back inside the apartment, kiss Ford, and then he'd call 911 and he'd tell them the goddamn truth.

Before. Not after.

He should have left a kiss on Ford's lips before the betrayal.

"Are you okay?" The car jerked. "Bubba. Talk to me."

Healey blinked away the irritation. Was that truly how it was? Was he remembering it the way it happened? Had he denied Ford that kiss? Or given it, like Judas?

He couldn't quite . . . remember.

"Healey."

"Hmm?" Opening his eyes, he saw his brother had stopped the car. "What?"

"You're going to the doctor, right fucking now."

With that, Nash whipped the car around, probably heading for the ferry, and Seattle, and another fine mess.

"Oh come on," Healey said tiredly as he glanced behind them. "There's no emergency. I'll make an appointment. I promise."

Nash kept driving, head down, jaw working like he wanted to say something but was holding himself back.

"What?" asked Healey.

"You were somewhere else for like . . . three minutes, man. You didn't even look my way when I called your name."

"I was thinking."

"I know." Nash's jaw was still going, teeth grinding.

"So what?"

"What do you mean what? You were gone. The lights were on, but nobody was home."

"And? Didn't I answer your question fast enough? I'm sorry, Nash. Sometimes it takes me a minute to process—"

"No." Nash pulled over again. "You did that exact same thing before. Don't you remember?"

Healey balled his fist. "I have no idea what you're talking about."

"After Mom died? You didn't talk for like . . . a week. Didn't look up. Didn't interact. It was like you were— I dunno, man, but it scared the fuck out of me."

"I—" Healey thought back. "I don't remember much about when Mom died."

"Ask Pop." Nash eyed him. "You were a ghost for a long, long time. I thought I lost you too." His fingers opened and closed on the shift knob while he met Healey's gaze.

Healey winced at the pain in his brother's eyes. "I'm sorry."

"A doctor might be able to help you process what's happening to you. They know more about emotional stuff now."

Healey's heart filled with fondness for his brother. He couldn't possibly understand the awful quagmire that was the pursuit of mental health. "The hospital gave me my paperwork and some referrals for doctors here. I haven't had time to contact anyone just yet."

"So? Let's get that ball rolling instead of moving boxes."

Healey groaned. Just the thought of making calls, of filling out paperwork, and waiting, and elevator music, and hushed voices, was exhausting.

"Tomorrow?" he whined. "Can't we spend today without thinking of any of that?"

While he gave the idea some thought, Nash's foot jiggled, rocking the vehicle. "You have twenty-four hours. By then Pop and Fjóla will be here, and it won't be up to you anymore."

"That sounds ominous."

Nash's smile was wry. "You have no idea."

CHAPTER NINE
DIEGO

The twilight before dawn was Diego's favorite time. No matter where he was, no matter what the weather, he always found something fascinating in the transformation of darkness by the subtle, gradual addition of light.

He'd never learned to appreciate sunsets, not the spectacular sunsets of the LA basin, not the many sunsets he'd filmed all over the globe. Morning had stillness. It had a peculiar, awakening scent. The air was different, the sky more vivid, more dramatic—even on days like this, when it was simply a vast gray expanse of light and shadow.

And when there were colors? Dawn's special rosiness, cold blues, and violets—the golden spears of first light through clouds—made even ordinary days magical, gilding the mountains and tall trees to the east, setting water droplets alight to hang on spider webs like tiny stars.

It hurt his heart to see it, but he made himself watch. Rising before dawn was both old habit and preference. Daybreak was his touchstone. His ritual.

"Light has something to teach us," his mother had once said. *"Even weak light, even filtered light, blocked light, travels at light speed."*

Diego could take his bearings anywhere in the world at daybreak and feel right at home.

So . . . what then, did that make this place? Bluewater Bay . . .

He took his breakfast out to the covered deck, where he made a mental note about refilling the bird feeder. It was peaceful there, if a little cold. The day was every shade of gray. Rain came down, and he liked its musical noise. He ought to put in some kind of fountain, maybe the bamboo kind that filled and tipped and *clunk*ed.

He could use some wind chimes too, maybe. Under the eaves where they wouldn't get destroyed by the elements.

Filming was on hiatus. He had no other work that day. No urgent errands to run. His mother used to say, *"It's times like this I get bored and start something reckless."*

She'd follow that up with a raised glass or a raised eyebrow.

"What should we do next?" she'd ask.

His mother had cared about her causes, and she'd never sat still. The way Cecil and Rachel pressured him about her photographs and papers, he could well believe she was still out there somewhere, fighting the good fight.

He unrolled his napkin and set his place. Then he went back for his coffee.

And it was exactly things like that which bugged him. He wouldn't have to make two trips to set the table if he didn't care how he ate, or what he ate, but his mother's voice was so insistent he didn't dare take shortcuts.

Not insistent.

Right.

Persistent.

Claro, Mami.

Footsteps caught his attention.

"Hello? It's me." His former tenant came around the corner of the house by the driveway. "Healey."

As if I wouldn't remember your name.

He rolled backward so he could turn and wave to his former tenant, who was being followed by someone who— "*Pendejo*. You multiplied."

"I'm Nash."

"I know." Diego gave him a nod.

"We've actually met, I think."

"Right." Diego held his hand out. "I'm with the postproduction team."

"Editing. I remember." Nash grinned and gave his hand a firm shake.

"How's Spencer?" Diego was absurdly pleased anyone would remember a tiny detail about him like that.

"Crabby. He's filming in Morocco, and the project is behind. They've had record-breaking temperatures for almost a week, and half the crew is sick with the flu."

"Sounds like most of the location shoots I've been on." Diego extended his hand toward the empty seats at his patio table. "Can I get you anything?"

"No, thanks." With a scrape of his chair, Healey sat. "We ate at the B&B. I came by to introduce Nash and see if you still want me to bring your stuff down from the garage apartment."

Diego wasn't as superstitious as his mother, for whom ghosts were a convenient way to explain away coincidences, but he gave a nervous glance around.

He was neither lazy nor credulous, but the hair stood up on his neck.

"Don't even worry about it."

Healey gave a glance toward the garage, a slight frown marring his ordinarily affable expression. "Photographic mediums are sensitive to moisture and temperature change. You'd probably better go through those boxes carefully and put the more delicate things in the house. Neither the garage nor the garage apartment were prepared for long-term storage."

"Nope." Nash snorted. "It was prepared to store me."

"But you're indestructible. Old photos are not." Healey gave his brother a friendly shove. "And anyway, you didn't have to share your room with entitled overachievers."

"How can you say that?" Nash gasped. "I'd spent my *entire childhood* with you." Nash gave him a gentle shove in return. "Anyway. I thought you liked your roommates."

"Not freshman year." After that, he'd been with Ford.

"As delightful as this homecoming is," Diego almost hated to point out the obvious, "neither of you live here anymore."

Healey chuckled. "All right, then. One time only offer. If you give me my cash back minus, I dunno, a few hundred bucks for the inconvenience, we'll bring your shit down from the garage apartment gratis, and we'll even stack it nicely in the garage so you can still park your SUV."

"We will?" Nash nudged him hard. "No. He doesn't even care if we bring the stuff down."

Diego shook his head. "You really don't have to."

Healey disagreed. "It's an honest-to-God apartment, and housing in Bluewater Bay can be tough to come by, especially when the show is filming. What if someone needs it, and it's full of boxes? What if you need some extra cash one month? It's a waste not to use it."

"Healey." Nash obviously wanted to end the conversation and go. Healey was the stubborn one. Like a reporter and his producer, they were a seasoned team. But Healey was definitely the talent.

Diego's conscience sounded suspiciously like his mother: *What if somebody needs that room and it's full?*

Without trying, Healey'd hit on the one reason Diego might listen to. A reason his mother would approve: the apartment might help someone in need.

He kept his eyes on Healey's haunting blue ones. Those were some goddamn stellar eyes. He wanted to know the name for their color. The real name: Cyan. Marine. Prussian. Periwinkle.

It wasn't because of those eyes he was considering taking Healey up on his offer. But it wasn't in spite of them, either.

"Yes." Before either brother realized he wasn't answering the question they'd asked, he quickly added, "Sure, you can clean out my garage attic for free. See how those words sound like a crappy deal? There's probably a reason for that."

"Awesome." Healey stood.

"You need to wait until it stops raining," said Diego. "I don't want my shit getting wet."

Now Nash was glaring at both of them. Diego was being such an ass, he half expected one of the brothers to slug him. Naturally, he added gasoline to the fire.

"So I can pencil you in for tomorrow morning? Weather permitting. Don't want to get wet while I sit on my porch and watch."

"We'll be here." Still smiling serenely, Healey started toward the driveway.

Nash gave Diego a nod. "Right now, I'm taking my brother to have his head examined. If they keep him, we'll reschedule. I assume he has your number?"

Diego laughed. "He does."

Of course, Diego's breakfast had gotten cold.

He gathered his food from the table and went inside. The remote was on the coffee table where he'd left it, a half-eaten batch of cookies beside it. He picked it up and returned to the show he'd been watching the night before, a Ken Burns documentary on the Dust Bowl.

"That's the golden ticket, right there, m'hijo," his mother had said about Dorothea Lange's photography. *"Facilitating empathy creates change."*

He retrieved his laptop from his backpack and opened it.

As a photojournalist, as a former news correspondent, he knew his mother's story was a powerful and—more important—a timely one.

Before her death, she'd started to tell it her way, and he'd have honored her wishes, done whatever she asked of him, provided her with technical help and physical support.

But how could he tell *her* story without her?

He tried firing up his editing software, opening the files he'd kept—informally—for his mother's projects.

Picking a random clip from the first videos—the ones she'd made with the borrowed camera from her first film production classes at night school—he tried to see his mother through a detached lens. She'd been an artist, but her real role was teacher. She'd been a mentor and a friend to so many local artists in LA, part of his reason for moving was to avoid being a sort of living monument to his mother.

He could never take her place among them.

He clicked Play and there they were, at the end of a long day in a field of strawberries. Mami sitting on the tailgate of someone's old blue El Camino. Him, laughing, clapping his hand to hers in a way-too-forceful high five. She mimed a broken hand for the camera. "*Ow,* papi . . ."

Diego remembered the clip, but not the day itself. He'd been six maybe? Mami was picking up extra work on the weekends, and he'd gone along to help. Few of the workers were women, but his mother preferred to work alongside them. "The strawberry ladies" were mostly very young—a little group of weekend day laborers who laughed at tabloid newspapers and shared tips on the best way to make up a smoky eye. They looked out for him, kept him in line when his mother wasn't around. They were all into some dude on *General Hospital*, and they talked about him constantly, like, what if he was in LA and what if they met him? What would he be like? What would they say to him, where they'd go out if they dated.

Again, always: what if, what if, what if?

If Diego was six, his mom had been not quite twenty-three, doing a work-study program at the college, going to school, and picking up odd jobs for cash on weekends with her friends—cleaning or farm work or yard work. Sometimes painting, whatever she could get.

"C'mon, papi," she called, "do that dance like MJ."

He could hardly watch himself leap lightly down from the truck to show off. At the time, Michael Jackson's latest video "Dangerous" featured his slim, athletic body, backlit, dancing in a doorway.

That was prime fodder for his earliest, most misunderstood fantasies. He'd been obsessed with Michael Jackson, imitating his dress, his walk, and his style, never leaving whichever crappy by-the-week motel they were crashing at without a black hat and aviator shades.

He'd had every move the singer made memorized, and now, even though the women obviously enjoyed his little performance, he winced, because he could see how earnest he'd been. How forthright and naive and completely ignorant.

Also, because he was the gayest kid ever, even then, and not because he swished—no. A man didn't navigate the uber-macho Latinx culture with a swish in his step. He became a pirate or a ninja. He developed untouchable swagger, or he hid and lied.

Diego had gone both ways—the swagger route, fighting with his fists, arming himself with whatever homemade weapons he could, *and* the lying route, because you can never be too safe.

He'd lied, and he'd lied, until one day, he simply couldn't lie anymore.

He'd kept his fists ready and his weapons handy, but he'd come out to his mother and Cecil and his stepsiblings.

By that time, even *he* had realized he had nothing to worry about from his large, loving family.

He didn't give a fuck about anyone else.

Finally, inevitably, the video ended. And for all the discomfort it caused, it made him smile.

They'd all been delusional: Mami, coming to the USA to claim her birthright, plus a better life for her unborn child. Those other ladies, who worked hard and lived pragmatic lives, but still cherished the hope they had a chance with a gay singer on a mainstream soap opera. And Diego, who'd converted from Catholicism to the church of Michael Jackson, never to return.

His mother's lens had captured one particular outsider's life in America as no one else's ever had—possibly, as no one else's could.

He picked up his laptop and rolled to his desk.

Cecil and Rachel had no idea what they were asking of him. It was painful, still, to see how they'd lived. How poor they'd been.

To remember people who'd treated them like garbage.

He sighed.

For his mother, then. Out of love and respect and to honor her memory, he made himself turn on his desktop. He'd transferred most of her videos and slides before he'd moved to Bluewater Bay. He needed to scan and upload her still prints and double-check the negatives were stored safely.

The first step in chronicling his mother's life, of course, would be to create an archive of the materials. The video recordings, photos, and diaries would have to be scanned and uploaded before he could begin. And since what he hadn't gotten to yet had been left in the garage apartment, he'd had the perfect excuse to put it off.

Until now.

Healey and his brother had come along at exactly the right time— or exactly the wrong time, depending. Finishing the work his mother started was the right thing to do. But he'd have to relive hard times and accept the painful reminder of a future he could no longer have.

He took a screen cap of his mother's face—she'd been younger than he was now, a single mom, wearing men's clothes, playing down her good looks so she wouldn't get hassled. Her smile was radiant. Despite the separation of death, he felt its warmth suffuse him gently, and that's what eventually made up his mind.

He wasn't superstitious, and he didn't believe in ghosts, but on the off chance...

Okay. He sighed. "All right, Mami. I'm on it."

CHAPTER TEN
HEALEY

As soon as they were back in the car, Nash turned to Healey angrily.

"So I guess *I'll* be moving boxes tomorrow. Your generosity knows no bounds."

"We'll open the trap door and set up the pulleys. No big. Did I tell you? I found the picture you left behind the footboard."

"Yeah?" He grinned. "You drink the whiskey?"

"Yeah," Healey admitted. "I'm kind of a mess."

"I know." The smile dropped off Nash's face. "What happened to you? Last time we talked, you and Ford were solid. Everything was going great. You defended! What the hell, man?"

Healey palmed his face, but it hurt too much to give it a good scrub, which was what he really wanted.

"C'mon. Talk to me." Nash's hand landed on his upper arm. It was one of the few places that didn't hurt. "What happened that night with Ford?"

Healey swallowed hard. "I can't talk about that. My attorney said—"

"Wait, you hired an attorney?"

"I—" There was a gag order in place where Ford's case was concerned. "Ford's family sent their attorney to represent me."

"Okay." Nash pulled out, creeping slowly along the street they'd grown up on. "Do you think that's wise?"

"What do you mean?"

"Maybe it'd be in your best interest to have your own attorney."

"I've done nothing wrong."

"Then why do you need an attorney?"

Healey closed his eyes. "I can't say."

Nash *humph*ed at that.

Healey groaned. "I can't believe I'm back in Bluewater Bay."

"And you're unemployed."

"Don't remind me. I've never done anything except study." Healey hesitated before asking a question he'd had for a while. "Were you ever angry about how it all went down? When the testing started, and they singled me out?"

Nash's cheeks darkened. "At first, yeah."

Healey swallowed hard. "Sorry, man. If I could go back and do things differently, I would."

"C'mon. I was jealous for, like, fifteen seconds. You got all this attention. Remember when those grad students baked you a cake?"

"I loved getting that cake."

"But then all you got to do after that was school." Nash gave a grimace. "You didn't come to Pop's workshop anymore, or watch cartoons on television, or play sports—"

"I played sports."

"Quidditch is *imaginary*, Healey."

That sent Healey right back to childhood. "Gaseous asshole."

"I know you are, but what am I?"

"You're a flatulating blowskunk." Healey rested his head against the seat and closed his eyes. He could remember everything. It was part of his gift. His curse. He could remember all the times he'd been the center of everyone's attention, all the times he'd looked over and seen a grit-teethed, long-suffering expression on Nash's face. As if he was *determined* to be happy playing with Legos in a corner while his brother undertook a series of complicated physical and mental tests.

Maybe Nash *was* only envious of the cake. At least he'd gotten cake too. One thing you could say about the Holly family is they shared, whether they had nothing or abundance.

"I missed having you around," Nash said quietly. "I missed you being just mine back then."

"I missed you too."

Healey pushed the audio button, and AC/DC's "Highway to Hell" came on. He laughed. Perfect way to break up a potentially maudlin moment. "Jesus, man. How can you still hear?"

"I was tired when I drove in last night. I kept the radio cranked up and the windows open to stay awake."

Healey needed a station that didn't offer his spleen as a sacrifice to the gods of rock and roll. He reached for the dial. "I'm here now. You don't have to wake the dead to keep you company anymore."

"No." Nash flicked his hand off the knob. "Keep your alternative hands off my radio."

"How does Spencer put up with you?"

Nash grinned like a hyena. "I'm necessary."

"You're what now?" Nash was so goddamn smug, Healey had to focus on finding something interesting outside his window. Maybe Spencer was Nash's figurative letter to Hogwarts. Or maybe he was Nash's Hagrid. In Hollywood parlance, Spencer was a big hairy deal. Healey thought the comparison apt.

Spencer gave Nash entrée to a world beyond loneliness. He'd drawn him into a global adventure, a passionate romance, and a new way of looking at himself.

And Nash was so happy. Probably for the first time ever. Healey didn't just hope, he *knew* deep in his heart that his twin was in a forever kind of love.

Nash said, "Spencer loves me. It doesn't make sense, but I don't complain, you know?"

No. I don't know.

I thought I knew a lot of things.

But now I'm not sure I ever knew anything.

Healey's head ached.

"Can we play a station that's somewhere between death metal and whatever banjo misconception you have about me?"

"Sure." With a grin, Nash found a station they could both live with. Then, he ruined everything by asking where Healey wanted to go. When the starkly true answer to that question came to him, Healey didn't want to say.

"Bayside Ridge?" Nash knew what he'd been thinking. He always knew.

Healey nodded. "Please."

He closed his eyes and tried to bring his mother's face into focus. As had often happened lately, he couldn't do it. He didn't remember her face anymore. Or her voice. Or how she smelled.

She'd been gone so long.

Pop and Nash visited her grave regularly, decorating with seasonal flowers, leaving trinkets and reminders. They sent him photos, even. He hadn't been to see his mother's grave since he graduated high school. For whatever reason, his father and Nash, the keepers of their mother's flame, never pressured him about it.

Now, he probably didn't need the grim reminder he'd almost joined her, wherever she was. Yet when they pulled into the cemetery and got out, the walk from headstone to headstone in the late-morning drizzle wasn't unpleasant. In fact, he wouldn't mind ending up in a place like this, next to his mother.

It was as good a place as any.

Smack. Nash swatted him, open-handed, across the back of the head.

Healey cowered away from a second attempt. "Ow. What the—"

"Goddamn it." Nash's breath misted the chilly air. "I told Pop you were going to fucking wallow."

"Jesus. I guess we filled that swear jar for nothing all those years." Healey's step landed him near a sprinkler head. He banged his foot hard. "*Shit.*"

About twenty-five yards away, an older woman turned to glare at him.

"Now who's waking up the dead?"

"Screw you." Healey said as he limp-walked away.

Finally, he found his mother's marker.

Just as he thought, it still didn't tell him a thing except what he already knew. Beloved Wife and Mother. The words were true—he'd heard the stories.

"I hardly remember her."

He had scenes, but maybe they only came from the videos and pictures his dad had shown him. He couldn't remember her singing to him, but he knew she'd done that every night. "You Are My Sunshine," sung to each of them in their separate beds.

"I don't remember much either," Nash offered. "I have feelings about Mom, but very few memories."

Healey nodded. That was nice to know—time wasn't only erasing his memories.

Misery loves company.

He swiped tears from his eyes before taking a deep breath.

In silent cooperation, they scooped rotting leaves away from the base of their mother's grave. Healey wanted to shine the marker, but neither of them had any kind of cloth. It seemed the ultimate irony—the person who most certainly would be carrying a pack of tissues was also the one buried under the headstone they wanted to use it on.

Later that afternoon, they bought a pizza and a six-pack of beer to take back to the B&B. Once there, they holed up in their tiny room, talking until neither one of them could stay awake any longer.

Nash took a call from Spencer, and Healey dodged one from their pop.

When they lay on their backs in the barest light, Nash turned to him. "This feels familiar."

"Be more familiar if we each had a bed," Healey said drily.

Nash gave a little shove with his elbow. "Only if we fight over the one next to the window for an hour."

"Or until Pop comes in, calls us 'you darn Furbies,' and says if we don't go to sleep, he'll invent the 'Kid Klonker.'" Healey smiled. "You're doing okay?"

"Hmm?" Nash could drop off like he was switching off a light.

"You got what you hoped for? Spencer and the traveling. You think you'll get married?"

In the low light, the smile that blossomed over Nash's lips was like a beacon. "Mm-hmm. I could, but Spencer still goes fight or flight when the word is mentioned. His eyes totally light up around kids, though."

"You'd be awesome dads." Healey drifted.

"What about you? I gotta call you Dr. Holly now."

Healey grinned into the darkness. "Hell yeah, you do."

Sleepily, Nash shifted so he was facing Healey. He propped his head on his hand and blinked. "I get that you're going through something painful. Ford didn't work out. But hang on to how good you did. You blew through the doctorate program at Stanford, for Christ's sakes."

"Wait—"

"You're ten times smarter than anyone I've ever met. And you're awesome. Plus, look at me? I am all. Fucking. That. And you have exactly the same DNA going for you. There'll be guys lining up to get with you, even though you're right-handed."

Healey laughed so hard he had to cover his face with the pillow. "I knew you were going to find a way to make this all about you."

"Nah. Cheer up, little fella. Even a copy of a copy says the same thing if you can read it."

"Fuck you." If Healey hadn't been so banged up, he'd have grabbed Nash and tried to strangle him. Eventually they'd have rolled off the bed. Then they'd get kicked out of the B&B for fighting and wrecking things.

As one does.

"It's not about Ford." As soon as Healey said the words, he knew they weren't entirely true. He jammed the pillow back under his head. "Well. Tangentially, it is about him, by the principles of—"

"English, please."

"I'm really not supposed to say. Ford's parents, his lawyers, don't want me talking about this."

"Like I give a limp-dicked fuck about them," Nash said. "What about you?"

"Ford is brilliant."

"Yeah, he is." Nash sighed. "And he made some poor decisions. Sometimes smart people do dumb things. And breaking it off with you—"

"It's not that." Closing his eyes was the only way to keep enough distance between him and Nash. "Shit happens. Scientists and statisticians factor that in. God, of course people make mistakes. Mistakes are easy. You own them. You move past them. This is different. This is—"

"Wait. What?"

"There are things so much worse than mistakes, Nash. You have no idea. I think I have a fundamental flaw . . ." Healey pressed his lips together. "I think it's like bad genes, man."

"Jesus." Nash gave him a bony-fingered jab. "What happened between you?"

"We were going to save the world together. Our brilliant minds. Gonna save everyone. God, I can't tell you how naive we were. How thoughtless and dripping with privilege."

Healey couldn't laugh or cry any more. He was numb.

"You gotta give me more than that to go on, bro." Nash's gentle voice killed him.

It *killed* him.

And because twins start pushing your buttons from their very first breath, it took nothing for his brother to strip all his artifice away. Healey gripped his pillow tightly. He couldn't let Nash see him like this.

Didn't want it.

Couldn't prevent it.

"Heals... Gimme... What the ever-loving *fuck* is going on with you?" More insistent, now, Nash got Healey's pillow-shield free, finally.

Healey glared at him. "I let Ford down. His meds needed tweaking. We all missed the signs. Not just me, Nash. His family. His doctors."

Nash froze. "I see."

"I know what you're going to say, but he's—"

"Like hell you do." Nash shook his head as if he couldn't believe what he was hearing. "Don't make excuses."

"It's not that simple. Looking back, the last three weeks before the accident seemed strange. I chalked it up to the stress of school. The last few months things weren't going so well. Now I think he must have started rapid cycling in late May. We talked it over."

"Then what?"

"You know what. We decided to take a last-minute trip."

"Why would you do that? Why would you—" He pinched the bridge of his nose. "You trusted him, even though you have tangible proof addicts can't be trusted."

"Ford is not an addict. Not only that, anyway. And I don't have proof *Ford* can't be—"

"You sure the fuck do now!" Nash said angrily. "Did you learn nothing from Pop and Christine? You have tangible proof that with addicts, everything can go to hell in an instant. Christine swore she wasn't drinking and look at what happened to Shelby."

"Goddamn it. Bipolar disorder is a diagnosis, not a character flaw. The substance abuse is a symptom—"

"What happened?"

"I can't tell you. I wish I could tell you, but I'm *under a gag order*."

"You will tell me, eventually."

"I can't, Nash. If there was anyone I would tell, it's you. I just can't."

Nash knew him well enough to let the words just lie there. To turn and offer his solid, warm back to lean against. Healey turned too, and let his back fall against his brother's.

Back to back.

They'd tried to come into the world that way. He hoped they'd go out of it that way too. Unlikely.

Spencer would probably have something to say about that.

But still... Healey was going to have to tell Nash what happened. He was going to have to describe the night Ford and he had ended up in a potentially lethal road rage situation together. How his highly overrated brains and his new diploma hadn't saved him from nearly getting himself killed.

They didn't have secrets, and he wasn't going to change the rules now.

Irrationally angry, Healey took an experimental breath.

Smelled like home.

CHAPTER ELEVEN
DIEGO

Diego never believed the Holly brothers would actually show up, but the black SUV rolled up at 7 a.m. and the twins practically fell out of it. They carried shopping bags with the Burnt Toast B&B logo on them. One of them had a carrier with three coffee cups.

As he watched through his security cam setup, they were smiling and laughing.

Who gets excited about moving a stranger's boxes at zero dark thirty?

They were hot. White boys with dark hair and solid, muscled bodies. They reminded him of American Staffordshire Terriers—especially Healey with his black eye. Now that the image was in his head, he'd never get it out.

Before they could knock, Diego glanced out the peephole. They'd arranged themselves side by side on his porch and were wiping smug grins off their smug faces.

Okay, maybe Nash and Healey Holly weren't smug, but Diego resented them anyway.

And he didn't know why.

But if he *did* know, it might be because he was lonely now that his mother was gone. He hardly ever got to see his brothers. Before his conscience could use his mother's voice to ask whose fault that was, he jerked the door open.

"Hello." Nash stepped back in surprise. "Were we that loud?"

"No, man. Check it out." Healey nudged his brother before pointing out the cameras Diego thought he'd hidden so well. "Dude's just paranoid. You keeping a grow op in there?"

"No," Diego said sourly. "I have high-end electronic equipment and some of it doesn't belong to me. Security system. Big deal."

"Only Healey is judging you," said Nash. "It's 'cause he's all judgy like that. But I wouldn't think you were paranoid, even if you put in a panic room."

"Thanks," said Diego.

"Did you?" Nash asked hopefully.

"There's no panic room."

Healey's sneakered foot lightly caught his brother's. "Where would he have put a panic room? There's no space for a panic room."

The American Staffordshire analogy deepened, solidified, and became a caricature. Oh, yeah. He could see it. Totally. And because he could never get enough of puppies, he started to thaw toward the Holly twins.

Which wasn't at all what he had planned.

Then again. Erstwhile tenant was hot. Identical faces, Nash's was harder. Leaner. Healey's was more elegant. Both had the sides of their hair shaved. Healey's hair, which looked thick and wavy, hung below his shoulders, while Nash's longest hair barely reached his eyes.

New tenant looked a little like the new James Bond's Q.

All Diego could think was, *How much is that doggy in the window?* The image popped predictably into his imagination.

"Wait. What are you laughing at?" Healey asked.

"Nothing. Here's the remote for the garage door." Diego gave them the new unit. "I'll be out in a minute."

"We'll set up your breakfast outside like yesterday." Healey pointed vaguely in that direction. Nash was already rounding the corner of the house.

After Diego closed the door between them, he sat in the foyer for a time, contemplating the plans he'd had for the day before the wrecking crew showed up. He'd found a thirty-second clip of his mother, standing in a field of sunflowers, and used it to piece together a very rudimentary opening sequence for the documentary Rachel wanted him to make. Over it, he'd laid the first words she'd penned for what she'd hoped would be her memoirs—the first of many books she'd planned to write:

"I never recognized the word 'No.' My parents were very religious. They wanted me not seen and not *heard, even when it came to expressing my joy. I am convinced the first time I heard the words, 'No, Gabriella,'*

I recognized them for the oppression they were. After that, I never listened to anyone who told me no again."

He hadn't gotten much sleep.

Through the slider, he could see his guests setting his patio table. He rolled outside to join them.

"Got coffee, cinnamon rolls, and some sort of—" Healey handed over a sandwich wrapped in parchment paper. "Egg and bacon ciabatta thing. Jim from the Burnt Toast sends his regards."

Bemused, Diego took his place at the table between them. He took a moment to study his guests. For a while, he simply watched them talk. Listened for patterns in their speech.

Healey wore a man-bun. *Kill me now.*

Probably, even if they wore their hair the same way, he'd be able to tell them apart. One twin was right-handed, one left. That was an obvious difference. Healey's hair had a cowlick that went one way from the center of his forehead, and Nash's hair swept in the other direction.

Nash was talkative and comical. Healey was reticent, but that might have resulted from pain. He wanted to ask about the accident but sensed Healey's emotions were still too raw.

After a few uncomfortable seconds, he saw the best way to tell the twins apart, even if they were dressed alike and wearing hats. Nash smiled more—warm happiness seemed to exude from him. In comparison, Healey radiated a kind of curious intensity. Energy Diego could feel in his chest like the vibration of a low-flying plane.

"I didn't expect you back, except to pick up your cash." He pulled a fat envelope from the bag on his wheelchair and slid it across the table.

Healey half stood to shove it in his back pocket. "You didn't think I'd keep my word?"

"No. That's not— Are you really here to move boxes because I might need that apartment someday?"

"That, and—" Nash took a long pull on his travel mug "—Healey's always gotta have a project."

"Are you saying I'm a project?" Diego put his sandwich down carefully. A silence descended over the table. In retrospect, he was prepared to say even the birds stopped chirping.

"Hell no." Healey looked between him and Nash. "Moving your boxes down from the garage is a project. *You* are a dude I'm trying to make friends with."

"Why?"

The twins looked at each other and then back at him.

"What do you mean why?" Healey asked.

"Why do we gotta be friends?" he asked. "Because I bought the house you used to live in? If you want to have some kind of old-home week, have at. You want to clean out my garage? I'd have to be an idiot to stop you, so I'm down. But you don't have to bring me breakfast. I don't *need* your help."

He'd backed his chair up and turned. Behind him, he felt tension build. Healey followed him inside. "Can I talk to you a minute, Diego?"

"Sure." Oh, Jesus. *Now* he wanted to talk too. Great.

Next you'll be calling social services on my behalf.

Motherfucking busybody.

Maybe another time he could deal with this. But with his dad and Rachel breathing down his neck and no work to speak of, he was ready to climb the walls. He so did not need do-gooders, church folk, or even well-meaning friends on his doorstep.

Eyes on the floor, Healey said, "First of all, I apologize again for any inconvenience we've caused you."

Oh, man. That again. Diego mumbled, "You weren't an inconvenience."

Healey sat across from him. "I'm no good at this kind of thing. I was in an accident. I came to Bluewater Bay more from instinct than any real desire to be here. I came to your house, and that was intrusive, and I apologize. My brother's here now, and I'll be okay. I guess I needed my family all along. But you know what?"

Diego didn't want to play a stupid guessing game. He lifted an eyebrow and waited for Healey to get on with it. After an excruciating few seconds he snapped, "What?"

"I keep getting this vibe here, between us." Healey gestured. "You don't seem to mind having the company. You don't *seem* to mind me personally, but then you're all like, *Fuck off* one minute later. What am I doing wrong here?"

Diego paused. The man was willing to communicate.

He was even... good at it.

"I'm not a project." Diego's brain couldn't move past that word.

"Of course you're not." Healey wrinkled his nose. "I think I might be, though."

Diego concurred. "Not my problem. In case you didn't notice, I have problems of my own."

Healey took a breath and let it out slowly. "Yeah. I get that. I'm sorry we bothered you. We'll move those boxes like we said, and then we'll get out of your hair, okay?"

Healey held his hand out for a shake, like a sandlot ball player agreeing to pay for a broken window.

Now Diego felt like an ass.

"You don't have to do that. Next time my stepdad is here, he'll move them for me. If I need anything before that, I'll just hire some kids from the high school to bring it down."

"Stubborn ass." Healey sighed. Stood to leave. "But just so you know, it'd be a piece of cake with the trap door. I'm sorry we bothered—"

"Wait. I have a trap door?" Diego glanced up.

"You never noticed? It's a rectangle in the ceiling with a folding ladder?"

"Oh, that." Diego swallowed his disappointment. "I never thought of that as a trap door, is all. Secret trap doors are much more interesting."

"I guess. But we rigged up a pulley system when Nash moved in. That was awesome. We can do that again, and have your boxes down and stacked in no time."

"I am not a project."

Healey's smile was a pathetic, momentary baring of teeth. He sighed. "Then we'll get out of your hair. Sorry to bother you."

Aw, dang. Now he'd *kicked* an American Staffordshire puppy.

"No. I'm the one who's—"

"Don't let him play you," Nash yelled from the other side of the slider. "When he gets all mopey like that, people give him candy. Plus, you gotta watch out for that pout. And his choir boy act."

"Don't give up all my secrets." Healey turned and flipped his brother off.

"Oh. And also he's into you." Nash double flipped him off right back.

"Right." Diego stiffened his spine so fast—the upper half anyway—it hurt. "I'm very sure."

"I'm not into you?" Healey's scorching blue gaze pinned him to his chair. "News to me."

"Don't you dare fuck with me." Diego's voice broke. "You and your evil twin."

"I—" Healey's hurt was etched in the lines on face. "We would *never*."

That singular spark—the gut-punch of wild attraction that would have made his cock lurch before the accident—now made his chest flutter instead.

Dude might be serious.

But why now?

Why did this sudden, inexplicable chemistry have to happen with Healey Holly—that chipper, entitled wreck of a man—*now*?

Diego didn't let himself look away. "You don't know shit about me."

"That's right. I don't," Healey agreed with a dazzling smile. "I'd like to, though. And it's weird, because I just broke up with someone, but that was a long time coming. Still I—I was pretty convinced I'd never meet anyone I dug that much again. And here you are. I can't stop looking at your mouth. I should probably shut up now."

"Probably." Diego whispered the word.

Healey nodded. "I didn't think this through, but I'll say this: I believe in chemistry. I thought you were hot when we first met, so maybe I've been gum you can't get off your shoe, but at least now you know why."

Tension knotted behind Diego's breastbone. "You don't even know if my junk works."

"That's none of my business until you make it my business." Bastard tried to hide his grin. "Full disclosure. Mine's, uh. You know. Pretty standard."

While that hung between them, Diego's heart got struck by lightning, and thunder echoed in his belly. The moment went on and on and on. He couldn't think of a thing to say to that. Well, he could think of one.

Yes.

If he met Healey in a bar, at work, at school, and if Healey wanted to hook up? He'd say *yes.* He'd say, *Take me home* and *let me suck you* and *come all over me,* and *fuck me hard* and . . .

Oh. By the way.

My dick works, thanks, just not the way it used to and not the way you'd think, and I'm not really comfortable talking about that with strangers.

Before Diego could say any of that, the words got caught in his pride. They disappeared, along with an apology for acting like an asshat when all the Holly twins had done was bring him breakfast.

"You okay?" Healey asked.

"Fine." *Goddamn it.* Why couldn't he just ask for what he wanted? Why was it always so fucking hard?

"Anyway." Thoroughly red now, Healey offered a second suggestion before Diego could make himself talk. "Come eat something and think about it while we work."

CHAPTER TWELVE
HEALEY

The garage was quantifiably different, but still Healey's chest hurt when the door rolled up to reveal... obviously not his pop, with his glasses on his head and his usual bewildered, yet fiercely joyous expression on his face.

Healey had known what he'd find, or what he wouldn't find, but it rankled to see the changes Diego'd made to what was once his home.

Diego had painted the garage floor with slick speckled paint and installed pristine white cabinets and peg boards to hold his tools. There was a refrigerator freezer out here, and shelves of sports equipment and free weights.

Gone was the cozy chaos. The tinkerer's workshop. The place where, together, he and Nash had found everything they'd needed for a thousand stupid, reckless adventures. He missed it. It hurt, because he didn't know if he'd ever feel that way about anyplace again.

They rigged another pulley system, and in very little time, Nash had lowered all the boxes down to Diego and Healey. After the upstairs room was cleared out, Healey cleaned it while Diego told Nash how to arrange things against an empty wall. Nash obviously got the worst part of that deal, being the designated muscle. But he and Diego made a decent team.

Diego had a dry, dark wit Healey liked a lot. He had a slim little smile sometimes, like the barest crescent moon behind a thick layer of cloud. How he wished Diego's figurative sky would clear so he could see Diego's full moon smile—but maybe once wouldn't be enough and why take a chance like that?

"Why not?" he asked himself. Why not take a chance on something that could be really, really good?

Jesus. Now I am my own evil twin.

Upstairs with Nash in his old apartment, he gave the place a final once-over.

"Miss it?" he asked.

"The apartment? No." Nash ran some water into the tiny sink and used a paper towel to wipe the counters down. "I miss you and Pop and Shelby and knowing all I have to do to see my family is walk down those stairs."

The apartment was guest ready. They'd accomplished what they'd come here to do. But it was harder to leave than he'd thought it would be.

Healey picked up the broom. "When Pop asked if I was okay with selling the house, I said sure. I mean... why not sell it, right?"

"You want to move back here?"

"No." He shrugged. "Yeah. Maybe. I don't know."

Nash shook his head. "Well, we gotta get out of Diego's hair while you decide. So what's next?"

"Hell if I know." Healey went to the window and looked outside. The view of the street was peaceful. "Nothing's the same—"

"I meant today. You know what? You should get with hot dude down there. Did you see the way he looked at you?"

"I was too busy looking at him. But I swear. I am not ready to start anything new with—"

"Who's talking about starting anything? I'm talking about getting busy. Hot dude is hot."

"Nope."

"C'mon. I know you," Nash said firmly. "You make a plan, and boom. You're done. You're sixteen moves ahead of everyone else. That's what happened with Ford. When things didn't go your way, you lost your shit."

"I did not. Where are you getting this from?"

"When you love someone, you'll do anything for them, even if it isn't in your best interest," he said, grimly. "Or theirs."

"This is all so *not true*."

"It is. But I'm here to look out for you," Nash told him. "You're a mad scientist, like Pop. Guys like you can't do it for yourselves."

Pfeh. "At least I'm not some actor's fancy man."

Nash preened. "I look fancy to you?"

"Yes."

"What if I do this?" Nash put a gentle headlock on Healey, and ruffled his hair. "I still look fancy to you?"

"Fuck. Off."

"Imma call Shelby and tell her you don't know how to talk to a boy you like," Nash threatened.

"*No.* She'll start sending me all those slash fic links again."

"Maybe you need a little fluffing." Nash let go and stepped back. "You're not filling me with confidence here."

Healey raked his good hand through his hair before winding it back up and resettling the wooden pin holding it. He capitulated under his brother's gentle prodding. "I like him."

"What's not to like? The man is hot. And he digs you, even if you're both being idiots."

"Shh," Healey hushed him. "He'll hear you."

"He went back inside the house to get something. Did you tell him you think he's hot?" Healey nodded. "Then what happened?"

"Nothing. He stared at me like I'd lost my damn mind."

"When we go back down, why don't you invite him out? Or maybe you should stay here and talk to him. Watch a movie together. Canoodle."

"I'll try, but you saw how receptive he's been."

"You just gotta get through all the armor with guys like that. He reminds me of Spencer. He needs an outlet."

Healey groaned. "According to you, everybody needs an outlet."

Nash frowned at him. "They do."

"Not everyone is a seething mass of unvented passions."

"Must just be everybody I meet, then. Anyway, you can't be saying Diego doesn't have some unresolved anger issues, because—"

"You're right, but maybe it's not any of our business. Out, we're done here."

"Unless you ask him out." Nash did as he was told, taking the broom, the dustpan, and half the cleaning supplies with him. "You will, won't you?"

"He's such a prickly bastard." Healey gave one last look at the place. He turned out the light and closed the door behind him.

"That gonna stop you?" Nash waited for him on the landing and they went down together.

"I—" Healey paused. "I'm attracted to him, all right? But it doesn't seem mutual, if you know what I mean."

"Ah, jeez. You're still such a child."

"And you'd do what?"

"I would hit that like the fist of an angry god, if I was you."

Of course you would. "In this situation, you can see where it might be politic to go slow, though, right?"

"Because he's in chair? Who would be better for a guy like that than someone who has some idea of what he needs?"

"I don't, though. I don't even know what I need, half the time."

"But you know the right questions to ask."

"If he doesn't bite my head off."

They found Diego on the patio, waiting, with a pitcher of lemonade and more of his homemade cookies.

Healey turned to Nash, hoping he'd provide some kind of an excuse for him to be alone with Diego—all he wanted was a plan or some subterfuge Diego wouldn't necessarily see as manipulation. *Please.*

Diego spoke first. "Your brother can take off now that the heavy lifting is done." He met Healey's surprised gaze with an unreadable expression. To Nash, he said, "I'll run Healey back to the B&B later if he wants to stay here for a while."

"Don't have to tell me twice." Nash pulled his car keys from his pocket. "I'm out."

"Nash." Healey hesitated.

"You want to go back with me or stay?" Nash asked.

Healey glanced at Diego, who was doing his best not to look like he cared one way or the other. Maybe he didn't. Or maybe he was trying to act cool.

Between them, somebody had to man up.

Healey shook his head. "I'll stay."

"See you later, bro." Nash grinned and made a fist. They bumped.

"I'll text you."

After Nash left, an eternity passed before either of them spoke. Diego eyed him warily. Healey stared Diego down, feeling awkward as hell. Finally, he pulled out a chair and turned it to straddle it.

"Hey." He opened with a majestic conversational gambit. "S'up."

"I get why you do that." Diego's smile was cautious. "You sit so I don't have to crane my neck to look up at you."

"Guilty. My sister uses a wheelchair. I've got habits."

"So. I have a rental apartment now?"

"Yep. It's all clean. Want to see?"

Diego shot him a sour look. "Sure, as soon as I sprout wings."

Healey sighed. "You're not a very creative problem-solver, are you? I say this not because I think you're dumb or anything. Many brilliant people can't find their way out of a walk-in closet."

"Name one." Diego's anger winked from his dark irises like . . . something else's eyes.

"Caught me." Healey looked away. "In the case of the indomitable garage stairs: One, I could carry you up there piggyback. Two, if my brother came back, I could put you and your chair in the pulley system and lift you that way. And three—" Healey'd had enough of Diego's sarcasm. He held his phone up and gave it a little wiggle. "I might have made a video of the place with my phone so I could show it to you that way."

Diego looked away. "A'ight."

"So my question is: Do you like taking no for an answer? Because I don't. If I want something and the answer is no, I find a better question. I'm a scientist. I can't help myself."

Even before Diego's face paled, Healey realized he'd gone way too far. Because *wow*. What an ableist, shit-for-brains thing to say. Too blunt, Healey. Too blunt, too soon, too everything.

But maybe if a guy's going to be that thin-skinned, he shouldn't be such a dick.

"Look, no—" Healey rubbed his temples. "God, I'm sorry. I didn't mean to be so—"

"Say that again." Diego's lips tightened.

First he screwed up with the word *project*, and now this. Was he destined to hit Diego's hot buttons every time? Shelby was going to kill him. She was going to laugh at him and then she was going to kill him.

Diego was a hot man with equally hot buttons all over him.

Diego was a human antipersonnel mine.

"I said, 'Do you like taking no for an answer?'" he repeated. "But I swear I didn't mean that the way it sounded. You—"

"Come with me, please," Diego said as he headed for the sliding door. "I want to show you something."

Healey followed him inside to the living room, where changes thoroughly distinguished the place from the home Healey had grown up in. It was a decent-sized room. Like their family had, Diego made the most of the space. It served as an office, a place to entertain guests, and a media room without being cluttered with furniture.

He'd given the walls a fresh coat of dove-gray paint and accented with vibrant blues. Light flooring and lots of living plants kept the room from feeling cold.

"The place looks nice."

"Thanks." Diego picked up the remote. "But what I wanted you to see is this." He played a video clip of a woman standing in a field of sunflowers.

Healey studied her facial features and turned back. "Mother? Sister? She looks like you."

"Mother." Diego nodded. "She used to ask me if I liked taking no for an answer too. That was... like... her thing."

Healey turned back to the screen. The woman had long dark hair and Diego's hooded brown eyes. Full lips. "She's very beautiful."

A smile lifted the corners of Diego's mouth. "Do you believe in ghosts?"

"No." Healey shook his head. "Sorry. I absolutely do not."

Like he'd smashed Diego over the head with a hammer, the conversation halted suddenly. Awkwardly. "For real?"

Aw, man. Healey knew where this was going.

He'd stopped arguing with his pop and Nash and Fjóla and Shelby about shit like this. They wanted the world to be full of magic and it was... it really was.

Just not the way they hoped.

Science is the magic of reality.

"Oh, wow. Nope, I'm sorry. No to ghosts, ESP, and religion. No to all the lies humans tell themselves to explain the way the world is. We would be much better off exploring things scientifically."

In the background, soft music played as Diego's mother and the sunflowers looped again.

"You and me could not be more different," Diego said finally.

"Because I don't believe in spooks?"

"What about God?"

"Er. Nope. Sorry. I kind of see religion as a form of medieval crowd control." Had Healey admitted that? Out loud?

Diego's face turned to stone.

Healey was quick to reassure him. "You can believe whatever you want. Just because I don't, doesn't mean you shouldn't if it makes you feel better about things."

"That's mighty magnanimous of you." Diego's cheeks darkened. "Knowing my beliefs are okay with you makes everything so much better."

Healey dropped his smile. "Likewise, you're allowing me to believe what I choose."

"But you think religion is childish."

Oh, for heaven's sake! "I did not say your beliefs are childish. I said *I* don't believe. If your faith is that fragile—"

"I did not say my faith was fragile," Diego shouted. "Goddamn it, you piss me off."

"You'll probably find it hard to believe"—Healey fought a nervous grin—"but I get that a lot."

Diego rolled a half foot forward, then back, then forward.

"You're pacing," Healey pointed out. "Why are you so pissed about what I believe?"

"You throw religion and superstition and ESP and ghosts in the same category."

"Magical thinking, yes. But there are a fuckton of naturally occurring things that are so magical you wouldn't even consider acknowledging something as silly as spiritualism."

Wheels still, Diego asked, "Like what?"

"Crystals, for one thing. You have no idea how awesome crystals are. And coral reefs. And fractals. And fireworks, and—"

"My mother believed crystals have metaphysical healing power," Diego admitted. "I guess you think that's pretty stupid."

"Anything can have a placebo effect," Healey said gently. "A simple belief can change your body chemistry. A smile can do that. You can call it magic or miraculous if you want, but in reality, it's biology."

Diego's gaze hardened. "And you don't believe God could be the architect of all this?"

This always happens. You know it always happens and you talk about religion anyway.

Wincing, Healey said, "I can't prove the existence of God. But I can prove the existence of the placebo response. The findings of scientists can be reproduced. My point is humans don't need pretend magic, Stanford Quidditch excepted. The world is magical enough. Biodiversity is magical. People use science every day to solve problems and make the world a better place."

Diego took up Healey's theme but sarcastically. "And modern medicine is making new strides, I should be so grateful, and on and on." Diego sounded exhausted. "I don't see why everything's always gotta be either-or with you people."

"Us people?" Healey pointed to himself. "I'm a *you people*, now?"

"Science doesn't explain everything."

"It doesn't," Healey agreed, "*yet*. Maybe someday it will. My slice of the science pie is pretty small. I'm afraid I don't have all the answers. Christ. This moment calls for a beer. When you move a guy's shit, he's supposed to buy you a beer."

"Yeah, all right," Diego agreed. "I have some in the fridge."

"Unless you'd rather go out."

"Don't wanna stay in with me?" Diego challenged. "There's beer in my fridge."

All the breath left Healey's body.

Diego seemed relaxed, his face blank. Yet he was tapping the tip of his pinky finger anxiously on the wheel of his chair. Healey doubted he even realized he was doing it. It was nice to know they were both nervous about this thing they were edging toward. Maybe if Healey was honest, it'd start things off on the right foot.

He got two bottles of beer, popped them open on the counter, and returned to find Diego putting away his laptop. The television was no longer on. Silence blanketed the house.

Diego seemed to be waiting for him to do something, because that's pretty much what he'd said he'd do . . . So, no pressure there.

Healey offered Diego his beer. "You should probably know I'm not very good at this whole small-talk thing. I'm more big talk. The cosmos. The big questions. Who was the first human to verifiably put the bop in the bop-she-bop-she-bop."

"What a surprise." Diego took a swig. "He's kidding around."

"So what do you suggest I do?" Healey dragged a chair closer to Diego's before sitting. "Got any ideas?"

"This is your seduction. What did you have planned?"

"Er . . . Begging, maybe?" Healey offered the sexy eyes. "Perhaps some groveling later if we get along?"

When Diego cracked a shy smile, Healey slipped from his chair, letting his knees hit the ground with a thud. He put his hands lightly on Diego's knees, skimmed them up his thighs.

"How 'bout I just start right here? And we'll see what comes up?"

"Wait. Stop." Diego took Healey's hands before they could unzip his jeans.

"Okay." Healey stilled.

"Just— Wait. Sorry."

"Okay?" Healey drew back warily, hands up like he was being robbed. "Better?"

"There are things we need to talk about—" Diego's face lost some of its color while he spoke. "And honest to God, they are not sexy things and you still have to listen to me."

"I'm listening." Wariness almost edged out curiosity. "Do I want to hear this?"

"The human spine is exactly like a bundle of telephone wires—"

"Wait." Healey gave the time-honored hand gesture for time-out. "What?"

"My little sister, Shelby, has a T7 spinal cord injury, remember? I'm well aware of what a spine is."

"Okay, then, in that case, there are two types of erections—"

Healey blew out a deep breath. "I understand the mechanism, really. I don't want to rush you. But can't we maybe push past the intro and go straight to how I can get you off? Because right now, the only thing I can think of is watching you come."

CHAPTER THIRTEEN
DIEGO

Aw...
Jesus Christ.
"You want to—"

"Get you off," Healey specified. "Do you have a preference?"

"No, no, no, no . . ." Diego pushed his chair back and wheeled around so there was plenty of space between them. "Sit."

Healey sat on the floor like a kindergartener. He was interested. Focused. He'd gone into student mode. Healey was a student of the universe and now Healey was ready to study him.

Awesome.

"It doesn't happen like that. I'm sorry. I really am. But there's things I need to do, and this isn't—"

"All right. We can go at your pace. I only want you to know I'm not scared of—" Healey indicated Diego, and his wheelchair, and pretty much everything below his waist "—what's going on there."

Kill me now. Just . . . please let a hole in the ground open up.

"You want to know what? I'm *scared*, all right?" Diego thudded his chest. "I'm totally out of my comfort zone here. I could not be more out of my comfort zone if I was on an iceberg suspended over an active volcano."

"So that's a no?" Healey got to his knees. Eye level again. The man was insufferable. "Are you saying no to getting off? Because—"

"Not no." As Healey drew closer, Diego gulped air.

When their lips were little more than a breath apart, Healey whispered, "I'd really like to kiss you. But that's it for now, if you want. Okay?"

Healey tilted his head before coming closer. Warm soft lips pressed his. The light scrape of a beard roughened his upper lip.

Healey smelled of coffee, hand sanitizer, and faintly, almonds. As he deepened their kiss, he tangled the fingers of his good hand in Diego's hair.

Oh. Pleasure.

To be touched, to be cradled in human hands.

Baptized by breath and spit and spunk.

Kissing he could do. Kissing was good.

Plus, Healey brought a kind of determination to it. As though kissing was an end in itself. As though he had all the time in the world to explore how pressure and proximity made Diego's breath catch in his throat. Made his heart race and his skin flush.

It's all gonna stop when he slides his hands up my thighs, only to discover my junk is literally disconnected to my brain.

Healey didn't seem fazed by that, but it was only a matter of time.

Awkward explanations would have to be made.

Understanding would dawn.

Healey would probably smile and nod the whole time they talked about it, but it wouldn't be genuine.

If he was desperate enough, or horny enough, he'd stick around for the big finale. Maybe.

In the meantime, Healey was letting the fingers of his cast hand drift over Diego's nipples—one of Diego's remaining bona fide sweet spots. Healey couldn't possibly know what he was doing, but ah, God, it felt so fucking good, Diego's head fell back and his mouth dropped open.

Smooth.

At this point, it might be politic to tell Healey what he was doing in all innocence would make Diego "spasm" if he continued it long enough, because whatever capricious gods had been in charge of his body after his accident had a little fun rewiring him before they put him back together again.

"Someone likes this," Healey observed almost clinically. "Need a little more pressure?"

"Mm-hmm." Diego decompressed his spine for a few seconds, then sat himself forward slightly in the chair for balance before removing his shirt. Healey helped, and when Diego's head finally popped out of the tight neck hole, they both laughed.

"You look like a baby owl." Healey smoothed his hair. "This okay? Me touching you like this?"

Diego nodded.

God, yeah. That is more than okay.

He leaned forward, and their lips met again. Christ, he could kiss Healey all day.

He'd been drawn to Healey from the first. To those incredibly blue eyes.

His face was pale in the late-afternoon light. Faint freckles stood out in contrast, and bright, coppery beard hairs glinted when the light caught them just right. Healey gazed back at him without artifice. When Diego pulled the single oversized wooden pin that held Healey's man-bun together, Healey's dark, wavy hair spilled from it like a silky waterfall.

Oh, wow. Healey's hair was so soft. That's where the almond scent was coming from too. Now its fragrance surrounded them like an Amaretto mist.

Healey kissed like he couldn't stop himself, and it was heady being on the other end of that. He dotted kisses over Diego's jaw, down his neck, into the tender skin behind his ear.

He used lips and tongue and teeth.

Thumb and forefinger took hold of a nipple.

Then teeth.

Ah, Christ.

There was no way Diego could even describe how good that was.

Since his accident, Diego's chest was a mass of confusing sensations, and it was utterly subjective—part arcane magicks and part performance art, he practically burst into flames wherever Healey touched him. Healey licked and bit his nipples, and then paid particular attention to his armpits.

Oh, that was a winner. Right there. Right. Goddamn. *There* . . .

Diego let his head fall back. A deeply embarrassing sort of chortle erupted from his throat, after which, it took him a minute to get control of his body again.

Healey stopped what he was doing. "What just happened here? Did you just *ejaculate*?"

"It's *complicated*." Diego pressed his lips together, because he couldn't prove it to Mr. I-only-believe-what-I-see. "There's no actual *ejaculate* . . . so I can neither confirm nor deny."

"I touched your armpit and you came. Jesus, I wish I could do that." Healey's eyes widened. "It's probably way not cool to say that though, huh?"

Diego glared. "Probably not cool at all. No."

"Sorry. But you made a really, really good face just now." Healey could be a smug son of a bitch when he wanted. "You liked that armpit thing, huh?"

Yeah he did. "It feels pretty good when you touch me there."

"I guess so." Insufferably smug. "You're a wonderful kisser, Diego."

Aw, now he had to go and spoil things by being sweet.

This time, it was Diego who reached out. He took Healey's face between his hands and kissed him thoroughly. "You too."

Maybe it was weird to get with a guy who'd only spilled into your life by accident one day, but it felt great.

He watched Healey's hand roam over his lower leg. "Okay if I take your feet off the rests? I can get closer if they're not there."

Diego nodded. "Okay."

Healey placed Diego's right foot carefully on the ground before moving the footrest out of the way. Then he did the same with the left. With Diego's legs loose, it was possible for Healey to push between his knees, bringing their bodies that much closer.

"You're still in charge here. What do you want?"

"I could suck you." Diego figured if Healey needed a little quid quo pro, he could oblige. He could offer his mouth. Teeing up an erection was like getting ready for a space mission, but things were what they were. "If you want me to fuck you, I need to shower. I have some things I do, and it takes time."

Healey's lips formed a small O of surprised understanding. "I see."

Diego rattled his pinkie finger like the Titanic hit an iceberg and it was up to him to inform all the ships at sea.

He always did that.

It was his tell.

His stepsiblings made a fortune off him before they'd finally told him how they always knew he was bluffing.

Healey studied him. "You look nervous."

"Uh . . . Maybe." Diego fidgeted.

Healey rubbed his face briefly, then held his hands out, wiggling his fingers like he was about to defuse a bomb. "In fact, you look ready to offer yourself up like a human sacrifice."

He got so close Diego started worrying about the size of his pores. Then he leaped to his feet. "I was wrong about the beer. We need to go to Denny's."

"What? Why?" Healey Holly was going to give him goddamn whiplash. "There's no Denny's."

"We don't have to go there specifically. We could go anyplace that serves breakfast all day." While Healey pulled out his phone, Diego pulled his T-shirt on. "I need to think about this. I have a billion questions. I mean . . . neural plasticity. It's fascinating. I get physics. That's what I do. But this is amazing. I've never met anyone who—"

"Stop." To his credit, Healey froze. "A minute ago you were trying to get in my pants, but now you want to study me?"

"Hell no." Healey took his hand and started backing up. Diego had no choice but to roll with him or put on the brakes. "I want to find out if you overcompensate for bad pancakes with butter or maple syrup. I want you to tell me your favorite memory, and what you drink to forget. I want to get to know you."

In spite of himself, Diego laughed. "Healey."

Healey bit his lower lip and let go. "I think that's the first time you've said my name."

Caught you off guard, huh, Mr. Wizard. "I like the sound of it."

Diego replaced his footrests before rolling to the foyer, where he grabbed the wall and stopped them both. "Keys." He picked them off a sturdy hook by the door, along with his backpack.

They left the house. Diego rolled to the driveway, and while he waited for Healey, he donned a pair of fingerless gloves.

"You driving?" Healey asked.

"We can walk."

Saying nothing, Healey fell into step beside Diego's chair. He jammed his good hand in his pocket and stared straight ahead.

"Nah, wait." Diego's hand shot out to stop him. "Lemme tell you how this should go. When I tee you up like that? You take the swing."

Flushing, Healey stared down at him. "I don't even know what you mean."

"Yeah, you do. When I say, 'We can walk,' you say, 'Well, I can, anyway.'" He pulled up to a light and pressed the button.

While they waited for the light to turn green, Healey fidgeted. "That's what I sound like to you?"

"You sound like all the dudes on Fox News to me."

"Not because of what I say." Healey had stopped beside him and was now glaring down at him angrily. "Not because I'm some . . . some . . . *nitwit*."

"Not a Friend of the Fox, eh?"

"No—"

"Point *one*, in your favor."

"Oh hello, I made you come from touching your armpit, so I think there's a couple more points to be awarded there." Healey was flushed, his eyes sparkling.

He apparently got a great deal of pleasure from the back and forth. *Good to know.*

"And as for Fox," he went on to say, "of course I'm not a fan. For one thing, hello climate change deniers."

"Okay. I'll give you that. But if we're going to get along, we've gotta acknowledge some things. You are Napoleon Dynamite."

"I know, right?" Healey rolled his eyes. "But *Fox News*. What a thing to say."

When the light changed, Diego rolled down the ramp and into the street.

Healey stepped out after him. "While we're being honest, you're way too young to be a curmudgeon. I wasn't going to say anything—"

"I'm a what?" Diego hit the ramp on the other side with some speed.

"You. Are. A curmudgeon. But all great curmudgeons are old and all the young ones are British, and also white, like Spencer. There's no one to star in your movie."

"They could find a Latino curmudgeon to cast."

"Be much more likely to spray tan someone paler."

"Are you going somewhere with this?"

"No. I don't even know where *we're* going," Healey said.

"You said pancakes." Diego turned when they came to Main Street—downtown Bluewater Bay. Built optimistically in the twenties and blissfully ignorant of werewolves for almost an entire century, it was growing quaint—instead of recessed—because of an influx of tourist dollars. "I thought the diner on Main Street?"

"Sunrise Café? Okay. Been a long time since I was there." The words were conversational, as though they hadn't been in a heated discussion seconds before. "Now where was I— Oh. Climate Change. Fox News probably believe scientists made that up because they have a personal grudge against hairspray."

"Hairspray?"

"Yes. Imagine a world without aerosols... oooh, scary. It's like the Michael Keaton version of Batman. A horrifying television landscape full of talking heads with flat hair."

"Do go on." Diego cracked a smile. "And on, and on, and on."

"Oh, I plan to."

Diego waited to the side until Healey got the old wooden door for him. To his credit, Healey didn't even hesitate. He seemed to know what Diego needed before Diego did. *Of course he does. His sister uses a chair.* Diego wouldn't wish that on her, but the outcome was going to be handy. Healey put his hand on Diego's shoulder, and Diego slapped it away.

"So that's how it's gonna be?" Healey asked. "Partial reinforcement. You're doling out affection in tiny little dribs and drabs, so eventually, I will be gagging for it."

"Maybe?"

"But you do like me, right?" Healey asked. "It's not beyond the realm of possibility you like me?"

"You're the scientist." Diego smirked as he rolled past. "You figure it out."

CHAPTER FOURTEEN

HEALEY

Pancakes were definitely called for.

Healey learned at a young age that sometimes all he needed was carbs. And coffee. And to shut his mouth and listen for a change.

Even if you're the smartest person in the room—and it wasn't misplaced pride to assume he was, except at Stanford where you couldn't swing a Nobel Prize without hitting a laureate or two—it paid to shut up and listen more often than not.

"It's all about perspective, isn't it?" he blurted, then asked to double-check, "Did I say that out loud?"

"Yeah, you did," Diego seemed pleased to inform him.

They'd been seated at a table in the corner and given menus. Healey vacillated between fancy pancakes and plain, and then worried over what kind of pork he wanted to go with it.

All kinds of pork.

That's what he wanted.

"I'll have the lumberjack special and coffee," he told their waitress.

Diego ordered a burger with fries. She gave them a bright smile, took their menus, and left. Apparently, Diego was still waiting for his answer, though, because he was . . . staring.

"Just thinking out loud."

"You see? Thinking," Diego told him. "That was your first mistake. Not the out loud part."

Healey hid his smile behind his mug. "I think all the time, I'm afraid."

"I figured." Diego tapped his straw on the table, pushed the paper off the rest of the way, then put it in his Coke.

Healey would have made a "growing" worm with his straw paper if he had one.

Missed opportunity.

"Any legitimate reason you believe I should stop thinking?"

Diego changed the subject on him. "What was your ex like? Any chance you'll get back together?"

Healey shuddered. "No."

"That was quick."

"Even if I wanted to get back together," Healey smiled sadly, "I suspect it isn't possible anymore."

"Because of the accident?"

Healey nodded. "Yeah. Shit wakes you up."

It was easier to blame the accident for their breakup than Ford's illness, or the distance that had grown between them, or the terrifying changes in Ford's personality during their last few weeks together.

It would be a long time before he'd think of Ford without the awful ache his cold anger and vicious words had left behind.

"You know what I did before this happened?" Diego slapped his wheelchair open-handed for emphasis.

Healey shook his head.

"I was a journalist. Got my degree from UCLA, worked for CNN."

Healey's eyes widened.

"You didn't even wonder?" He sipped his coke.

"How'd you end up doing that?" Healey asked. "You mind talking about it?"

Diego's chin lifted. "Does your sister like talking about herself? Or just her accident, because it seems to me that all people really want to know is how I got in the chair and what I'm doing about it."

Fair enough. "*I* want to know more than that. Do you want to know about Shelby?"

"Can you tell her story without her SCI?"

"No, I can't. I'm not sure she'd want me to."

"But you don't know."

"No, I don't." Healey contemplated his coffee. "My stepmother—Shelby's mom—is an alcoholic. She was drunk and ran a red light. Her car got T-boned, passenger side, right where Shelby was sitting. We're lucky Shelby survived."

"That's awful."

"It took our family a long time to find a new normal."

"What happened to her mom?"

"Prison, because it wasn't her first offense. Shelby's our prize for surviving that." Healey didn't live with daily outrage and anxiety for Shelby's future anymore, but he'd never take his sister for granted.

Diego's mouth softened. "I was on vacation in Colorado. Mountain biking. I got hit by a truck. Thrown for fucking miles. I actually landed in a tree. Spoiler alert: I lived."

"I'm so sorry." Healey's gaze snapped back to Diego. "Shit. Not that you lived."

Diego shrugged. "T11 fracture. Part of my spine is fused. I'm paraplegic, which means we need to have a frank and serious talk about sex."

"Yes. Sex—" Healey offered. "And by that I mean sex with me specifically—is inevitable from here on out, so we should discuss it. Sex with me, and death, and taxes."

Diego's bright smile turned into a lazy smirk. "Decisions, decisions."

"Why do you sound like you'd prefer the latter?"

A slight redness crested Diego's cheeks. "I can't feel anything below my waist. I have specific routines for peeing and a regular bowel routine—"

It was at this precise moment their waitress arrived with breakfast. She stood there uncertainly, all color fleeing, wearing a pale, hospitable smile.

"Er . . . Who's the lumberjack again?"

"Me." Healey sat back and let her serve him.

Oh awkward, awkward.

She finished putting their plates down, double-checked her ticket in a high-pitched nervous little girl voice, and then left them.

Please God.

Don't let me laugh.

"You should know I laugh when I'm nervous." Thank heavens, he'd spoken in time. "Ah, hahah. Hahahaha. Shit. Oh my God. I'm so sorry."

Diego reached for the glass ketchup bottle, took off the cap, and tried pouring it over his fries.

"What're you nervous about?" He started patting the base of the ketchup to get it to flow. *Pat, pat, pat. Pat, pat, pat.*

Healey wanted to keep his mouth shut, but in the end, he couldn't stop himself from pointing out, "It works best if you hold the end and wiggle the tip sharply from side to side."

"We still talking about sex?" Diego asked. "Because you're not inspiring me with confidence here."

Healey groaned. "The ketchup."

Jesus. Diego could be sarcastic. Maybe he was off-balance? Maybe Healey had thrown Diego as off-balance as he was, and his surly attitude was some kind of test?

"Are you testing me?"

"No."

Good to know this isn't a test. On the other hand, Diego's answer could possibly be part of a more elaborate test. Healey propped his chin on his hand, gave Diego a frustrated shake of his head.

"But if I *were* taking a test, how would I be doing? Because even though test taking is normally something I'm really good at, it's extremely stressful for me."

"You're fine." More blushing.

Healey saw what put Diego off-balance.

Honesty.

Confidence.

"What do you need from me, Diego?"

Diego cleared his throat. "Nothing, man."

"I should have expressed myself better." Healey picked up an extra-crispy slice of bacon and let it shatter on his tongue. Oh God, that was so tasty. "One, how can I give you pleasure? Oh, and B, if we were to fuck, what would you need from me to make it good for you?"

Brown eyes blinked at him.

Uncomprehending? Curious? Confused?

Maybe that was too much, too soon? Oh God, it probably was.

Had he crossed the line?

"Of course, hahaha." Jesus. *Demented laughter and all.* "All of that would be predicated on you still being interested in me. If you were. Are. That's all I mean. *If* you are still interested, *then* . . . blah, blah, blah. You could say something anytime at all now and it would be awesome."

Diego's expression was still doubtful. "*You've* got a PhD?"

"Mm-hmm. But it's in physics. Not dating."

Diego appeared to digest that information.

"Okay. But why me? I mean other than I bought the house you used to live in, you know nothing about me."

Healey narrowed his eyes. Ford might have been Healey's first real lover, but he'd hooked up plenty before. They'd occasionally picked up a third. Sometimes even another couple. Sometimes men, sometimes women, although that was more Ford's thing. Ford's attitude toward sex was the same as his attitude toward great whiskey and music and mostly... everything.

If some is good, more is better.

He'd taught Healey to go after what he wanted. A silent *thank-you* shivered over Healey's skin—like one of those fucking feather things all the sex shops sell since *Fifty Shades*.

"For me, attraction is instantaneous." He cut a triangle of pancake and slid it around in the syrup. "I lock eyes with a dude, and it's either on or it's not."

When he ate, it was on. No doubt about it. Diego couldn't take his eyes off Healey's mouth. Healey could practically feel the heat coming off him.

"So you're attracted to me? That's why we're here?"

"Why else?" Healey asked. "I like you well enough, but I don't know you yet."

"Right. The thing is with me? It's super inconvenient. You'd be a lot better off looking for someone less challenging right now. You're on the rebound. Go hook up with some hot guy at a club. Get that shit out of your system and move on."

"That's your advice?"

Diego cut his burger in two before picking the closest half up. Despite that, it only took a single bite for it to fall apart, with bits of bun and lettuce and tomato and bacon raining onto his plate like confetti.

"In the long run—" he politely finished chewing before speaking again "—going out to look for someone able-bodied will be a lot more fun for you than using me as a sex toy."

Oh God. Is that what Diego thought?

"Am I not making myself clear enough?" Healey asked. "I find you incalculably hot. Fine. Sexy. Primo stuff." He'd already lost himself in Diego's scent, his skin, his flavor. Was insecurity Diego's hang-up? Healey winced. He was practically a walking hard-on for Diego.

Diego laughed behind his napkin.

"It's not funny." Now Healey was pissed. "At the very least, there's nothing funny about me finding you attractive. Admit it. You're not a troll."

"So you're for real? This isn't some... fetish for you?"

Stung hard, Healey barely sputtered, "F-fetish? Fuck off. *Fetish*. I have a sister who... Christ."

"I have to ask, don't you get it?" Diego glanced around before lowering his voice. "There are people who search out guys like me online, man. They dig watching me pick up my legs like they're inanimate objects. They'd pay me for it, if I let them."

"I— You must know I don't feel that way?" Healey hated that Diego even asked, but he knew his sister sometimes succumbed to similar dark thoughts. She'd admitted as much to him, privately.

Diego pushed his plate away. The move was largely symbolic. It only slid two inches before it hit his glass. "How do I know having a sister with a disability hasn't *given* you some kind of fetish?"

Healey lost focus when he realized where this was going. It *was* a test. Another test. And despite how utterly creepy it was to even suggest such a thing, sometimes tests were creepy and you had to pass them anyway.

"Hmm." He thought about it.

"So..." Diego probably figured that would be the end of it.

Healey nodded as he mentally lined up what he knew to be true.

"All right." He nodded some more. "I can work with that. Either I'm genuinely interested in you, or I've got a fetish, is that it? And you can't tell which is true, because I'm not ignorant. I understand the biology of a spinal cord injury. I know what gives"—he coughed—"and what doesn't, as it were."

It was the most natural thing in the world for Healey to glance toward Diego for confirmation or argument.

Diego picked up a fry, dunked it in ketchup, and popped it in his mouth.

Ooh. Nice mouth. It drew Healey's attention right back to the problem at hand.

"You can *choose* to believe I am genuinely interested in you. Where does that lead us?"

"Boinking." Diego's reply was immediate.

Healey hoped so too. "Undoubtedly. But hypothetically, if you're with a guy and he looks at you and his dick gets hard and he says it's because of you, you . . ." He waited expectantly.

"I'd have to wonder if it's because he's into guys like me. The fetish thing." Diego frowned. "It's always there in the back of my mind."

"Okay, so, let's back up. You're with a guy and his dick is hard right now. If you believe him when he says he digs you and you end up in the sack, everyone wins."

"If he's not a selfish asshat? Yes." Glancing away, Diego shoveled another couple of fries into his mouth. "But say I don't believe him. What if I think he's probably a weirdo?"

Healey really had planned on begging and then groveling, but that was out of the question at the Sunrise Café. It was already late in the afternoon. The knees of his jeans would stick to the filthy floor.

There was only one thing left to do.

I am going to nonexistent Hell for bastardizing Pascal's Wager like this.

"If you can't believe anyone *would* want you because of the chair or whatever, then you are pretty much going to be celibate."

"I can masturbate, you know—"

Healey saw the waitress coming and put his hand on Diego's to warn him, but of course, he didn't take the hint in time.

"—and use a sexual surrogate. I've had a couple guys over. It's not like I'm a hermit."

"Hello again. Sorry to be . . . um . . ." The waitress put a second soda down on the table for Diego.

He didn't touch the new glass, but gave her a nod. "Thanks."

She backed away with his empty glass.

He heaved another sigh.

"Thirsty work," Healey remarked, "scaring the wait staff like that."

Diego craned his neck as much as he could to see her skitter away. "I didn't know she was there. It's easy for you, with your back against the wall. You could see her coming."

"I put my hand on yours to warn you."

Brown eyes widened. Healey noticed faint flecks of gold and orange for the first time. Nice eyes. Dark as black coffee with hidden surprises.

"I thought hand-holding was the next part of your seduction plan. You were saying."

Healey leaned his chin on his hand.

"I was saying either people are attracted to you or to the chair, which is part of you, sort of. If you choose to believe it's you, you act accordingly, boink, and that's awesome, right? But if you don't believe and you want to boink anyway, so what? Maybe you'll get your heart broken later when you find out someone had a fetish. Has that happened?"

"Yeah." Diego's jaw muscles tightened, and his finger *tap-tap-tapp*ed its little SOS to the world. "Kinda."

"If the alternative is DIY sex and hookers, is that really what you want?"

"No."

"So there's probably no harm in acting as if you believe someone could want you for yourself. If only in controlled situations . . . say, for example, when you *haven't* met through a Craigslist ad?"

"You make a pretty good point," Diego grumbled.

Me and Pascal.

I hope you never learn why it's all bullshit.

"If you'll please just give me a chance," Healey offered, "I'll prove my dick gets hard around you with regular, almost alarming, frequency. And that has nothing to do with your SCI."

CHAPTER FIFTEEN
DIEGO

Diego'd believed a good line before, only to find, more often than not, the person using it was interested in him because of his SCI. They were curious. Morbidly fascinated. Concerned for him. They pitied him.

After the accident, the competitive-level fitness, high-risk job, and lofty principles he fought so hard to balance fell away, one by one, leaving him in a desperate struggle to relearn physical tasks he'd mastered before he could talk.

The worst times were long past, but on the way he'd had to learn a whole new set of social skills too.

There were workarounds for everything, but most of it pissed him off.

"The waitress asked you a question," Healey pointed out.

"No, she didn't."

She tried again. "I said, does your friend want—"

"I see. Wait." Healey turned to her, benign quizzical smile in place. "Since we're not using sign language, I wonder why you would think my friend is deaf?"

Aw, thud.

That rubbing sound? That was Diego's heart, humping Healey's leg.

Not that he'd admit it.

"I'm so sorry, sir." The girl looked faintly sick now.

"It's nothing." Diego was used to interacting with people who lost their shit. He smiled to put her at ease.

"I tell you what. Why don't you take this—" Healey took two twenties from his wallet and gave them to her. "And bring us a couple of boxes. All right?"

"Oh, thank you. *Thank you.*"

Diego could see he still rattled her. He didn't get why, though. Because he was brown? Because he was in a wheelchair? "Aw, fuck it." He quit worrying about it.

"What?"

"I don't even get what her problem was. I was nice. I don't fucking bite."

"You act like you will. I think at first she thought you were hot, and then you said, 'bowel routine' like a grumpy old man and fucked it up."

"Okay, yeah." *My fault. Right. I scared the girl.* "Must have happened exactly that way."

"It did, man. And if it didn't, fuck it. What do you care what she thinks?"

"I don't." *Petulance, your name is Diego.* They boxed up the remains of their meals and headed outside without going over it again.

The sun wouldn't set for hours yet, and it wasn't too overcast. As they passed through the downtown streets, traffic seemed light. The denizens of Bluewater Bay must be eating dinner before making their way back outdoors to enjoy the fairly nice evening.

Diego rolled along the sidewalk. Healey stayed in step beside him, carrying the bag that held their leftovers.

"I'm sorry about dinner," Diego apologized. "I realize that was an unappetizing conversation."

"That was nothing." Healey gave an uncaring tilt of his head and turned to walk backward, so he was facing Diego.

"For you maybe."

"I'm not saying I love autopsy dinner theater, but on an intellectual level there's nothing gross about the human body."

"Watch where you're going," Diego warned.

Healey turned around just in time to avoid a newspaper box.

"What's autopsy dinner theater?" Diego asked.

"What Ford used to call *Bones.*"

"Ford's the ex, huh? How come you broke up?"

Healey's blue eyes appeared to glitter briefly but then he blinked. Gone. "We were leaving school. Heading in different directions."

Healey's answer tripped all Diego's early bullshit detectors. It didn't have emotion behind it, and Healey was an emotional guy. The words sounded rehearsed, like a jingle, or a political sound bite.

Healey needed a warning label: *Fragile. Handle with care.*

"So I'm Rebound Guy?" Diego asked.

"Yep."

"Because you think I'm hot."

"That's right."

"Stop," Diego ordered. "Close your eyes right now."

Healey did as he was asked.

"Tell me everything you remember about me."

It was a risk. He might find out Healey was a lying loser. He might find out just how naive he could be about a man, again.

But if Healey was some kind of bullshit artist, Diego would know.

Of course, they'd stopped right outside Red Hot Bluewater, and Healey's eyes were closed, but Diego had to stare at the most blatant display of sex toys he'd ever seen.

They didn't used to put those in the window, did they? Because, *wow*. There was a sign in the window:

Blow-XXX Sale.

(Pick your favorite three-letter word)

"You want me to describe you physically?" Healey asked. "Or should I add in character traits?"

The nerve of some people.

He'd said it before, and he'd say it again. Smug. Healey was smug. "Physically would be fine."

"All right. You're wearing Vans. They're black suede and canvas and they feature a white pin-stripe on the side. Black cotton socks. Your jeans are Levi's. Low rise. Washed to perfection. They look and feel like you ball them up every night and sleep with them in your arms. How am I doing so far?"

"Fine." Diego's mouth dried as he watched Healey's dick thicken behind his zipper.

Healey kept on—utterly *sinvergüenza*.

"You're wearing a T-shirt with all four Doctors from the new *Doctor Who* series on it. They're in a crosswalk, mimicking The Beatles

Abbey Road cover. Your hoodie is probably Hanes, but I'm only guessing there."

"All right." Diego had to call it. "I believe you. You actually see me."

But no. Healey could not see him at that moment, because he kept his eyes squeezed firmly shut, ignoring Diego's order to finish up.

They were going to have to talk about the word *consent*.

"Your face is oval. You have a very determined chin. High cheekbones, brown eyes, angry eyebrows, and a nose that's a bit hawklike. I like your nose, by the way. You probably caught some shit about it in school, but it's majestic. At one time, your ears were pierced, as was your left eyebrow. How come you took it out? I think you'd look hot with a barbell. You have a faint scar on your jaw in the shape of an inverted V. Every time I see it, I want to lick it."

"Is that all?" Diego asked hoarsely.

"For now. I was hoping I'd find tattoos. You had your shirt off, and I didn't see any. I like them."

Diego pressed his lips together. Licked them nervously.

"Did I do okay?" Healey opened his eyes, anticipating a treat like a puppy performing a trick.

Diego's gaze found Healey's belly. Fell to the fabric stretching over his cock. "It's early yet." He spoke without looking up.

"Yeah it is," Healey agreed.

Healey's answer was careful. Diego appreciated the way Healey felt his way toward whatever it was they were doing. The way he didn't pepper him with questions, or ask for gory details.

Diego saw how hard Healey's cock was and how hard Healey was holding himself back. Like a Thoroughbred at the starting gate, Healey was ready to race. He wanted to go as fast as his mind and body could carry him, but he'd agreed to go at Diego's pace.

He honored his word.

After the light changed, they crossed the street. Diego caught sight of himself in the reflection from one of the old shop windows.

He was *exactly* as Healey described.

He was average. Hot average. Not scrub average.

Healey asked, "Do you want me to come home with you, Diego?"

Diego gripped his wheels, ready to turn left, toward his house.

"I have to decide now?"

Healey pointed to the right. "It's just that I could leave you here and get back to the B&B pretty easily. You wouldn't have to drive me."

"So?"

Healey took time to adjust the pin that held his hair. "I don't want to misread the situation. If you want me to come with you, I'd like you to tell me."

Okay. Wow. No need to discuss consent with Healey after all.

This was it.

You either ask for what you want, or you fuck off.

The man knows what he's getting into.

He sees you.

If he's a creep, he's done a terrific job of not making things weird so far.

"I have a few things I need to get caught up on before bedtime."

Diego let himself roll past Healey, but turned to give him a look so incendiary they should have both burst into flames.

Just so there was no mistake about what and who he wanted, he said, "Heel, Healey. There's probably something for you to do while I'm busy, but I'll for sure want you there when I finish."

CHAPTER SIXTEEN
HEALEY

Healey saw himself from the outside in. As if in a documentary of his life, he sat in the living room of the house that was no longer his, but that still felt familiar—like an actress, aged by makeup, or the photograph of a long-dead relative whose features you share.

Familiar enough that the differences were more obvious than the similarities.

"C'mon. Pick up, pick up, pick up," Healey whispered, glancing toward the hallway, beyond which Diego had spent the last hour doing God knew what.

"You need a ride?" Nash's voice boomed. Way to be on stealth mode.

Why didn't I text?

"He's in the bathroom. I'm waiting in the living room. It's been like . . . an hour."

"You check he hasn't gone out the window?"

"No, but he should, probably. The longer I wait, the less confidence I have. By the time he comes out, my dick's gonna be like an elevator button and he'll just keep pushing it and pushing it and the car won't rise—"

"Don't panic. How often do I gotta tell you: it's only sex."

"It's not. Not for me. I told you—"

"When your mind starts racing, and you're feeling nervous, what do you do? Grab your dick. Your brain can't do two things at the same time."

"I can't do it, Nash. I just wanted to be with this guy I like, but this—"

Diego's cold voice interrupted him. "Didn't believe me about the inconvenience?"

At the sound, Healey turned sharply.

Diego waited in the hallway, shirtless, wearing only boxers, slightly hairy feet bare.

Erect.

How had he managed to leave his room and wheel all the way back without Healey hearing a thing?

He looked so vulnerable, Healey's heart hurt.

"As you can see," Diego's voice dripped with quiet dignity, "it's not just inconvenient to be with me. Do you think you're the first to point out the lack of spontaneity?"

"I need to hang up now, bro."

"I'll drive you home." Diego turned his chair to move past.

"The hell you will." Healey blocked his way. "Listening to half of a conversation is like trying to solve one side of an equation. That was Nash."

"I guessed."

Healey nodded. "Sure, but don't guess what we said, okay?"

"I heard what you said."

"You heard half, maybe. Not the part where I said I'm nervous I'll mess this up. Or where I reminded Nash I don't have a fuckton of experience because I don't really screw around all that much."

"Yeah?" Diego rolled forward about ten inches.

"Not *by myself*, no." Healey took a step toward him. "And you didn't hear how much I want to be with you but waiting seems to ratchet up my anxiety and I feel like I'm taking a test again..."

Diego's posture softened a little. "Your boyfriend play around on you?"

Healey laughed. "Nope. He liked to add more than divide, if you see what I mean. He brought people home. Singles. Couples. I think he was probably—" He put his hand over his mouth before he could say, *pathologically poly*, in that one man or woman never satisfied Ford for long. "We were safe, sane, and consensual. I was with Ford. And Ford might be with anyone."

"I understand." Slowly, Diego nodded. He rolled forward until he was close enough to take Healey's hand. "I wouldn't share you."

Healey had to think about breathing. In. Out. Not too loud. No snorting.

"I don't really want to be shared, anyway."

"Come with me, Healey."

Healey laid his cast hand on Diego's strong shoulder, memorizing the play of muscle beneath all that silky smooth skin. He let Diego lead the way to his bedroom, which should have been weird, because—duh—his little sister had grown up in there, for God's sake.

But no.

The room was completely transformed.

"Shelby would kill for this."

He turned in a complete circle to get the whole picture. The wall between Shelby's room and what used to be their pop's study had been opened and a brand-new arch allowed passage between the two.

Shelby's room was now Diego's dressing area.

It felt like a spa with a bath and shower area enclosed by glass bricks for privacy, and a large padded platform under a nice bright window for . . . Healey was trying to figure it out when he caught Diego staring at him.

"Massage table? Reading nook?"

Diego's expression was unreadable. "I lie down to dress."

"This is a great setup. Wish we'd have thought of it for Shelby. It would have been so much easier for her. She'd have been our little queen in a place like this."

"My stepbrother designed the room, and the rest of my family came up to help with the build."

"Sweet." Healey ran his fingers over the glass. "Where do they live?"

"Glendale." Diego wrinkled his nose. "When we stripped the old fixtures out and did the painting, we kept running into your family's memories."

Healey laughed at that. "The dings where Nash put my head through the wall?"

"Open the closet." Diego jerked his chin toward Shelby's old walk-in.

Curious, Healey opened the door.

"Behind it."

Warmth filled Healey's heart when he saw they hadn't painted over his sister's girly pink Sharpie-marker scrawl: *Mr. And Mrs. Spencer Kepler. Mrs. Shelby Holly-Kepler. Shelby Kepler.* <3 <3 <3.

"Aw, that's priceless."

When Healey whipped his phone out to take a picture, Diego pushed his hand down. "You do that and shit will be weird around the holidays forever."

Healey thought about it, chuckled, and then snapped the picture anyway. "Weird family holidays? You have no idea."

"You're a lousy brother, you know that?"

"I don't like to brag, but I do what I can." In the archway, Healey got his first look at Diego's bedroom.

"Am I looking at a layout for *Architectural Digest*? Or *Modern Bondage*?"

Diego's grin faded. "Not sure I see what you're seeing."

The room was small, but there was enough space around the bed for Diego's wheelchair to turn. The monochrome beige linens matched the walls. White crown molding and baseboards would have made the room soothing, except for the queen-size four-poster with a frame made of welded pipes defining—literally dominating—the space. The industrial bedframe mimicked a canopy. The gymnast's rings suggested The Doms of Dick-Licking. Healey's cock got hard just imagining all the things he could do on a bed like that.

Or.

Maybe the rings were a great way for a guy with an SCI to get himself out of bed. His blood rebelled. Half went toward his brain, half charged his dick. Some must have got lost, because for a second he didn't understand what Diego was saying.

"Hmm?"

"That for me?" Diego brushed his fingers over Healey's zipper.

Healey grunted when Diego deepened the caress. He caught Diego's hand—strong and square; veiny, as was his forearm. Healey dropped kisses on Diego's fingers, leaning in and pressing his lips to Diego's firm, full ones. He tasted like cinnamon mouthwash and smelled like soap. Like clean man. One of Healey's personal kinks. He loved it when a man smelled fresh, but not . . . perfumed.

Healey sank to his knees and fumbled with footrests, which led to touching Diego's perfect, shapely bare feet, and more kissing. Healey used lips and tongue and sharp little nips of his teeth because Diego'd liked that before, but it occurred to him: maybe he'd like something else?

"What should I do?" Healey asked, in a whisper.

His mouth was dry, his tongue thick with desire. Diego's lazy smile was dangerously close to a smirk again, but Healey was too turned on to give him any shit about it.

"Undress for me?" If Diego saw Healey's fingers were shaking, he gave no indication.

"Sure." Healey could do this. Some men liked a slow seduction. He stood, keeping his focus on Diego, meeting his hot, hungry gaze. He winced when he pulled his shirt over his head.

"You should maybe wear a sling."

"I should do a lot of things." Healey dropped his shirt and toed off his shoes. As soon as Diego loosened his belt, his trousers, which were too big, pooled around his ankles.

"Nice." Diego snapped the elastic on Healey's Hugo Boss boxer briefs. "I did not see those coming. You choose those?"

Healey gave a shake of his head. "Labels were Ford's department."

"Drop 'em?"

Healey let them fall. Once he ditched his socks, he waited for Diego to say something.

And waited.

And waited some more.

A smile won its way onto Diego's face. Healey saw it for the victory it was and grinned back shyly.

"Sit on the side of the bed?"

Healey laughed as he sat.

"The bed's an excellent height, don't you think?" Rolling forward, Diego caught one of Healey's calves, lifting his leg until Healey had to lie down or suffer a hamstring pull.

"That's it. Relax, papi." Diego rested Healey's leg on his well-muscled shoulder while he reached down to pick up the other one. "Let me take care of you?"

"Okay." Healey pulled one of Diego's pillows beneath his head.

Diego's cool finger slid down Healey's treasure trail. "We cool if I do this?"

"Sure."

"Touch you?" He used one hand to cup Healey's balls, the other wrapped around his cock. "Jack you?"

"Yeah." Healey breathed the word. Face flushed, Diego grinned from between Healey's legs and took him to the back of his throat. *Christ.* "Diego."

Diego knew his way around a dick, for goddamn sure.

He laved and mouthed and teased, tugged and drew away, leaving Healey boneless, speechless. Leaving him open and vulnerable and mindless with desire.

"You like that, Mr. Wizard? I'm going to open you and plunge inside you and fuck you so hard. You want that?"

Diego's sex talk?

Healey's bulletproof kink.

Healey laughed nervously, manically, and pulled a second pillow over to cover his face. Just so Diego couldn't see him. Not so he couldn't hear.

"Shy? Yeah. But you like feeding me your cock. You like it so much. So I can suck you? Want me to pinch your nipples? Spank your ass? Like it a little rough?"

"God, yes," Healey gasped.

"You like when a guy licks you open? Want me to put my finger in you? Fuck you? You want to get finger-fucked? Or fucked for real?"

"Yeah." Healey's hips shot up, hungry for that exact thing. "Do it. Do whatever. Just don't—"

"I've got you, papi. Don't you worry your AmStaff-puppy ass about that." Diego's hands left his skin. Healey heard the ubiquitous *crinkle* of plastic and *snap* of a lube tube cap.

"Are we—" Healey lifted his head, dazed "—really? You want to fuck me?"

Diego hesitated. "*Or* I injected my penis with a needle full of drugs for nothing."

"Wait. Is that how you get people to put out?" Healey squinted at him. "The old I-just-gave-myself-a-penile-injection-and-you-didn't-even-take-out-the-garbage guilt trip?"

"I've been meaning to ask what you've done for *me* lately?"

"Good point, I guess. I hope to be screaming your name. Will that help?"

Diego let Healey's legs down. Then he rolled around to the other side of the bed, reached between the mattress and box spring, and dug out two canvas straps with loops on the end.

"Wow. I'd ask if you were a Boy Scout—"

"Nope."

"Or... you know. A serial killer."

"Not that either." Diego rolled back around. "Yet."

Healey chuckled. "God, I hope your dick is as much fun as your mouth."

"You like my mouth?"

"I like everything about you so far, but that's probably my cock talking."

"Shush, Healey." One finger, then two; lube and patience.

Prep out of the way, Healey got the show of a lifetime when Diego grabbed the rings to pull himself almost to standing. Fierce concentration twisted his mouth with the effort of letting himself sort of come in for a hesitant, hopefully one-point landing.

It was a trust fall. Diego sank onto Healey's body and Healey caught him. The struggle seemed like the best foreplay ever—to simply slide and grunt and rut and tumble together like that until they were balanced on the edge of actual fucking.

Healey cradled him in his arms. They took advantage of momentum and upper body strength—Diego, to kiss Healey and pull himself far enough across the bed to catch the straps with his hands; Healey, to help him by hanging on.

"Where are those tethered?" Healey asked breathlessly.

"Side rails." The fierce strain on Diego's face while he pulled himself into position was sexy as fuck.

Diego Luz was sexy as fuck.

Healey shifted subtly, rocking Diego with him until he had his legs wrapped around Diego's hips and Diego's dick was poised, hard, waiting for a signal from Healey to go.

"Shit, Heals." *Okay. Now that was funny.* "Fuck, you know what I mean. You gotta get me in, Heals."

"Go . . . *Go*." Healey positioned Diego's cock while he let the unconscious use of the nickname slide. "Oh, yeah. Go." He adjusted to the invasion that was both an ache and a need.

A distraction and a necessity.

Between Diego's grip on the straps, and Healey's grip on Diego, they found a way to start. Found a rhythm that worked between them.

Inevitably awkward during sex, Healey couldn't stop laughing, which pushed Diego's dick out until they got down to serious business. He tried to deploy the tricks he'd learned about Diego's body earlier.

"Oh, Christ." Diego shivered from a simple touch to his throat or his ribs. Rubbing the muscles on his back made him arch and groan and shiver.

Fiercely masculine, beautiful, tender, caring. All those adjectives could be applied to Diego the lover.

Healey writhed beneath him as pleasure built and built and built. Until sweat slicked his skin, and his incoherent cries filled the air.

"This it, Mr. Wizard?" Diego's words got sharper, his breath heavy and hot on Healey's skin. "This? Is this how you need to be fucked?"

"Harder, please," Healey begged. "Harder."

"You got it." Diego was right there to oblige him, biceps bulging, forearms straining as he hammered Healey's sweet spot, even as his weight drove Healey into the mattress and gravity pinned Healey's dick between his hairy belly and Diego's nearly smooth one.

Friction. Heat. Energy. Combustion. *Bang*! Physics. He ran his hand down Diego's arm—muscle like iron rippling with strength, with vitality—massive, like his chest was massive.

Enthralled, Healey sought out more of the erogenous zones he'd discovered earlier...

"Ah, Christ." Diego let his head drop until it pressed against Healey's cheek. "That makes me shiver all over. Keep doing it. It's... indescribable... It feels so fucking good."

"Ah, Diego, fuck." Healey went off like a rocket, spurting come between their bellies. All the breath left him. He lay boneless and gasping hard, shivering in the aftermath of a whole-body orgasm that took him like a tornado and dropped him back on the bed, still spasming. He wrapped his arm around Diego, kissing the surprise off his face before grinning. "Oh my God."

"You don't believe in God." Diego's face was a breath away and his eyes... they were so warm and brown.

He sighed. "But now I totally believe in you."

Diego reached between them and carefully pulled out before pushing off to lie on his back, breathing heavily. *Okay, so. Not a cuddler.* Healey reached for his hand instead. His *toes* were weak. Jesus. He couldn't feel his thigh muscles. When was the last time he'd come like that?

Startled when Diego's warm fingers gripped his just as tightly, he bit his lip. They lay looking through the supports of a modern, industrial canopy monstrosity. Already sleep was reeling him in, but he fought it off, with the idea of making Diego more comfortable.

He sat up. "I'll bring you a towel."

"I can go. I know where everything is." Diego wrenched himself over, pushed himself to sitting, and pulled off the condom. He dropped it into a waste basket by the side of the bed, and then positioned his chair.

Healey watched Diego slip his boxers over a cock that was still as erect as it had been before they started, enjoying the play of muscle beneath Diego's warm dark skin. He sensed these few minutes after sex might be dangerous ground between them.

"I'm okay with helping clean up after sex," he offered. "With taking turns?"

"I don't like it when guys do that for me." Diego gripped his rings and used them to transfer without incident. "It reminds me too much of the hospital. You want a beer or anything?"

"Yeah, some water?"

"Anything stronger?"

"Just water. Hey." He caught Diego's hand before he could roll away. "You're a machine and I dug it."

Diego shot him one of those patented *You think I care?* looks.

But Healey was beginning to recognize when Diego fronted.

Diego wanted him, but he needed to establish he was the fucker and not the fuckee, which was perfectly fine with Healey.

Better than fine.

Getting fucked was Healey's wonder drug.

Harder. Faster. Longer. Better.

Words to live by.

Stop the world for me.

Stop the mind-racing, problem-solving, and test-taking.

Stop the guilt.
"Back in a sec."
Diego left him there, contemplating round two.

CHAPTER SEVENTEEN

DIEGO

Diego cleaned himself in the bath. A quick wipe-down. A cool cloth and an inspection of his skin for damage. He found nothing, but sometimes there was bruising or an occasional abrasion. You had to be careful with skin you couldn't feel.

He left Healey with a damp towel.

Now he was sitting in front of the open refrigerator, mind blown, unable to remember what he was there for, but . . .

Oh yeah. Hydration. Jesus, it was fucking cold in the fridge.

He grabbed what he needed, closed the door, and sat alone in the glow of the ice maker's "welcome" lights.

He thought about Healey and sex. *Smoking.*

Of course, there was a chasm, a fathomless divide between his life before and his life after the accident. Everything came down to before and after. Sleep and digestion and moods and yeah . . . even fucking.

He didn't compare before and after. No one who wanted to move forward sat around thinking about things like that.

Like an accountant, he'd drawn a great big double line beneath the date of his accident on his mental calendar, balanced the debits and credits, and paid his debts. Now there was nothing before. No pages, no notes, nothing worth looking back at. Nothing worth thinking about.

He'd never had a lover that attentive, that determined, that supple and giving . . .

He'd never had a lover that attuned to his every breath—

That was *after*. Wasn't it?

Because his memories were exactly like his legs. They were there, but the connection had been lost. All the telegraph men, ossified and cobwebby at their lonely posts.

That was still true.

But because Healey had a gift for transporting him back, for erasing the crack in his timeline, for negating the damage to his pride, if not his spine, he'd forgotten for a minute or two.

Diego let the idea sink in.

He'd *forgotten* about his SCI, his workarounds, and his need to settle for less. All his preconceived notions got obliterated by the extraordinary, massive new concept named Healey Holly.

Diego's courage failed him. The truth of his situation . . . Well, everything *but* his medically enhanced penis wilted—the pathetic, insensate javelin producing a nice tent in his boxers, but doing nothing for him, feeling nothing.

He felt affection for his penis. Like Poe, a dog he'd owned once who'd chewed up his pot plants, vomited on his leather couch, and had cost him a bundle at the animal hospital before finally—years of shenanigans later—passing quite contentedly in his sleep, Diego loved his dick.

He'd acclimated to living with disappointment with both, his dog and his dick.

Then, along came Healey Holly. Healey got what he needed, if Diego's come-spattered belly was anything to go by. Closing his eyes, Diego tried out this latest memory . . .

He'd had better sex.

But he'd never had a better lover.

If what he and Healey had going now could get better with a little planning and communication and trial and error?

"I'm down." The words, a declaration to no one.

Everyone.

The universe.

"I. Am. Down."

He gathered a box of cookies and some chips and a jar of salsa, dropping things in his lap as he rolled along the galley-kitchen setup, then back to the hall, and to Healey, and the next conversation they needed to have.

That one would not be easy either.

Healey had shifted onto his side and drifted to sleep in a pose Diego called "freshly fucked West Side frat boy." His eyes opened. His smile was welcoming and warm.

Diego unloaded food onto the nightstand, saw his phone, and asked, "Okay if I take your picture?"

"Sure, go ahead."

Diego hesitated. "Not with my phone. A camera."

Healey's knee jiggled a little. Excitement? Anxiety?

"Video?"

"Still photos."

"Okay, Diego." Healey's cock had started taking interest in the proceedings. He threw the sheet off and posed. *Clown*. "I want you to take my picture like one of your French girls. Wearing this."

"Okay." Diego shot Healey a wink as he rolled to the closet, where he dug out his camera bag.

"Wearing *only* this." Healey's cock was hard and veiny. Its plum-colored head dripped a string of glistening pre-ejaculate.

"Very funny." Diego set the auto-focus for low light and red-eye reduction. Sure he could grab lenses and shit. But like *Wolf's Landing*, a lot could happen in post.

He wanted a lasting memory. To hold on to Healey a little longer, a little tighter than the other guys who'd been here . . .

Wow. Not good.

Healey's smile faded. "What?"

Diego took a deep breath.

"Look over my shoulder at the window." *Snick*. "You have a great face, you know that, right?" *Snick, snick, snick.*

"You think so?" Healey preened.

"Mm-hmm. Are you Irish?"

"I don't know, maybe. Pop thinks so. Holly is Irish or English."

"You look Irish. You've got freckles."

"Yeah. You?"

"I'm not Irish."

Healey's expression was wry. "Okay, then. Mr. Luz. Your family name could come from practically anywhere."

"I'm from LA."

"Angeleno." Healey considered this. *Snick*. "With no tattoos? Nope. Can't be."

Diego held the camera idle in his lap for a second. "Don't know why I never got one. Before, it was because my mother wanted me to.

And after, I was either too hypersensitive or it seemed creepy to write on all that lifeless—"

"Not lifeless. Insensate."

Who was Healey to correct him?

"Shut up. What do you know." *Snick. Ding, ding.* Fierce Healey was hot. Righteous indignation looked awful good on him.

"Mami kept telling me what kind she thought I should get. '*Por mi madre hermosa, piedosa, gloriosa.*'" He mimicked her, but gently. *Con afecto.* "'Get something with a rainbow, *m'hijo*. No, get "*Sí, Se Puede.*" No, get "YOLO."'"

"Oh no, she did not."

"She did." Diego shuddered. "I don't speak ill of the dead, but Mami, *que Dios la tenga en gloria*, was meme trash."

"You're *wonderful* when you speak Spanish." *Snick.*

Diego studied the shot on the DSLR's screen. Being behind the camera all those years, observing everything through the filter of his lens and then finding the threads of the story the images had to tell, was his private thing. It was an internal thing. His work went on largely behind the scenes and for him, the end result was always tangential to the search for the next story.

Nobody looked at him if he did his job right.

Nobody saw him unless he wanted them to.

Now, nobody saw him at all, except Healey Holly, and that made him dangerous not just to Diego's routines, but to his heart.

He'd forgotten the magic words. Go carefully. Handle with Care.

You are rebound guy.

"I'm down for fucking, but I'm not in the market for a boyfriend, Healey."

Healey's expression—an awful cocktail of blind-sided and natural optimism losing ground to disappointment—was the picture Diego didn't take. Couldn't, wouldn't. He shouldn't have started this in the first place. Healey wasn't a player. Healey wasn't a guy you fuck and forget.

Healey sat up. "I see."

In a word, he looked resigned. He looked kind and caring and warm and *resigned*. Diego set the camera in his lap and rolled forward.

"It's not that I don't think you're a great guy."

"No. I know. You're a great guy too. I'm not even in town for very long, really."

"Right. Of course. How many companies are trying to hire you?" he asked brightly. "Or will you teach? You just need to get back on your feet, is all."

"Said the man who knocked me off them." Healey waited a few seconds before taking the camera from Diego's nerveless fingers. "Too soon?"

Diego laughed, and the tables got turned. *Snick.*

"Wait—" Healey lowered the camera. "You mind me taking your picture? I should have asked."

He shook his head. "It's my camera. I can erase them if you make my butt look fat."

Snick. "Tell me more about your family. Your mom believed in metaphysical healing and she wanted you to get a tattoo? What was that like?"

"Exhausting," he said truthfully. "And solid. My mom was a force of nature. When I had my accident, she spent so much time learning about SCIs, caregiving, finding new therapies, new doctors. She pulled me through that. She didn't give me any choice."

"She advocated for you when you couldn't advocate for yourself."

"Exactly," Diego said. "I don't know what I'd have done without her. Probably given up."

"You the type for that?" *Snick. Snick.*

"Nah." *Caught me looking stupid that time.* "I'm no quitter. Haven't given up yet, anyway."

"Did you ever think," Healey's gaze narrowed, "the people who love you should have made the doctors stop? Did you ever wonder, 'Why is my mother doing nothing while someone hurts me?'"

"No." Diego leaned toward him. "I knew doctors needed to do certain things, and it wasn't always going to feel good."

Healey nodded. "My sister was very young."

"I'll bet that was tough as fuck on her."

Healey set the camera down, uncapped a bottled water and drank half down. "She was in a coma for several weeks. Sometimes I'd sit with her and talk. She'd open her eyes and look toward me. She heard my voice maybe?"

It was possible. "They told my family to talk to me."

Healey nodded. "What do you remember about the accident?"

"Nothing."

"What about the time you spent in the hospital?"

Noise. Endless, mind-numbing pain. Nights that turned into days that turned back into nights. "I remember waking up in the hospital. Getting my hand free and yanking out my catheter."

"*Ow*." Healey winced.

Diego wished he had a picture of that face, right there.

"Not for me," he reminded Healey he couldn't feel a thing. "I don't remember what my thinking was, but no man wants to see something sticking out of his junk."

"I wouldn't say that. I mean. Sounds. People do—"

Diego snickered. "You're a kinky motherfucker, aren't you?"

"No." Healey flushed. "Not me. But sometimes—"

"Relax. I got you." Diego put him out of his misery. "I'm kidding anyway. I don't care what people do. I used to do shit. Plugs sometimes. Cockrings. A little rough play."

"Rough play gets me hot." Healey raised both hands again, as if now they were back to the awkward handwringing and bomb-defusing gestures from earlier. "That's, uh . . . full disclosure."

Without thinking it through, Diego hooked his hand around Healey's neck and hauled him in for a kiss.

When they broke apart, he smiled. "You're going to make someone a great pet someday."

Healey glanced at Diego's still-rigid cock. "In the meantime, I could do something with that. Waste not want not."

Diego's gaze followed his.

He liked the sparkle in Healey's eyes. Liked where this was going, despite the fact he didn't want or need a boyfriend. "This old thing?"

"Sure."

"I've had it for years. I'm not even sure it's in working condition."

"Well, some of those are quite valuable. I could buff it up a little for you there."

"No harm in that."

Healey glanced up, flushed and eager. "How long can you hang on to those rings?"

"Whoa, whoa, whoa. We walk before we run, cadet."

Healey relaxed. "All right. What's your best-case scenario here?"

"Can I position you?"

Healey waved him in like a plane. "I'd be disappointed if you didn't."

Diego decided to surprise him by rolling him onto his stomach, cushioning his arm and positioning his legs half off the bed.

Healey glanced over his shoulder. "You sure about this, Corrigan? This doesn't seem like the way we came before."

"Trust me."

Healey's blue eyes met his, and his flippant words came back like a boomerang. Healey did trust him. Healey surrendered his body and his will. He waited like a penitent, like a student, an acolyte. It was heady fucking stuff.

Fingers testing Healey's opening, Diego found him soft and ready. He put on a condom, used a discreetly placed wipe—because slipping is never sexy—and reached up to grip his rings again.

He poised, tensed, and hoisted himself up. It was a test of nerve to do this, to drape his body over Healey's and have the faith he could make it work . . .

He hovered there briefly, wondering if Healey could see how tough this was. He deserved an award for this, it was hard to do with any swagger. Diego could make it look easy.

Healey watched over his shoulder.

"Be ready to catch me if I fall," Diego teased.

"Um. Between my ass cheeks?"

Diego snorted, his concentration broken. He had to regroup after that. "You do not want to make me laugh while I'm vertical like this. Just saying."

"You have done this before, right?"

"I can hang from a single ring too," Diego muttered. *Smack.* "That red-hot handprint on your ass is going to feel great against my skin."

Healey grunted happily and even gave a bit of a wiggle. "Do it again."

So Diego smacked that fine bubble ass a few times, listening, getting used to the sweet sound it made, skin over muscle over bone, solid, earthy. Strong and real, like Healey himself.

Diego put one hand in the middle of Healey's back, and let himself go.

He braced on Healey's shoulder. Pulled up so he could wrap both arms around his lover and position himself at Healey's entrance, gripping Healey's shoulder from beneath for leverage.

"Okay?" he asked when he was a simple biceps curl away from plunging into Healey's tight heat.

Healey shivered all over. "This is different."

"It works, mostly." Effort roughened Diego's voice. "Grab my hips."

"If I could visualize the angle better—" Healey did as he was asked "—I could calculate the combination of our separate weights, which, theoretically, could be really useful when it comes figuring out the amount of energy—"

Diego gave an experimental shove. "Should you really be making plans out loud right now?"

"Oh, yeah." Healey encouraged, "Okay. Go—"

"Wait." Why did this feel like an amusement park ride? "You've gotta compensate for the fact I can't roll my hips."

"Like this?" Healey tried twisting slightly and pushing back.

Sweat burned Diego's eyes. "Sweet Fred Wallenda. Fly, if you have to. As long as we keep my dick in, we win."

"Okay." Healey hesitated. "But you can't feel any of that, right?"

"Later you lick my armpits again and we're golden."

"Got it."

Healey lifted his hips and pushed back.

Things looked up after that. Way, way up.

Diego couldn't feel that part of the action, but Healey had one hand wrapped around the back of his neck, and he was dotting kisses over whatever skin he could touch, which turned out to be a whole load of other places like his upper arm and his biceps and the inside of—

"No, stop, not there."

Healey froze. "How come?"

"Too sensitive. Not fun."

"Kay." Healey tried another place. "Better?"

"Oh, Christ yeah."

And later, when Healey was so slick with sweat Diego could hardly hold on to him: "Oops, wait."

Healey reached down to capture Diego's dick and reinsert it. That? Should have been awkward, but nothing seemed like a big deal with Healey.

"Okay, we're good, go."

"This good?"

"I don't know if— Christ. Ah, yeah. That's good. You can stay there all day, baby."

There was no watching Healey's face for cues, but Diego'd never been with such an uninhibited guy. Healey was open to anything. Game to try anything. He treated sex like a conversation they were having together. It evolved while it was going on.

And holy cow. Everyone got their say.

Diego'd gone to a great deal of trouble learning how to safely shove a hard dick into somebody's ass, but it was his partners who had to make the magic happen. Healey was fluid and graceful and quick to pick up on cues. He understood he had to be careful, but he was easy to get off—he fucked like he had nothing to lose, flashed over quickly, and chased the finish line with the dedication of an Olympian.

Diego gave him a reach around, and as soon as he touched Healey's dick, Healey tensed and drenched his fingers with a delightful, fragrant splash of hot come.

That's how it's done, fuckers. Fierce pride filled Diego. He allowed himself the moment. 'Cause fuck yeah. Who wouldn't? He rolled off. Healey turned over, hair hiding his face like Cousin Itt. Diego had to brush it away to see his eyes. He looked almost giddy.

"You're perfect." Healey's eyes closed slowly, and just like that, Diego realized he was in way over his head.

They were fucking, weren't they?

Fucking, for God's sake.

You don't look at a guy like that when you're fucking. You look at your boyfriend like that, and Diego didn't think he *could* be a boyfriend. Not like Healey wanted, anyway. Not like his ex, whose education and backgrounds dovetailed with Healey's. Whose future was as certain and full of promise.

Diego could admit now, maybe, that he'd been hiding in Bluewater Bay too. Doing grunt work—stuff he could have done straight out of college—to get by because he didn't believe he had his old job in him anymore.

All people saw when they looked at him were his limitations and no photojournalist wants to be noticed. In his chair, he became the story often enough that it sickened him to contemplate even trying again.

Trying *anything*.

Why did he keep torturing himself with possibilities when life had handed him one great big nope?

Long after he kicked Healey to the living room couch, he frowned into the darkness.

The darkness frowned back.

CHAPTER EIGHTEEN
HEALEY

Awake, Healey studied whatever he found in plain sight. Magazines, books, photographs. Even when he did nothing but lie there, he felt like an intruder. Eventually, he left Diego's house and started for home. He simply stepped into the foggy, sea-scented darkness and made his way back to the B&B.

On the way, he stopped for a drink.

He recognized the bartender as an old friend from school, Sana. She smiled brightly when she pulled his beer, and let him know she had a break coming up. He found a nice quiet corner table and waited for her.

Alas, it was fighting flannel night—in one corner, you had your Pendleton, and in other, L.L. Bean. East Coast–West Coast rivalry, alive and well. These were not hipsters, though, for the most part. They were people he'd known all his life. They dressed the way they always had. The rest of the world had simply climbed on board.

"So . . . Healey Holly." Sana finally got time to stop by. "As I live and breathe."

"Hey, hi." He stood to give her a kiss on the cheek. She didn't look any different than when they'd been mathletes together.

"You're are my twofer today. I saw Nash earlier." Brainy as hell and way too beautiful for her own good, Sana was the Lebanese Christian girl who challenged everyone's rhetoric about women, about the Middle East, and about stereotypes. Since then, she'd undergone a retro-pinup-girl transformation, and it didn't seem weird at all. He took her hand in his and saw her wedding rings.

"Married? You look great. Sit down. How are you?"

"Fine." She glanced around fondly. "Better than."

"But you're bartending?"

She rolled her eyes. "While I get my MFA, yes. I'm bartending."

"You're—"

"Still in school." She sat across from him and used both hands to fluff out the crisp, puffy skirt she wore, before taking out a phone. "I'm a mother now."

She showed him pictures of a beautiful boy and girl. The girl appeared older. "A brilliant one, no doubt."

She blushed. "It makes sleep torture a daily reality."

"And you are more beautiful now than you have ever been."

Her nose crinkled, and he remembered that about her. She was a face maker.

"I read about your accident in the paper. Are you okay?"

"I walked away." He shrugged. "Can't ask for more than that, right?"

She nodded. "You're done with school?"

"All done." Scratching the label from his beer, he said, "Unless I decide to teach, I'm finished with school."

"Future plans?"

"None, except to supplement this—" he jiggled his bottle "—with a double shot of Maker's Mark when you're back on duty."

"You've got it."

He turned his chair toward hers. "Catch me up on Bluewater Bay."

She grinned. "You probably know everything you give a shit about. Your dad sold your house?"

"Yep." He asked too casually, "You ever meet the guy who bought it?"

"Diego? Sure. He's hot. Well-liked. Plays for your team."

There's always an advantage to knowing a small-town bartender.

"I tried to rent Nash's old apartment. For a lot of reasons, that was a crap idea." He leaned forward. "What do you think of Diego, though? He party a lot?"

"Not at all." She cracked the cap on her water bottle and took a healthy swig. "He comes in with the postproduction crew during filming. Always sits right where you're sitting. Gets one beer and nurses it all night. Tips great, though."

"By himself?"

"Wait." She wagged a long, purple-tipped fingernail in his face. "Oh, I see where this is going. You like him."

The smile fighting his face was probably just *idiotic*. "Maybe."

"You are still such a *pumpkin*." She sighed. "I could eat you up."

He shot her a look that said how well that would go over.

"That man you were with," she asked, "in the accident. He was your boyfriend, wasn't he?"

Healey drained his beer. "I can't talk about that."

"My husband's on the job." She leaned forward. "I know it's wrong, but he has friends and they talk. Because it was you, I asked."

Alarmed, Healey thought of the gag order and what it might mean if Ford's lawyers thought he'd violated it.

"Can he do that?"

"He asked around privately. Friends of friends. You know how law enforcement is. I'm only saying because if you need the name of a therapist who specializes in that kind of trauma, I could—"

"I'm fine."

She pressed her lips together.

"It's not the way it seems from the outside," he insisted. "Really. I was never scared."

He paused. Waited.

No lightning.

He was probably right about God not existing. Or God didn't mind liars.

"I know Ford," he continued. "He wouldn't hurt anyone, so it was really only a matter of waiting him out."

She listened patiently while he excused the inexcusable.

She was not buying it. "That's some fragrant bullshit there."

"It's too easy to judge something you don't understand." Aware he sounded like every other sap, he finished feebly, "Anyway, I lived with him for years, so I think I know what I'm talking about better than people who don't know him. He would never hurt me."

"Oh, sweetheart."

He tightened his grip on his bottle. "For the last time, I'm fine."

"All right." She fretted. "Anyone tries that shit here, they'll have to go through your family and friends."

"I'm really not stupid."

"No one ever said you were. God, if it were only a matter of brains—" She shook her head. "But naive? Yeah."

"What do you suggest?"

"Take care of yourself like you take care of others. Build some walls, honey. That's all."

"The minute I do that—" he jutted his chin out "—fear wins."

She stood, leaned over, and kissed his cheek. He let his head fall against the wall. The bricks were rough against his neck.

They smiled at each other. When she took away his empty, longing rose in his belly like the smoke of an abandoned cooking fire. He ached for home. For normal. For a place with no excuses or blame. For his pop, and what he now understood was unconditional love.

When Sana brought his drink, she said, "The world can be a nice place."

"One Maker's Mark at a time. Thank you." His mother used to look at him like that. At least, he imagined she did. Which reminded him he needed to thank Clara Underhill too. "I'm planning to ask Ms. Underhill for brunch at the Resort at Juan de Fuca some Sunday. Want to come? You could bring your family."

"God, why would I bring those heathens." She pulled her phone from her pocket. "Lemme text Sahil and ask if there's a Sunday that works for both of us. It'd be great to get together. Should I see if anyone from school wants in? Make it an unofficial reunion?"

He must have flinched, because she patted his back.

"All right, we save that for later," she crooned. "It's all good."

"Thanks." He squeezed her hand before she left.

As she slipped behind the bar, he studied the way she handled the bottles, the glasses, and the customers. She'd learned to juggle in middle school, they all had. It had been some project designed to keep their bodies as active as their minds, probably. But now she'd found a way to use it to supplement her income.

She was a bright spot.

She was fresh air.

There were really good people in Bluewater Bay.

When she brought him his third drink along with the business card of a local medical practice, he took it, thinking maybe she was right about that too.

"This is last call, sweetie. Where are you staying?"

"I'm at the B&B." He took his drink and downed it. The cool air would surely wake him up once he got outside. He put a few twenties on the table and thanked Sana.

"I'll be done soon. I can run you home." Her expression was concerned. "You can pick up your car tomorrow."

"I'm not driving. No worries."

"You're such a *boy*." She laughed. "It's no trouble, really."

"I need the walk. Thanks."

"Have it your way. See you Sunday."

"I'll be in touch. Same email?" he asked.

"I'll remember to check the old one, yes."

Healey stepped outside. A few more feet put him into the glow of an old-fashioned streetlamp. At night Bluewater Bay's downtown was no longer a mistakenly nostalgic tourist trap, but a run down logging town whose genteel poverty hinted at problems with infrastructure like lighting and roads.

Currently it was cold and spitting rain. Moisture brought the scent of tire rubber, dirt, and God knew what else up from the earth. He liked the musty smell.

Rain washed everything clean.

It sobered him up a little too.

No. It woke him up. He was still good and drunk.

Not one to wake others when he could do for himself, he let himself into the B&B, got a glass of water, and headed up to bed.

Nash was already asleep, but apparently in the years they hadn't lived together, he'd become a much lighter sleeper.

"Didn't expect you back."

"*Shit.*" Healey startled. "Diego doesn't share his bed and the couch sucked. Plus, he has this clock with a fucking regulator. *Tick-tock, tick-tock* all night. Felt like a horror film."

Before Nash could respond to that, Healey left him to do a quickie wash up and brush his teeth. When he returned, he hoped Nash was asleep. No such luck.

Nash yawned like a bear. "Did you have a good time?"

"Yeah, Pop." Caustic tone of voice for caustic words. "He fed me candy and soda and let me stay up way past my bedtime. But he kept trying to get me to call forth Satan. It wasn't weird or anything."

Nash sat up. "Healthy sex rarely includes Satan, bro. I thought I taught you better."

"Fuck you. I'm just a little . . ." Healey sat down hard on the end of the bed and the whole bed frame levered up, nearly launching Nash off like a catapult.

"*Whoa!*" People probably heard that on the first floor.

He and Nash scrambled to redistribute their weight.

"Off-balance?" Nash asked drily.

"I'm still coming down from that test-taking feeling. You know how I always get nervous and—"

"Sex is not a test." The words could have been considered Nash's mantra.

"Not for you, maybe." Healey toed off his shoes and let them fall to the floor one by one.

"You gotta think of it more like a road trip than a test. I keep telling you."

"It's not a road trip. On a road trip you don't have to worry whether the countryside you're traveling through likes you or not."

"What do I always—"

"You don't have to worry if your tourist face is ugly."

"Tourist face," Nash chuckled. "That your 'T' face?"

"If I fuck up on a trip, miss a connection, arrive too soon, or get totally lost and have to ask for directions, I don't give a crap, because I'm not going to see any of those people again."

"I see one solution."

Healey sighed, long and drawn out. "What?"

"How many billion people are there now?" Nash tried to kick him off the edge of the bed. "You have a lot to choose from. Say you only screw each person once. All the people in the world, not counting the women, not counting the ones who wouldn't have you on a bet, it'd still keep you pretty busy for the next few days."

"Fuck. You." Healey flopped beside him. His entire body ached.

"You get weirded out by his SCI? Worried you'd hurt him?"

"Know how Shelby gets? I try to be so precise with words, but I'm always going to say something stupid. I'll go, 'Don't you walk away while I'm talking to you—'"

". . . And you make her cry." Nash laughed.

Healey mimicked her, "'You know I can't walk. How could you be such an insensitive dick?'"

Nash nodded. "Shelby plays us. All except Fjóla. Those two are hashtag 'RideNDie' these days. Mama bear and her cub. Even Pop doesn't make sudden moves around them."

"I guess," Healey said into the darkness. Fjóla was strong and calm and fearless. Pop lucked out, finding someone like that. Healey yawned, already half-asleep.

Nash didn't let it go. "Now tell me what you're really worried about."

"I like him," Healey admitted. "I'm not ready to like someone. I don't want to do that anymore."

"How come?"

"Maybe I take things too seriously, or—" He let out a long, shuddering breath. "Maybe I just care too much, but I want to build a new world with somebody, not just show up and eat and fuck. Maybe to someone like Ford or Diego, all that energy feels suffocating. I want to be with someone without drowning them."

"If one dude can't handle the intensity, find someone who can." Nash turned, making the bed shift fractionally—enough for Nash's shoulder to make contact with Healey's. Enough for the warmth of Nash's skin to permeate the T-shirt he was wearing. "Or do you think you'll need more than one? Like a ménage?"

"No." Healey noticed the contact. Smiled into the darkness. "God no. I'm a one-man man."

"It's going to be fine." Nash's breath stank. Toothpaste over a background of Flaming Hot Cheetos. "Don't worry. I can fix anything."

CHAPTER NINETEEN
DIEGO

Goddamn it. Healey was gone.

Diego usually slept like a rock after fucking. This time, he'd woken with a strange sense of foreboding... He'd decided to check, and when he got to the living room, there was nothing on his couch except a neatly folded blanket and pillow.

His insides did a funny stumble, like they expected solid footing and a sinkhole opened up instead. He rolled to the coffee table and looked it over. The neat stacks of papers he'd left were untouched, but Healey had looked through the photographs. He'd even written a note about one: "Best use of light. Interesting juxtaposition of ideas. Negative space."

Diego frowned at the image, a 4X6 of his mother with her first brand-new car.

Negative space? Maybe.

Maybe...

Not the subject—he rolled to his desk and hit the switch on his workstation.

"Let there be light, and fans, and monitors." Getting an energy drink from the fridge, he added, "And caffeine."

The back of all his photographs bore a number he could use to find the image on his hard drive. He'd printed, scanned, and stored all his 35-mm work. When the right picture came up on the screen—his mother, relaxed and smiling, a hip-cocked badass leaning against her lipstick-red, '92 Nissan Sentra.

He let his mind drift.

They'd been coming back from New Mexico, so the picture must have been taken somewhere along I-20. He'd had too much pop at the Cracker Barrel, where they'd eaten lunch.

On the drive, he'd bugged her and bugged her and bugged her. "I have to pee."

Unconcerned, she'd shrugged. "Do you see a bathroom?"

"I'm a dude, I can pee anywhere."

"Not on my watch, you can't. What are you? Some kind of hoodlum? You'll wait."

But he'd nagged at her and whined.

As one does.

Eventually, he'd worn her down so much, she'd said, "Ah, fuck it."

They'd pulled over to the side of the road . . . And parked directly in front of a Coca-Cola sign that read, *Love, America.*

He'd been so relieved, he'd run off behind a rock and peed his brains out. Looking back, he couldn't remember whose idea it had been to take the picture.

Frowning, he zoomed in on the letters.

There.

Someone had carefully painted the ", America" in matching Coca-Cola red. The original sign simply read *Love.*

Someone had gone to all the trouble of altering that sign—doing the 1992 equivalent of Photoshop on it.

With ninja-level irony.

Now that he looked closer, it was obviously graffiti, and his mother was obviously posing with the sign, not the car. How had he missed that? It *changed* everything.

Before he could stop and think about the consequences, he picked up the phone and dialed.

Rachel answered with her usual rough-voiced charm. "What?"

"Good morning to you, Harvey Fierstein. Can I please speak with my Aunt Rachey?"

"I am not bailing your ass out of jail again."

He winced. "That was *one* time, and you were like twenty minutes away."

"By *plane*. I boarded a plane to come and save your ass. You're welcome. What do you want?"

"I think I found a theme."

His phone was silent for way too long.

"Rach?"

"Getting my bearings." He heard footsteps, the tinkle and slosh of glass, ice, and liquid. "We should both be asleep."

They should.

Why wasn't he sleeping again? Oh, yeah.

Healey.

"So tell me." She was finally back.

"Emailing you a JPEG file," he said. "See that? I don't think that billboard is legit."

"You Photoshop that?" she asked.

"Nope. Is there a way to find out if they ever made a billboard with that slogan? I didn't think anything about it until someone pointed it out."

She typed while she talked. "Be a mess trying to find if it's a real billboard, because they do alternative billboards at the holidays and I seem to recall a 'Love' one."

"Coke's been around since the nineteenth century. I've pulled up a list of their official slogans," he said.

"I remember 'Coke Is It!'"

"Mami had coasters that said, 'You Can't Beat the Real Thing.' When I was ten that was the dirtiest joke I knew."

"You're such a brat. Tell me your epiphany, then. Spill. I need sleep."

"You can't see it? 'Love *comma* America'?"

"Oh my God. Commas do save lives. What am I looking at here?"

"I think that's her work." He hesitated. "No, I'm sure of it."

"What is?"

"Taylor Swift's latest album cover—what do you think? I think Mami painted that sign. And I'll bet if I look through all my pictures, I'll find other photographs that seem random like this, but aren't."

In particular, he was remembering this one time when he'd taken a great picture of her, and she'd sent him back to get a picture of her and the wall of the barn she was leaning on . . . What had that barn wall said?

"I thought she just liked—" He typed the word Nebraska into his search box and found what he was looking for. "Ah. Here." He sent the picture to Rachel.

His mother, standing in front of a likeness of George W. Bush with the words, *Miss Me? Nyet.*

At some point, the sign had quite obviously read, *Miss me yet?*

"She did these, right?" he marveled. "This is totally something she'd sneak out in the middle of the night wearing some dumbass Lucha mask to do."

"If she did, she never said a word to me."

"Me neither." He looked for some trace of his mother's touch in the paint and found nothing. "The joke? That's all Mami. But why not take credit?"

"Whoever altered the sign intended it to be sly," Rachel guessed. "It's hard to say if she painted them, or if she simply saw them and liked them. She did collect pictures of other artists' work. And she liked kitsch."

She *loved* kitsch. Using the world as their classroom, they'd taught themselves to document the things that interested them in all sorts of different ways. He could almost hear his mother's voice, *"Get a picture of that, baby. I have to look it up when we get home."*

Together, they'd created whole vacations around roadside attractions.

Why not leave a little something behind?

"One year, we spent two weeks driving old Route 66 looking for Muffler Men. I think she painted these signs. I think they're like hidden Mickeys at Disneyland and she *wanted* us to find them later."

"Such a Gabbi thing to do. She'd get the last word in from the grave..." Rachel's voice trailed off. "I'll never believe she could keep a secret that big, though."

Oh, he could. Easily. She'd never felt safe. Not outside the bubble of the art world and the few men and women who protected her interests there.

"She kept everything about her art a secret until you came along, Aunt Rachel. If she did these things, the reason was personal. She didn't want credit. She just wanted to have her say."

"Now *that* I can totally believe." Rachel yawned audibly. "Is that the time? Go to bed. Call me tomorrow."

"A'ight. Love to everyone." He hung up, pushed himself away from the desk, and simply sat there, watching the screensaver float pictures into the void. He didn't want to ghostwrite his mother's memoir. He was too close to the subject. Plus, she'd wanted to remain something of a mystery. She'd been a phenomenon—yet there remained a part of her nobody had got to see, not even him.

That hurt, at the time.

Cecil and Rachel had no qualms about unearthing her secrets now. If they expected encouragement from him, they'd be disappointed. He didn't want to write about who she'd kissed. He didn't want to talk about the petty jealousies, scandals, the time she was bitter—when her faith deserted her.

But if there was a legit story here about her career? If there was a hidden facet of his mother's work no one knew about? He'd put aside his qualms, because that was a story he wanted to tell.

After a while, he lay down. The couch where he'd left Healey the night before wasn't uncomfortable. He used it all the time. It had to be his imagination when he discerned the faint hint of Healey on the cushions. The almond scent came from Healey's hair. That fragrant, wavy, light-brown spill of hipster-camouflage.

Ah, Jesus. He should call.

He should, but it would mean admitting he'd woken up in the middle of the night worrying about Healey. It would mean waking Healey up and demanding answers he didn't have any right to.

Where are you?

Didn't you care for the accommodations?

Are you all right?

Did you call Nash for a ride?

Does Nash think I'm a total dick now because I didn't take you home?

Did he even care what Nash Holly thought of him?

"No, goddamn it."

He didn't do boyfriend shit.

He distinctly, succinctly, did not.

He lay there feeling vindicated. Knowing there was no one in the world who could see he was acting like an ass, and there would be no evidence to prove it either.

He wasn't boyfriend material, and not because of any goddamn SCI.

"Boyfriends are Labrador Retrievers named Jake," he spoke the affirmation out loud. "They are precursors to marriage. To children. I am not looking for a boyfriend."

He closed his eyes.

Smiled at the memory of some stupid shit Healey had said.

Opened his eyes.

Healey would call. Probably, he would.

Or they'd bump into each other around town.

Diego spent a lot of time at the ridge, where the cemetery looked over the water. That was right next to the B&B. Plus, you couldn't help meeting up with people all the time in a town the size of Bluewater Bay. Even if you didn't want to.

He checked his phone. It would be dawn soon—time to decide whether to try to get a couple more hours' sleep, or start his day. He was missing his favorite time, goddamn it.

In the end, he packed his bag for the gym and donned the *Every Day Is Arm Day* T-shirt.

By the time he'd dressed, gotten in the car, and driven through the silence of Bluewater Bay, faint light cracked the eastern horizon. He swiped his key card at the desk, and headed toward the nearly empty locker rooms.

"Diego." Ginsberg Sloan, one of the stunt men from *Wolf's Landing*, was inside, wearing nothing more than a towel. "How's things. Enjoying the hiatus?"

"I'd rather be busy." Diego shoved his things into a locker. "How about you?"

"Just flew back from Romania, man. So fucking wet and cold all the time. I'm getting too spoiled for crappy location shoots and bad food and weather I don't like."

"And an empty bed?" Gins was with Derrick, owner of the B&B.

"Lumberjacks do have their uses." Gins grinned and headed for the showers.

"A'ight. I'll see you later."

As he left the locker room, Diego congratulated himself on not asking Gins if he'd met the B&B's new tenant. He'd handle things if he saw Healey. He'd play it loose. He'd decide if he wanted to hook up next time—if there was a next time—on the fly. Like always.

Despite his resolve, he checked his phone again.

"You going to use that machine? Or what?"

Diego frowned up at the guy standing with his arms crossed, peering down at him. Dude had a lazy smile. Nice green eyes. Also, awesome full-sleeve tattoos. Diego's first instinct had been to tell the dude to go fuck off and die, but he wasn't going to war over an ab machine he didn't plan to use.

"Sorry, man. You take it."

Lazy-smile guy winked. "You don't remember me, do you?"

"Should I?" He felt pretty safe saying so. He hadn't slept with anyone in Bluewater Bay except Healey. Not that he only remembered people he slept with . . .

"That's okay. We only met once. You thought I was hogging the cream at Stomping Grounds."

"Ah God, yeah. I—" that hadn't been one of his finer moments "—I'm real sorry about snapping that way."

"No, you had a point. I didn't see you there because I didn't bother looking down."

"I should have just said something instead of unloading on you."

"We've all done it. I'm known for my tats, not the sweetness of my disposition."

"They are nice." The sleeves were inked with vivid, colorful tropical flowers. "I'm surprised I don't remember those."

"I had on a long-sleeved shirt that day probably. Rigoberto Villa—Ringo—from Ink Bay."

"You're an artist?"

"Mm-hmm." He looked Diego over. "I don't see no ink on you. When you gonna bust your cherry?"

Diego shook his head. "I can't, man."

"Health shit or religious reasons?"

"Hypersensitivity."

"You look pretty tough to me."

Diego explained. "It's a real thing. Comes with the chair. Sometimes I can't stand to be touched. Sometimes I need people to touch me extra hard. The problem comes and goes."

"I didn't know that." He threw his towel over the bar. "Too bad. You've got a pretty awesome canvas."

"Yeah, yeah." Diego shrugged off the obvious line.

"No, I mean it." Ringo pointed at his shoulder. "I'd do a whole round shoulder thing on your delt there. Celestials or the Aztec calendar or something. You're a beast."

The admiring looks went straight to Diego's ego. When he was done with his reps, they made their way to the free weights. Ringo started adding weights to the press bar.

Diego asked, "You want me to spot you?"

Ringo glanced up. "You can do that?"

"Probably," he teased. "Maybe? What's the worst that could happen?"

Of course he couldn't spot someone who was pressing a ton of weight.

"Got me. I wasn't about to trust my thorax to a seated dude. You try out a biceps curl with the weight I press?"

Diego admitted it wouldn't happen. "Got me there."

"I am the Thorax, I speak for the trees." Ginsberg stopped at the head of the bench and spotted Ringo's reps before saying good night on his way out. "*Ciao, bello.*"

"Night, Gins. Soon, okay? Margaritas and darts. Guy with the worst location stories buys the drinks."

"Only if we're counting film locations and not your days as a news producer."

"Deal." Diego bumped fists with him, and he left.

"Cute kid." Ringo watched Gins walk away.

"That was Carter Samuels's stunt double. I wouldn't call him a kid where he can hear you."

"No way! I seen him around, but I thought he went to the college or something."

"Nope. He gets his ass kicked for a living." Diego turned back to Ringo. "Sorry I can't spot you. You mind spotting me, anyway?"

"Sure."

After three reps he was breathless and bathed in sweat. He counted off the last few while his muscles screamed with effort. He let Ringo take the bar, and pushed himself into a sitting position. With one hand on the bench and one on his chair, he made the transfer.

"Goddamn. No wonder your chest is massive." Ringo wiped his face with a sports towel. "You wouldn't believe the ink I could do with a canvas like that."

"I'll think about it some." He got his own towel and wiped off. "I could try."

"I've never seen anyone like you. Lifting like that, moving from chair to bench and back."

"I had a lot of upper body strength 'cause I did gymnastics in college. I'm used to building specific muscle groups."

"Still." Ringo shook his head. "Don't hide your light, man."

"Hard work is a great way to kill time." Diego lifted his water to his mouth, took a deep swig, and sighed with satisfaction. "Sometimes it needs killing."

"I hear you," Ringo said. "When my partner died, I felt the same way."

"I'm sorry for your loss. Has it been long?"

"It happened years ago. Motorcycle accident."

"Sorry."

"You can't kill time. It keeps getting back up like a zombie. Time kills *us*. Don't let it." He draped his towel over his shoulder and started toward the locker room. "Nice working out with you."

"You too." Diego meant that, for a change.

"Don't be a stranger."

"Hey, wait." Diego thought of something he wanted. "You do piercings?"

"Need yours redone?"

"Yeah." Diego did not even consider where the idea came from. "I think my ears are still okay, but my eyebrow closed. Can you redo it?"

"It happens all the time. I'm going to shower and then open the shop. You wanna take care of that this morning?"

"Sure."

Wait. Did he? Healey was pretty perceptive. He'd make the connection between remarking on those piercings and suddenly seeing them repierced if Diego showed up with jewelry on.

Fuck it. It was his face. He had a right to redo his piercings if he wanted. He was going to foster a soul patch again too. Or maybe he'd grow a Van Dyke, like Cecil's. Mami said Cecil looked like a modern Don Quixote.

Maybe he'd get a haircut too. If he was going back out on the meat market, he could use a little grooming. He needed it for a reason—he'd look like himself again, with his piercings in. He checked an old picture on his phone.

Yep.

Not only had he looked better back in the day, he'd taken a lot better care of himself then too. Diego didn't have far to go to see how he looked this morning. The gym was full of mirrors. He was effing swole, and damn proud of it. But there was a time when he'd been far more fastidious about how he looked and how he dressed.

He used to have a lot more self-respect.

So, hell yeah, he was going to put his piercings back in. And he should dig some better clothes out of his closet.

None of which had anything to do with Healey Holly, the man who reminded him of what he used to be by making him forget what he was.

CHAPTER TWENTY
HEALEY

When the early-morning knock sounded on the door to their room, Nash leaped out of bed, but not before elbowing Healey on his already-bruised eye.

"Christ. That's gonna leave a new shiner. Tonight, you get your own damn room."

"Last night, you weren't even here." Nash dragged a T-shirt over his head on the way to the door.

"That was a hookup."

"So. Make it happen again." Nash opened the door, and their pop stepped into the room.

"Land Shark!"

"What the hell, Pop? You can't call ahead?"

Ace wrapped his arm around Nash's shoulders before dragging him over to capture Healey, so he could hug them both at once. "I've missed you two."

He let go of Nash and held Healey by both shoulders, eyes narrowed.

"You okay, Heals?"

Healey shook his head. "Sure. Sore and sad."

Understanding was his pop's stock in trade. "Goddamn it. I liked Ford."

"I still like him," Healey said quietly.

Nash let out a snort of outrage. "Don't defend him, he almost got you killed."

"We don't know everything yet, Nash," said Pop.

"We know Healey's got broken bones."

"Anyone can have an accident."

Healey stayed silent while Ace and Nash argued about taking personal responsibility and entitled people and making tough choices.

When he was a kid, he'd stopped his ears when Nash and his dad argued. Ace was a softie, but Nash had a pretty black-and-white way of looking at things. He condemned Shelby's mother, Christine, even though she'd been a hopeless addict. Healey and their pop had a tougher time blaming her, even considering what had happened.

After a while, though, they noticed he was staying silent.

"Healey?" Nash studied him. "What is it?"

"The pressure on Ford was immense." Immense and toxic. Ford's parents threw money at his problems, but withheld empathy. "And a diagnosis of BPD in young adulthood—"

"Don't make excuses for what he did," said Nash. "He made a choice to stop taking his meds."

"I don't make excuses. But there are *reasons*. If Ford had a brain tumor, no one would blame him for what happened."

"But if Ford had a brain tumor that caused him to act out in dangerous ways—"

Pop cut him off. "Leave it alone, Nash."

Nash turned on Pop. "Healey could have been killed."

"We don't know what happened," Pop reminded him.

Nash pointed Healey's way. "Because he won't tell us."

"It's none of your business," Healey insisted. "Ford's out of our lives now, anyway."

"I'm sorry, son." Pop's voice softened. "I know you loved each other. That's rough."

"Don't be too hard on him," Healey pleaded. "None of us can know what goes on in someone else's head."

Nash gave a disgusted grunt. "I hope you brought Fjóla. We could use someone rational around here."

"Absolutely." Pop beamed with pride. "She's getting her place ready for guests. I came to take you home."

Healey glanced at Nash. "Getting pretty serious, huh?"

Pink crescents made Pop's cheeks look painted on. "It hardly makes sense for me to go to a hotel."

"We're not judging you." Nash grinned. "But we should probably have a talk about when a boy likes a girl and sometimes he feels things."

"You can't be my kid." Pop turned to Healey for help. "Tell him you had a fateful accident with a copying machine."

"Are you sure Fjóla has room for three guests?" Nash asked.

"Her place is a bit small. We'll manage." Pop was always an optimist. Whatever, it had to be bigger than this.

"I'll pack." Healey padded to the closet to get his duffel.

"Does this mean I won't have to share a bed with Mr. Sleeps-Like-a-Top?" asked Nash.

"Look who's talking, Mr. Snack Breath," Healey muttered.

"Are you two still in preschool? Seriously." Ace checked each drawer of the tiny bureau. "I did not fly halfway around the world to hear you two argue."

"Yeah, you did." Nash brought Healey's toiletry kit from the bathroom. "You realize leaving here means no more of Jim's tasty breakfasts."

"Oh, shoot." Healey could practically taste Jim's lemon bars, but he was still glad they were leaving. He squared his shoulders. "Nope. Not even Jim's pastries are worth sharing a bed with you."

"You couldn't get a second room here?" asked Pop.

"There's a fan event," said Nash. "No room at the inn for Jesus, even. We were lucky they hadn't fixed up this room for guests."

"There's always a fan event." Healey zipped his duffel while Pop double-checked the bedding for anything forgotten.

Nash got dressed and packed his things in short order. "We just need to tell Derrick we're checking out. And to say thanks."

The three men looked at one another.

"Weird, us all being here like this—" Healey's gut tightened "—without the house to go to."

"Come on." Pop patted him gently on the back. "Fjóla will make you comfortable. That's her superpower."

"And if not, you can always hook up with Diego again," said Nash.

"Wait, what?" asked Pop.

"Never mind." Healey glared at Nash before he grabbing the handle of his duffel. "Just for that, I won't let Jim pack you a doggy box."

"He will." Nash closed the door behind them. Pop followed them down the stairs. "He likes me."

"He likes me better," Healey said.

Nash laughed. "Says you."

"Victoria Beckham likes me better too."

Nash turned to sneer at him. "Her, you can have."

"Say what?" Jim brandished an empty coffeepot. "Don't ask for anything fancier than drip after that crack about my Queen Victoria."

"I'm sorry, but we have to go." Healey held his good hand out to shake. "My pop's here, and the room is way too small for three of us."

"Of course it is." Jim wrapped both hands around Healey's. They shook warmly. "But don't be a stranger."

"Be seeing you." Nash barely managed to exit the door without Victoria Beckham's pointy little teeth taking a chunk out of his leg.

Pop followed, and Healey turned back. "Thanks again. Let Derrick know I'll be by later to settle up."

"No worries." Jim picked Victoria up, put her under his arm, and waved.

Pop and Nash both had rental cars, so Healey went in Pop's. Nash drove alone.

As soon as they were under way, he regretted it.

Pop turned to him. "You can give Nash that need-to-know bullshit, but this is me you're talking to. What happened to Ford. Was it the Illuminati?"

"No, Pop. I'm sorry, but I don't think the Illuminati are for real."

"No?" Pop's eyes twinkled. "Shelby says that Beyoncé and Jay Z are in charge of it."

"Pretty sure not."

"Yeah, yeah. I guess it's need to know, huh?" Pop watched the television show *Numb3rs* religiously. It had been tough convincing him the grad students at Stanford weren't called in all the time to solve crime or thwart terrorist attacks.

"Pop."

"All right, all right. Keep your secrets."

He was playing. There was a wry twist to his lips and a little bit of an expectant air. As if he was waiting for Healey to call him on things. Healey didn't want to give him the satisfaction.

Still . . . you never knew with Pop.

Pop stopped at a stoplight and turned his way. "You know who is named Diego? The guy who bought our house."

"Yeah." Healey's face caught fire. "I met him. He did a pretty nice remodel."

Pop narrowed his eyes. "Is that what the kids are calling it these days?"

Healey let that go without comment.

"What's he like?" asked Pop.

"Prickly."

Pop nodded. "Been in the chair long?"

"I didn't ask, but I don't think so."

"How bad is it?"

"I don't know if he'd want me talking about his health."

"Probably not." Pop shrugged. "I guess I shouldn't have asked."

"Ask him."

The light turned green, and they entered the intersection. "Think I'll get to meet him?"

Healey didn't know. There was Diego's whole *I don't want a boyfriend* thing. That was pretty clear. "I like him, but I won't be staying in Bluewater Bay, so I doubt we'll date or anything."

"Don't be afraid to make new friends, Heals."

"Pop."

"I'm just saying. It's hard, after you lose someone. You start to wonder if that's all you get. If it was some kind of fluke. If there can ever be anyone else."

They sat through the next light cycle with loss like a wet blanket weighing them down.

"Obviously, it's not a fluke," Healey offered. "There were other women for you, after Mom."

The small smile his pop wore probably had its genesis in Fjóla. "They say third time's the charm."

Genuinely pleased, Healey gripped his dad's shoulder. "You're tying the knot?"

"Probably not." He shrugged. "Why bother? Not like we'll have kids."

"I guess not."

"*You* could have kids. Don't let anyone tell you how to live." His father had always advocated on their behalf. "Make the family you want and the haters be damned."

Wow. How long had Pop been storing that up? "I will, Pop."

Pop turned on the radio and some kind of New Age, Pan-flute music flooded the car for a second before he changed it and Guns N' Roses took over.

"Hehehe," he chuckled. "Fjóla likes that world music stuff."

Healey smiled at that. It was weird seeing his pop fall in love, but Ace Holly was young enough and fit enough that watching him and Fjóla was kind of like Thai food. Sweet and hot.

Plus, Pop was due something good for a change. Something wonderful. He'd been a great dad.

Pop was owed.

"Fjóla's good people," Healey murmured.

"The finest." Something had shifted subtly in his tone. "When your mom died, I thought I closed the book on love. Christine was different."

"Understatement of the year."

Pop didn't deny the charge. "It was nice being needed for a while."

"I know." Healey liked being needed too. He liked solving problems. He liked fixing things. He—

"Did Ford need you?" His pop stared at him, unblinking. "The way Christine needed me?"

Something gritty caught in Healey's throat. "I don't want to talk about Ford."

After studying his face for a minute, Pop muttered, "No need."

He probably saw Healey's unspoken answer. He checked oncoming traffic before making the turn onto a side street where three pretty houses sat in a row, like cottages for woodland elves. Pop pulled into the farthest one and killed the engine.

"I can make a pretty good guess what happened. Ford started partying a little too heavily?"

"Ford isn't Christine."

In the shadows, Pop's face fell. "No. Probably not."

"Ford's family asked me not to talk about the things that led up to the night of the accident, but Pop, you don't know how it was. He was scared. He took the medicine they gave him, and it just didn't work all the time, and he was scared—"

"Oh, son. I'm so sorry."

"It's not my story to tell." Healey felt sick saying that much. "That's why this is so hard. One minute we were on top of the world, and the next, it all turned upside down, but not because we partied too much."

"I believe you. But you can see how worried we've been, and no one is talking."

Healey rested his head against the seat cushion. In the silence of the car, far enough away from all the people involved, Healey was able to say it. "We'd been having problems for a long time. You know about the BPD, but things were getting worse. He started resisting treatment. Missing appointments."

"Why didn't you tell us sooner?"

When he let the memory play out, Healey gave an involuntary shudder. "After he came back from spending the holidays at home, things changed, but it was so gradual. He withdrew. He wasn't sleeping. He got seriously back into running—he drove himself relentlessly."

"Did his family know?"

"Of course. I told them. But they weren't there for the day-to-day and he was good at hiding things. I don't think they really understood. At some point, I don't know when, because he was still keeping up a pretense, Ford decided to stop taking his meds."

"I'm sorry you had to go through that alone."

"I wasn't alone. I was with Ford."

His statement seemed ludicrous now. Fraught with ominous warning. He'd always depended on Ford to anchor him, even though Ford had problems of his own. And he'd failed horribly to return the favor.

Maybe he'd been unable to help for reasons wholly forgivable. But maybe he'd simply been blind, and Ford had suffered.

The front door of the house opened and welcoming light spilled onto the porch—along with Fjóla. She waved happily at Nash, who'd pulled up behind them, but gotten out of the car first.

Healey and his father joined them.

"Welcome to my home." She hugged Healey gently when he got to her, and then his pop hugged her, and Nash hugged everybody.

This.

This was what he'd been hoping for when he got back to Bluewater Bay. He needed his family, and here they were, *here for him*, like always.

"C'mon." Nash tightened his arm round him. "I gotcha."

The sheer joy of having his family here was brilliant. Knowing he could sleep without fear of anything or anyone. Without keeping one eye open. He could let go.

He could simply—finally—rest, because his family had his back.

Healey's voice was choked with relief when he spoke. "I don't know what I'd do..."

"Me neither. Shh." Nash shook him like a puppy. "It's going to be okay."

CHAPTER TWENTY-ONE

DIEGO

When Diego didn't hear anything from Healey for a week, he was frankly relieved.

Guys like Healey, men with siblings who kept in touch over minutiae—men with parents who flew halfway around the world to be with them after a college romance breaks up—weren't his usual hookup fare.

Diego's usual hookup fare left when he was done, and everyone was okay with that. He'd dodged a bullet, as far as he was concerned. A guy like Healey could easily get clingy.

Of course... Healey had left. It had been over a week, and Healey hadn't sent so much as an emoji.

Goddamn it.

That didn't feel very awesome.

Healey had left without being told to go. Without saying good-bye. Healey wasn't presuming they were a couple, like he'd feared. So, that was great, right?

Why did it feel not great? Why did it feel like he'd been rejected, when the only thing that had happened was he'd been given the gift of not having to spell things out to a one-night stand?

"What am I so worried about?" he said out loud.

"At a guess, I'd say talking to yourself?" Tori, owner of Stomping Grounds and maker of the best Cuban coffee—well, probably the only Cuban coffee—in town, stared down at him. She looked mildly amused. "You should see your face. Want another?"

"I'm good." Diego put away the phone he was fiddling with. Was he the only person over five years of age still playing Pokémon Go? "Caught a Magikarp."

"My condolences." Tori sat in the chair opposite his. With filming on hiatus, lethargy could turn into depression at light speed. Since his routine was to get coffee and a protein pack every weekday morning, rain or shine, Tori had become Diego's unofficial mother figure.

"As if there aren't enough wide-eyed idiots around here staring at their phones, not watching where they're going, walking out in front of traffic—"

"What's got you muttering to yourself?" When he didn't answer, she guessed. "Guy trouble? That's men for you. Can't live with them, and in all but a few progressive states, you're not allowed to shoot them unless you have a pretty good reason. Tell Mama all about it."

"There's no guy," he corrected.

"Is that the problem? Because I know a whole bunch of guys who'd be awesome for—"

"No. Jeez. Not everything is about relationships or whatever." Diego hoped to hell he didn't look as crusty as he sounded. "I have to do some things that aren't going to be easy, is all."

She gave a slow nod. "Anything I can help with?"

"Unless you have an encyclopedic knowledge of billboard advertising in the last half of the twentieth century?"

She shook her head.

"I have to go through my mother's papers and photographs." He explained finding the picture of the altered billboard, and how he was searching through his archives for others. "I've been putting off looking through her things. You know how it is."

Tori shook her head. "The only thing my mom left behind was empties. I lined every single bottle up along the fence and spent an entire day shooting at them."

"That's two gun references in a single conversation."

Red lips curved up in a pretty white smile. "Wow. Guns and sex. Maybe it's me who needs to get laid, huh?"

"Yep." The sooner they could talk about anything besides getting laid the better, as far as he was concerned. "Anything interesting going on around here next weekend?"

"I'm so glad you asked." At last, he'd triggered a new direction for her thoughts. She nodded happily. "We're doing a movie party on Friday the thirteenth. I'll be showing *Weird Science* and *Real Genius*. Can you tell Healey to call me?"

"And how would I do that?" Shoot. He might have sounded a bit snappy, there.

Her mouth twisted wryly. "Because he's living in your garage apartment?"

"My garage was the last place he needed. His brother's in town—"

"Yeah, I saw Nash a few days ago. I just assumed he was staying with Healey. They said Ace was coming too, huh?"

"How would I know? Healey stayed in the apartment over my garage for a single night—" *true* "—a week and a half ago. That's all there was."

Most definitely *not* true.

"They must be staying with Fjóla, then, you think?"

"I don't know. Why the interrogation, Tori? Why do you even give a shit?"

She gave his arm a playful shove. "I don't. I'm trying to figure out why you're so cagey about the Holly boys. Those two usually make a hell of an impression, especially on men who like men."

His face got hot. "I'm not cagey. They're gone. I bought their house. It's mine now. I'm not their fucking gardener."

She scooted her chair back. "Wow."

"No. Sorry." He was so ashamed, he just gave up. "I am so sorry."

"Just wow." She stood slowly, mimed backing away in terror, and picked up her chair as if he were going to maul her. "Who pissed in your Cheerios?"

"Knock it off, Tori. Can I just have a fucking brownie please? I need sugar and caffeine."

She swallowed anything caustic, even going so far as to allow a fleeting maternal expression to escape as she went to get the treat for him. She picked up a bottled water from behind the counter on her way back and returned, sitting down again.

"Thank you." He took the brownie while she uncapped the water and took a big swig. "I appreciate you for more than your brownies. You know that right?"

"I do know, and—" narrowing her eyes, she tapped a bright-red fingernail on the table "—I've given you chocolate. You must now give me truth."

He sighed. "Healey and I hooked up."

As casual as he made the words, he knew she wouldn't let things go at that.

And of course she didn't.

"Oh my God. That's perfect. The two of you make so much sense—"

"It's no big deal, okay?" She looked like she almost believed him, but then he went and spoiled everything by adding, "It was only once, and he hasn't even called or anything since. So I doubt—"

"I see." Only Tori could invest those words with so much chilling portent.

"It was nothing." Keeping her from learning the truth was hopeless. He couldn't stop himself from revealing too much. Like catching a falling knife.

Or . . . Tori was just that good.

"Really," he finished lamely.

"*Really.*"

She smiled and . . . *boom*. There it was. The laser-like focus of the inveterate matchmaker. The crafty, knowing expression. The hint of self-congratulatory delight.

And her aspect—beatific.

"Movie Night is Friday," she said warmly. "I was thinking of inviting the Hollys. Who better to facilitate the event than Bluewater Bay's own Weird Scientist. Here's what we're going to do—"

"I'm really busy these days," he said. "Sorry."

She clutched the edge of the table tightly. "What could possibly be more important than Movie Night?"

"I told you. I'm doing something for my stepdad and my mother's friend Rachel. I doubt I'll have the time to stop by, but—"

"Oh, you'll stop by all right." She had the nerve to finger-point. "You are the only one I trust with my precious audio-visual equipment. That's a sacred responsibility, Diego. And it's one I know I can count on you to do your best at because that's just the kind of fine young man you are."

Tori's tone was so familiar. "You used to be a nun, didn't you?"

She dimpled at that. "That is one thing *no one* has ever accused me of."

He finished his brownie in one last big bite. After chewing, he agreed, "Okay, I'll run your movies, *Madrina*. But don't count on me hanging around for the festivities. I don't feel so much like partying these days."

At this, her teasing demeanor disappeared, leaving only his concerned friend. Her gaze calmly searched his.

"Hey," she said gently. "I've made some guesses as to what brought you up to Bluewater Bay, and why you've chosen to stay."

He fiddled with his cup. "I came because of *Wolf's Landing*, but I moved here because . . . I like the Sound."

She put her hand over his. He didn't move it, even though the urge to draw away came naturally as breathing.

"You once told me you were a gymnast?"

He snorted. "I did gymnastics. I wasn't exactly some elite athlete."

She nodded. "You know about momentum. Bluewater Bay is a good place to land, but it's also an excellent place to find your balance. To spring back from."

"How many moms I gotta have?" he teased.

"As many as you need, *mocoso*."

"Oh, you did not just call me that."

"I did." She stood and stretched. Tilted her head and peered at him. "So are you ever going to talk about those piercings?"

"What about them?" He glanced up. "They're not new."

"No, but you've started wearing jewelry again. And I know for a fact you had to have your eyebrow redone. I saw you go into Ink Bay with Ringo."

"Stalking me much?" She had the grace to look contrite. "Healey noticed the scars and it reminded me, is all. He's observant like that. I didn't think about my piercings after the accident. It wasn't a priority, and they healed."

She leered. "You look hot today, Rico Suave . . ."

"Oh, for God's sake. I didn't have a makeover."

"What can I tell you. I like piercings. Got any others?"

Cagily, he replied, "I don't have to answer that."

Her grin widened. "So that's a yes."

He shrugged. "Can't anymore, but yeah. I did have."

"Okay, so seriously. I want to set you up with one of my baristas. Will you let me? I could give him Movie Night off, and you could get to know each other. Alternatively, I could ask him to work and you could be a super attractive distraction for him."

"Not interested."

"Because . . . ?" she asked, slyly.

Oh, he knew what she wanted to hear. She figured the mention of Healey meant something. If he started down this path with her, there'd never be an end to it.

"Not interested."

"You want to know what I think? Someone's going to change your mind about that sooner than you think."

"All right. Place your bet. You pay your money and you take your chances." He shoved all his trash in the single bag on his lap and rolled toward the bin. To leave no doubt that he wouldn't be changing his mind anytime soon, he said, "I'll let you know if it happens."

As she waved good-bye, she called out, "Town like this one, poppet, everyone will know before you do."

Right. She was actually right. Why had he moved to Bluewater Bay again?

He followed the same path he always took, zigging and zagging along the grid of streets with numbers and tree names. Pretty boring shit. He had his camera with him, so he stopped and took the time to pull it out, to drape it around his neck in case he saw anything worth shooting.

It was taking a while for him to get used to the damp chill of the Pacific Northwest. The wind coming off the water picked up the leaves on the ground and whirled them, stiff and chilly, around his wheels. Diego donned a beanie, zipped his hoodie, and wound a colorful scarf—the hand-knit product of his stepfather's enforced captivity after knee surgery—around his neck several times.

The sun was breaking through the clouds, arrowing icy light onto the trees guarding the old cemetery. He rarely saw anyone other than Derrick from the B&B there, so it came as a bit of a surprise to see a handsome, silver-haired man standing in an older corner of the property, arms folded.

In a flash, it came to him who the man must be: Ace Holly. Healey's "Pop." The resemblance was unmistakable. He had that American Staffordshire look, but the gray-muzzled version. A happy, healthy old dog who turned, saw Diego, and came bounding over with a genuine smile on his face.

"Hey, are you Diego Luz?"

"What gave it away?"

Ace laughed in chagrin. "I deserve that for presuming. How are you enjoying living in Bluewater Bay?"

"I like it fine." He'd picked up his camera to take a couple of shots from the ridge, and he subtly caught Ace. Didn't really know why, except he wanted a picture of the man. "You miss it?"

"Sometimes. My wife is buried over there." Ace pointed toward where he'd been standing. "When we put her in the ground, all I could envision was standing here, year after year, looking into the distance as time crawled by."

"It's a nice view."

Tranquil. Cool and pleasant for the people who came to visit, unlike the manicured mediocrity of big business cemeteries that feature traveling art exhibits and live theater. Old cemeteries were peaceful. Modern cemeteries were practical. His mother was at Forest Lawn. You couldn't get more practical than that.

"Funny thing. You can look into the distance, but not the future."

As if there was a city-wide fire sale on pithy advice, Ace offered his wares.

Diego heard his mother's laugher on the wind as he echoed, "Funny."

He'd resigned himself to the chair and everything that went with it. But he wasn't ready for some new "life" to begin. He didn't want to be wrapped in the web of interconnected lives in Bluewater Bay, and yet...

Bluewater Bay was a typical small town. The people there drew him in and tested and plotted and probed. He was resigned to that too.

He held up his camera. "Mind if I take your picture?"

"What for? Doesn't matter." Ace beamed at him before striking a dignified pose. "Sure."

CHAPTER TWENTY-TWO
DIEGO

On Movie Night, Stomping Grounds was total chaos. The kids danced to Oingo Boingo. Tori's staff served coffee. More than one person snuck sips from a flask. Healey was just a big kid himself—wearing a lab coat and Docs—whose wavy hair had been sprayed Poison Ivy green and secured in a bun with a different wooden pin.

Diego set up the video feed while Healey took the microphone. Tori had set tables for mini "science" experiments. She and Healey'd found fun things for people of all ages to do—vats of borax-and-school-glue "Slime," mint-and-soda-pop carbonated fountains. Someone had even brought a "plasma" ball.

Healey had a way with kids. "The noble gasses," he said with a laugh, "are not the kind your dads make when they fart, because unlike dad farts, they are what?"

When he advanced his Powerpoint presentation, the audience called out each property with him: "Colorless, odorless, tasteless, and nonflammable."

Everyone ended up laughing.

"Boys will be boys." Tori grimaced before turning to Diego, who was double-checking the sound.

"I wouldn't know," he said sourly. "I'm a man."

He didn't want to be here. Didn't want his body lighting up like a beer sign whenever Healey looked his way. Parts of his body. Weird parts.

He could taste Healey's kisses. Feel his tongue glide, slick and languid, over the highly sensitive hotspots they discovered together—his armpits, nipples, the side of his neck.

Being that emotionally interested without the corresponding physical sensations sucked. It frayed his nerves. It filled him with inexplicable rage.

Attraction crackled between them, and he had nothing to do with it. Healey drew him in, even if he was only talking about Nikola Tesla, high-voltage electromagnets, neon-filled glass spheres, and the value of additives like argon and krypton.

While Healey talked, probably three dozen adults and half again as many kids learned science wasn't an ominous, clandestine club, but a hands-on, fun, family pastime.

When they started playing with some kind of high-tech bubble juice, Diego rolled outside for a breath of fresh air.

"Hey. Diego!" Across the street, Ace Holly emerged from a dark SUV waving happily. "Crazy night here, huh?"

Diego waited for Ace to cross. "Sure is. It's hopping in there."

"Healey had a lot of fun devising the experiments." Diego followed Ace back inside, where they had to speak over the crowd to make themselves heard.

"Tori comes up with some good ideas." He should know—because he knew his way around Final Cut Pro he'd gotten roped into half of them lately.

Ace nodded. "I was worried Healey was trying to do too much at first, but it's been okay."

The object of their scrutiny stood on the stage, one arm in a cast, one holding the microphone while a child produced an entire room's worth of bubbles from an old aluminum tennis racquet. Glasses that Healey probably didn't need rested on the tip of his nose.

Diego suddenly realized Healey was staring at him. Waiting for something? Diego met his gaze. "What?"

"Ready to start the film, Igor?"

He couldn't help chuckling at that. He dragged out his best Boris Karloff. "Ready, master."

Amusement crossed Healey's face. And quiet longing. *Wait.* What the hell?

"Someone get the lights?" Tori called.

Volunteers scrambled. Seconds later, everyone was looking at a pair of gross gym socks, chicken legs, and... pimply nerds.

Andrew McCarthy. Girls doing gymnastics. Leg warmers.

"Welcome to a land that time forgot . . ." Healey intoned before leaving the stage and slipping quietly out through one of the side doors. Diego caught his slightly pained grimace and winced for him. It couldn't be easy doing all that running around with a broken arm. Which hadn't stopped Diego from fucking the hell out of Healey when he'd had the chance.

Of course, that was what Healey'd asked for. Wasn't it?

In Tori's words, *"Just wow."*

Better judgment thrown to the wind, Diego followed Healey outside. He found him by the dumpster, staring up at the sky.

"See something you like?"

A sad smile crossed Healey's face. "What's not to like? You know there was a spike on one of the radio transmitters we sent into space? We may have found alien life."

"That must have been kind of exciting, huh?"

"Sure." Healey winked. "Right now, 65 million light years away, there's probably a guy in a tinfoil hat saying, 'Fuck. I *knew* it.'"

God, he liked Healey Holly. Why did liking a guy make everything so much harder?

"You okay?" Healey looked so tired. "Are you still staying at the B&B?"

Healey shook his head. "Staying with my dad's girlfriend."

Diego nodded. "Wondered."

"Did you?" Healey's direct gaze was all challenge.

Diego shrugged.

"I wondered about you too." Healey's voice rose.

Diego shot a side-eye glance Healey's way. "You didn't call."

"You didn't either. That's the thing about cell phones. I'd know if you had."

"A'ight. I know." Diego let his head fall back. The full moon was a ball-shaped lantern behind gauzy curtains. It cast a pale halo over a church spire in the distance. "I told you I'm not good at this kind of thing."

"On the contrary." Healey sighed and turned to him. "I'd argue that you're masterful."

A spike of anger pierced him. "What do you mean by that?"

"When it comes to letting people know where they stand? You communicate very well."

Diego fidgeted with his wheels. "Don't be like that."

Healey stared—he was waiting for more.

"I didn't have a shitty time or anything," Diego added.

"High praise." Healey laughed. "Be sure and leave me a good Yelp review."

"Shut up." He reached out impulsively and slipped his hand between the buttons on Healey's lab coat. He caught hold of a belt loop and gave it a little shake. "I met your pop up at Bayside Ridge. I guess your mom is buried there?"

Healey frowned. "I didn't know he went out there recently. How'd he seem?"

"Okay." Diego recalled the memory. "He went there to tell your mom about Fjóla."

Healey sighed. "You know how they say people 'never met a stranger'? That's Pop. Sorry he bent your ear."

"He's going to send me one of his inventions. A sandwich maker?"

"You'll like that. You can make your own hot pockets."

The employee door at Stomping Grounds opened, and light spilled into the alley. Tori stood just inside, waiting for their attention.

Diego didn't let Healey go. "You want to come by later?"

Tori called, "Remind me: the play clay is nontoxic, but the slime isn't appropriate for little kids, right?"

"That's right." Healey patted his pockets. "Be there in a second."

"Okay." The door closed, and Healey did that thing—he squatted against the wall so they were on the same eye level. It was a decent thing to do and also a reminder that Healey wasn't a trick and Diego had no right treating him like one.

"I could come by," Healey said. "No promises, but if I get a chance? Sure."

"Sure." Not the enthusiasm Diego had been hoping for, but he was stupidly pleased. He didn't want to examine the thing too closely. If he did, he'd have to face the fact that after two weeks, Healey Holly was constantly on his mind.

"You can let go now." Healey's amused voice.

"Right." Diego pulled his hand back.

Healey was almost to the door when he turned. "So if I come over, I can expect to be left alone for an hour, fucked hard, and then exiled to the living room where I can either lie there wondering what I did to deserve it, or leave?"

Diego's mouth opened, but no words came out.

"I'll think about it." Healey opened the door.

Healey would have left him sitting there by the dumpster like an old couch, like something too big to throw away, something that someone else might find useful but was no longer needed, except Diego rolled after him angrily.

"Wait. You want to know the truth?" he snapped.

"No, I want you to lie to me some more." Healey didn't turn around.

"It's fucking creepy, is all," Diego blurted. "I can't sleep knowing someone is touching my body where I can't feel it."

Healey turned sharply. "*That's* why you didn't want me in the bed?"

"I don't like sleeping with people anymore. Fucking toenail gouging—"

"It makes you feel vulnerable." Healey stared at him long enough to paint a portrait.

Diego acknowledged the not-question with a bob of his head.

The wind of indignation fell from Healey's sails. "You could have said that."

"It's not something I really gave a lot of thought to. There haven't been that many guys, since . . ."

"So it's not me, it's you." Healey edged a tiny bit closer. "I mean, I totally knew that. I just wanted to make sure you knew."

"Are you going to bust my balls for every little thing?"

Healey's amused look was patrician. "Are you going to stop looking at me like I'm the last cupcake at a birthday party and then ignoring my ass?"

"I never."

"Please." Healey turned around, and this time, he didn't look back as he headed inside.

Tori stepped from the shadows, holding a couple of stuffed green trash bags.

"Eavesdropping?" Diego asked.

"Of course. I brought these from my car, but I heard you arguing and decided to let you finish."

"What've you got there?"

"For the kids." She pulled a rainbow unicorn piñata out of one bag and a SpongeBob out of another. "I want to do this during intermission so the parents can head home with the littler ones. I should have put them up earlier."

"We can do it."

She toed a weed growing hopefully in a crack in the blacktop. "You and Heals sound like more than a one-night stand."

He appreciated the darkness concealing his face. "I like him, but I don't know how to do this stuff."

"Gossip travels fast in Bluewater Bay—"

"Is everyone talking already?"

"Not about you." Laughter rumbled from inside Stomping Grounds. He had to hand it to Tori. People loved her events. "Not yet. Do you know what happened with Healey's ex?"

"There was a car accident. That's what I heard. The ex is in trouble over it, and Healey's not talking. Was it substance abuse?"

"Mental breakdown." She glanced back toward the door where Healey'd disappeared. "I only heard this third hand from Sana, who got it from her husband, Sahil, but he's in law enforcement, and he got it straight from a friend in the CHP."

"Healey had a breakdown?" Unable to stop himself, he turned to the door where Healey'd been standing a moment ago.

She shook her head. "Ford."

"Oh, man." He had it all wrong. He'd figured a couple of privileged airheads got their asses handed to them by the highway patrol and everything went back to normal for them afterward. "What happened? Do you know?"

"Not the whole thing. I just have this feeling Healey is recovering from more than broken bones."

Had Healey been that into his ex? He was on the rebound. He'd admitted as much. How long had they been together?

"If I'm right about what he's been through," said Tori, "it'll be hard for him to trust someone new."

"Then maybe he shouldn't be trusting. Maybe he'd be smarter to keep people at arm's length until they prove they can *be* trusted."

"One—" she pinched his arm harder than he'd admit "—that smacks of victim-blaming, you asshole."

Ow.

She rubbed the mark, making the pain worse. "And two, where's the fun in that?"

Once he had feeling in his arm again, he and Tori scanned the area for a nice place to put the piñata. She finally hung it from the branch of one of the oak trees along the side street, under a street light so when the kids broke it open, they could find the candy.

Thankfully, that part of the evening went off without a hitch. While he was still outside supervising candy pickup, Diego texted a friend in the CHP to ask if he could get any information on a certain car accident.

For you? came the reply, *Maybe. Depends. What you got for me?*

Gratitude?

It's a start. Skype?

I gotta roll home.

See you then. Looking forward to it. Long time, man. Great to hear from you.

Me too. Diego told Tori he was going home.

"I've got to set up the second movie?" she asked.

"It's already set up. Just press Play."

Together, they dodged the people returning to watch the second film. "Don't you need your laptop?"

"That's my spare. It's crap anyway. I just talked to an old friend, and I want to go home and catch up with him."

"All right."

He almost ignored her doubtful expression, but she was a friend. He owed her. "I could stay and make sure everything works, if you want."

She considered it. Maybe if he gave her his puppy-dog eyes? She frowned to prove she was above that sort of thing, but let him go anyway. "No, I guess not. I'll be fine. Go home and have fun. See you in the morning. You're a brick."

"Only my head." He took off.
She called after him. "You got that right!"

CHAPTER TWENTY-THREE
HEALEY

The last thing Healey expected when he walked into Diego's place was soft music and candles. The smell of vanilla perfuming the air.

Diego invited him in, rolling backward. He'd obviously taken a shower and changed. He was wearing a pair of cargo shorts and a whimsical, retro Hawaiian shirt. He'd put in his piercings, sparkling stud earrings and a barbell over his left eye. His feet were bare.

Not previously a foot man, Healey still got a hot little clutch in his gut when he looked at Diego's lovely, masculine feet.

Diego could be surly. Rude. Tough. Muscled. He was a full-on alpha dog, but his feet were big, velvety, silent paws. Healey's mouth watered just looking at them.

"I have a confession to make." Diego stopped before they made it to the living room.

Healey passed him and waited. "You're not gay after all. You just fucked me to make a point?"

"Let me apologize in advance." Diego's voice filled with something that didn't sound the least remorseful. Jesus. Did he even *want* to hear whatever made Diego's face look so serious? He doubted he was going to get a choice. "I burned through some favors to find out about the accident you were in."

It was a good thing Healey had been about to sit. When his knees buckled, the couch wasn't that far to fall. "You what?"

"Believe me when I tell you I would never have done it if I knew why you wanted to keep things a secret."

Healey's mouth went dry. "You don't get to decide what secrets deserve to be kept secret. If Ford's family thinks I'm talking about this—"

"But it's—" Diego stared at him. "What happened to you was—"

"You should never have found out." Healey got up and walked restlessly to the window. The yard looked the same in the dark. His face, ghostly in the glass, appeared to hover over the shrubbery. "Not even addressing my trust issues for the moment, because we will get back to that, there are vital legal and medical privacy issues. Plus, it isn't any of your goddamned business."

"I am not sorry." Diego didn't budge. "Either you tell me what happened or I'll guess."

"If you asked around, then you know what happened."

"My contacts indicated that the two of you were victims of a hate crime, which later became a violent road-rage incident during which your boyfriend pulled a gun and opened fire."

"Well—"

"But that's not exactly what happened, is it? And it is my business if this thing we're doing"—he gestured between them—"goes any further."

"How do you figure that?" Healey's chin shot to the moon. "Because you're fucking me, you get to know everything about my past? I don't think so."

"Can't you see how offensive this is?" Diego closed the distance between them.

"What?" *No one* looked at him like that. Like he was stupid. He wanted to scrub the smug off Diego's face. With soap.

"What do you think would have happened to you if you weren't rich white guys in your twenties? What were you driving?"

Healey toed the ground. "Ford's car."

"Right. What is it? Beamer? Jetta?"

Healey shook his head.

Diego huffed a sad laugh. "It doesn't even matter. Let me see if I've got this straight. Your boyfriend had a BP episode, so you decide to do a Vegas turnaround?"

"Yeah," Healey lied. "That's exactly it."

Diego's hands stilled in his lap. "Do you have any concept what would have happened to me if I had been in that situation? Or anyone with skin darker than a sheet of copy paper?"

Healey winced.

"You and your privileged boyfriend—" Diego closed his eyes. "I can't even."

"Ford is mentally ill."

"He used a gun in the commission of a felony," Diego shouted. "My God, you have to see how outrageous that is given everything that's going on—"

"I know." Healey held himself together while memories that were still too fresh tore him apart. "I know. I should have done something to stop him. I should have—"

"Nobody's blaming you."

A burst of anger escaped him as a snort. "Either you're a hell of a lot more naive than I ever gave you credit for, or you're deluded. Ford's family—"

"Fuck them." Diego hands curled into fists. "I realize I don't have all the facts—"

"Ya think?" Healey asked furiously. "You think maybe second-guessing the last three years of my life might be a little much, even for an omnipotent guy like you?"

"Okay. Fine. Want to talk about it?"

"I can't." Talking about Ford made him queasy, plus . . . "Gag order."

"Pretend I'm your lawyer, give me some cash."

"What? Is that even legit?"

"No. Do you really give a shit?"

A lump formed in Healey's throat. He'd become so used to keeping the events of that night secret, he wasn't even sure he *could* talk about it. But he wanted to. He wanted to tell someone—not Nash, who would call him a dumbass, and not his dad, who would be disappointed and sick with worry for his future.

Did he even care what Ford and his family thought anymore?

If I talk, will I be throwing Ford under the very bus Ford's attorney's planned on running me down with?

A glance at the clock, the window, and the ceiling didn't provide answers.

Diego's eyes, though . . . Warm. Understanding. Kind.

Diego has seen way worse, and maybe he'll help me understand everything better.

"All right."
Those were the eyes of an honorable man.

CHAPTER TWENTY-FOUR
DIEGO

"I wasn't aware Ford had been rapid cycling." Healey sighed deeply. "I was busy with my own work, my dissertation and defense. Spencer had come along for Nash, and Dad met Fjóla. Shelby was going to Spain. I wasn't at home, but all those things affected me too. Things were changing. It was a challenging time."

Diego led him into the kitchen. "Coffee?"

Healey shook his head. "Wine would be a whole lot better for this conversation."

Diego flipped him off. "We have Chateau Anchor Steam or Napa Corona?"

"Beer's good. Don't go to any trouble."

"Best not. I could get exhausted from all the hard work." Diego popped the top on the counter and handed him the bottle. "Ford wanted to go to Vegas to celebrate graduation?"

Healey nodded. "Normally I love a road trip, but something felt off. We'd officially broken up. I was relieved."

Diego brought out a plate of cookies. "How so?"

"Things felt forced for a long time."

"Something felt off?" Diego prompted.

"He was funny. Restless. Doing carpool karaoke and streaming live Facebook videos. We fucked in the car at a rest stop, and he wanted me to blow him again in the parking lot of the Andersen's Split Pea Soup in Santa Nella."

"That wasn't normal behavior?" Diego ruthlessly suppressed an irrational surge of anger. He didn't give a shit what Healey had done before him. "Never mind, forget I asked."

Healey flushed. "It's okay. Yeah. No. It wasn't normal for him to come on to me like that when we were alone. It hadn't been normal for over a year."

"So you blew him at the split pea soup place? Happy and Peewee must be so proud."

"You know the place?" Healey chuckled. "I forget you're from LA."

"I used to hit the one in Buellton all the time with my mother."

"That place is kitsch heaven, and Ford loves their Monte Cristo sandwiches."

Diego frowned and went back to the fridge for bottled water. "That where things went south?"

Sighing, Healey closed his eyes. "We attracted the wrong kind of attention."

"Easy to do when you're in flagrante delicto."

"True dat." Healey's wince acknowledged the fact. "This pickup truck followed us onto the freeway. Chased us. I tried to get Ford to pull off I-5. Tried to get him to drive to the highway patrol substation. There's a 'find an office' function online."

"Did you find one?"

"Ford wouldn't pull off." Healey picked up his bottle and scraped at the label. Flakes of the green spray he'd used to dye his hair had fallen, giving him green freckles alongside the copper ones. "He said he'd be damned if he'd let some rednecks ruin our trip. They started chasing us. Swerving around Ford's SUV and braking hard so we'd have to slam on our brakes, not just kid stuff. I figured if it went on like that, we were dead."

"Is that when Ford grabbed your phone and threw it out of the car?"

Healey's eyes filled. "You know what happened?"

"I regret prying, now. I should have waited for you to tell me."

Healey shrugged. "Why do you want that?"

"I want the man who"—Diego picked at an imaginary thread on his jeans—"might or might not be my boyfriend to tell me about a traumatic event from his past."

"Ford wasn't himself. I—" Healey licked his lips "—I guess he believed I meant to have the police arrest him. He thought I—"

"He was paranoid, in other words." Healey nodded. "So if I understand correctly, he—"

"His mood went south, that fast." Healey snapped his fingers. "He pulled a gun from the console and pointed it at me."

"Christ." Diego set his water down with a *thunk*. "Where'd he get the gun?"

"The fuck should I know! I'd never seen it before. He didn't fire it—just waved it around. But the guys in the truck saw it. After that, they took off, and Ford floored it. I couldn't believe he wanted to go after them. We clipped the back of their truck and spun out. Rolled maybe... three times?"

Healey's eyes lost focus. His speech slowed. Diego clasped his hand and, finding it ice cold, rubbed it between his own to warm it. "Then what?"

"I got this weird sense of calm. I remember thinking if I could only get my phone back, I'd record my thoughts for Nash and Pop and Shelby. It seemed like hours before the car stopped moving."

Diego lifted Healey's hand to his lips. Healey cupped his jaw and stared at him. Diego read confusion, anguish, and resignation on Healey's handsome features. Despite that, his instinct for the story took over. "What about the gun? Was Ford still in possession of the gun at that point?"

The abrupt question seemed to snap Healey back to his senses. He shook his head minutely. "The gun flew out of Ford's hand during the accident, I guess. It disappeared somewhere. There was dust and debris in the air. The threat of fire. Ford was in a rage. He crawled out and threw himself at the men in the truck. They were injured and in no condition to fight. Ford had to be restrained."

"He wasn't injured?"

"I'm sure he was concussed. I was. He had burns on his face from the airbag. Two black eyes. I don't know if they were anything more than superficial injuries. I didn't see him after the accident because I was still trapped in the car."

"That must have been awful." Diego pressed their foreheads together. "I'm sorry."

"Firefighters and police arrived on the scene pretty quickly, I think. I don't even remember that part, only when I was free.

They took initial information at the scene. The dudes in the truck talked plenty. They interviewed the guys from the truck again at the hospital. Ford and me separately, at the hospital and at the station."

"I'll bet their story didn't line up with yours."

"There were a couple of witnesses. A lady in a blue Prius pulled over. She got video. I guess I was starting to go into shock. I was cold."

Diego's eyes narrowed. "So why the gag order?"

"I don't know."

"Normally, it's to keep from prejudicing a potential jury pool. I have a suspicion what's involved here is privilege. I think someone's trying to cover it up."

"I doubt that. That's—"

"Business as usual." Diego rolled to get him another beer. "Rich white college kids like you get special treatment every day."

"The gag order is Ford's attorney's doing. He's looking out for Ford, though, not me. I haven't been charged with anything."

"Not even indecent exposure?"

"They couldn't legitimately prove it, so it was our word against theirs." He wrapped a hand around the back of his neck. "The attorney kept me from answering the question."

Diego sat up. "What did Ford say?"

"He said he doesn't remember. Everything got ugly after that. The press made us look like entitled college pinheads marauding on the taxpayers' dime. They kept out the sex angle. The gun. Ford's illness. Ford's family is well off. I'm . . . you know."

"The stalking might meet the burden for a federal hate crime but the gun escalates everything."

Healey shook his head. "That *fucking* gun. How the hell . . .?"

"He didn't use it?"

Healey gave a violent shudder.

"But he threatened you with it?"

"Obliquely."

"What does that mean, 'obliquely'?"

"Neither parallel nor at a right angle to." Healey recited. "Slanted."

The automatic reply tickled Diego's funny bone. "Golly, Mr. Wizard."

"Sorry."

"Did you feel threatened?"

"I felt—" Healey blinked slowly "—shocked. I felt horrified. Ford was my lover, my *best friend*. I nearly shit myself. What do you think I felt? My heart was fucking broken, and it was all my fault, and . . . I still can't believe it happened."

Diego drew in a deep breath before letting Healey's hand go. He sensed that Healey hadn't admitted to himself how scared he'd been. Sensed that doing such a thing would be as painful as the event itself.

"And Ford's email said his dad's lawyers will try to shift the blame onto you somehow."

"He used the words 'throw,' 'under,' and 'bus.'"

"Why didn't you tell me this before?"

"I'm just some hookup to you. You knew about the accident—just not the whole story." Healey pulled his car keys from the pocket of his lab coat. "I'm leaving."

CHAPTER TWENTY-FIVE
HEALEY

Diego caught Healey's hand and even though he tried to pull away, Diego held fast—reasonably, assertively willing Healey to stay for a moment longer.

To his notoriously unreliable eye, Diego looked pretty sincere.

And enticing, strong, and . . . *God!* Who didn't want a strong man?

Who didn't want to lean on someone instead of being the one leaned on, for a change?

Diego whispered, "Please, don't go."

Healey stepped closer to the crumbling edge. "I just—"

Shameful, shameful tears gathered in his eyes.

"C'mon baby. Stay with me." Diego held his arms out, and Healey let himself fall. "Let me take care of you."

He didn't need a whole lot more than a hug every now and again.

Normally, he was self-sufficient, not some privileged, ivory-tower-dweller with no concept how to give as well as take.

Normally, he didn't require quite this much . . . hand holding.

"Shh." Diego wrapped his arms around Healey's neck and cradled him. Just fucking cradled him in those massive arms. Healey let himself be folded up and loved on, hard.

"Jesus Christ," Diego whispered. "You know what you are? You're a magnificent dumbass. You took good care of Ford. Of course you did. Don't even question that."

Did that sound come from me? Oh my God, that's not even a human sound.

"You did everything you could for him." Diego pulled the pin from Healey's green sticky hair and stroked his hand over it, smoothing the long waves over his shoulder. "It's time to let others do for you, okay? No strings, man. Just take a load off."

Sucking in a long, slow breath, Healey regained his composure. He nodded into Diego's shoulder before sitting up and eventually leaving him in the kitchen.

Healey washed up in the guest bath. He let a few minutes pass before—feeling like he'd come out of a dense fog—he returned and found Diego at the counter, drinking a beer and scrolling over something on his phone.

Once again, Diego left subtle space between them.

Probing the idea, Healey discovered he dug having someone who knew when to leave him alone. Diego read him pretty well. Or he was just that easy to read.

"What's got you frowning now?" Diego's brow rose.

Asked and answered, then. "Is there a teleprompter on my forehead?"

Diego took a swig of his beer. "Say again?"

"Am I transparent to you? You act like I'm some kind of... I don't know. Cliché. Like I bore you. Like I could never surprise you."

"Is that what you think? Yeah, okay." Diego idly rubbed his eyebrow and grimaced—must have forgotten he'd replaced his piercing. "At first? I saw what I expected to see."

Before Healey could jump on that, Diego held up his hands.

"That was when I didn't know you. Before we hooked up."

Healey nodded. "Okay."

"But stuff didn't add up until now. I know your story and now you're real for me. I got some perspective. People's lives can get fucked up through no fault of their own, I understand that."

Healey was pretty sure he'd never get control of his throat again.

Diego handed him his beer, and he took it, gratefully. After a few swigs, he said, "I asked for help. I wasn't trying to be some hero with Ford. It's not about me, anyway."

Diego had a way of peering at him and tilting his head. Looking inside him.

Irritably, Healy scrubbed at his eyes. "I asked for help. But I still fucked it—"

"Even from what little I know of you," Diego said firmly, "I would trust you with my life."

"Holy cow." Healey rejected that like a mismatched organ. "I hope not."

Diego gave his neck a rueful scratch. "It's not as amazing a thing as you'd think. Trusting you with my life doesn't mean trusting you with my body while I'm sleeping."

Ah. With communication comes the light of understanding.

Healey sat back down. "Thank you for telling me why you don't like sharing a bed. I never meant to put you on the spot like that."

"It's— I never had to talk about it before." Diego's expression was best described as *having teeth pulled*.

"Sorry." Healey genuinely meant that.

"'S'nothing personal," Diego explained. "Nobody ever cared before."

Healey's heart hammered. The resulting surge of blood drowned out every other sound but his quickening breaths. "It's all right," he promised. "I'll earn your trust eventually or I won't. We go on your schedule."

"My God, Healey." Diego reached for him. "Shut up and kiss me."

Surprised, Healey complied. He was already into Diego way deeper than he wanted to be. Past friendship, past hooking up—not that he'd admit it, for sure.

Not that it made him feel good.

He and Ford were *over*. Healey hung on to that. They'd been over, and they'd let it drag on for far too long after, in his case, because he'd figured life had enough endings and beginnings, and graduation seemed to be a natural boundary. Like a river or a mountain range.

It had been years since he'd believed he and Ford would end up together on the other side. Most guys wouldn't bet on a guy like Healey for the long term. Or Ford.

"Wait." Healey gripped Diego's upper arms to keep from falling at his feet. His inner kink hound was deeply, earnestly ready for someone like Diego to come along... but his heart wasn't.

It really wasn't.

"Okay, papi?" asked Diego. "What do you need?"

"Nothing," Healey said. "Everything. Don't let go."

"Ah, c'mon. *Shh* . . ." Diego brushed Healey's hair out of his face. "You've had a real tough time, huh? How about this. You go watch something on television while I—"

"Wait." Healey stopped him with another gentle kiss. "If this is about you having a hard dick, don't go."

Diego pulled back sharply.

"Don't get me wrong." Healey changed tactics. "I am all about the D—it's awesome. But some other time, okay?"

"Healey." Diego studied him.

Healey shook his head. "I hurt—just—everywhere."

Closed. As if he'd flipped some invisible sign. "I hate that you hurt because of your *chingada* ex—" Diego sighed. "Some other time, then."

Healey blinked. Was he being dismissed? If this was a booty call and he wasn't . . . um . . . up for action . . .? Was that it for Diego? Was he supposed to leave now?

He didn't know. And maybe that should *tell him something*. He hesitated for a fraction of a second too long and then things just got awkward.

"Sure." Wrapping his hand over the warm skin at the nape of Diego's neck, he gave him a gentle massage. But not a kiss, because that would be . . . "Hit me up some other time. I'll be down."

As he stood to go, he *felt* Diego's exasperated expression. He also felt vulnerable. Exposed. For the first time in his life, he was really into a guy who didn't seem all that into him back.

Wow . . . that was . . . really conceited. And shitty. But now he thought about it, it was also possibly true. The idea shouldn't have blindsided him—he'd been the aggressor all along.

Still, he lost control of his mouth as he backed toward the door. "Um . . . You did a great remodel here. At first I thought I was going to be sorry to see the changes, but I like them."

Diego frowned at him. Maybe that was too abrupt? Maybe he should have just said he had to go? Diego's expression grew more and more thoughtful.

"So. I'm gonna go now."

"Healey?" Diego stopped him.

Healey closed his eyes. "Yeah?"

"Stay and watch a movie with me."

Healey opened his mouth. Closed it. He was afraid to ask the questions on the tip of his tongue.

What did that mean?

Were they friends?

Were they boyfriends? Extended hookups with film-watching privileges?

Maybe he didn't want to know. Maybe naming this little flame they were fanning would smother it, and he sure as hell didn't want that. Diego's face had gone unreadable, but his body was . . . too tight. Too controlled. He held himself stiffly, as if he was expecting to get punched.

"Sure," Healey said carefully. Smiling, he unbuttoned his lab coat again, grateful to rid himself of his scientist costume and tie, once and for all. He took off the flannel shirt, under which he wore a Mountain Goats T-shirt.

When Diego didn't make a crack about his taste in music—or more precisely Ford's taste—he figured they'd leveled up, relationship-wise.

Maybe they were even actually *having* a relationship right then.

He doubted Diego was aware. Just to be on the safe side, Healey decided to keep it to himself. "Okay then," Healey said as Diego led him to the living room. He watched Diego transfer to the couch and gave a surprised laugh when Diego patted the cushion next to him.

"C'mon. I don't bite."

After he sat, Diego slung an arm around him, bravely digging his fingers oh-so-pleasurably through Healey's green, yucky hair . . .

Oh. Wow. It felt so good. Healey closed his eyes.

The sparks were there. Their mutual attraction was undeniable. Whether they were canoodling on the couch or seeing each other across Tori's place. Whether he was awake or asleep, he felt the chemistry that bound them together, and it was like some experimental drug.

If he and Pop could invent a way to share this feeling, they'd be richer than they'd ever dreamed.

He had no hypothesis, no idea of the outcome. He only knew he wanted more.

This was uncharted. Unexpected. Unprecedented. He was Goldilocks and this was too much and not enough and exactly right. Diego carefully cupped his chin. Pulled him closer.

"What are we doing?" Healey asked.

Diego's hot gaze found his. "You want to talk right now?"

Healey shook his head.

"Then shut up." Diego's barbell winked in the faint light.

Heart thudding wildly, Healey watched him come closer...

CHAPTER TWENTY-SIX
DIEGO

*T*he movie was something with aliens. Or monsters. When he pointed out the film was over and he had no clue what it was about, Healey's laughter warmed his lips and they kept on kissing.

"This just in." Healey took a deep breath. "Diego Luz masters distraction."

"Masters *what*? Masters Bation?" Diego laced their fingers together. "You walked right into that one."

Healey groaned. "Yeah, I did."

Amused, he ran his thumb over Healey's lips. Healey mouthed it playfully.

Healey's hand fell lightly on his chest. "Your heart's a little speedy."

"Wonder why?" Diego laid his forehead against Healey's. They bumped noses, scraped bearded cheeks together, and found each other again. Healey got him. Healey had him. Healey had almost walked away twice—*twice*—because he'd pushed him too far.

Stupid pride.

Stupid stubborn asshole mouth.

He could put on the sex playlist, light candles, and crab-walk into Healey sideways, but coming at him straight on, the way Healey took on the world . . .

He didn't know how to do that.

"You comfortable like this?" Healey'd switched off the big screen. For a long moment, Diego saw only the huge purple spot it left in his vision. "Can I stretch out?"

Diego nodded. "Go ahead."

Healey shifted around so his head was in Diego's lap and his feet dangled over the couch's arm.

"'S'nice." Healey closed his eyes while Diego messed with his hair.

"What is it with this hairstyle?" Diego rubbed his fingers over the buzzed-off hair at Healey's nape. "Can't make up your mind?"

"Next you'll say I need to turn off my rock and roll records and get a job."

Diego let his head fall back against the couch cushions. "You thought about what you'll do now?"

Healey shook his head. "Not yet."

"I thought guys like you were recruited by the Illuminati out of middle school."

Healey's laughter shook Diego's lap. "My pop must love you."

"Your pop is a scream."

"You aren't the first person to say that. Some people actually screamed when they said it." He turned his head and kissed Diego's palm. "I've had job offers, but so far nothing's come in on the Illuminati's letterhead. I'll keep you posted."

"Are you going to teach?"

"Hell no. I've been in school since I was two and a half. It's time I saw the world from outside the bubble."

Diego brushed his fingers over Healey's cast. "What's next, then, after this?"

"I'll probably travel until my savings run out. Six months, maybe a year if I stretch things out. Strip for tips."

"You should get yourself an old VW van or something. Just fucking drive around America and see it from the ground. It's amazing out there. My mom and me, we used to put a pin in a map and take off. I'd do my homework while she drove. We stayed in the crappiest motels. Sometimes she left me with friends at night."

Healey didn't appear to share his enthusiasm. "Sounds like that sucked."

"I didn't know better." He smoothed Healey's T-shirt. "As I go through her papers, I'm discovering things about her I never knew. You know she had some kind of secret hobby? In fact, I think you broke that story."

"I did?" Healey opened his eyes.

"You know that picture you made notes about?"

"The cute pic with the car and the Coke sign? Your mom looked young in that."

"I think my mom altered that sign. If I'm right, it's not the only time she ever left a private joke behind."

"For real?"

Diego shrugged. "Nobody knows what went on in my mom's head. It certainly seems like something she'd do."

"I don't remember my mother." He glanced down.

"Mami was a free spirit." Diego had a head full of memories. Some, he wouldn't trade for a solid-gold mountain, and some he'd just as soon burn. "I wouldn't be surprised if she was responsible for the Nazca Lines."

A shy smile curved Healey's lips. "Secrets are as cool as trap doors. Can I help?"

"It's out of my hands for a while. I sent my stepfather copies of the photographs and Mami's corresponding notes. Family project."

Healey's slow blink seemed more sleepy than seductive. "Sounds like a good thing for everybody."

"You're such a glass-half-full guy." Diego ignored the mild itch from his eyebrow piercing. "Like a kid."

"I'm not naive." With a regretful sigh, he sat up. "I should probably get going."

"You have to?"

"Imma fall asleep here if I don't. Pop and Fjóla will worry."

Diego let it go. They stretched and yawned in tandem, making Healey chuckle self-consciously. He truly was a nervous laugher. Maybe they'd play poker sometime. The information could be lucrative.

Diego brushed Healey's hair off his face. Soothing, smoothing his hands over Healey's shoulders and back. Healey melted beneath his touch, pushing forward, trying to get closer. When Healey nuzzled into the junction of Diego's neck and shoulder, they both let out little sighs.

Christ.
Am I petting him?
He's digging it. Oh hell yeah.
Yeah, I'm petting him. That's a goddamn haiku, right there.

"You're fun." Surprised to find how sincerely he meant the words, Diego cupped Healey's face and kissed him again.

Green and disreputable, Healey broke away. A lazy smile stretched over his face. "I haven't made out like that in years."

"What'd you think? Thumbs up or down?" Diego asked.

"You don't know?" There was nothing discreet about Healey's dick. Hard the whole time, it stretched his jeans enough to be resurfaced by them, plus he'd leaked a pool of pre-come like a blinking neon sign.

"That's so hot." Diego's mouth watered while he contemplated what, if anything, he should do about Healey's erection.

It would be nothing for him to blow Healey. He'd actually enjoy the hell out of it. But giving a dude a blowjob just because he was hard felt like paying for his company in some way—a joyless, unwanted obligation.

Even though he was into Healey, the whole situation felt strange and complicated. The other dude's expectations mattered. The look on his face mattered. He was an audience Diego could lose, even after he'd told all his best jokes.

Plus, once he got past the indecision, he'd require prep. Like a corpse at a banquet, Diego's problems weren't going to magically disappear when he figured out where to sit.

But wait... This was Healey. He liked Healey.

He wanted Healey to like him back.

Taking hold of Healey's belt buckle, he tugged. "I could take care of you, if you want."

Healey's head tilted like he was listening to angels. His expression said he'd been afraid this was going to happen, and now it had. Maybe he was working out how to let Diego down? Alternatively, he could have been wondering how it'd look if he took Diego up on the offer of a blowjob without returning the favor.

Get your dick sucked with no reciprocity and look like a Grade-A asshat, or go home with blue balls. *Can I show a guy a good time, or what?* Diego would have given anything in his possession to never see that expression on Healey's face again.

"No." Healey smiled his regrets. "Some other time."

"Sure," Diego nodded. Tried not to look disappointed.

Wait.

If Healey regretted and Diego was disappointed, they were both on the wrong page. "For the record: I'd actually love to suck your dick."

Having to say that out loud made his whole body blush.

Blue eyes studied his. Looking for sincerity? He'd probably used his allotment up in kindergarten. He was not that guy.

"You mean that?" Healey asked.

"Don't think I like sucking dick?" Healey's belt buckle was turning out to be a pretty good handle. He dragged Healey closer and brushed the knuckle of his other hand across the bulge in Healey's jeans. "Don't you?"

"Oh, I do." Healey's eyes sparkled. "Very much indeed."

Baldly, Diego shook his head. "I don't ejaculate."

"I do." Healey's fingers drifted over Diego's cheek. His thumb rested lightly on Diego's barbell. "Unless you tell me not to."

What?

Oh! Breathless, dry-mouthed, Diego considered the possibilities Healey's invitation presented. "Yeah?"

"I won't like it." Healey's creeping flush told him otherwise. "I might even struggle a little."

Keeping a small smile hidden, Diego gave him the badass eyes. "It'll go harder on you if you struggle. I might have to tie you up."

Subtle tension grew in Healey's elegant, muscled frame.

"Why doesn't this feel like a test to you?" Diego wondered out loud. "You don't like taking tests. You have exam anxiety, you said so."

"This"—Healey let his hands drop to his sides—"is a game, not a test."

"And you like games."

"I *love* games." The word itself was a sigh of relief.

Diego had never guessed how deep his freak-streak ran before he met Healey Holly, but there wasn't going to be any doubt after. Healey Holly was a living doll. A life-size, good-looking action figure of the analyst type rather than the agent type. And he was asking to be played with, hard.

Balloons and confetti didn't fall from the ceiling, but Diego thanked God for—and didn't question—his good fortune. He must have climbed on board the kink train too quickly though, because Healey's smile evaporated.

"Um." Healey caught Diego's hand before he could take down his zipper. "Just don't be mean."

Diego froze. "Am I mean? Have I been—"

"No." Healey shook his head. "You're aloof."

"Because—"

"Don't say cruel things to me. Don't humiliate me. Some guys dig that, but I don't."

"Ah." *Limits.* Diego got it. Wouldn't think limits would come up with a guy like Healey. "You do this a lot?"

"Some."

Irritation, like sand in his shorts, made Diego ask, "Don't tell me, Ford was into this?"

"*I'm* into this." Healey's tone made him look up. Ford was apparently a sore spot. Of course he was. Blue eyes glistened. "Ford has nothing to do with what happens between us."

"A'ight." *Sold. Can I touch you now?*

Real sensitive, asshole.

He held up his hand, and Healey walked into it. It caught him squarely in the gut. Feeling possessive and full of shit, Diego gave his belly a good rub.

"Get in my bed."

Healey's hesitated. "Okay. But you don't have to do the thing." He mimed using a hypodermic.

"I wasn't planning to. I have to pee."

Healey nodded, eyes gentle. He had to know Diego used a catheter. He'd guess, at any rate. He'd know it was private. What was he standing there for?

"Would you ask me for help if you needed anything?"

"I would. But I don't."

Please, let this be the only time you ask me that.

Except, it's never the only time.

Healey leaned over and kissed his cheek. "I'll be in your bed."

As Healey padded away on his soft hipster feet, he practically glowed from the calm he exuded. God*damn* him. Diego rolled angrily into the second bathroom where he could get ready in private.

Footsteps outside the door made Diego's mouth dry. A knock sounded.

"I wanted to say"—breathless-voiced Healey—"when I said I wasn't afraid of... anything about... I'm not squeamish about medical shit. I'm strong and good with my hands. I've given injections. It's um... not a hobby or anything but—"

Diego sighed. "You got a point to make?"

"Not really."

Minutes passed.

Another knock, this time, more insistent. "Wait. I do have a point. If you like your privacy, fine. But if you're hiding back here because you think I can't handle the shit show, I've had season tickets for ten years." Footsteps, heading away again.

Right.

He's right.

"Healey?" Footsteps slowed. Returned. "Think of it like this: until we've dated awhile, the bathroom doors stay closed."

Healey asked, "It's a preference, then?"

"Yes."

"So if we keep the bathroom door closed, we preserve the mystery for that much longer. Is that what you're saying?"

Diego sagged with relief. "That's exactly what I'm saying."

"So we're *dating*!" Footsteps, quicker this time, carried the voice away. "I fucking knew it."

CHAPTER TWENTY-SEVEN
HEALEY

While he waited for Diego, Healey explored the bed like a bored cat, testing the rings and straps. Imagining the possibilities. He figured he had a while, so he was hanging over the edge, looking beneath the tailored bed skirt when he heard Diego roll in.

He gave a quick glance up and saw Diego wearing nothing but briefs.

Also a frown. "What are you doing?"

"Just looking. There's not a single dustball under there." Healey studied the empty, immaculate space. "What is wrong with you?"

"I can operate a dust mop with great efficiency."

"It's not the fact that you can use one." Healey backed onto the mattress. "It's that you *do* which has me in awe."

When Diego reached for him, Healey scooted back.

"Can you—" Healey bit his lip "—I don't know. Meet me up here on the bed?"

"I guess." Positioning his chair and locking the wheels, Diego gripped the rings to hoist himself up. Once seated, he grabbed his legs and used momentum and leverage to position himself.

"Never seen a bed like this before." Healey ran an admiring hand over the bars of the headboard. "Custom?"

Diego nodded. "It's a permanent installation. We'll have to cut it up to get it out of here."

"It's badass. You think it could support a sex swing?"

Color surfaced on Diego's cheeks. "I'm not getting in a sex swing."

"Never said anything about you."

"Healey—" Diego's tone spelled doom for the idea.

"Uh-oh." Healey flopped down beside him. "I'm getting too far ahead again?"

"Little bit." Diego covered his eyes with his forearm. "I know you understand about these things. Your sister—"

"We tell Shelby she can do anything she wants to do."

"That's because you're a well-meaning idiot and a total and complete clod."

"That's not fair—"

"Shelby can't do *anything she wants*." Diego propped himself up on his elbows, changed his mind, and pushed himself to sitting with his back against the headboard. "She has a spinal cord injury that makes it impossible for her to do certain things, despite your cheerleading, despite your best intentions. You don't have a fucking clue."

"Nobody knows someone else's pain," Healey muttered. "But there's empathy. There's compassion. I can use my ingenuity to try to help and that's no small thing, right?"

Diego swallowed. "I don't want that."

"No, I don't suppose you would." Healey tucked his good arm behind his head.

"You like rough sex?" Diego asked. "It's really your thing? Not a whim? You want a lifetime of that?"

"Little bit," Healey echoed Diego's earlier words. "I have to stop thinking, sometimes. Being restrained helps. Ford showed me."

Diego groaned. "Did Ford also show you how a paraplegic might accomplish that on a regular basis?"

"Sorry."

Diego let his head fall back. "Don't be. You need what you need. But take into consideration that it could be sort of scary for me."

"I'm sure—"

"Don't. God. Just let me say this. We can't fuck as hard as we both want because—" he started snickering before he could even finish the sentence "—I'm a delicate flower."

They laughed together, even though it wasn't funny.

"I don't see you that way." Healey laced their fingers together.

"Doesn't matter what you see," Diego said. "Doesn't matter how I front. You know this. You have to know. Did Shelby live in denial too? Or did you all do that for her too?"

Hurt, Healey paused. He sat up on his haunches and stared into Diego's eyes, refusing him anywhere to hide. "Why is it I always feel like I'm playing checkers and you're playing chess?"

"I have to protect—"

"Your skin, I know. And your heart. And your dignity." As he spoke, Healey found new places to kiss, an exposed dimple, a promising smile line next to Diego's closed eye, a vulnerable earlobe. "You have to protect your autonomy. Your independence. You have to protect your self-concept, and by that I mean how you see yourself and how you want the world to see you. How am I doing?"

Diego pursed his lips. "Pretty good."

Healey wished he had a picture of Diego's frown just then. Pout. Pout/frown. Frout. "I understand all those things. Just not the same way you do."

"Then what are we doing?" There went that chin shooting up. Unmistakably *Hit me with your best shot, I can take it,* and *I dare you.* It said, *I'll outlast all my disappointments, including you.*

"Shh." Healey eased himself up. "I'm just saying."

He ran the fingers of his cast hand over Diego's shoulder. Down his arm.

When Diego would have spoken, Healey kissed him.

"Let me try, okay?" Healey shifted closer. "Tell me where you trust me to touch you."

He held his hands out, palms open, and waited. Meeting his gaze, Diego took them and placed them on his chest. "Here."

"Okay." Healey stroked the skin of Diego's nearly hairless chest. Nipples pebbled in anticipation. He couldn't resist tasting one.

He ran the tips of his fingers down Diego's arms. Massaged the palm of one hand, then the other.

"How about here?" Touching Diego, stroking rhythmically over his skin was soothing to him too. Comforting, like petting a cat. "This okay?"

"Mm-hmm."

He retraced his path, drawing his hands back up Diego's arms, down his pecs and chest and belly. "Can I go lower?"

Diego nodded before closing his eyes. That slight hesitation served as a caution flag.

Slower, slower.

"I'll wait until you trust me."

Diego licked his lips. "I don't know why you want to touch what I can't feel."

"I'm greedy." This wasn't the first time he'd admitted it. "I'm impatient."

"Big surprise." Healey tried to back away, but Diego stopped him. "Don't retreat. It's okay."

"I think—" Healey bit his lip. "I might have trouble compartmentalizing you."

"Unless you're a flight attendant or a serial killer, I can't see why you'd need to compartmentalize me." Diego touched a button on his phone, and the overhead light dimmed to a soft, golden glow.

Much better—more romantic.

"I have the self-control of a honey badger in heat. Tell me now if there's any place you don't want me to touch, and I'll respect your wishes. I just need to know. And I might fuck up. But not on purpose."

Their eyes locked. Seconds felt like whole days. Diego slid slowly, sensually onto his back. Subtly provocative. Inviting.

He licked his lips. "Why don't you point to something, and I'll let you know if it's off-limits or not."

"Okay. But don't try the '*Ow!*' maneuver. Thanks to Shelby, and every rom-com ever, I'm wise to that."

"I'll make a note. No practical jokes." Diego nodded. "Good to know."

"Let's start with the basics," Healey muttered as he made his way to the foot of the bed to point at Diego's big toe. "How about this?"

"You want to touch my toe?"

"I want to suck it. Ever since the first time I saw your naked foot, I've wanted to put my mouth on it, which is weird because I'm not usually a foot man, but, Christ. Just look at that gorgeous foot."

Diego covered his eyes. "You are a mental case."

While he swallowed his ire, Healey said, "Some people don't have the first clue they're talking to a dude whose life was recently torn apart by mental illness. You don't have that luxury."

Diego paled. "Christ, I'm sorry."

"Not a big—"

"You're right, though. And I'm sorry. It's just something I say—a line from a cartoon. I never meant—"

Healey waited while Diego got all over himself backtracking from that.

"I won't be saying it anymore, I guess." Diego jammed a pillow under his head. "Are we ever going to do this?"

"Do what?"

"Get off?"

"We're dating now. We've got all night."

"You may have, but the clock is ticking on me. I like to sleep. Do you have any kind of plan?"

"Again with the plan." Healey backed away. "You didn't like groveling or begging and now I have to ask which body parts are off-limits one by one. My only plan is to hang in here until I come, no matter what."

"Is talking foreplay for you?" Diego asked. "Are you getting paid by the word?"

"How would you like me to answer that?" Healey glanced over, all eyebrows and attitude.

"Honestly." Diego's tone didn't allow for argument.

"It's not foreplay." Healey sat up and crossed his legs. "I talk when I'm nervous. I don't want to fuck this up—"

"C'mere. It's obvious we're just going to have to get this over with."

"Oh, because that's sounds so—"

"Shut up." Diego hooked his hand around Healey's neck. "Let me get lube."

Healey braced himself to anchor Diego when he leaned over to open the nightstand drawer. Diego's quick nod reassured him he'd done the right thing. Plus, neither of them fell off the bed. Sometimes, Diego was like a dance partner. If Healey figured out his steps, then things went smoothly. If he tripped over his feet, then *boom*. Square one.

Diego withdrew a small bottle of a superior lube brand. At first, when Healey tried to take it from him, he didn't let go.

"Don't compartmentalize," Diego said before his fingers loosened their grip. "It's all yours."

Healey nodded. "You'll tell me if—"

"I will."

Decision made, Healey wrapped his arms around Diego, delivering kisses and bites and licks to the side of his neck. "You smell delicious."

"Stop talking now."

"Okay." Healey got his fingers on the waistband of Diego's briefs. "Can these go?"

Diego nodded.

Healey helped him out of his briefs—on fire for all that tan skin. Muscles defined Diego's chest, along with the sparsest line of hair arrowing down to a patch of trimmed pubic hair and a gorgeous, flaccid cock. He kissed the top of one foot, and then the other, and then climbed, taking turns, alternating his kisses between one leg and the other: arch, instep, ankle, shin, calf, knee. The back of the knee.

He laved all that warm soft skin. So vital. So vulnerable and undefended.

"I'm up here."

Carefully, he lifted Diego's foot so he could see. Kissing the instep again, he smiled.

"I'm earning your trust."

"This is trust." Diego's voice shook with emotion. "You have no idea."

"I think I do." Healey took his time kissing the rest of his way up Diego's legs. "Thank you."

The inside of Diego's thigh got special attention. Healey fondled his balls. He even got a reaction from Diego's dick, which surprised him.

"You get hard?" he asked.

Diego nodded. "Physical contact with my cock. Sometimes fabrics or rolling over a bump in the sidewalk... one time I was holding a cat. I'd rather not go there."

Healey leaned over and whispered, "Roll over?"

Diego started the process of shifting his body. After a few seconds, Healey asked, "Need a hand? I've only got one, but it's yours if you need it."

"It will be quicker if you position my legs."

He helped Diego as casually as he could. "Sure."

Before he could pull away, Diego gave him a kiss that lasted until he couldn't catch his breath. Healey was dizzy when they broke apart. Diego caught his jaw.

"But for future reference, unless I ask you to," said Diego, "don't move me."

Healey promised he'd never do such a thing, all the while reaching for the lube. He probably would have promised to hold his breath forever and drink the ocean too, he wanted Diego so badly. He was too desperate, almost sick with wanting him.

Two more of those devastating kisses and it might be too late for the lube. Finding a position Healey could manage proved difficult. Between his arm and Diego's circumstances, they'd probably require stacks of pillows . . . but . . . oh yes. He let out a groan of satisfaction when his slicked-up dick slipped between Diego's thighs.

There was no wrapping Diego in his arms. No long, passionate kisses to lead up to slow lovemaking. No penetration of any kind. Just a lubed dick and some friction. Impersonal and a little perfunctory, it still proved too much for him. Healey froze, indecisive for one terrible moment, before he jerked twice and shot his load.

"I'm sorry. Wow. I'm so sorry."

"For what?" Diego had to torque his body around to see Healey's face. "Premature ejaculation?"

"Yes. *Shit.*" Healey's head spun. "Oh God. I have ED now too."

"Shut up," Diego said affectionately. "You do not."

"That's never happened before. Wait. That's what everyone with ED says, isn't it? But no, you'll say that it isn't and—"

"Healey." Diego rolled to his side and cuddled against him.

"It's a normal thing, though, right? It happens?" Healey clutched at the idea. "Sure it does. I've been through a traumatic incident. Plus, I'm not exactly at one hundred percent, physically. You know?"

"Heals."

"Only my family calls me that." Healey bounded out of bed to pace. "Oh my God. I have ED. I'm too young to have ED."

"Healey Holly." Diego used a tone of voice Healey'd never heard from him before. "Stop."

Before Healey could get to the switch on the wall, Diego changed the lighting with his phone. Healey didn't want to turn around.

Even in the fading light, he felt aglow with jizz, as if he was standing underneath the searchlight of a police helicopter, dripping with bioluminescent spooge.

"Come here," Diego ordered.

After the lights dimmed to almost nothing, Healey returned to the side of the bed.

Diego patted the mattress next to him. "You are just ridiculous when you're nervous."

"I am," Healey admitted before sitting down.

"You also talk too much."

Healey's gaze headed heavenward. "To be fair, I only really do that when it becomes necessary to take a position on a subject that matters a great deal to me because I have to thoroughly consider all the potential outcomes—" One look at Diego's face and he clammed right up.

"You get nervous when you take tests." As Diego reiterated this, he ran a finger idly over Healey's stomach, gathering a sizable glob of his come on one finger before sucking it into his mouth. Healey couldn't take his eyes off that finger. Or that mouth.

No compartmentalizing here. Healey liked the whole goddamn package. Diego lit him up inside and overwhelmed him and subsumed him.

"I repeat." Diego's come-hither smile melted Healey's spine. "This is not a test."

CHAPTER TWENTY-EIGHT
HEALEY

Healey's eyes snapped open at exactly 3 a.m., according to his phone. For a microsecond, he didn't know where he was. Didn't recognize the man lying next to him. Physical sensations, too, seemed strange. Cast on one arm, aching body, muscle pain, stiffness. Then reality poured over him—the levee holding back his memories failed, and everything came rushing in.

Diego knew about the accident.

He'd been able to find out what happened between him and Ford with relative ease. And he probably thought Healey's secretive behavior, his reluctance to talk about the case and the past, were due to the trauma of the event or the gag order. But neither was precisely true.

Guilt and grief flooded his heart.

The night of the accident was still so very clear in his mind. He'd missed every sign that Ford was spiraling out of control. He hadn't seemed secretive. He hadn't appeared erratic or anxious. He hadn't been extra talkative or unusually silent or obviously self-medicating. Healey'd been so caught up with his own worries, with defending and graduation, he missed troubling behavior on Ford's part.

Then again, maybe Ford had simply gotten brilliant at hiding his paranoia...

The end result? Healey let everyone down, especially Ford.

"What's got you thinking so hard?" Diego's voice was a sleepy diesel-rumble, like a bus engine starting up.

"Ford. I forgot for a minute and everything was all wrong."

Diego went oddly still. "What's that mean, 'everything was wrong'?"

"The light. The room, the furnishings, the bed. I woke up just . . . lost for a minute."

Diego's let his body fall back. "Better now?"

"Sure," Healey lied. "But it's late. You sleep. I'll see myself out."

Diego nodded and turned away. "Night."

Healey leaned over and kissed Diego's temple. "Pleasant dreams, hot stuff."

A small smile found its way to Diego's lips. "You too, when you get to bed."

Healey picked up his discarded clothing before stepping into Diego's bathroom to dress. Turning around, he saw again the changes to Shelby's little room—changes that didn't seem benign in the cold, predawn stillness.

The feeling of uncertainty he'd woken up with, the eerie sense of things not being right, persisted.

A new homeowner could erase his family's tracks and paint over their personal touches, negating their ownership of the house, but now it felt like someone was trying to erase their past in Bluewater Bay altogether.

But that wasn't fair, was it? The closet where Shelby had scrawled her schoolgirl crushes on the wall was still there. Diego wasn't that guy. He wasn't trying to erase anything. He was trying to build something new for himself, and it wasn't fair to impose old memories and sentimental garbage on him, any more than it was fair for Healey to blame himself for what happened with Ford.

God. He had to stop doing that. No good could come of second guessing that awful night.

On the way out, he stopped for a glass of juice. The picture on the fridge intrigued him. Diego and his mother, who had almost identical lovely, intense dark eyes. She looked barely old enough to babysit him. Another picture showed Diego as a stocky kid with his arm around a road-weary dog.

Photos had been piled in neat stacks on the counter by Diego's fax machine—Diego, at various kid milestones. Always with his mother. Always smiling and happy and posing. It gave Healey the shivers to think of them—if it was just the two of them—so vulnerable to the world. Healey was a pack animal. His need for community, for tribe, had never been so clear to him as it was after Ford's arrest.

Healey needed a network of family and friends. He reached out to people when he was lost or lonely. He always had done.

Who did Diego have, now that his mother was gone?

Did he need someone? Not everyone did. And some people had family and it didn't matter, they could take them or leave them at will. That's the first thing he'd learned from Ford.

Some people got pushed from the nest, and they were expected to fly. If they didn't want to fly, or for some reason they couldn't, then they fell. *Splat.*

Some families practiced a ruthless kind of social Darwinism—even among their own offspring.

Was Diego from one of those?

No. The evidence—the photos—all showed a loving mother and her respectful, caring son. This wasn't about Diego.

The feeling Healey couldn't shake, of wrongness, of being out of sync, out of touch with everything important to him, only got worse the more he worried about it.

He'd come home to find answers.

He'd thought he would find them in Bluewater Bay, but he'd only found more questions. Now, he'd gone and let himself get distracted.

Diego was a magnificent distraction—no doubt about it. In fact, Diego was well on his way to being more than a distraction. Diego was like playing the best kind of video game—the kind where the rules changed with every encounter. Diego could become an obsession.

There's a problem when the distraction becomes as important as the mission.

Healey'd come home to find his center. Instead, he'd run into a whole new set of balls to juggle. He'd moved on too fast. The past hadn't quite let go of him, and until it did, he shouldn't confuse things by starting something new.

Not that he believed Diego was "starting" anything with him.

They were fucking.

That's all it was and that was absolutely fine.

Probably, Diego hadn't found his center yet, either. He'd lost his mobility. His mother had passed. He'd had to give up a job that was important to him—maybe Diego had some grieving to do, as well. Healey looked back toward the bedroom. He pictured returning to bed. Remembered his dad, hoping for the best with Christine. Relived the smile on Ford's face when he'd produced the G26—the Baby Glock—out of fucking nowhere and started firing out the driver's-side window.

With a shaking hand, Healey jotted a note for Diego to call him. He signed it with a smiley face, and left.

CHAPTER TWENTY-NINE
DIEGO

"**N**ight."

That sounded normal, didn't it? His voice hadn't had a catch in it when he said it, or...

He'd been half asleep, for fuck's sake. Healey'd said he was thinking about Ford and he was leaving, and Diego had said, *"Night."*

"Okay." Diego spoke the word several minutes after Healey closed the front door.

No reason to feel especially vulnerable.

It locked automatically. "Okay."

Diego lay back with his eyes closed. His body felt . . . full. Energized. Alive.

His only bruise, a deliberate love bite to the tender skin inside his upper arm, throbbed. It ached just right if he lay with his hands behind his head, so of course he did. And every time he felt the slight, sweet sizzle of pain, he thought of Healey's mouth, Healey's teeth, Healey's mesmerizing blue eyes, and the way Healey's lashes swept down to hide his unhappiness when he left.

"I woke up and everything was all wrong."

Healey's first thought was for Ford.

Diego would have argued, even pleaded, with him to stay, except for that.

The memory set off a depth charge inside Diego, breaking him open in some new way, unearthing a hidden trove of grief and rage.

He would not be left behind again.

In his ignorance, he'd believed a few nights with Healey couldn't hurt. He'd believed Healey could walk away and he'd be fine. He could walk away too, after all. *Roll away.*

Yet when Healey did that very thing, he got butt-hurt and cranky and...

Back when he'd talked to the doctors and the physical therapists, they said he'd have to "accept" a new normal. Full stop. He'd met with the occupational therapists, the advocates, the allies, and yes... he'd even talked to some of the new-age quacks, and he'd come away with the determination to "define" his normal for himself. He'd been in control of his normal since, and he'd never looked back.

This wasn't normal, "new" or otherwise. No one could call this normal, to be so hung up over a guy he'd only just met.

Nothing from his experience—neither his outsider childhood nor his days filming the news—offered relationship guidance. The key to his entire existence before the accident, his secret, his most basic survival skill was dodging disaster.

"Get up, papi, we have to go now."

"It's cold."

"I know, baby. Pull up your hoodie. Look what I made you. See? Like Slytherin." Green and gray felt, stitched clumsily together, cut on the ends to resemble fringe. She had a similar felt scarf in Ravenclaw colors.

Be ready to move. Be spontaneous. Be crafty. Be mobile.

Be *able*.

Be able *is fine, Mami, but what if the world throws a great big* Impedimenta! *in your way? Or a* Crucio! His sad little laugh spilled over again. There was no way to keep it in. He was losing his fucking mind.

It was a long time before he closed his eyes and went to sleep.

CHAPTER THIRTY
HEALEY

*B*luewater Bay hummed faintly under slithering fog. Healey crept along the street, barely able to see ten feet ahead. Mist like this could be eerie as hell. It had a disorienting way of reflecting his headlights. He and Nash used to sneak out and head for the beach on nights like this one, with one of Pop's earlier inventions—a radio-controlled, drone-like flying saucer he'd originally designed to carry small parcels between rooms of the house. With LED lights, it made the perfect UFO for nighttime mischief.

Healey and Nash had gotten up to all kinds of stuff with that.

Tonight, barely anyone was out and about. The glistening streets hissed beneath his tires. Instead of heading home, he took the highway toward Port Angeles, restlessness and a persistent sense of unease driving him.

Finally, he pulled over to the shoulder and made the call he'd been dreading.

"Healey?" The sleep-tinged voice belonged to Beryl, Ford's younger sister, the only member of Ford's family still willing to take his calls.

"Hey, B."

"I'm not supposed to talk to you."

"Who said that, your dad?"

"No. Of course not. The lawyers." The snick of a lighter was followed by a deep indrawn breath. "Everything is so fucked up."

"I just—" He tried the wipers before realizing it was his eyes that were cloudy. "I need to see him."

"Ford doesn't 'see' people."

"Can't you ask him for me? I promise, I won't—"

"He won't let me visit anymore. He asked to be moved to a new facility. He won't speak to anyone except our father's attorney."

Healey's heart sank. "Since when?"

"Since the arrest. I wish I could tell you that it's going to be okay, or that he's going through something and he'll change his mind. But we don't do that, do we? We don't change our minds. We lose them."

Somewhere, an owl hooted. "Ford could change his mind."

"He won't. So you know what we're up against," she commiserated. "Mom thinks she understands, but she keeps talking about how Ford is going to get better and come home and everything will go back the way it was. Dad sees Ford's problem as primarily medical. He's hoping someone will fix Ford and send him back to us. Like taking a dog to board and train."

More sounds on her side. Familiar. The *pop* and *hiss* of an energy drink. And it would be an energy drink. Something expensive and natural. She'd never just drink an ordinary pop.

Zebras, not horses. It was always zebras with Ford and his family.

"It's going to be hard for Ford to prove there's nothing wrong." Her bitter laughter was just short of frightening. "He's had his chances."

"I'm sure once Ford's meds are stable, your parents will—"

"It can't go back the way things were. Ford doesn't want it to. He says life is suffocating. He hates every minute of it." Exhalation break, although how she had breath left after those pronouncements when he certainly didn't... "I don't know how much more plain he's going to have to make things. Move on, Healey. Even when he gets better, he wants nothing to do with any of us anymore, and I don't blame him."

Healey disconnected the call before Beryl could. She and Ford had always been especially close, and if he was refusing to see her...

Dropping his phone on the seat beside him, he sat there, numb with grief. In the far distance, a foghorn warned passing ships against the local coastline.

Growing up, he'd expected to run into certain types of problems. His gifted status didn't spare him from being gay-bashed, nor did it prepare him in any way to defend himself against loving the wrong man.

Privilege wouldn't keep him from throwing his life away on drugs or alcohol.

He'd prepared himself as best he could for all the things that could trip him up, existing in a strange kind of limbo, bobbing along, hoping for the best. Preparing for the worst.

Life had thrown Diego at him, in much the same way it had thrown Ford. And there was nothing bad, nothing inherently wrong with taking what life offered.

But what if he hadn't learned his lesson the first time? What if Diego was equally bad for him, in the long run?

And how come—if he was really as smart as everyone said he was—he didn't know the answer?

Ford was done with him. He'd declared as much the last time they were together. He'd said it through his actions, his parents, his lawyers, and now, his sister. Ford's life was *suffocating* and hopefully now he could breathe.

So why did Healey still feel this awful burden—guilt and shame and something far worse? A kind of self-loathing. The feeling he'd let everyone down. He'd cheated somehow. Been unworthy. Unsympathetic.

He'd *abandoned* someone he loved.

Was *forced* to abandon him, despite the fact that now was probably when Ford needed his friends and family most. The nature of Ford's illness isolated him. Depression caused him to shut himself away, mania made others shy away from him. Balancing meds meant weird mood swings. Some days Ford acted perfectly normal. Others, it was beyond his capability to get out of bed.

And now Healey wondered, how long had it been since he'd done a check on his own mental health?

Too long.

Way, way too long.

Before he could pull back out onto the road and drive home, flashing lights lit up the rearview mirror. The sheriff's deputy who pulled in behind him exercised caution, coming to the passenger side window instead of standing in the street when the visibility was so poor.

Healey wiped his eyes discreetly before rolling down the window.

"Something up with the car?" The man was polite. Dark and handsome. Healey felt no sense of alarm.

"I stopped for a phone call." Healey leaned over the console while still keeping his hands in plain sight. "I was waiting a minute before heading out."

The deputy did a surreptitious visual check of the car. "Bad news?"

"Nothing unexpected." Healey didn't explain he was the one who made the call.

"It's obviously not the best time to park here in fog like this." The man's wide, white smile surprised him. "My wife, Sana, would kill me if anything happened to you."

"Oh gosh." Healey winced before offering his hand across the console for the officer to shake. "You must be Sahil?"

Sahil nodded. "I was just about to get a cup of coffee, would you like to join me?"

"God yes." Healey wasn't ready to sleep. "Where can we get coffee at this time of night?"

"Gas'n'Sip?"

"Has their coffee improved? Never mind. It's not about the coffee, is it?"

"Is it ever?" Sahil quipped before he left to return to his patrol car. The black-and-white edged onto the street, and Healey pulled out to follow him.

CHAPTER THIRTY-ONE

DIEGO

The following morning, Diego realized two things. One, his sheets smelled delicious, like Healey Holly, sex, and cookies. And two, he wished like hell Healey was still sharing them with him.

A sick pool of yearning formed in his gut—presumably the condensation drip from his thawing libido. Because he couldn't be missing Healey's warmth in his bed, next to his body, bad-breath kisses, and the awkward of having someone see his morning routine. All his routines.

He shivered, and not from the cold.

That longing couldn't be his heart, coming back to life.

It could not, because that would be so fucking unfair... For his dick to lie insensate forever while his heart started beating happily again, hoping things could get back to the very "new normal" he'd been dreading...

He pulled a magnifying mirror from his nightstand drawer and minutely examined his skin. There was nothing like clinical medical shit to shoot Cupid down like a MiG over Miami. His dick, perineum, and anus looked fine. There were a couple marks on the skin of his ass from Healey's tight grip. No problems.

There wouldn't be, would there? Healey was gentle and capable. He wanted things rough on his end, as it were. He didn't so much as scrape a nail over Diego's skin. At least, not without asking first.

Memories made Diego want to pull a pillow over his head and relive the experience in great, whacking-off detail. Except, yeah. *Not possible.*

Another reason to wish Healey had stayed. He was starting to crave that armpit thing.

"Your own fault." Diego transferred to his chair and rolled toward the bath. "It's your own goddamn fault. You told him to go because you—"

Didn't believe. Didn't have faith. *Didn't listen to your mami.*

"You know, Healey doesn't believe in any of your metaphysical shit."

He knew what his mother would say to that.

He said it himself, using her voice. "Yeah? Well. I don't believe in him either. He's weird."

Healey's weird?

Right.

Morning routines accomplished, Diego rolled out into the odd serendipity of a sunlit, golden morning. While long-time residents of Bluewater Bay got a slow start on Saturdays, the tourists had no such scruples. On Main Street, Stomping Grounds did brisk trade, but that was a given. His plan to bypass Tori's place in favor of a fast cup of coffee at the Gas'n'Sip was thwarted by a long line at the register there too. He shot Roy a wave as he rolled past. Waved to the nervous kid in the Tourist Info place. Familiar places. Familiar faces.

He gave up and headed for the Sunrise Café, where the wait would theoretically lead to actual food.

One face—a patron wearing a flap hat, seated in a four-top table by himself—caught Diego's attention and made his heart clench happily, at least for the split second it took for him to realize he was looking at Nash, not Healey.

From his face, Nash knew he'd been mistaken for his brother. As he took his hat off and set it on the bench beside him, the sparkle in his eye formed a wry apology for not being the proper twin.

Am I that obvious?

Nash made a *come here* gesture and mouthed, *Join me?*

Since he was seated at an accessible table, the hostess moved one of the chairs. She smiled brightly as soon as Diego rolled up to the table.

"Coffee?"

"Yes, please." He picked up a menu and started to read. His smile dimmed when he realized they were going to have the same waitress from his pancake trip with Healey.

She brought the coffee pot over and hovered for a second.

"Hey, Lisa, I want you to meet someone." Nash added a casual wave of his hand in Diego's direction. "Do you know Diego yet? He works with the *Wolf's Landing* postproduction team. Edits and stuff. He's dating my brother."

Diego looked up. "News travels fast."

"I saw you in here with Healey the other day." She smiled so brightly, it seemed a little scary-clown. "How are you today?"

Poor woman had no idea which word to stress, *you* or *today*, so her voice wobbled, hovering uncertainly on each word as it came out.

"Fine, thanks."

"What can I get for you?" She made such sincere eye contact his irises burned in sympathy.

Oh my God. She's afraid to blink now. "I'll have Huevos Rancheros with no sour cream, please." He said the words quickly to put her out of her misery.

"I'll get that." She noted his order before backing away.

"Lisa's kind of shy," Nash said, after she left. "She's, like, always been weird around me. Maybe she's super-religious or something, and she gets spooky around the gay."

"Healey and I were having a frank conversation last time I was here, and I think I freaked her out."

"Ah." Nash rested his chin on his hand. "So. You and Healey are dating."

Diego couldn't help the eyebrow that twitched at that. "So he told me."

Nash's eyes narrowed.

Diego dumped cream and sugar into his coffee. "He doesn't seem to be over Ford."

"Would you be?"

Of course, he wouldn't. Not if he loved someone and an illness took them away from him. If they were still around, still in trouble, and he couldn't do anything to help them, it would kill him.

"Did Healey tell you what happened?" Nash asked. "His accident?"

He shook his head. "I'm ashamed to say I dug into the story using some old news contacts."

"Uh-oh. Does Healey know you did that?"

"I apologized." Guilt made Diego flush. "I'm not sure I wouldn't do it again, though."

"Healey blames himself for what happened."

"I guessed."

"He hasn't even talked to me about it yet." Nash carefully neatened his flatware. Fork on the left, knife and spoon on the right, knife edge facing the plate, just the way Mami taught Diego to do it. "Wish he would. It's hard to stay on the sidelines, waiting for him to decide he's ready."

"It wouldn't be right for me to—"

"Damn right. I can wait until Healey's ready." He aimed a harsh gaze Diego's way. "Maybe *you* should've waited."

"I didn't have the *luxury* of waiting." Who was this guy to tell him how to handle his shit? "Your brother showed up on my doorstep at night, banged up to hell, determined to rent a room I had no desire to—"

"I get that. But you check his *references*. You don't go digging up information like he's a criminal."

"I know, a'ight?" Diego's defensive growl startled the waitress, who hesitated behind him, holding their plates.

Once she'd placed them and slunk away, he continued.

"Some of the things he was saying sounded sketchy. I figured I should find out what I could. He isn't all that stable himself, you know that, right?"

Diego's cell phone vibrated. He dug it out of his pocket and took a look. "Speak of the devil."

"I'm surprised he's awake. He didn't roll in until around six thirty."

Diego glanced up. Had he mistaken the time Healey'd left? Mistaken drifting in and out of sleep alone in the stillness of morning? Healey'd headed out around three. "Six thirty?"

Nash nodded. "I guess he met up with an old friend on the way home from your house."

Healey's text read, *Free for brunch tomorrow?*

Diego considered his options. Admittedly, they were binary. Go for brunch or stay home. *Where?* he texted back.

Resort of Juan de Fuca? 11:30 okay?

Sure, Diego typed, before putting his phone away. "Your brother doesn't have a clue what he wants."

"I know. Here, Lisa." Nash moved things out of the way for the skittish waitress. She poured each of them more water. "Oh, that's great. Thank you."

"You're welcome."

Diego watched her go. "She's like some frightened woodland creature."

"Speaking of which, I hope to hell you like watching every fucking documentary on Big Foot ever made."

"Big Foot?"

"Healey didn't tell you?" Nash grabbed his fork and started smashing butter into his pancakes. "Oh my god. Why would he? He's probably still trying to impress you with the power of his awesome. Healey's a closet cryptozoologist."

"What?" Diego asked, incredulously. "That *fake* fucker. He says he doesn't believe in anything he can't prove with science."

"That's probably why he didn't mention it. Crypto is Healey's Achilles' heel. He really, really wants to believe. You're welcome."

"That lying bastard."

"I know, right?" Nash's eyes were the same disconcerting shade of blue as his brother's, though they seemed . . . older . . . somehow. As if he'd lived more, or harder . . .

"You know what my favorite thing in the world is?" Nash asked suddenly.

Diego took a sip of his coffee. "I could not begin to guess."

"Getting Healey's goat." Nash leaned back against his chair as if he had all the time in the world. "You're a photographer. How well do you use Photoshop?"

"Holy shit." Diego saw the possibilities immediately. "You're really not a very good brother, are you?"

"Do you have an identical twin who happens to be a verifiable genius with a PhD?"

"Nope."

"You can call me anything you want if you ever get one of those." Nash shoved a piece of super-crispy bacon in his mouth and gave it a hard crunch. "In the meantime, let's just make his life a little more exciting. Shall we?"

Diego grinned. "You are a serious shit-stirrer."

Blue eyes lit with cold fire. "I know, right?"

CHAPTER THIRTY-TWO
HEALEY

*I*t was 11:31. Diego was late. You couldn't really count a minute as late, but Healey had been anxiously looking toward the parking lot since 11:15, and therefore, when the second hand passed the half-hour mark, his anxiety ratcheted up ten notches.

Not that he had anything to be anxious about.

He wanted this to go well, is all. He wanted Diego to meet his friends. He wanted his friends to meet Diego. He wanted everyone to get along. And he wanted it to be over so he could go back home and put on sweatpants.

Not necessarily in that order.

"You look so nice." Sana adjusted his tie. Again.

He'd borrowed a suit from Nash, who had much better tailors now that he'd hooked up with Spencer than they could have imagined back in the day, when suit separates from JCPenney were an extravagance Pop could barely afford. Even when Pop's ship came in, they'd never had stuff like this. Nash was broader than him through the shoulders, but it didn't look like he was wearing his pop's clothes or anything.

It's only breakfast.

They'd done that already. He wondered if Diego liked the same types of foods he did. He hadn't ordered anything gross like hash or liver and onions. Did Diego liked his eggs sunny side up? Did he dipped his crusts in the yolks?

What if he thinks it's weird to invite a hookup to brunch with old friends?

He said you were dating.

Wait. No.

You said you were dating. He just didn't tell you otherwise.

"What's that face for?" Sahil asked.

Healey checked his watch again. "Dating is stupid."

Clara laughed. "You can take the boy out of high school, confer on him three degrees, but—"

"Is that him?" Sahil pointed toward Diego's SUV. He pulled into the parking lot and took the handicapped space.

Healey breathed a sigh of relief. "That's him. It will take him a minute to get out of the car. Everyone chill. Just act normal."

"I saw this movie," Clara deadpanned. "I hope you didn't make some kind of bet about prom. That always backfires."

"Not helping," Healey muttered.

"Who said I came to help?" She smiled sweetly. "Can we go inside and drink now? I'm starved."

"Who are you, really? And what have you done with my Ms. Underhill?"

She peered past him. "Ooh, your young man is very good-looking."

Healey whipped around to look. "How can you tell? He's not even—"

"Like shooting piranha in a punchbowl." She had the nerve to snicker at his lack of chill.

"You monster. Please, marry me?" he begged, for the hundredth time. "I don't want a wife. I just want to sit at your feet and worship until you die."

"As much as I'd like another pet..."

"Sorry I'm late." Diego's arrival spared Healey another cruel disappointment at Clara Underhill's hands.

"You're right on time, and you look good enough to eat." Healey jammed his good hand in his pocket in lieu of punching himself in the face for saying something so idiotic.

"I'm Clara." She held out her hand.

"Oh, excuse me." Healey turned on his best Vanna White, extending his arm to introduce his friends. "Allow me to introduce Clara Underhill. She taught math at the high school before retiring to spend more time in her primary role, Queen of Hell. And these are my friends Sana and Sahil."

"How do you do." Sahil shook hands with Diego.

"Pleasure."

Then Diego shook hands with Sana. "Nice to meet you."

When he'd made every introduction mathematically possible without repeats, Healey wound up standing there, arms akimbo.

"Okay, this way?" At least one of his arms was useful, as it was pointing toward the entrance.

He hung back, going last, with Diego.

They made small talk while Healey hid a sudden rush of hunger that had nothing to do with food. Diego's mouthwatering tan skin looked luscious against a crisp white shirt and brown leather jacket. Khaki pants. His turquoise choker and matching bracelet looked handmade.

Wholly unable to stop himself, Healey leaned over to kiss Diego while he held the door open for his chair. Surprise and something oddly sweet crossed Diego's normally taciturn features.

"You look good." Diego rolled past, but not before Healey noted the flush on his cheeks. "You dress up for me?"

"Yeah, I did." Healey followed the party to the host station. "That okay?"

Diego let his gaze drift over Healey's entire body. "I said you looked good, didn't I?"

The host picked up a stack of menus before asking, "Everyone here?"

"Yes." Sahil led the way with Sana, and Diego followed. Healey held out his arm for Clara.

"Oh, I'm to be *led into dinner*, am I? How very English country estate." Her eyes sparkled. "If we don't discover a murdered corpse at some point, I'll be so disappointed."

White tablecloths, burgundy carpets, and a fresh coat of paint gave the Inn a certain vitality, despite the old school, cholesterol-laden banquet food. Sana and Clara kept the conversation lively while they caught up, leaving Healey, Sahil, and Diego to make the usual conversational gambits with regard to sports and weather.

Brunch was an endless buffet of the usual things: omelets, waffles, a carving station, an acre of prepared salads. Hungry enough to embarrass himself after his exertions the night before, Healey nevertheless prepared himself to carry a plate for his date, but Diego preempted that by requesting a serving tray.

As they went down the buffet line together, Diego placed food on the tray in his lap, and when he got back to the table, he set up his breakfast and placed the tray against the wall, next to his chair.

Living with Shelby, Healey'd learned to anticipate her needs. But Diego didn't need or want minions. Maybe they'd spoiled Shelby a little? He guessed they had. And she'd let them, because she enjoyed watching them do her bidding.

"What's got you thinking so hard?" Diego asked during a lull in the conversation. "Ford?"

That startled Healey. "I was thinking about my sister."

"How about your family, Diego?" Sana asked. "Do they live in the area?"

Diego shook his head. "My mother passed away last year."

"Condolences," Clara murmured.

Diego lifted his napkin to wipe his lips—unnecessarily, it seemed to Healey. Anything that hid Diego's spectacular mouth, even for a second, was not only unnecessary but frankly suspect, as far as he was concerned.

"My stepfather and his children live in Los Angeles. I'm solo up here."

"Yet you put down roots," Sahil said. "You like the area?"

"Since I'm with the *Wolf's Landing* production crew, it's a handy base of operations. I can easily get to projects in Vancouver and LA from here. I'm close enough for work when I can get it, and I'm still living somewhere relatively untouched. I can indulge my favorite hobby."

Healey snickered, earning him a put-upon expression from both Diego and Sana.

"Which is?" Clara sent him an arch look that should have stopped his heart.

"Nature photography."

"Very nice." Sahil sat forward, excited now the conversation was going to turn technical. "I indulge in some photography myself. May I ask what kinds of cameras you use?"

"Yeah, what did you take those naked pictures of me with the other night, Diego?" He dared Diego to wipe the grin off his face.

"Oh, that kind of nature photography." Clara held her G&T up for the waiter to signal she needed another. "We'll definitely need details about that."

"That's enough out of you." Diego gave Healey's forehead a playful poke before he and Sahil launched into an intense discussion of macro lenses.

Clara leaned over to whisper in Healey's ear. "I like him."

His heart did a silly wiggle. "I do too."

The rest of the meal featured lots of topic-hopping, memories of school, and letting Diego in on every dumb thing Healey had said or done back in the day. Afterward, they waved good-bye to Sana and Sahil, who announced cheerfully that they'd taken the kids to her mother's and had the afternoon child-free.

Healey wished he was going home with Diego, but he'd promised to drive Clara back to her place.

Diego didn't invite him to come by after.

Healey hadn't asked, either, which added a slightly stilted flavor to their parting. But after his disorientation on Friday, and his subsequent talk with Beryl, his heart faltered whenever he thought about calling Diego to hook up again.

In some self-imposed limbo, he couldn't move forward and he couldn't move back. That was, he thought he'd already moved *forward*. But obviously the guilt he was feeling, the sense that he'd cheated, meant he wasn't over *something* yet.

He was over the romance. God's honest truth. He was way over the romance.

When he and Ford first got together, they hadn't had a clue how hard life could be. Looking back, the writing had been on the wall. Healey wanted a constructive, creative, productive life with someone, and Ford wasn't capable of that.

Despite his new understanding, despite what Ford wanted, despite what Beryl said, "moving on" felt like giving up on Ford—something Healey could never do. Not ever. Even if they weren't romantically involved, Healey wanted the best for Ford, and it hurt like hell that Ford wanted to move on as if they'd never met.

"Diego's remarkably mature for a man his age." Clara had clearly liked him. "He seems very serious."

"I think he believes in ghosts."

"What's wrong with that?" Her smile was probably due to that fourth G&T.

He waited for a red light—when it was safe for him to glare at her.

"Don't tell me you believe in metaphysical nonsense too."

She waved a weathered hand. "Blah, blah, blah, heaven and earth, Horatio, than are dreamt of in your philosophy—how does that go again?"

"I'm pretty sure Horatio was only there for the skull part."

She put on lipstick, left a "kiss" on the passenger window, and giggled about it. "He was *also* there for the heaven-and-earth-slash-philosophy part too. It was the same scene, wasn't it?" Clara got her keys from her purse—a ladylike little thing made from something decidedly not vegan. "Anyway, you'd be a fool to let that get in your way. He seems pragmatic where it counts."

"Yeah."

"But I sense an artist's soul." She asked, "Have you seen his pictures?"

"No." Then he remembered the ones of Diego's mother. "Some. He hasn't shown me his portfolio or anything." He pulled up in front of her house and killed the engine.

"I think you should ask to see them."

He turned to ask why, but she was already spilling out of the car. He considered running around to help her, because if he knew anything, it was that women her age shouldn't *spill*, but she'd already closed the door between them, waved, and trotted up the walkway to her house.

While he waved back, his phone vibrated.

Thanks for brunch. Your friends are nice.

So polite. Was Diego's text a figurative good-night kiss? Or a good-night kiss-off?

Healey positively could not tell.

Healey typed, *You want to get together maybe?* in the text box. His thumb hovered over Send.

Hovered . . . *hovered.*

He locked the screen and pocketed the phone before pulling away from the curb. When his phone vibrated again, he assumed the call was from Diego, but it was Nash.

"How'd it go?"

Healey switched the phone to speaker. "Not bad. The food was decent."

"Did my suit survive?"

"Don't you have people living in your basement whose only job is to spin straw into this magnificent suit? Tell them to make another one. Me *likey*."

"You are such an ass."

God, I am. Healey pulled over. *I am totally an ass.* He confessed. "I am an ass without even a hat to cover me."

"Excuse me?" Nash's voice was not perplexed. Not precisely. More... "Where are you? Are you drunk?"—*angry*—"Are you driving under the influence?"

"I am not even"—Healey's hand tightened on the wheel—"remotely caffeinated."

Nash blew out a breath. "Then what's up now?"

"You say that like something's always up. Like I'm a leaky radiator in need of constant maintenance."

"So?"

"You *know* what's up. I don't feel safe. I don't feel... grounded."

"Then come back to the house. Pop's here, and Fjóla. We'll make popcorn. There's still time to Skype Shelby."

"No." Healey turned on the defroster when the windshield started looking cloudy. "I don't want to come home, because that means I can't handle my shit. And I can't call Diego, because the last thing I want to do is land on the next guy like a ton of bricks, and he doesn't need that either—" He jammed his fist into his mouth to keep from saying more.

"Aw, man." Nash's voice was soft. "Talk to me."

"I smother people. All right?" Healey closed his eyes. "Even mom said it. I suck the air out of a room."

"*Twins.*" Nash stressed the word. They'd both heard their mother say it a hundred times—every time they played their video of the Christmas before she died. "She said, 'Twins can suck all the air out of a room in nothing flat.' And you know she only meant the work and the noise and—"

"I know that. I do. But I *don't* handle my shit very well. Maybe Ford was right. I have too much energy. I care too much, only not always about the things other people want me to. I need too much. I am! I'm *suffocating*."

Nash cursed Ford's ancestors colorfully. "I swear to God, bro. I'd let you believe that if it was true."

"Then why won't Ford see me, even just to say hello? Why has he cut me off without a word, as if he has to be rid of me to get better? Was I that—"

"Ford is mentally ill, bro. By definition, you can't believe everything he tells you. I dunno, man. Maybe we'll never know. But all those years ago, when he told me he loved you, I believed he meant it. And I believe you love him. But things don't always work out."

Healey tried to think back, but when he was upset, the older memories got tangled together with the more recent, painful ones. "You asked him?"

"I had to warn him I'd kick his ass if he didn't treat you right. I've got your back, don't I?"

Healey smiled like a goofball. "Bullshit you asked him if he loved me."

"All right. He volunteered the information. You never suffocated anybody, Healey. That was Ford's illness talking. You've gotta believe that."

"Thanks," he said, before disconnecting the call. He laid his phone on the seat beside him. Looked at it for a long time.

No. He wouldn't text Diego back. He'd let things percolate for a bit. Let the idea of them dating settle. Maybe generate a little fondness through absence.

Because he could certainly learn from his mistakes. If he was going to be dating Diego, it wasn't going to be the same messy free-for-all it had been with Ford. He'd be dignified and ask for dates. He'd send thank-you texts and let time pass.

They both had lives.

He wasn't in college anymore, where simply flopping down on some dude's couch meant you were down, and borrowing his sweatshirt meant you were together.

Healey Holly was not about to be accused of suffocating anyone, ever again.

CHAPTER THIRTY-THREE
DIEGO

After brunch at the Juan de Fuca, Diego pounced on his phone every time it rang. By Wednesday, he felt young and dumb. He felt *rejected*, but still, when his phone rang while he was eating breakfast, he snatched it up, only to experience a sense of keen disappointment that his caller was not Healey Holly, and how stupid was that?

He *could* call Healey.

He could simply pick up the phone and call Healey and say, *I really dug falling asleep next to you. Come back and let's do it again.*

But every time he picked up the phone, he went through several iterations of holding it, staring at it, and finally putting it down again, unused.

Instead, every time it rang, Diego's heart went into overdrive.

"Yeah." He tried not to sound disappointed when he saw his caller was Cecil.

"Hello, sunshine." Unperturbed by Diego's mood, Cecil chirped, "What's got you so cheerful this morning?"

"Sorry," he muttered. "I should have taken a job while the show's on hiatus. Christ, I'm so bored I'd be willing to shoot a wedding at this point. A bar mitzvah."

There was a long pause before Cecil spoke. "Er . . ."

It took Diego a minute to realize that Cecil—never in his life at a loss for words—was now tongue tied.

And like a clap of thunder, he knew why. "When's the happy day?"

"Diego—"

"Oh, please. You're not going to try to explain the concept of *ménage* to me now, are you? Because I gotta say, I figured that out before I knew I liked boys."

"Oh. Wow." The words came out chagrined.

"You guys should have kept the blinds closed, huh?"

"Okay. I'll, um . . ." Cecil coughed. "Keep that in mind."

"So when are you and Rachel tying the knot?"

"New Year's. It's not a big deal. Just family, in the house here. You're sure you're not"—another pause—"in any way unhappy that Rachel and I are going to make things official?"

"Aw, man, of course not. Congratulations, Cecil. I want you to be happy . . ." When he realized he'd let the words trail off, he winced. Why couldn't he just leave it at that? Cecil was a fucking mind reader, even over the phone. He'd have heard the doubt in Diego's voice, and—

"But?" Cecil prompted.

Diego let out a long slow breath. "It's more like an *and*."

"Ah." Sounds indicated Cecil was settling into his favorite chair, maybe with a cup of coffee, or a breakfast sandwich. For a lawyer who charged a king's ransom for his time, he was sure free with time for his kids.

A rush of warmth hit Diego along with the thought: he was still one of Cecil's kids. That hadn't changed. Wouldn't change, even though his mother wasn't there to bind them together.

"What's on your mind, *m'hijo*?"

Cecil's kindness, his common sense, and his lawyer's reticence when it came to carrying tales made him an ideal person for Diego to share his almost too-painful thoughts with. He explained about being blindsided by Healey. How normal—*Christ* how he hated that *chingada* word—how like himself Healey made him feel. How dating and sex and—God, he felt idiotic even saying it—*love* were something he believed he'd only ever see in the rearview mirror and now . . .

Now he wasn't so sure that was true.

Now, the terrible reality of getting back into dating shimmered faintly in the distance, taking shape in ways he'd never dreamed.

It was just *beautiful*.

And . . . scary as hell.

"What's the worst thing that could happen to you if you fall for this guy?" That was kind of a disingenuous question, because Cecil knew the worst that could happen to someone like Diego. A guy with

Cecil's long experience in the criminal justice system knew the worst that could happen to anybody.

But... what could be so bad? Healey leaves. He says, *I can't handle all your problems*, and he leaves. That would be... awful. But people leave. Even if they don't walk away, they die. People leave all the time. That's why— Wait. Cecil asked *"What's the worst thing that could happen to you...?"*

Because "the worst thing" wasn't what happened to him. He could take anything.

But when Mami died, even though he knew she was in a better place, he'd been devastated. Because *he* had to stay here, alone.

The worst thing *was* falling for someone. Love made you too vulnerable.

"I don't know if I can do this," he said quietly. "I don't know if I'm strong enough to fall for him and then watch him walk away."

"You can protect your heart too much, you know. Is he the type to quit?"

Healey? Probably not. No.

He'd stayed with Ford, despite his journey with mental illness. He'd stayed and been part of Ford's treatment plan. He'd done his best, and he was eating himself alive that he couldn't do more.

Christ.

"He's the little engine that could. He'd never abandon a friend in need." Diego ground the heel of his hand into the ache over his eye. "Never. What am I even thinking—"

"Don't do that," Cecil chided. "Don't make that a bad thing. This boy you like is the loyal type?"

Loyal enough to defend the guy who'd practically killed him. "To a fault."

"And he's nice?"

"Yeah."

"That's awesome." Cecil's sappy happiness came through loud and clear. "You deserve loyalty and love and laughter. You deserve a decent guy."

"I don't exactly know if he's decent. He's not a bigot or a homophobe, and he'd be nice to his mother, except she's dead."

"Mmm." Cecil's thinking sound.

"What?"

"Two motherless boys. That makes me sad, somehow. When I lost my mother, I thought the sun would never feel warm again. I thought the soil would spit her right back out, and the earth should simply stop rotating—"

"A'ight, Clarence Darrow. That's a little grim." He snapped his mouth *shut*.

Knowing when to silence Cecil's penchant for oratory had been his mother's specialty. He'd never done such a thing before. Couldn't imagine what made him do it now.

"Gabbi must be sitting on your shoulder right now." The warmth in Cecil's voice absolved him. Gooseflesh covered his arms.

Yes... he could feel her.

This belief in things unseen was the one thing he couldn't share with Healey—the feeling he had that sometimes, some part of his mother's essence remained with him, as vital and vibrant as ever. There were days he could feel her inside his heart, quarterbacking every little play, as controlling as she'd been in life.

Today appeared to be one of those.

"I've been feeling her presence a lot lately."

"Yeah?" Cecil prompted. "Then you know you're on the right track. Gabbi won't steer you wrong. You are her world."

Are. *Are.*

Cecil believes.

Diego tapped his trackpad, and his computer came to life. His voice was little more than a croak when he spoke. "I'm sending you a link. Let me know what you think."

Diego uploaded the most recent video he'd created, using one of his mother's podcast interviews to give voice to another part of her story. He sent the link to Cecil, listening to Cecil's movements as he opened the file on his end. Music signaled he'd started playing it right then, so Diego waited while he watched.

There was something so comforting about the presence of another human, even on the phone. Before Healey, Diego hadn't let himself consider things like whether he might be lonely. Now, as he soaked up each little tick of Cecil's fingers on the keys, the clink of a pencil, and the sound of a mug hitting the desk, he knew he'd been kidding himself.

The clip showed how Gabriella Maria Montenegro, a birthright citizen of the United States, was deported with her family in the late eighties. How from an early age, she was determined to return and make a life for herself. How getting pregnant out of wedlock at fifteen forced her hand when her parents threatened her with placing her baby up for adoption whether she wanted that or not.

While Cecil watched the clip, Diego opened a bottle of water. He told himself his suddenly dry mouth wasn't because he was worried what Cecil thought of his efforts so far. He told himself that Gabbi was his *mother*, after all, and no one except maybe Gabbi could tell her story better than he could.

He told himself these things, but still he wasn't satisfied. The voice-over wasn't dynamic enough. The images were bland and unemotional. The journey the young Gabbi had taken to get to the States had been frightening and perilous, but the clips he had didn't leverage enough emotion, and therefore, they lacked tangible tension.

If only he could travel to Mexico, to his grandparents' place, and start from there. Because he knew . . . *he knew*. To tell his mother's story properly, he had to walk in her shoes.

Walk.

He wanted to cry.

"I'm not sure this is going to work." Diego waited until Cecil had finished the clip to speak again. "It's not very compelling, is it? I keep reaching for the tone I want to take, trying to find the right pictures, but it seems so goddamn static. Maybe I'm just too close to the subject this time."

"Of course you are. If you weren't, it would be easy."

Diego muttered, "I guess."

"I don't need to tell you hard things can be worth doing."

"Yeah, yeah." Diego was glad Cecil couldn't see the color in his cheeks.

"Only you can do this for her, *m'hijo*."

"But no pressure," he groused.

Cecil snorted. "Pressure can be as good as hard. You'll find your road. I have faith in you. You have a good eye."

"Okay." As an afterthought, Diego asked, "You know what? You've probably heard about this dude I'm seeing. Remember that Stanford student who got arrested?"

"There have been a couple of Stanford students in the news recently. Made me glad I went to CAL. You're not seeing one of those guys?" Worry hovered on the edge of his voice.

"The man I'm talking about was the passenger in a car chase. In fact, he's going to want a consultation, eventually. Or a name. Someone he can trust."

"I don't remember the details." Cecil's fingers tapped on the keys again. "Ah. Yeah. What did your young man tell you?"

"There's a gag order in place, so he wouldn't talk at first. That didn't stop me from finding things out. Probably not the best thing to do, researching him like that."

"The plot thickens."

"I know, right?" Diego gave his arm a scratch before lifting himself off the seat to decompress his spine and give his skin some air. "I'm a journalist. I can't stand secrets."

"That's what makes you good at your job."

Hold, hold, hold. Diego's had to strain to keep himself off his chair. It felt good, to stretch like that. "Used to." He relaxed back into his seat.

"Your curiosity is still perfectly fine."

Cecil's fatherly tone signaled the point he was trying to make was important to him. Also that he thought Diego was being a bit of a dumbass. He could do that in such a loving way you never felt it. That was part of Cecil's charm.

"Your brain works," he continued. "You are on the sunny side of the grass. I leave it to you to MacGyver the rest. Of all my boys—and I would never say this to them, mind you—you're the toughest. It's because your mom was a bona fide badass."

"You have no idea."

"Hmm?"

"I'm working on a theory right now. I'll let you know if it pans out."

"Is this about the graffiti? Rachel showed me those billboard pictures. I totally buy Gabbi painting those signs. It's exactly the kind of thing she'd get up to."

"She didn't sleep well," Diego mused. "Sometimes on the road, she'd get restless, and I'd wake up in an empty motel room. Used to scare me shitless until I got old enough to take care of myself. She always came back."

Until she couldn't.

"Gabbi was—" Cecil seemed to choose his words carefully. "There were things about your mother I never understood. She could be hard sometimes. She could be selfish. Did she know you woke up while she was gone?"

"Yeah." Cecil saw his mother clearly—loved her despite her flaws. It took a heavy weight from Diego's shoulders. They both loved Gabbi, but neither had any illusions. Cecil wouldn't want him to staple a posthumous halo and wings on her.

Gabbi was no angel.

"It was unconscionable for her to do that." Disappointment laced Cecil's voice. "I would have talked with her about it if I'd known. I'd have put a stop to it."

Those weren't idle words. He adopted Diego immediately after marrying Gabbi, giving him his name and his protection. He treated Diego the same as his biological kids, leaving a seven-figure job to spend more time with them when Gabbi got sick. Now, he advocated for her causes.

"She wasn't an easy person," Diego said finally.

"She loved fiercely." Cecil took a deep breath, and if Diego wasn't mistaken, he was probably wiping his eyes with one of his ubiquitous, white tone-on-tone monogrammed handkerchiefs. "This conversation is too serious. Tell me about this man you've met."

Diego hesitated. Did he want to jinx things? "How about I'll tell you if anything more happens?"

"If you want to play it that way for a while, it's okay." Cecil let himself be diverted by talk of the weather, the video, and what his kids were up to.

They spent a little time talking about whether Diego should consider returning to journalism. Diego argued he wasn't fit for the work anymore, but lately . . . lately lots of things that seemed impossible—

"Like Gabbi, in her way, you have a unique ability to shine the light of reason on *unreasonable* things," Cecil offered. "You have a good eye, and a gift for telling a very human story through the lens of your camera. This will be needed more than ever in the coming years."

"*Dad.*" Any more than one syllable would break him open—Pandora's piñata, with all his shortcomings and fears and failings tumbling out.

"When you've licked your wounds enough, you won't be able to stay in your cave. You don't run away from hard things."

"I can't."

Cecil took a while to respond. "Let this new guy storm the castle walls, Diego. Let yourself have something good for a change. You deserve it."

"Okay. Maybe... A'ight." Diego took a deep swig of water, capped his bottle, and put it down. "After I get this thing with Mami squared away."

"No. No waiting," Cecil said firmly. "Don't let anything pass you by anymore. Time is short."

Diego's resolution wavered only so long. "Okay, counselor. Anything to make this line of questioning stop." Witnesses probably got better treatment.

"I expect you to promise." The teasing note was back in Cecil's voice.

When they hung up, Diego felt lighter, especially later that night, when he got a text from Healey. *Why haven't you called me? I've been slow-playing this jam but I'm a seriously hot motherfucker even though I am right-handed and I would love to*

It ended there.

Diego waited.

Another message two seconds later confirmed his theory that the original message didn't originate from Healey Holly's smooth white, mathematician's hands, but Nash's calloused mechanic's mitts.

Christ, I'm sorry. That was The Evil One. That fucking bastard, I'll kill him. Look, I'm sorry, okay? He's, like, emotionally seven

A second later, he had another message: *inches flaccid*

And another: *I will kill him*

Diego typed, *Are you guys through puberty yet?*
You should know.

Diego used the puking emoji. Healey wasn't capable of manipulation. But Nash . . . Oh, well. *Someone* had to put him and Healey out of their misery.

Nash had clearly lost patience with them.

Why don't you come over, Heals. Leave that ugly brother of yours to sext with his movie star. I'll let you put your dick down my throat . . .

He stared at his phone. Waited. Waited . . .

The phone rang.

"This is Nash. Healey left, but he's going to realize his phone is still here in three . . . two . . . one . . ." The call disconnected.

A few seconds later, Diego got another text. *OMW*

CHAPTER THIRTY-FOUR
HEALEY

Rainclouds gathered over the sound—a storm, blowing in fast. As Healey left Fjóla's place, the first fat droplets drummed on the roof of his SUV. His windshield wipers moved in time to Green Day's "American Idiot"—at least until he changed the radio station and The Killers took over.

He wondered what Diego would think of them. On second thought, he didn't wonder, he already knew Diego thought he was a geek with craptastic taste in music and— Were they even friends?

Healey took his foot off the gas.

He had a couple of preconceived notions where Diego was concerned. Maybe his ideas were all wrong too. Maybe Diego hadn't been completely unmoved that last time. He'd *seemed* to soak up all the affection Healey wanted to give without a fight.

Healey's hands tightened on the wheel. "What am I doing?"

Diego ticked off every one of Healey's secret buttons. He was tough and strong and bright. Kind and not easily won over. A little angry. A little proud. Diego wasn't a fairy-tale prince. But when Healey made him smile, when he made Diego forget himself for a minute, he earned a bare, brief glimmer of the man behind the mystery.

And what a glimmer it was . . .

Diego—the guy waiting to be discovered if only he could learn to trust—was *crack* to Healey.

Just like Ford had been crack.

Oh, geez. He coasted onto a side street because he needed to think things through.

Slowing to a stop, he left the engine running—the wipers rocking—as he used clumsy fingers to message the one person he knew would understand.

Am I like Pop?

Nash's text reply was instantaneous. *I knew you'd freak out.*

His phone rang in his hands, so he answered Nash's call with a swipe of one finger. "Am I?"

Nash growled, "Don't overthink your shit all the time."

"I stuck with Ford. Sometimes I enabled him and ultimately, that hurt him more than it helped him. I was like some well-meaning idiot who—"

"Wait a damned minute. You weren't his doctor. You weren't his therapist. You were his boyfriend. If anyone dropped the ball, it was them."

"But—"

"Look. I've thought about this, all right? It's not the same. You were with Ford long before he had his first breakdown," Nash said. "But Pop went all in with Christine *despite* knowing she was an addict. By the time he realized how badly things could go, they were already married, and he stuck by her, trying to help because he's a decent guy. He was a frog in hot water. He hoped for the best and never even realized that soup smell was our family, boiling alive."

"Jesus, Nash."

"The difference is," Nash said irritably, "Ford wasn't Christine. Diego isn't Christine. You see people for who they are, and Pop sees them for what they could be. If you're worried you won't pull the ripcord and save yourself? Well. You're a decent guy like Pop. Probably you wouldn't. That's why you have me."

"Wow."

"Getting to know Diego is the only way to find out who he is. Just go in with your eyes wide open."

In a small voice, Healey asked, "Does this say something about me? Is Diego's fear that I might be some kind of freak or fetishist, even... maybe... partly true?"

"I don't think so. But what if it is?" Nash asked. "I dig repressed English guys with freckles. People have types."

"That's hardly the same thing."

"Maybe you resonate to complex personality issues. Or maybe you see how a dude's challenges make him stronger and you admire him for it. Look at Shelby. She's a fucking badass. When she's ready to date, there'd *better* be a guy or girl who can see beyond the SCI to how amazing she is. You can't separate her from her chair. That's part of what makes her who she is."

That felt almost true. "But—"

"Maybe you should assume you like complicated people because you love the labyrinthine. Liking someone who is intricate is a good thing."

"When you put it that way . . ." Healey swallowed. "I—I owe it to Diego to think this through going in. The last thing I want to do is hurt him."

"Yeah, but don't overthink. Let him decide when he's ready. Don't you dare make the decision for him. You know how much you'd hate that."

Healey grimaced. "I know."

"And you could try talking to him instead of me," Nash chided. In the background, there was a game on the television. "Tell *him* all this shit."

Healey frowned into the darkness beyond his rain-spattered windshield. Nash didn't need to hear him agree. He disconnected the call and put the car in gear.

CHAPTER THIRTY-FIVE
DIEGO

Opening the door to a timid knock, Diego found Healey beneath the porch light, good hand shoved in his pocket. He rolled backward so Healey could step inside.

"I need to tell you something." Healey leaned against the wall just inside the door. He didn't look like he was going to come all the way inside until he could get whatever it was off his chest.

Diego braced himself for disappointment as he closed the door behind them.

"I'm not a freak or a dude with a fetish, but I don't know how I'd feel if you weren't in that chair." Healey's face was pale in the light from the door's glass window. His gaze didn't move from Diego's feet.

Diego stiffened. "What the actual fuck?"

Healey spoke softly. "I know that's not what you need to hear from me."

"You don't know what I need," Diego said tiredly, since it sounded like this might be the beginning of the end for them. "But that's sure the hell not what I want to hear."

"But I know what *I* need," Healey said. "I know what *I* want."

"And what's that?"

Healey dragged his hands through his damp hair. "To tell you, I have to confess something."

"What?" Diego braced himself for anything.

"I've never had to worry about anything except passing a test. Can you imagine?"

"Not really."

"I can say unequivocally I do not have a fetish. I am attracted to people who have faced adversity. I'm attracted to people I perceive as strong. People who live lives outside the bubble of academia and—"

"That's only another kind of fetish," Diego said slowly. "People are pre-programmed to survive."

"I understand that. My sister would kill me for saying any of this."

"And?"

"I told you. I can't compartmentalize you. I admire your strength. I admire your sense of humor. Your poise. None of that has anything to do with the chair, except in my mind you and the chair are inextricably linked."

"Fuck you," Diego said angrily. "I don't know which is worse. Care-taking or hero-worship."

"That's just it!" Healey snapped. "You need to hear all these things I have in my head and then you'll be able to decide, am I *that guy*? Am I the guy who doesn't get it because they're wrapped up in the momentary idea of being with you, the guy who wants to care give or the curious guy or the one who fetishizes you? Or am I a guy trying to see past all that to who you are?"

Diego frowned. "You make a point."

"You're smart and funny and because of your disability I see you as resilient. I admire resilient people. I can't promise I'd feel the same way if you were able-bodied, because I never met you before. And I worry about everything, all the time, so that's me being an—"

"Ass." Diego watched Healey's big confession with a jaundiced eye. "You're being an ass."

"I don't know if I like you for you," Healey stated baldly. "I do like you very much, but I can't promise my motives are strictly pure. You deserve someone who—"

"Oh for God's sake, do you talk this much all the time?" Diego's heart lifted. Warmed. What-the-fuck-ever. Was Healey even capable of subterfuge? The way his mouth ran on, Diego doubted it. Laughter bubbled up inside him.

Healey narrowed his eyes. "Um—"

"That was a rhetorical question." Diego rolled forward and gripped Healey by his belt buckle. "Stop."

"What?"

"Healey. I *trust* you." As soon as the words were out of Diego's mouth, he realized he meant every single one. He trusted Healey's motives and his kindness. He trusted his empathy. He could trust him as a lover, too, because Healey was simply... good. He was a *good* man. "I see you too, you know."

Healey's mouth opened, then he closed it again. "Yeah?"

"Yes." Diego imbued the word with finality.

Despite Diego's shy smile, Healey still didn't leave the safety of the wall. "What now?"

Diego gripped Healey's hands, willing him to pay attention. "Now you stop second-guessing. Because I know what's here, papi. I understand you. You understand me. Let's get this party started."

Diego jerked his head, indicating Healey should follow.

His bedroom was just down the hall.

CHAPTER THIRTY-SIX
DIEGO

Holy fuck. Round *three* was on the horizon.

Jesus. Diego gathered Healey into his arms, half-asleep, half-aroused. A minute ago Healey had seemed sated. Now he was rubbing little circles on Diego's back. Smiling lazily. Offering kisses that drew Diego in, teased him, tempted him to risk just a little more of himself—a little more of his privacy and his autonomy—with each interaction.

Healey, it seemed, risked everything, all the time.

He existed in a perpetual state of "all-in." Minutes ticked by while Healey dazzled him with shy kisses. Somehow, they wrestled into a not-too-uncomfortable position. Healey looked down at him, fingers on his good hand tweaking Diego's nipples, smoothing his armpits. Stroking his earlobes.

Oh. Who'd think that'd feel so awesome?

The spot on his ribs, just above the flat places he could no longer—

"Motherfucker." Diego gave a crazy laugh when the wave of pleasure hit him like a weirdly erotic hiccup. Or . . . no words for that sensation. None.

He let silken lethargy settle into his bones while Healey pushed against him. Their cocks rubbed together—Healey'd lubed up again, and he was being so careful.

It was hard to think with Healey close. He smelled so good.

"May I move your legs?"

Diego froze.

May I, instead of *can I.* So . . . polite. A well-brought-up boy, he'd asked nicely.

But the translation: *Can I position you like an inanimate object?*

Can I move the parts you cannot feel for my pleasure? Ohgodohgodohgod.

"Give me a sec," he said gruffly, calling time-out on the play.

Not because he wanted to halt Healey's forward motion. And definitely not because he couldn't say no. Diego called a time-out to double-check: *Is this what I want?*

Healey was too important to leave his feelings to chance. Being with Healey was a choice and that choice had consequences. If Diego said yes, it meant he was giving Healey his unqualified trust, and there would be no going back from that.

"Yes." *How easy was that?*

"Are you sure? I have your permission?"

"Revocable at any time," Diego qualified. "You understand?"

"Always." Healey's fierce gaze set off a depth charge of hope in Diego's chest. "Say the word."

"Yes." Diego wrapped one arm around Healey's neck and pulled him down. "Yes... Yes... Yes."

Healey slipped between Diego's legs, going so carefully he trembled—not with the effort of holding himself up, but of holding himself back from penetrating Diego instead of simulating it.

That had to be killing him.

"Wait," Diego said suddenly.

"What?" Healey's cock wilted between them.

"Jesus, you're literal. We could—" He gulped. "You could."

"What?" Healey asked again.

"Penetrate me." He glanced at the ceiling above Healey's head. Was that ceiling fan dusty?

"I thought that was like crossing the streams." The one thing you could say about Healey, he was responsive to changes in mood... "I thought we don't do that because Bad Things can happen."

"I like getting fucked." *Excruciating* to say those words. "But with a medical vibrator. Just—"

"Ah... Okay. I'll be careful." Healey traced his lips with little kisses. Dotted them over his face and chest. "And if at any point you decide it's not what you want, or whatever, no worries."

"Fuck off." He turned his suddenly too-hot face to the side. "I'm not made of glass."

That was how Diego let Healey inside him.

Inside his body.

Inside his heart.

Healey took his responsibility like a sacred obligation. He was so deliberate, Diego had to tell him to get on with it more than once.

Only two fingers to work him open. That was far enough. He gave Healey some lube and a condom-covered, remote-controlled vibrating device to slip inside him. He worked the controls while Healey used Diego's Frankencock to get himself off.

God, he wished he didn't have to think about sex.

Thinking about it made it matter-of-fact any way you looked at— *Oh.*

That was nice.

Whatever the vibrator was doing below, Healey hadn't let up with his good hand. He was brushing his thumb over Diego's nipples while he lifted himself on and off Diego's cock.

Ooh. Healey scraped his nail over Diego's nub just so—

"Oh. That, Mr. Wizard. Do *that*."

"Mmm." Healey used his teeth where his nail had been. The Force was strong with him. He learned well. And once Diego emptied his mind of all the reasons he couldn't do it, post-SCI-sex turned out to be almost like every other kind of sex he'd had. It was embarrassing and funny and silly and gruesome.

It was as easy as falling off another mountain bike—*boom!* He flew upside down again—this time figuratively. Floating, falling. They strained and crashed together. Dipped and spun and rose and fell. Fucked in whatever way made sense in the moment.

The vibrator added an elusive warmth—a rush so heady it left him gasping with laughter. God help him if Healey saw. There might have been a couple of unmanly tears.

Despite the antispasmodic meds, in the middle of everything, his jumpy goddamn legs took off on their own, going all Andreas Fault 8.0 earthquake, shaking the entire bed, rattling the chains like he was Frankenstein's Monster—all of which gave Healey a ride he'd probably never forget.

"Ah, Christ, I'm coming." Healey gasped. "Ah, shit. Wow."

And suddenly, the vibrator was no longer Diego's new best friend.

"Get it out." Aftershocks. Diego's entire upper body warmed so fast his vision grayed. "Get it out."

Healey removed the vibrator gently and laid it aside before shoving a pillow beneath Diego's head. "Problems? Autonomic dysreflexia? You said you had a T11, and I—"

"No. It wasn't that. I think—" Diego fell back, exhausted. "It was just too much stimulation."

Healey curled next to him. "What's it feel like?"

"The vibrator? I don't feel it." Diego shrugged. "I get a warmth, a rush. Imagine having a climax you can't feel. It still does all that heart racing, head spinning shit."

Dizzying, pleasurable sensations that made his whole body burn. Whatever chemicals had been dumped into his bloodstream gave him the post-fuck lassitude he remembered from before the accident. Like ripples crossing his skin, leaving him flushed and relieved, relaxed and ready for sleep.

For a change, he had no regrets.

None.

He even let Healey clean things up without complaining because if this was a thing—if they were going to do this thing—well . . .

Healey deserved "normal" sometimes too.

"You okay?" Healey's concern was touching. Embarrassing. Misguided. "I mean, that was wild, man. Does that leg thing happen often?"

"Sometimes." Diego gritted his teeth. "I'm fine."

"You don't always have to be so tough."

"It's not like I can turn it off." Diego shot him a wry grin. "I'm a tough hombre."

"But you feel good?" Healey's voice was mild. Pleasant. Not invasive. Just . . . right.

"Yeah," he sighed. "God, yeah."

His legs rattled a little more, so he repositioned them with a sigh.

"You look good." Healey traced a finger down Diego's nose, over his lips, into the space just underneath. "Can you grow a soul patch?"

"Yeah. I was thinking about it, actually."

"How about a little beard?"

"You'd like that?"

"A little scruff, maybe," Healey admitted before licking a long line up Diego's throat. "Yeah."

"I can forget to shave for a couple days. I'm on vacation. I'm not sure what it will look like. I don't grow a lot of facial hair."

Healey hesitated. "I'm on vacation too, so to speak. You want to go somewhere?"

"Like a road trip?" Healey nodded. "Where?"

"Down the coast? Across the border into Canada? I like Chicago. Kansas City. What floats your boat?"

Diego rolled himself to his side, facing Healey. "Don't you have doctor appointments and shit?"

"Yeah." Healey gave his shoulder a careful roll. "The cast comes off my arm in two weeks. And I'll probably need some therapy."

"Maybe we should wait until you're one hundred percent."

Healey's disappointment showed.

"What?"

"I don't want to wait." Healey rolled to his back, letting his head fall on the pillow. "But you're right. I feel like there's this huge pile of unfinished business hanging over me. I can't really begin anything again, I shouldn't start anything *new* until—"

"Ford." Diego said the word tightly, but that wasn't fair. Things were awkward. They were new together. They both had ghosts that needed exorcising.

Healey nodded slowly. "I need to see Ford one more time. I want to forgive him face-to-face. Say goodbye and wish him well. I have to. He won't talk to me on the phone. He may not even see me. But I can't move forward until I do."

Diego was silent for a long time. "Fair enough."

"Backup would be awesome. Not—not when I see him. But I don't know if I could face the trip alone."

"You're not alone. You have Nash. Your family."

Healey shook his head. "Not for this. They're too close. Too— angry on my behalf. They took everything between me and Ford too personally. It's not about that. I just have to speak my piece, and—"

Diego nodded. "Okay. I'll ride with you, if you want. I'm in."

Healey caught his hand and kissed it. "I appreciate that more than I can say."

"I need something from you, too."

"Yeah? Name it."

Diego paused. Goddamn it, he only had to ask. Why was that so hard?

He swallowed. "My stepfather is getting remarried on New Year's Eve. Will you come with me?"

"A wedding?" The tension left Healey's body. "Oh, Christ. The way you were acting, I thought it was going to be something like a class reunion or one of my kidneys. Of course I'll go."

Healey's whole body relaxed. Obviously he'd never been to a Luz family wedding. He was gonna look back on this moment.

Oh, yeah. He'd learn...

Diego wrapped both arms around him. Their eyes met again, Healey's blue ones were so full of warmth. God, Healey was sexy. Sinewy. His hair slithered over Diego's shoulders like he was some hipster saint, come to perform a miracle.

Diego strained against laughter, but then he said fuck it and let it go. Healey laughed with him like it was contagious.

So then they were kissing and laughing. Healey's chest hair scrubbed across his nipples. Their sweat-soaked skin stuck together, and Healey's beard stubble burned. Droplets of sweat snaked down Diego's skin—more flowing tendrils of new sensation.

For the second time, Diego forgot all the things he needed to remember.

Stupid, *stupid* to fall for a fearless boy.

Healey sighed. "You think you could get me a towel? No way am I leaving this bed right now."

"You think." Diego reached into the nightstand and grabbed a couple of wipes for him. "Here."

Healey's expression went from sated to serious. "Need me to go?"

"Not yet..." Diego rocked up, used momentum to drop his legs over the side of the bed, and transferred. "Let me be a decent host."

Reaching for a pillow, Healey subsided onto the mattress. "If you're sure."

"I'm not sure about anything anymore." Diego made his way to the bathroom to get towels, and on the way back, he opened the refrigerator and pulled out some water bottles.

Healey's eyes were on him the whole way, making him as self-conscious and tongue-tied as he had been the first time he brought a man home. That was back when he could carry a dude up several flights of stairs and throw him down and fuck him through the mattress.

That was back when he could give Healey what he needed.

"What's that face for?" Healey asked.

"Water and a towel." He handed them over. "Your majesty."

"Nuh-uh." Healey propped his head up on his hand. "You don't get to roll off and come back with an attitude. Come up here."

Still desperate to make a good impression, but as out of his element as a landed fish, Diego gripped the rings to pull himself onto the bed.

Healey drew in a quick breath. "That is my new favorite floor show."

Diego flushed. Okay. So, Healey admired his body. There was no mistaking that. Healey dug his muscles.

And he can barely take his eyes off my mouth.

Diego promised himself he wouldn't get caught up in how hot that was. Greedy eyes, looking at him like that. He didn't want to get too used to such a thing. He fell to the bed, allowing himself to be scooped up, folded into the sleepy embrace of a lover.

First time in years.

Felt like the first time *ever*.

Breathlessly, he examined the wonder of fate. The sheer cosmic coincidences that had to happen before he ran into Healey Holly. His accident, his change in careers, his mother's death, which led to settling in Bluewater Bay.

Ford's illness, his breakdown, the accident, everything that led Healey home.

No matter what, he wasn't about to block a play like that one. Not when all the forces of the universe seemed lined up to make it happen.

Whether Healey believed in that sort of thing or not.

CHAPTER THIRTY-SEVEN
HEALEY

Healey's eyes drifted open when the sun was high enough in the sky to crack through the mini blinds. Shafts of light arrowed across the floor while pale-yellow sunshine drizzled over the foot of the bed.

Diego's lashes lifted a second later, as if he knew Healey was wide-awake and watching him. He captured Healey's jaw, a smile ghosting over his lips. "Pretty boy." Diego blinked sleepily. "This isn't so bad."

"Ouch." Healey rubbed his nose to Diego's. "That's some faint, faint praise you got there."

"I meant waking up with you in my face." Diego shoved an errant pillow more securely under his head. "Last night was . . ."

Healey waited.

And waited some more . . .

"Off the charts?" he finally supplied. "Off the hook? Off the chain. Off the wall? Off-brand? Off-kilter? Offenbach? *Work* with me here."

Diego shot him a fond look. "You don't need your ego stroked. Want breakfast?"

"Sure." Healey thumbed Diego's barbell before giving it a kiss, after which he felt like a tool.

Diego smirked. "You really dig that piercing, huh?"

"I do."

Diego's expression turned calculating. "You pierce something, if you like it so much."

"Oh. So that's how it's going to be?" Diego's challenge made Healey purr. He was not averse to the idea of piercings. "What'd you have in mind?"

Diego let his gaze drift over Healey's body. It was a hungry perusal. A shockingly intimate one. He pinched one of Healey's nipples.

Healey grunted with pleasure. "I could do that."

"Really?"

"I'm in." He already had morning wood, and now it throbbed with longing. "Anything else?"

Diego's big hand cupped Healey's balls. Rubbed his taint. "I'm sure I'll think of something."

"You're going to kill me." And what a way to go.

Without giving permission a single thought, he ran his hand down Diego's side and over his hip. A gentle nudge made Diego's knee fall forward.

For a second they both stared at it. Then Healey reached out to put it back, and Diego stopped his hand. "No."

While Diego put it back, Healey pulled away with an awkward groan. "Sorry."

"Naw. Shit." *Eye roll.* "Nothing's off-limits. I'm—"

"You said the word *no*, okay? It's fine. It's all good."

Diego's nose-wrinkle was . . . out of character and cute. "I'm still getting used to this."

"I understand."

"I'm glad. Because I don't." Diego used momentum to bring himself upright. Then he swung his legs over the side.

Healey couldn't read his expression. "Which bathroom do you want me to use?"

"Use this one. It's fine." Diego focused his gaze on some point over Healey's shoulder.

Sensing another potential landmine, Healey took his time getting out of bed. "Okay."

"I'm going to just—" Diego transferred himself to his chair "—do my thing. Don't mind me. I'll be done when I'm done."

Now, Healey understood.

The access Diego granted him was unprecedented. His heart read it as acceptance. As a step forward. As a relationship milestone.

At the same time, Diego didn't need to prove anything to him.

"If you're more comfortable, I'm happy to give you privacy."

Diego's fingers drummed. "I didn't give a shit about privacy before this happened to me. That's the thing."

Healey took a frank look at Diego's body. "It's not like you've got anything to be ashamed of."

"It's not anything like shame." Diego squinted as if he were trying to see through the floor. "Half of my body divorced me, and now I'm like some weekend dad, only my kid is a surly teen motherfucker I have to reacquaint myself with every time I spend time with him. I don't really know or understand him anymore. I can't control him. Can't get him to do what I want. But I still have to drag him around with me wherever I go. I can't explain how I feel any better than that."

"Using that analogy, you love this kid. Right?"

"I'm too tired for my Mensa test today," Diego bitched.

Healey wished he could do better too. A better boyfriend might know what to say to make things easier. In this instance, he didn't trust himself to react without more data.

"I don't know what you need." He gave Diego his game face. "But whatever it is—privacy, an extra hand, a jet pack ... whatever—I'm in. As long as you tell me. I'm sorta smart. Not psychic."

Diego's eyes widened. "I can have a *jet pack*?"

"Not like you think." Healey smiled at a memory. "Shelby used to play field hockey with a leaf blower in a pack on the back of her wheelchair. Her friends took turns pushing her while she mastered ball-handling. The only problem was games got called on account of limited battery power. Weight issues."

"Oh, batteries. That was your mistake. Those things are shit."

"*Di-AY-go*." Healey chided in Shelby's voice. "We are not monsters. We don't strap a gas-powered *engine* on the back of a little girl."

Diego pouted. "It's not a real jet pack, then."

"No, but it was awesome. You had to aim the air stream just so, and the ball would go flying, and then they'd all take after it like little brightly colored penguins. The other players used their sticks, and Shelby'd blow. *Whooosh*."

"I could get behind that." Diego nodded. "If only for yard waste."

"Anyone can get a leaf blower, man. This was a full-on Ghostbusters-style backpack with sound and blinking lights and a laser sight." He picked his phone off the nightstand. "I'm going to get it for you . . . Let me text Nash right now and see if it's at the garage still . . . There's no way Pop got rid of that. It was—"

"Oh, shit."

"What is it?"

"New message from Ford. 'Get a lawyer. Watch your back.'" Healey swallowed. "Okay. There's nothing scary about that at all."

"Let me text my stepdad. You know he's a lawyer, right?" Diego picked up his cell and started typing, but before he got very far, he hesitated. "If you want, I mean. I don't want to overstep. But if anyone will know if something is actionable—"

"Sure." Stunned, Healey thumbed a quick reply to Ford. He got an autoresponse in return. No end date. Just, *I have no connectivity. I don't know when I'll be back. If you need something, please refer to my family.*

Was anything Ford said even true? Or was this lawsuit some nebulous idea that had Ford's anxiety ratcheting up for nothing? Was it because of the meds? His dreams, his paranoia?

Had Ford worried and chewed on and fretted over the consequences of the accident until he believed he ought to warn Healey to make plans to deal with it? Until it had become so frightening and real that he'd felt the need to act on his fears? Because that had happened before, over tests and taxes. Over imagined slights from neighbors.

How *real* was the problem?

Healey never knew. The hardest thing he'd ever done was accept the fact that Ford's reality was suspect. That even with a terrific mind like his, he could still get things terribly, horribly wrong.

Diego asked, "Have you gotten anything from these people who are supposed to be suing you?"

"No. But I'm not sure anyone knows where I am."

"Believe me, they could find out in minutes. You aren't trying to hide anything. You've used your credit cards, your cell phone." He gave the smartphone clutched in Healey's hand a little poke to prove his point. "Plus Spencer's Twitter feed has hinted at your location at least once because of Nash."

"You've been cyber-stalking me?"

"Maybe." Guys didn't really do that did they? It was . . . boyish. Earnest. Endearing. It was another nail in the lid of Healey's heart-coffin, slamming down. Putting an end to the two of them being some temporary fling...

"My life is going to be a circus," he confessed.

"I always wanted to join the circus." Diego's mouth softened into an almost-smile, but his fingers tapped. Healey looked pointedly at them. Diego stopped, shook his nervous hands in the air, and then folded them in his lap. "Obviously, I'm crap on the high wire. But I can function as a pretty good net."

Almost too touched to speak, Healey nodded. "I'll hold you to that."

"I should . . ." Diego jerked his head toward the toilet. "I'm going to need coffee and some kind of food after all the bio-medical engineering."

"All right. I'll be in the kitchen figuring it out." Healey caught Diego's hand before he could leave. "Thanks. I mean that."

"Sure." Diego's expression warmed Healey right up. "Don't forget. We have a date to get your nipples pierced."

Healey nuzzled into the skin behind Diego's ear. "I am counting the hours."

In the kitchen, Healey discovered a refrigerator stocked with fresh food. Some spices in the cupboard. Bread. He began breaking eggs into a bowl he found, enjoying the clean workspace and the homey chore of cooking for Diego for a change.

His gaze fell on the picture of Diego and his mother. If it was just the two of them, Diego had probably learned his way around the kitchen at a young age.

In point of fact, both Healey and Nash had learned to feed themselves and Shelby while their dad had worked long hours at the garage. Their single-parent household made being tough and independent a necessity.

Ford had grown up with a stay-at-home mother who'd nevertheless employed a string of nannies and housekeepers. But Ford was strong and stubborn, and he'd been independent by nature, not necessity.

A self-described control freak, Ford took losing control over his emotions as the ultimate betrayal. There was a metaphorical parallel between Diego's divorce-from-his-body and Ford's wayward brain chemistry. It was as if Ford's rational mind took off on him, like a cheating spouse—it was worse than a divorce, really, because when Ford's rational mind came back, he had to deal with the fallout from the wreckage his absence left behind.

Nobody liked to lose control.

Healey'd lived in Ford's invisible fun house for a long time. He couldn't see the things that made Ford so angry or sad or frightened, but the emotions were tangible—as real as the wheelchair Diego sat in. Healey'd wanted to be with Ford. And now he wanted to be with Diego.

So what did that say about him that from the moment of Ford's diagnosis, he'd lost faith they'd stay together.

Was he a quitter? Or disloyal?

Had he given up too soon? Given Ford even more reason to distrust?

He heated up a pan before putting some bread into the four-slice toaster. Four slices? *Boy must like him some toast.* He went back to scrambling eggs. Thoughts of Ford—memories—some good, some bad, flooded back.

A squeak on the wooden floor made him turn. Diego, fresh from a quick shower, had rolled in and was watching, waiting while he stood there, *not* stirring a bowl of raw eggs.

How long had he been standing there?

"Cecil's the man—he's got connections everywhere. He's going to help. He'll try to get you in to see Ford. Is that what you want?"

Healey wished he didn't. The caution on Diego's face—the almost wounded resignation—hurt him too.

"Yes," he said. "It's probably not the best idea. But I want that very much."

CHAPTER THIRTY-EIGHT
HEALEY

Later in the day, as Diego negotiated the terrain leading to Fjóla's place, Healey was struck again by how much thought went in to using a chair. The chair was why Nash had lost his shit when Shelby announced she wanted a year abroad. She had to plan a strategy for getting from place to place well ahead, anywhere she went. She could get stuck, get tipped, get injured. It made them all sick to think about it.

Still, they had to stand by and watch and wait. They couldn't help because that took something fundamental away from Shelby, something wholly personal and profound and essential. And it was fucking hard.

As with Shelby, Healey wanted to be mindful of these things. He had to let people do things for themselves or accept the sometimes salty consequences. Healey went up the path and rang the bell. By the time his pop answered the door, Diego'd caught up with him.

"Hey." Pop's wide grin made him feel ten years old again. "Welcome. We were just making popcorn. Come on in."

He held the door open as first Diego and then Healey entered.

"Come on back. Nash and I are going to watch a movie."

Healey got a glimpse of the screen. "*Airplane?*"

Pop nodded. "It's still Nash's favorite."

"Whatta surprise." Healey gave Fjóla a kiss on the cheek. "Hi, pretty lady."

Fjóla pinked up. "Flatterer."

"It would only be flattery," said Diego, "if it wasn't true. Hey, you."

She came over and hugged him tightly. "So good to see you again, Diego."

"You've met?" Pop asked.

"I was hired to work with the actors." Fjóla nodded. "But the *Wolf's Landing* production crew has been a pet project of mine. Meditation and yoga are magic for stress."

"She suggested Adaptive Yoga for me," said Diego. "It's a lot harder than you'd think it would be."

"Your upper body is very strong. Yoga can be part of the program to help you keep it that way."

Healey tried to keep his face blank, but lost control when his brother turned a knowing gaze his way. He returned the look with a quirk of his brow.

"Captain America would kill for Diego's chest," Healey boasted. "Just sayin.'"

Diego threw a self-satisfied smirk his way.

"I came because I need to tell you guys something. It looks like there are going to be lawsuits involving my accident. I'm named as a defendant—"

"So they plan to blame you?" Nash's outrage was palpable. "To make it your fault that—"

"I don't think that's the case," Diego offered calmly. "My stepdad, Cecil, will get in contact with Ford's family's lawyers to let them know he's representing Healey. When I talked to him about it, he didn't seem all that concerned. It's standard to cast a big-ass net in these situations. It puts pressure on everyone. Whoever blinks first, settles."

Pop sat heavily. "Is this because of the accident? Or because of Ford?" He caught it when Healey and Diego exchanged glances. "What is it?"

"It was Ford who let me know about the lawsuit—"

"*Ford's* suing you?"

"No. I only mean—" Healey shook his head. "I don't know for sure if anyone is suing me. I don't know anything but what Ford told me."

Pop made a distracted, disbelieving sound.

"Ace. What can we do?" Fjóla joined them. "There must be something."

"I hate this." Pop sighed. "Ford is such a decent kid. He's got a real good heart. It's tough to be that smart, you know? Not that I'd know or—"

Fjóla kissed the rest of his words away.

Healey studied his pop, wondering again if the resemblance between them went deeper than simple looks. No doubt his pop's thoughts ran along similar lines.

"You know..." Pop looked at his hands. His glasses were perched in his wavy silver hair, which, wow, was way too long. "I wasn't a very good role model."

Nash frowned. "Knock that off."

"You worked hard for your family," Fjóla said gently. "Your children grew up knowing they were loved. You seem like a wonderful father to me. A good man."

Pop reddened. "Maybe you're a little bit prejudiced, huh?"

"All the way prejudiced." Her warmth suffused the very air. "Go Team Ace! It's such a shame about Ford though. Is he in terrible trouble?"

"Yes. I think he might be. On the positive side of the ledger," Diego offered, "Ford's health will be re-evaluated, and possibly, he'll get better treatment in a residential program."

Healey had heard that before. "Another round of pharmacological roulette."

"Slow down, science boy," Diego teased. "I thought you were a believer."

"In gravity. Not Big Pharma. You couldn't pay me to break bread with those jackals. Not since my EpiPen went over a thousand bucks."

"You're allergic to something?" he asked seriously.

"Bees." Healey nodded. "And amoxicillin."

"How oddly specific." Diego took out his phone. "I guess I should make a note, if we're hitting the road together"

"You're going somewhere?" Ace asked.

"We're thinking about a road trip," Healey answered for both of them. "I'm ready to take a break. See some sights. Diego's not working right now. We thought it would be fun."

Diego put his phone away with a wink. "I don't know, man. There are bees everywhere."

"Fewer and fewer every year." Pop's forehead wrinkled like he was getting one of his ideas. "I'd like to try beekeeping—it's been a lifelong ambition of mine. I wonder if there's a way to do it here?"

"In Bluewater Bay?" asked Nash.

"In my backyard?" Fjóla stopped with a handful of popcorn halfway to her mouth.

"But I'm allergic," Healey said.

Pop glanced between Healey and then at Diego. "You should both keep EpiPens on you at all times if Healey's going to be around bees. Last time, he just got hives all over his upper body, but they said the reaction can increase, and there's no way to know what the effect will be next time."

"Probably best not to borrow trouble." Fjóla's fond expression included all of them. "Popcorn?"

Nash blanched and turned to Healey. "I'm warning you now. There are anchovies in there."

"In the popcorn?" Diego asked, incredulously.

With a defiant glance Nash's way, Fjóla passed Diego the bowl.

Diego gave the popcorn a look, and with a what-the-hell gesture, he took one of the red-plastic cups off the coffee table to scoop some out. Everyone stared while he tasted the anchovy-laced snack.

"I didn't see that flavor coming," he said finally. "I can't tell if I actually like it, or if my taste buds have finally given up on me."

"You might or might not like it?" Fjóla asked. "Not inspiring praise."

Healey shot Diego a pointed look. "There seems to be a lot of that going around."

Diego jerked his head toward the seat next to his wheelchair, and Healey scooted into it. A fond smile creased his lips as he leaned forward to whisper in Healey's ear. "You know what's what."

Exchanging another look, this one full of promise, Healey shifted so their shoulders touched. Fjóla brought tall, cold glasses of iced green tea for everyone before starting the movie. Nash belly-laughed at all the well-worn but crude jokes while they took turns with the dialogue.

"You guys have this memorized?" Diego asked.

Pop didn't take his eyes off the screen. "I can neither confirm nor deny."

Diego whispered, "I see exactly how you got so . . . you."

Nash winked at Healey. "*I* am taking that as a compliment."

Healey watched his brother's occasional sly glances at his phone. Somewhere Spencer was out there missing Nash. Texting him. Healey was lucky Nash was the kind of brother to drop everything for family, but he didn't want Nash to spend all his time stamping out the little bonfires in everyone else's life at some unknown cost to his own.

At some point, Nash ought to have a life too.

Nash read him like the phone book, reaching out with one sneaker-clad foot to give Healey's ankle a sharp kick.

"Don't overthink."

Healey sighed. Shot a look Diego's way and found warm brown eyes regarding him thoughtfully.

"You okay?"

"Sure." Healey nodded, eyes growing heavy. His head lolled and he drifted off.

When Diego's phone gave a loud squawk, he woke again.

The film was over. Fjóla and Pop were no longer in the room. A glance at the clock on the wall said it was almost suppertime.

From farther away, productive cooking noises came from Fjóla's sleek, small kitchen.

"Have a nice nap there, sunshine?" Nash asked.

Healey blinked. "Must have been more tired than I thought."

"My stepdad sent a text," Diego murmured. "He wants us to come down."

"So there's something to what Ford said?" Healey asked.

"From what I understand, Ford's lawyers want to depose you, preemptively."

Nash sat forward. "What does that mean, 'preemptively'?"

"They want to find out what Healey will say if this goes to court in a civil trial."

"I'm going to tell the truth." Healey's eyes stung. "What else would I say?"

Diego hesitated before saying, "One of the men from the truck chasing you suffered a traumatic brain injury. He's still in a coma. Did you know that?"

He was going to be sick. "I—I haven't followed the news to find out their condition, no. They terrorized us for thirty miles at high speeds. Can I get a glass of water?"

"I have pop, will this do?" Diego handed him his can.

Healey drank gratefully.

"Do we have to do this right now?" Healey asked.

"Ford terrorized you inside the car. If you don't talk about that—"

"First I've heard of this," said Nash. "What the fuck, man? What the hell happened that night?"

"I'll talk when I'm supposed to." He glared at Diego, who merely shrugged.

"Your family is probably exempt from the gag order."

"Never mind that gag shit," said Nash. "What is Diego talking about?"

Healey hesitated before admitting, "Ford wouldn't stop when I asked. Wouldn't let me call the police. It's over, yeah?"

"What do you mean he wouldn't let you call?" Nash visibly tensed. "How could he stop you?"

"He threw my phone out the window, okay?"

If Nash'd seemed shocked before, now he was furious. "Christ. *Heals*."

"I see where your mind is going with this. It's not—"

"That makes you some kind of hostage. Did you ask him to let you out?"

"Gee, no. I guess I didn't think of it during the eighty-mile-an-hour car chase we were having with rednecks out to beat us into mochi."

Nash blew like an angry cartoon bull. "I'm going to ignore your sarcasm in favor of—"

"Rational discourse?" Healey asked. "Since when can you even manage such a thing without jumping to—"

"*I'm* jumping to conclusions?" Nash thumped his chest. "Because I have new information you did not—"

"*I* didn't see fit to share it because I knew you'd act like this."

"Whoa." Diego mimed *cut*. "Twin powers, de-activate. One person finishes his own sentence. Then the other one speaks. That's how it's done."

Pop stood in the doorway, looking at all three of them with benign affability. He sighed. "It's the first act of the screaming twin show. I know it by heart."

"How does it end?" Diego asked. "Should we check for dueling pistols and remove any sharp knives?"

"It's a three-act play." Pop's eyes lit with amusement. "In the first act they try to kill each other. In the second, they shift responsibility for any unfinished chores, and in the third act, they unite as a terrifying single entity to kill their common enemies. The end."

"Happily ever after." Healey said the words, but Nash initiated the fist bump.

Boom. Exploding fingers.

"This is fascinating," said Diego. "Mami was my only blood relation. Is it always like that?"

"Twins may have something special." Pop moved the empty popcorn bowl and sat on the edge of the coffee table, opposite. "These two share a brain."

"I only have stepsiblings." He turned to them. "You guys are echoes of your pop. Alike—both in looks and temperament, from what I can tell. It's really interesting. Can I bring my camera over sometime? Take some portraits of the three of you?"

Pop lifted a shoulder. "Fine with me."

From the kitchen Fjóla called, "I would love copies, if it's not too much trouble."

Nash nodded and Healey took Diego's hand.

"I like being the center of your attention," he told him.

Nash flipped his brother off. "You are an attention *whore*."

"I know you are, but what am I?" Healey cranked up his middle finger. "Creak, creak, creak, creak."

"Nash has a point." Diego smiled softly. "Somehow, Healey always gets my attention."

"Can I get some help carrying?" said Fjóla.

"Hold that thought. I'll *earn* your attention later." Healey said the words for Diego's ears alone. He was so busy looking into Diego's eyes, moving in for a kiss, actively stealing Diego's breath to seal the deal—it wasn't until he glanced up that he realized his pop and Nash had left the room. "I'll be back in a minute."

Diego caught his hand. "Cecil wants us to come down in the morning. Friend of a friend has a corporate jet heading his way. We can catch a ride."

"Wow. Really? That's kind of overkill, isn't it?"

"It's empty. En route to pick up clients. And I'm sure there's some kind of back scratching involved. Nobody does shit for free."

"But—"

"I've flown in it." Diego laughed. "It's awesome, if that's—"

"But tomorrow? That's really quick."

Diego's eyes narrowed. "I'm sorry. I thought you were worried. Wanted closure. If it's too soon—"

"I didn't say that, exactly." But now that it was real, Healey wasn't ready.

"If we go, you can talk things over with Cecil. He'll be straight with you. Tell you what's likely to happen." Diego smoothed the worried lines between Healey's eyebrows. "He'll tell you everything you have to be worried about."

"Oh, no. No, no, no." Healey's gut clenched hard. "I don't think I can do that." Already his skin prickled with the sting of anxious sweat.

"Hey." Diego's soda-pop breath gusted over Healey's cheek as he came in for a tender kiss. "You okay?"

"I wish."

"You want me to call Cecil? Tell him forget it?" His expression softened. "It's okay. You can fly commercial any time. There's no pressure."

Healey closed his eyes. He had to find out exactly how much trouble he was in and he dreaded it. He also dreaded seeing Ford.

Oh my God. Ford.

How could he face Ford? Had he really been single when he met Diego? Nominally, via Facebook, he was single. Technically they'd broken up, in person, before that awful night. In reality they'd been drifting apart for more than a year before that. Why was it so hard to wake up without Ford's head on the pillow next to his? Why did the scent of Thai food and weed still catch him on the raw? Make him long for things with soul-deep, full-body yearning, that he had barely tolerated while he had them.

The accident had been far worse—physically—for Healey than for Ford. He'd been in the hospital when Ford's family had taken him away. No one had answered his calls except Beryl, and she'd given him no reason to think he and Ford would ever be together again. Quite the opposite. She'd told him to move on.

But he'd fucked Diego without getting his own post-accident closure *with Ford*. Without saying, *Be well*, and without offering real forgiveness, and after so many years—after all they'd been through—Ford deserved better from him than that.

But the gun. Oh my God. That fucking gun.

Healey shivered despite the warmth of Fjóla's homey living room. He could not forgive that gun.

It would have been a deal breaker for Healey, if he'd known of its existence. Not because he had any particular hatred of guns, but he had a healthy skepticism about people with mental illness and impulse control problems owning them. And he had certainly not known, not until he'd first seen the Baby Glock in Ford's hand, that Ford would ever be able to obtain one...

In that moment, Ford had been...someone else. Someone Healey didn't know and didn't trust and didn't like. The gun changed Ford's DNA in a way Ford's hypersexuality, depression, anxiety, and even his flashpoint temper and the violent rage that came with it had not.

Healey would not be a party to the kind of tragedy a gun could add to their lives.

Ford knew his stance on handguns, and still, Ford'd managed not only to get hold of one, but to turn it on *him*...*Me*.

The gun was a declaration of war.

Dizziness. Burning sweat. Ice-cold hands.

I can't catch my breath.

"What?" Diego asked.

Healey shook his head. He couldn't form the words.

Ford looked you right in the eye and threatened you with a handgun Was it loaded? Was the safety on? How real was that threat?

"I can't."

No. No. No. No.

Their pop had taught them to treat *every* gun as if it was ready to fire.

He pointed it at you.

You could be gone now. A ghost.

Nash could be mourning your passing.
With a sigh, he made up his mind.
"All right. I'll go. Thank you."

CHAPTER THIRTY-NINE
DIEGO

Not-quite rain freckled the shoulders of Diego's peacoat as two good-looking bodybuilder types carried him up the boarding stairs.

It was done matter-of-factly. Over in mere seconds. One gripped the arms of his chair and the other the wheels.

Together they made short work of a complication Diego dreaded every time he flew. Healey had offered a piggyback ride. Now he wondered if that wouldn't have been (a) way more fun, and (b) less undignified.

On the tarmac, Healey snickered behind his back.

Healey didn't have a mean bone in his body, but his funny bone seemed tuned to the key of awkward—being carried was awkward as hell. Bastard.

"If you tell anyone we know about this, I will end you," Diego shouted. Narrow plane plus wheelchair equaled hot mess. Once he'd gotten himself comfortable in one of the attractive white leather seats, he nodded that it was fine for Healey to board.

Healey sauntered up the stairs wearing a tan trench coat over a suit and tie. He carried a leather messenger bag. This was professional Healey. Not date Healey, or busted-all-to-hell Healey.

This was Healey as his peers saw him.

This Healey made Diego's knees go weak, the irony of which was not lost on him.

He glanced around, eyes lighting on the third passenger with some surprise, because apparently, there was a third passenger after all.

In fact, he . . . she . . . What did it matter with cats? Turned out to be the reason the plane was flying to Los Angeles in the first place.

"Jesus Christ, what the fuck is that?" Healey gasped.

Diego, who had already given their cabin mate the once-over, laughed. "It's a cat."

"That's . . . a cat?" Healey gave a grimace.

"Yep." Lashed to one of the seats in case of turbulence, a tiny gray inside-out monster with bat ears peered malevolently from behind the mesh of a sparkly white cat carrier.

"It's still young, but yeah." Diego leaned over to get another look. "Someone apparently needs their Egyptian Sphynx kitten in Los Angeles, stat."

"Someone is flying a cat. In a private jet." Healey glared doubtfully. "On purpose."

That was not a question, but Diego answered. "Yup." He glanced out the window, embarrassed to be part of such a thing. "People do."

"I didn't grow up with money," said Healey, "but it's not like Pop's doing too shabby now. Ford's family has legacy wealth. This . . .?"

Diego waited.

"*This* is why people should eat the rich."

"Says the Stanford PhD. I know what your education cost."

"And in terms of return on investment, the work I'll be doing will help save our planet. What's green energy worth to you? A couple hairless cats? A private jet? We have to start asking ourselves: what am I willing to *give up* in order for the species to survive?"

"Okay, wow. Not my plane. Not my cat." Diego waved his hands helplessly. "But you're hot when you talk green energy."

Healey flushed.

"This jet was flying, with or without us. This little kitty—" he grinned at the thing "—has to get to LA. So . . ."

"Hello, gentlemen, and welcome aboard."

The attendant's warm smile was well-practiced but appeared sincere. She had blonde hair in a neat coronet of braids. A thin nose with a bump, like Meryl Streep. She was just as sleek and elegant as the jet itself. Diego had never met her before, but it'd been almost a full year since he'd last hitched a ride on this particular aircraft.

"I'm Olivia. Can I get you anything to drink while you're waiting for lunch?"

Healey looked to him before asking, "There's lunch?"

"Since you're traveling with us today, I brought supplies. I can offer bruschetta topped with an heirloom caprese salad featuring fresh buffalo mozzarella as an appetizer, and your choice of grilled skate or peppercorn steak for your entrée. Garlic smashed new potatoes and caramelized Brussels sprouts. Sound all right?"

"Mm-hmm." Healey's lips compressed. With laughter? Or horror. Or some unseemly combination of both?

"Which sounds good to you today?"

"We'll have the steak," said Diego. The woman had to be a first rate chef to work aboard this aircraft. The owner—a production company executive whose last sitcom had garnered a planeload of Emmys—was known to be a gourmet cook himself.

And okay. Sure. It was *ridiculous*. But getting a ride on one of Cecil's client's planes—when he could—made traveling so much easier. Asking yourself if you should do something like that when it was on offer—whether taking advantage of someone else's excessive lifestyle was morally and ethically right—was like asking if you wanted a pain reliever that worked.

Of course he was going to take advantage.

"Mr. Luz, your stepfather is a favorite passenger of mine. I always bring the Alquimia Reserva on board for him. Would you care to try it?"

Diego turned to Healey. "Say yes. It's my favorite tequila. Aged three years. I can only have a thimbleful, because of my meds. But that shit's off the hook."

"You'll enjoy it," Olivia coaxed Healey. "It has notes of cinnamon and spices and a lovely fruity finish."

Healey eyed her. "Everyone knows I dig a lovely fruity finish."

Olivia smiled prettily. "You will enjoy it. I'll bring it and let you settle in here before we secure the cabin. We'll have permission to taxi in no time. Back in a moment."

The cat took that opportunity to give a screeching meow.

Olivia turned toward the carrier. "I haven't forgotten you, Asphodel. I have the skate, grilled to order, and steamed liver dumplings."

The cat appeared unmollified. It narrowed its eyes at all of them and hissed.

When Olivia left, Healey leaned toward Diego to whisper. "I am now *positive* this is an episode of *American Horror Story*."

"Funny you should mention that show." Diego had shared this very jet with one of the *AHS* cast members, the last time he'd flown.

An hour later, Healey had reclined his seat and put his feet up. He now sipped his second cut-crystal glass of the pricy tequila. He was obviously feeling it. He looked relaxed and happy.

Luxury looked good on Healey. Diego said something to that effect.

"Oh God. See? *This* is the problem with indecent wealth." Healey sat up guiltily. "You get used to it so quickly. It's addictive... How will I ever fly Southwest again, now that I know?"

Diego laughed. "You're drunk."

Healey gave a just-shy-of-sloppy grin. "This *delicious* tequila does seem a little strong."

Diego checked his email. "Message from Cecil. Everything is all set. You'll meet with Ford this afternoon. Cecil is sending a car."

Healey rubbed at his beard shadow before setting his glass down with an audible *clack*. "I don't know."

Diego frowned. "Changed your mind?"

"Honestly? Whenever I think about it? I get this sick dread in the pit of my stomach." He covered his gut protectively to illustrate. "My senses go on high alert. Even my skin prickles. That's not normal, is it?"

"That's anxiety."

"Yes." Healey yanked the pin from his too-long hair and raked his hand through it. The sight of him with those French cuffs lifted to his head, cuff links winking in the overhead lighting...

The scruffy, half-dead bastard who'd shown up on his doorstep turned out to be a seriously hot motherfucker. Everything, the suit, the plane, the fancy clothes, Healey's full lips and arctic blue eyes...

Everything turned this moment into Diego's favorite type of porn. He could only stare.

"What?"

"Olivia," Diego called out.

She peered around the bulkhead. "What can I get for you, sir?"

"Do you think it's possible we could have complete privacy for about ten minutes?"

"Certainly, sir. Just press the call button if you need anything."

Olivia was far too experienced and professional to react to his request with anything more than hauteur.

Diego nodded. "I think I have this particular thing covered."

She gave him a small smile before retreating.

"Are you kidding me right now?" Healey asked.

"Stand up."

"Um. Air turbulence..."

"I'll be gentle." Diego crooked his finger.

"I don't know if I should take the chance." But he stood, leaning precariously before making his way to Diego's seat. "I don't want to get my dick torn off."

"I don't want to hold it. I want to suck it."

"Okay. Wow." Healey shivered. "YOLO, whatever."

Diego repositioned his legs and pulled Healey closer. He took Healey's hands and placed them on his shoulders before unfastening his belt buckle, which was slim this time. Silver and elegant. The fabric of Healey's trousers felt great to his touch.

"What can I do?" Healey asked.

Diego met his slightly off-kilter gaze. "I've got this, honey. You can just remain in the upright and locked position until I bring you in for a landing."

"A-*ha*." Healey squeaked when Diego took his zipper down and mouthed his balls through his briefs. "I'm never flying commercial again."

"That's how it starts." Diego sucked in a deep lungful of warm moist air. "Christ, you smell good."

Healey's briefs were very brief. The head of his cock surged above his waistband while Diego nibbled the fat column of his dick. God, he wanted that cock in the worst way. Wanted it every way. He was done feeling crappy about sex. Done thinking all the good stuff was in his past.

This is the good stuff. This. *Right now.*

His dick didn't care, but the rest of his senses were still perfectly fine. Healey was beautiful. Diego loved his man-scent. His crisp pubic hair fairly crackled beneath Diego's fingers. He tasted of salt and sweat and the sweetness that simply oozed from him.

The rumble of Healey's voice sent shivers down his back.

When he gripped Healey's hips, excitement made his fingers tremble. Not precisely from sexual arousal, but Diego couldn't discern between the arousal and excitement anymore. He *wanted* Healey. Wanted to suck him, fuck him. Mark him.

He leaned over and did just that, pulling up a bruise in the hollow of Healey's hip. Healey hissed, either with pain or passion.

When Diego had no breath left, he thumbed the mark. Healey's hand came up to increase the pressure. He liked things a little rough, he'd said, and he proved it then.

"I love that, baby," Healey urged. "Use your teeth."

Diego licked and bit. He regressed, turning Healey around and going caveman on his pert ass. *Smack*!

Healey groaned. Someone definitely liked that.

Almost frenzied, Diego left a cluster of slight pink bite marks and fingerprints on his pale, faintly freckled skin. So fucking pretty. Warm to the touch.

Next time he'd use his mouth and his tongue and his Frankencock Monster until that sweet pink hole was goddamn full...

Healey turned and gripped Diego's head between his hands. Desperation looked good on him. Diego wrapped his lips around Healey's dick and sucked him in. Moving slowly at first, he savored each stroke of his tongue over the slick, lumpy-veined, gorgeous length. He went down on Healey with reverence. With precision, and passion, and awe.

He needed this. Needed to suck and slurp and worship this cock. He needed the moans and sobs, and that final sweet burst of seed that filled his mouth.

Healey cried out.

Diego pulled Healey into his arms. Enfolded and held him. As much as he'd ever need an orgasm, he needed to redefine what it meant to be a whole, human man.

Now he could see without question, without ego or artifice or pride. He was a man. He was the man who made Healey Holly *burst*, and gasp, and sigh. His sexual reality had changed, but it wasn't over.

It was only different. He could have a man in his life, in his heart, in his bed, and he wanted that man to be Healey Holly.

Healey ran questing fingers over his lips. "Something funny?"

Diego shook his head, too moved to speak.

Healey's fingers continued to explore—his chin, his neck, the hollow of his throat. Lips followed.

Blue eyes, half-dazed, fluttered open. "So fucking good, Diego."

"See?" Diego swallowed past the thickness in his throat. "No turbulence."

"You don't think so?" Healey's gaze found his.

"Let's make you respectable."

Healey smiled. "Good luck with that."

It wasn't easy putting Healey's clothes to rights, considering Healey kept trying to crawl inside Diego's skin while he did it.

"Does wearing a suit make you more affectionate?"

"I don't know." Healey used his hair to tickle Diego's shoulder. "Does it?"

"Knock it off," Diego teased. "Olivia will be back any minute with food."

Cheeks pink, eyes shining, lips full and moist from Diego's kisses, Healey stood before nearly falling back into his own seat.

"You are something else." Diego didn't know what, but it didn't matter.

Healey was his.

CHAPTER FORTY
HEALEY

Since 1972, the sign said, *Gladstones has been serving the freshest fish in Malibu.* The restaurant was right on the beach.

Diego wanted to wait in the restaurant's bar while Cecil's driver Cameron took Healey up the Pacific Coast Highway to see Ford at the Nautilus Center.

"No offense," he'd said. "But I'd rather have something to look at for an hour than the back of Cameron's head."

It was late afternoon when they pulled away from the restaurant's parking lot. Healey's last view of Diego—sitting backlit against the Pacific, wind playing with his slightly stubborn hair, lingered. It anchored him.

Fog crept onto the land. The atmosphere was exactly right, emotionally—as if someone from *Wolf's Landing* had scripted the scene. At sunset, the fog-shrouded coast would appear gone completely.

Healey shivered. Sometimes things he had to do were hard. He had no idea what to expect, and for someone like him . . . maybe that was the worst thing. If you couldn't plan, you couldn't prepare. You couldn't protect yourself from wrong answers, bad calculations, and failure. Most people who knew him, figured him for a happy go lucky-type, like his pop.

And he was. But he'd been through tragic things and terrifying things, too. And his way of coping was to learn everything he could about every problem ahead of time, coupled with the certain knowledge he was smart enough to figure out solutions. When he didn't know going in what was going to happen, that's when things fell apart for him.

At last he found himself outside the very expensive, very private residential treatment center where Ford waited for his trial. Healey braced himself for whatever he'd find.

But first, he had to pass through a level of security he'd rarely seen before—one that, in key areas, featured fingerprint identification and ballistic glass.

Outside the steel and glass building, tree-shrouded gardens fielded enough greenery to camouflage its primary function—rehab for celebrities suffering from all manner of "work-related exhaustion."

Inside, the building looked like the campus of any post-millennial dot com business, but without the aura of productivity. It was possible those companies took their cues from forward-thinking wellness centers, but it was more likely this "campus" took its lead from Google. An administrator—a man who clearly considered any visitor of Ford Robertson Keyes a VIP—took Healey into an office with a floor-to-ceiling ocean view to introduce himself and explain the rules for visitations.

He offered to take Healey to see Ford personally.

At reception, Healey was asked to empty his pockets into a secure locker, to give up his phone and any other electronics. He was briskly and efficiently searched. They walked down three pristine beige marble hallways before going through a set of automated glass doors and into a courtyard with outdoor seating and unlit fire pits.

Ford sat at a fancy bistro table on the wide veranda overlooking the churning waters at the foot of the cliffs below. An eight-foot glass wall separated him from the edge. He wore blue scrubs under a hoodie featuring a stylized Nautilus shell logo on the back. When Healey approached him, he saw the words *Relief, Respite, and Recovery* embroidered beneath it. Ford had what looked like a chai tea latte. Next to that, some chocolate-dipped madeleines were fanned out on a white china plate.

The view was spectacular here too.

The man who'd led him here melted away to give them privacy. The many cameras, with their ever-changing angles, followed their every move, destroying the illusion.

Healey's first thought, despite the monitoring device on Ford's ankle, despite the vacant apathy in Ford's eyes, was how can *I* get a room at this establishment?

Ford didn't rise to greet him. He didn't look up.

In fact, Ford didn't react at all.

That was the final straw. The final insult.

Final, final, *final* . . . and still Healey could not let things go.

Suddenly, like a thunderclap headache or a really bad case of food poisoning, his entire body rebelled against the idea of being here. Nausea roiled in his gut and the bright sun blinded him. Sweat popped out on his forehead and trickled down his neck. Stinging sweat, prickling all along his skin.

He was *exactly* like his dad after all.

He was here to fence with windmills—here because it wasn't in his nature to give up, especially not on a person he cared about. Despite that, despite the sick-making frustration of loving someone who could not love him back, he couldn't simply leave.

What was it going to finally take?

The thing between him and Ford hadn't been romantic love for a long time. Not since the real Ford started bringing randoms home to mess with his head.

Now, it appeared his Ford had left the building entirely.

You couldn't love someone who wasn't there.

Or you could love. *He* did. He still loved Ford. But Ford couldn't love him back even if he wanted to.

Healey sat in the chair opposite Ford, sick with sorrow.

"A plate of cookies . . ." Ford emptied out the pocket of his sleep pants onto the table, studying a pill that clattered on the clean marble surface after he shook it from his hand ". . . three nasty tissues and a risperidone. I think that's what that is. For your thoughts. And don't spare me. I deserve whatever."

"No, you don't." Healey sighed. "Neither of us deserves any of this."

"It's possible I do. Likely, even. I've never been a good person."

"It doesn't work like that." Healey made the familiar argument. Like perfunctory sex, he went through the motions even as Ford sighed. Even as Ford let him explain something Ford lived with every day. "The brain is a fragile ecosystem. The body is a machine. A single cell mutates, and things go wrong. It's not because you're bad. It's not anybody's fault. It just *is*."

"I've been reading the Bible—the New Testament, where Jesus heals the sinners." In the microsecond before he could rein in his thoughts, Healey must have let his true feelings show, because Ford exploded. "Fuck you. Fuck you! You don't know everything."

The cup flew, flinging foamy tea everywhere.

Healey got down to pick up the pieces, and while he did that, he took several deep, calming breaths.

"You're right. I don't know everything. Just because I don't believe, doesn't mean—"

"Don't *handle* me, Healey." Ford put both hands up like claws, as if he was going to spring and rend Healey to bits. "I can't stand it when you do that."

"I'm sorry." Healey clasped his hands together, unafraid. If Ford came at him, he'd deal with it. "I want to thank you for seeing me. I know you didn't want to. I appreciate you letting me come here today."

Ford snorted. "It's not like I had a choice. It was a condition of the... thing. Whatever. They said I had to see you. My lawyers."

Lawyers. Plural. Wow. "Regardless of how it happened, I appreciate it."

"What do you hope to achieve here, Heals?" Ford's eyes narrowed. "You can't save me. You never could."

"No," Healey agreed, "I can't save you."

"Remember when we met?"

"I do." But maybe he didn't.

Was it drum circle, or Quidditch?

Or had Ford just passed by his dorm room and seen him alone and come in? The fact was... he couldn't remember. But Diego—how Diego looked the first time he opened the door to the house that once belonged to Pop—Healey remembered that.

Remembered the shock of recognition. Not that he'd ever seen Diego in his life, but... he remembered feeling like he knew him. Or was it just the house he knew, and now... was he making connections that weren't there? He blinked.

"You've met someone." Ford's words weren't a question. "I can see it all over you. Happiness looks like yellow frosting."

"You're the one I'm holding in my heart right now. You're the one I'm looking at, *right now*. What color frosting is that?"

Ford sighed again. "Blue."

"Make it warmer," Healey begged. "Make it purple. I love you, Ford. I never stopped loving you."

"I don't know what that means."

"That's okay. You don't have to know. What I feel is about me. I *love* you. I will be here for you if you ever need me. If you let me know what I can do..."

Ford blinked his wide brown eyes slowly, disconcertingly. It fell into an eerie cadence. Almost like normal human behavior, it was at the same time decidedly medicated and mechanical.

"What about the yellow-frosting man?"

Healey shrugged. "That's separate. Make my frosting when I'm with you purple, then it can be separate. Different and separate."

"I guess having someone new means you won't blow me anymore." He bit his lip. "Imma miss that."

"Sorry." Healey shook his head. "That's for him now. But love is a separate thing. The love is still yours. I'll never take it away. It's not a resource issue like land or food. The more I give away, the more I'll have to give."

"The gospel according to John... Lennon. My God, Healey." The old Ford made a brief, astounding comeback. "How did we end up here? I'm the smartest kid in coloring class."

Healey had no answers for him. Some mischief made Ford reach out and pluck the pin from Healey's hair.

"That's better. Relax."

"All right." Healey removed his jacket.

"Nice threads."

Healey gave the fabric a rub. "They're Nash's."

Ford snorted. "Pull the other one."

"No, really. This is his. The suit, the shirt, this cuff link." He gestured to the sleeve over his unbroken arm. "My stuff is still—"

"At our place?" Ford winced. "I think Beryl cleaned out our apartment."

That wasn't good. He hoped she'd simply put his things in storage but very much feared she'd tossed them.

"There was nothing there I need right away."

Ford turned his face. "I hate sad things."

"I know." On instinct, Healey took Ford's hand between his.

Ford didn't react. "It was always going to be good-bye between us, wasn't it?"

"I don't know. I guess."

"I thought maybe we should be like Thelma and Louise..."

Healey's turn to blink. "They *died*."

"Spoilers, hello." How did Ford convey such pain with laughter? "*Now* you tell me?"

A long time passed before Healey could make himself speak. "Is that what you wanted?" he asked. "For us to go out in some... blaze of glory?"

"I don't know what I wanted." Ford gave eye roll like a CW network soap star. "I certainly have no idea what I wanted that night. Except... maybe..."

Healey waited. "Yeah?"

"I wanted to believe it wasn't going to end."

"I'm so sorry."

What they'd had was fated to end—no matter what—*before* Ford tried to get them both killed.

But it was over now, sure as fuck.

Healey imagined that kitten monstrosity from the flight down in its white sparkly cat carrier, only marked S's Cat—simultaneously dead and alive.

That's what happens when you drink on the way to visit people in fancy rehab centers.

Ford leaned forward. "If you say one word about Schrödinger's fucking cat, I will call security."

Healey started guiltily. "What?"

"You were thinking it."

"So now you're psychic?" But he had been thinking it. "Okay, fuck, you know me pretty well, don't you?"

"I should think so." Little by little, pressure increased on Healey's hand. "I never wanted to lose my best friend."

"But it's complicated, right?"

Ford nodded. "I'll be here for a while, you know?"

"Yes."

"Did you get your own lawyer?" Ford let go of his hand and folded his neatly, almost primly on the table.

"I have someone helping me out right now."

"Yellow-frosting man?" The blank expression was back in place.

"His stepfather is an attorney. He's going to advise me. I don't know what will happen."

Ford craned his neck first one way, and then the other. Healey recognized the move as a technique he'd learned to weigh his thoughts, rather than blurt out the first thing.

"I'm sorry I broke your phone."

Healey laughed out loud. He couldn't help it. That was not the worst thing that'd happened that night. He had to say it. "You broke a hell of a lot more than my phone."

Ford stood abruptly, folding thin arms over his chest. "I said I was sorry."

"No. I'm sorry. Sit down."

"I broke your arm. I know that. I just—"

"You broke my trust." Healey gritted his teeth. "You broke my heart."

"Not your heart," Ford said woodenly. "That was never really mine."

Healey winced. "Where the hell did the gun come from?"

"I'm not supposed to talk about that."

Visceral, painful emotion always welled up around that fucking gun. Healey's throat tightened just thinking about it. "That was—"

"A deal breaker. I know."

"That was more than a— You— I—" Healey swallowed and tried again. "The pain is gone. But I relive that fucking gun every time I close my eyes."

"Shut up." Ford stepped away to pace back and forth between the posts holding up sections of the glass wall. "I knew. I knew you'd never forgive me for that. Never in a million years."

"Is that why you did it?"

"I have no idea why." Ford turned to him, mouth half open. Maybe it was surprise, or maybe he had a song stuck in his head.

"I guess it doesn't really matter now."

Ford dropped his arms, suddenly, and turned, holding out his hand for a single, awful second. Healey flinched, expecting to see a gun. His heart practically exploded. He tried not to let it show, but he was pretty sure his pulse was rattling like a pressure-cooker top and Ford could see it in his throat.

Fucking nonsense. He blew out a deep breath.

"Good-bye, Healey." Ford waited to shake his hand.

That was a fucking test and you failed.

Healey's heart broke all over again, and he stayed where he was. "Good-bye, Ford."

Without looking back, Ford entered a code on the keypad. He left Healey standing outside, waiting awkwardly for security to notice him there and come let him in.

Fucking Ford. Always had to have the last word, even if it wasn't a fucking word at all. Healey waved his arm toward the camera. He wanted to go back to Bluewater Bay. He wanted to go—

Wait. *Not* home.

Healey wanted to go wherever Diego was going.

CHAPTER FORTY-ONE

HEALEY

The sleek black SUV pulled up in front of the facility. Cameron got out and opened the door for Healey. Diego waited inside with a bottled water for him.

"It's official. I'm a luxury whore." Healey cracked open his water. "Didn't take long for me to abandon my principles, did it?"

"You had principles?"

"At school," Healey said lightly.

"I'm not used to luxury, believe me." Diego picked up a water, then slapped it back into his cup holder. "I didn't grow up with this, you know."

"I know." Healey wondered at the heat in Diego's voice.

"I was embedded with soldiers in Afghanistan. We didn't have executive cars there." Diego picked up his backpack and dug through it. When he found his phone, he thumbed at it for a bit, and then handed it over. "Look. Those are some of the places we called home for months at a time."

Healey looked through picture after picture. Crowded military encampments, soldiers sleeping on mats on dirt floors, men and women digging shitholes with grim affability, convoys of Humvees traveling over endless roads—rutted and pockmarked with potholes and burn marks and shrapnel.

"Wow."

"Just saying . . . it hasn't been all private jets with me."

Healey met Diego's gaze. Where was the resentment coming from? He smoothed Diego's frown lines with his thumb.

"Are you okay?"

With a huff, Diego glanced toward his window. "LA makes me itchy."

"Why didn't you say so?" Healey asked. "You didn't have to come."

"I miss Cecil." Diego keep his face averted. "It was a free ride. What can I say?"

Happiness blossomed under Healey's ribs. "You can say whatever. But I know you're only here because I—I needed you to be here. If it's weak to say that—"

"It's not." Diego turned back. "But I think there are things I need too, so maybe you can help me out with that? Cecil and his fiancée, Rachel, are going to want to know what I've been doing about my mother's papers and photographs, and I'm not sure what to tell them."

"What do they want?"

"We're supposed to be working on some projects together." He pursed his lips. "I'm creating a short documentary."

"Your mother was a photographer?"

"She did everything. Painting, sculpture. Graffiti." Diego let his head fall against the seat cushions. "But if you want to get the real picture of my mom, you have to talk to her students."

"She was a teacher." Healey could see that.

"And a mentor."

"You have pictures of her work?"

Diego's lips twitched. "Google Gabriella Maria Montenegro Luz."

Healey did, and as he scrolled, and scrolled, and scrolled, he was drawn in by playful colors, joyful people. Light that felt like it pierced your heart.

"Those are gorgeous."

"Here. These are my favorites." Diego took Healey's phone and brought up a recent image gallery from one of his mother's last shows. "Mami went through a fascination with doorways just before she passed. Her final works were little jewels."

Healey studied them, miniatures featuring vibrantly colorful doors, cracked open just enough to reveal vividly imagined slices of magical worlds beyond. "How come you don't have one of your mother's paintings hanging in your house?"

"I don't know." Lips pressed into a tight line, Diego shook his head. "It hurts."

The words went straight to Healey's heart. "You have lots of photographs *of* your mother."

"The public Gabbi Luz and my mother were two very different people."

"Tell me something about her?"

"You really want to know?" he asked. "Or is this about making conversation?"

"Of course I want to know." He fussed with his window shade. "Only I don't want to pry."

"My mami was born in LA, but her parents got deported after her dad got busted for a DUI. She was about three then, maybe? Her father had a legit work visa, but it had expired. That's how most illegals get here, by the way. They don't all crawl through some tunnel, and a wall's not going to stop them."

"But being born here," Healey asked. "That makes your mother a US citizen, doesn't it?"

Diego's hard expression said he'd been asked this before. "Yes."

"So when did she come back?"

"She got pregnant with me at fifteen. I guess she talked an old dude into smuggling her into the USA in the trunk of his car. Everything was easier before 9/11."

"Wait—" Healey allowed the reality of that to set in. He did the math. Fifteen. Pregnant. Alone in a new city—a new *country*. "Why the hell—"

"Her parents wanted her to get rid of it—me, I guess," he corrected. "She supposedly told some guy her sob story, and he agreed to help. Maybe that's the sanitized version. One time, I overheard her say the dude who brought her across the border was the frat rat who got her pregnant."

"God." *Shelby* was older than that.

"She was tough. Smart. Didn't take shit from anyone. Or she did, but she kept this"—his gaze drifted to a point over Healey's shoulder—"ledger in her head. Wrongs got righted. She didn't always move in a straight line, but she expected justice when people hurt her."

Diego picked up his phone and thumbed through his image files. "Here." He pulled up a painting that could only be about his accident. She'd re-imagined the crash in her trademark bright colors. The mountain bike, Diego, and his wheelchair, all flying across a cloudless blue sky—flung there from some invisible point of impact. They were being watched over by stylized brown angel, holding an extra pair of wings...

"Holy cow."

"That's Mami for you. She had really unfortunate expressionist tendencies."

"No wonder you're superstitious as all hell."

Diego gave him a shove. "Wait till you get your nipples pierced. I am going to give you such a *pinch*." He sat back and gave his chest a light tap. "I feel my mother here. She's on my mind. Looking over my shoulder. She's talking to me all the time. I don't care whether you believe. I believe."

Healey watched as one after another light cycle passed without more than a single car making it across the intersection. Part of his brain was caught up with traffic solutions, while the other came to a screeching halt with a single, sudden thought. "You want to know the truth?"

"Sure." *That sigh.* Maybe he'd stretched Diego's patience a little thin, what with the science and the five senses and the teasing about superstition.

"It's only sour grapes that make these things so hard for me to believe. I can't remember what my mother looks like. I can't remember her voice. And I wish I could."

Diego's face fell. "I'm so sorry."

"What will it take for you to write that book? Is there anything I can do to help?"

"What do you mean?"

"It makes sense to go backward sometimes. I went home after my accident. I went to ground in the last place where I felt safe."

"I can relate to that."

"But didn't you do the opposite?" Healey preempted the argument he saw building in Diego's eyes. "No. Hear me out."

Terse nod.

"Didn't you do exactly the opposite? Didn't you leave the place where you grew up? Your family is here in Los Angeles. All your touchstones are here. They must be. You put the photographs you're talking about in a room you couldn't even reach—"

"I don't know where you're going with this, but I have doctors for it—"

"It was an observation," Healey admitted. "I can't go anywhere with it. It's not really any of my business."

This time it was Diego's turn to frown. Neither of them spoke for a while. Not until Healey saw the low curtain of clouds meet the blue-green water of the Pacific ocean in the distance.

Diego leaned forward to speak to the driver. "Could you pull into the parking lot of Gladstones for me?"

Healey glanced at him with some surprise. "Are we making an unscheduled seafood stop?"

"Didn't you read your texts? We're meeting Rachel and Cecil here for dinner later. I'd like to talk for a few minutes first. Do you mind?"

Something in Diego's manner worried Healey. Cameron pulled into the restaurant's parking lot, curved around, and parked. While they watched, he stopped by the kiosk to talk to the parking lot attendant. Healey got out and waited for Diego.

In the background, surf rushed against the cliffs. Gulls wheeled overhead. If Healey closed his eyes, he could almost feel sand between his toes.

Was this the point at which Diego was going to say they came from different worlds? That they wanted different things?

Diego stared out over the railing. "I *was* trying to bury the past."

Healey nodded, not trusting himself to speak.

"And you just kept picking and picking at it—"

"I literally dragged it out of your attic," Healey supplied. "But you never really wanted to forget."

"No," Diego admitted. "The past is part of the story. You can't just start anywhere you want, you know?"

"I know." Healey's heart sank.

"I need to go back all the way. Not just to my beginnings, but to my mother's. I need to find out who my mother really was. I need to help Cecil and Rachel honor her memory. Can you understand that?"

Healey heard the words but didn't quite comprehend what they meant. They'd come to Los Angeles in order for Healey to get closure with Ford. Whatever happened after, whatever those dickheads and their lawyers threw at him, whatever Cecil said, whatever happened in court, he now understood that what he'd really come for was to end things with Ford so he could *start* something with Diego.

It looked like Diego wanted time, as well. It sounded like he was asking for the chance to put his past behind him before starting his future too.

Healey could hardly blame him for that. "I understand."

But where did that leave *them*?

"My mother's life, her 'journey' for lack of a better word, is topical right now."

"I'll say." With anti-immigrant sentiment on the rise all over the world—even in the so-called American melting pot—it could hardly be more topical.

"I'm torn." Diego glanced up at him, and then back toward the ocean. "I could cobble together a nice presentation of pictures and art, and call it done. But there's a longer, deeper story there. A good story. And I want to tell it from start to finish. It's a much bigger project than anyone anticipates. A novel. A full-length documentary. I'd need to crowdfund it. I'd need—"

"How can I help?" Healey's heart filled with unexpected things. Admiration, chief among them. If Diego wanted to dig deep into his mother's past, if he was willing to face his own past with that kind of unflinching courage, Healey wanted to help.

"God. You are so—" Diego broke off with a laugh.

"What?"

"This shit terrifies me. How can you always be all like, '*Allons-y*, Alonso! Mush. Let's go.' You're always ready to lead the charge, so confident. So—"

"I'm privileged." Healey nudged Diego when he glanced away. "Don't say you weren't thinking it."

Diego nodded. "I wasn't."

"Like hell."

Diego grunted. "A'ight."

"Because it's true. I mean, I'd be crazy to think otherwise. Shelby pointed out a long time ago that, despite being in the queer minority, I'm able and male and white. I might *feel* isolated or oppressed because back in the day I couldn't marry or serve in the military. But if I wanted to *hide* my otherness, I could do anything I choose. I could easily pass for straight. I could enjoy my privilege and suck cock too."

Diego's brows rose. "Your little sister said that?"

"I blame Tumblr." Healey followed the progress of a pigeon that decided since Diego was sitting down he must have food. "But at the same time, I'm kind of awed by how painfully perceptive her observation was."

"I want to meet her."

"I'd love for her to meet you." Healey's heart was so full, he couldn't help but smile.

Diego smiled back, and it looked dopey and totally wrong on him. And sincere.

Completely sincere.

"So..." Diego gave him a little pinch. "Instead of a hundred things you could say about a creative endeavor that could cost a fortune, take the better part of a year, and ultimately, be a total failure, you ask, 'How can I help?'"

Healey resettled the pin in his hair. Charging ahead was always easier when his hair was secure.

"I'm in. What do you need me to do?"

"Just like that?" Diego asked.

"Name it." Healey cupped Diego's strong, solid jaw between his hands. "I'm *in*."

Diego's lips twitched with mirth, maybe. Emotion, possibly.

He didn't answer right away, and Healey wondered how much more anticipation his heart could stand.

Diego turned and kissed the palm of Healey's hand.

"Have you ever been to Jalisco? That's where they make tequila."

"Oh." Healey pressed his forehead to Diego's. "I like this plan already."

EPILOGUE
HEALEY

Healey stepped through the French doors, leaving the heated, candlelit house. Cecil's back yard was huge. A hundred thousand fairy lights winked in the trees. A million more points of light twinkled from the city beyond. In the shadows at the far end of the property, Diego sat gazing into a koi pond. He held his camera idle in his lap.

The ceremony was supposed to start in five, but of course, Diego lingered in the quiet, keeping his thoughts to himself—which, granted, looked like a pretty great idea. But if Healey couldn't get out of this, then Diego couldn't. It was Diego's family after all.

Tables had been set up on the lawn and cater waiters were putting the finishing touches on Cecil and Rachel's wedding dinner. The pool was glowing with submersible lights, full of little flower islands with flameless candles inside acrylic hurricane lanterns.

Diego was a genius. Inside, there was nothing but human chaos. Out here Healey could think. He could even see some stars. Still, a promise was a promise. Healey flexed his fingers—his arm ached from the cold since he'd broken it. He shrugged the pain off.

"I think Cecil is starting to get a little worried you won't show."

"I'm right here. How can I not show?" Diego glanced up, caught sight of Healey's formalwear, and opened his mouth to speak. Then he closed it.

How disappointing.

"You've got nothing?" Healey twirled, causing the sharp pleats in his kilt to flip dangerously. "You have nothing to say to me right now? This is the real thing. Spenser got them for us. All the Holly men have them now, they're official."

"Nash wears it?" Diego asked, incredulously.

"I can neither confirm nor—"

Diego's laugh was sharp. "Man's gotta pick his battles, I guess."

Healey leaned over Diego with his hand cupped to his ear. "I didn't quite hear you? Are you saying you don't like my nice outfit?"

Healey loved the look on Diego's face. It said, *Holy shit*. And, *What the actual fuck?* and more pathetically, *Are you really going to make me say it?*

He smiled down at the man he'd come to depend on in so many, many ways...

And let Diego off the hook. "You're going to blow a gasket if you don't let yourself have a good laugh at my chicken legs."

"Who says I'm laughing?"

God, the man had eyelashes for miles ... and no. That wasn't laughter Healey saw in Diego's expression. It was heat and desire. It was longing for this—this *something* they were defining together.

An unaccustomed shyness struck him. "You like?"

"Oh, yeah." Diego's hot gaze devoured Healey while he cupped the back of his bare thighs, sliding up, and up. "What is not to ... like....?"

"You're about to prove all those nothing-under-the-kilt rumors true. Conclusively."

"Easy access. Me like." Diego grinned wolfishly.

"Whoops." Healey leaped when Diego got his fingers involved.

"I could really dig this. Wow." Diego groaned. "First time I've had a distinct advantage because I'm seated."

Healey quirked an eyebrow in disbelief. "First time?"

Diego flushed.

Probably, he was remembering the massive shower in Cecil's guest suite. Or all those times that tooth-brushing and shaving in Diego's big bathroom gave way to blowjobs and fucking and more. Was it Healey's fault his dick was always bobbing inches away from Diego's face?

They'd ordered toys together online. For a straight couple, that'd be like buying a house. Now, Healey was thinking the sorts of stupid thoughts that moonlight and roses and candles make a man think. He looked at Diego, who looked back at him as if he'd never seen him before.

"What?" Healey patted his jacket, his belt, his sporran. He twisted to check as much of his ass as he could. "Do I have visible panty lines?"

Diego smacked him. "Wouldn't you need *visible panties* for that?"

"Ah." Healey went along with the gag, but added, "Don't be cryptic."

"I was thinking about midnight."

"You worried I'll try to kiss you in front of your whole family?"

Diego stopped, turned his chair, and rolled into the light. "Do you really think that?"

Healey shook his head. "No."

"Healey, I *expect* you to kiss me up in front of all my relatives."

"Of course you do." But Nash was the brave one. He was the in-your-face Holly twin. Healey was more circumspect—not shy, but not entirely public. Not since Ford, certainly, and not ever, if he'd had a choice in the matter. Healey guessed they'd find balance there too, eventually...

Saying good-bye had helped him let go of some of those other Ford things too. Each piece, each memory, glittered sharp as a shard of glass under his skin. He unearthed them painfully. Quietly.

Diego had his own memories.

Diego offered wisdom or silence. Both helped. They shared the ride, the workload, the storms, the sunrises, and the nights when sex between them was as fierce and filthy and treacherous as the currents in the sound. When passion held them under the surface of their pettiness and ground them down and refined them.

Like life.

"You'd better come in." Healey stepped back, so Diego could precede him over the path. Healey followed, less aware of his own footsteps than the sounds of Diego's wheels.

The ceremony started on time. The music began. The lights dimmed.

Healey's breath caught when Diego took his place beside his stepdad. His black tuxedo, white formal shirt, and red-and-gold patterned tie were elegant and understated. He looked so fucking hot.

Diego had let Healey tie his shoe laces. He was not getting enough of that anytime soon. Kneeling. Performing any tiny little act of kindness, of service—any of the few offers of help Diego allowed—was only possible because Healey finally admitted he wanted it.

He'd asked permission to do it again, and that one little gesture—the symbol of all the give and take between them, placing a kiss on the tops of his feet afterward and then buffing his lip prints off the too-shiny surface—was a compromise, rather than a sacrifice on his part. Diego ruffled his hair when he did it. It was an invocation. A benediction.

Healey could admit that much, at least.

The wedding march began. Rachel entered with her eldest son, Ricky. He was handsome, half-Tongan, half-Mexican, built like an ox with thick curly hair. He was beautiful, the men were all beautiful, yet to Healey's eyes, there was no one but Diego.

Someday, Healey fully expected to get an invitation to Nash and Spencer's wedding. Pop raised them to do the traditional thing. Even if Pop didn't plan to marry again, he'd always urged both him and Nash to start families of their own. To have kids, if they wanted, and it stood to reason Nash would go first. Nash was always first through the airlock. Whether he was stepping in to console his twin when their mother died, or stepping *up* to support his dad when Shelby was injured, Nash had the quickest reaction time. And despite the fact that his extended family took up every available space in an admittedly immense house, it looked like Diego was the type to put family first too.

Maybe that's why they worked?

Healey glanced up and found Diego watching him. The lady in front of him shifted, blocking Healey's view for several irritating seconds. When she moved back, and Healey caught sight of Diego again—oh, how he wished he had his camera.

Diego sat, chin lifted, watching Rachel and Cecil exchange vows. They obviously shared a deep and genuine love. Diego watched with such hope. With naked longing. In that moment, he was the image of his mother, whom Healey had now seen in countless film clips and photographs. Whom he'd heard about in dozens of interviews. Whom he felt he almost knew, through the devotion of her son.

I love him.

The thought was as startling as any he'd ever had. It came as a quiet epiphany, like the intuitive leaps that are sometimes necessary for great problem-solving—

Someone tapped on his shoulder. Frowning, he turned, but whoever it was, no one was looking at him now. Maybe some kid had let a Jordan almond fly.

I love him, was where he'd been when he was so rudely interrupted. The idea made him shiver. A delightful wave of roses and orange blossoms went by with the bride as she and the rest of the wedding party made their way to the yard.

Although there were professional videographers as well as still photographers on hand, he knew Diego wanted to take pictures of the family later. Healey was expected to be in them. Apparently, news of their couplehood had made the Feliz Navi-Dad(!) newsletter. He'd even been featured prominently in some of the Christmas pictures. Diego's family was like a colony of space aliens, complete with a hive mind. Resistance was futile. Healey didn't even fight it anymore. His new plan? Give Diego a lap dance he'd never forget, take him to bed, and remind him that keeping an ingenious guy like Healey around had an upside.

Dinner was being catered by El Cholo, served family style. Big vats of rice and refried beans, tamales, carnitas and carne asada, chicken mole. Everything melted in his mouth.

Diego had ditched his jacket and tie somewhere and rolled up his sleeves. They sat together at the family table, laughing, talking. Leaning over and taking whatever liberties they wanted, because champagne melted away Healey's inhibitions and sweetened his disposition.

"We're drinking champagne all the time from now on." Healey whispered the words.

Diego lifted his napkin to his lips. "You think it's the wine?"

"What else?" Healey teased.

Diego ran his thumb over Healey's lip. "I forgot what it's like to think about the future. This feels . . . good."

"Maybe that's why people hold weddings," Healey offered. "To reaffirm life."

Diego laced their fingers together. "It's sex that does that. We could reaffirm life later."

"I'm down." Healey's breath caught.

Diego shook his head slowly. "I think your family may be more optimistic about the future than mine. Your dad could fall out of a plane and be totally 'Hey, I'm okay so far!' on the way down."

Healey had to laugh, 'cause... yeah. Wow. "Very true."

"But that's good." Diego squeezed Healey's hand. "That's good. Optimists should be like... sacred or something. You guys are blessed. You guys just gotta each stick with a realist. Buddy system, you know. You gotta stick with me..."

Healey noticed the little catch in Diego's voice, and turned to meet his gaze. His gorgeous, unfathomable eyes glittered with unshed tears.

His own voice was hoarse when he replied. "Hell yeah."

"My mami was like you." Diego rubbed at a spot just above his piercing. "She wasn't easy."

"No." Healey's voice came out funny. "Doesn't sound like she was."

"But wherever she went, she made things happen. You know what I mean? She could find the most interesting thing about a total stranger and magnify it. She made people feel good about themselves. She rejected authority. She lit things on fire just to watch them burn."

Healey winced. "As a physicist, I plan to err on the side of caution."

"You know what I mean. Most people just march in line, point A to point B. It takes someone like Mami to blaze a new path. Someone like your pop. Outside-the-box thinkers. People who try new things. These are difficult times. It's okay to be scared, but it's not okay to quit."

"So, we're going to spend the next six months on the road making an expensive documentary film because you finally admit your mom was cool?"

"Hello, *I got a grant*. If we're super careful, it might last the whole first week."

"I can strip for cash, if you need me to. Wasn't there a movie like that?"

"Sorry." Diego leaned over and gave his cheek a quick kiss. "Your stripping contract was exclusive. Didn't you read the fine print?"

The back of Healey's neck heated. "Exclusive?"

"You want to share me?" Diego asked.

"No." The wallop of rage that hit Healey's gut did not lie. "No. Nope, *nyet, non.* Iie."

"Okay. I guess you don't like the idea of sharing me."

Healey showed his teeth. "I do not."

"So." Diego shrugged. "I guess that makes me your man."

"Yeah it does." Healey glanced around. "Hell yeah it does. You are *my* man."

"And that makes you my boy."

"Wait—" Healey's smile flatlined. "How come I'm your boy, but you're my man?"

"It's just an expression."

Glasses clinked again, while they argued playfully. The orchestra played "My Heart Will Go On" and the children ran unsupervised with sparklers—which, nobody asked Healey, but seriously he could see a whole lot of problems with that.

At midnight, they kissed while fireworks exploded overhead. Instead of cordite and ozone, the scent of orange blossoms teased Healey again. He glanced at the centerpiece, which featured a puff of hydrangeas in a white ceramic bowl, then at his plate. Flourless chocolate cake with a raspberry coulis...

"Do you smell orange blossoms?" He had to shout over the noise to be heard.

Diego narrowed his eyes. "What?"

"I smell orange blossoms." Oh god. Healey'd forgotten the *connotation* of the flower. Orange blossoms were for brides. "That's not a metaphor or anything. I actually smell it."

Diego froze then relaxed and gave him a wistful, wide white smile. "Cali used to be one big orange grove."

Duh. "I know."

"They're everywhere." He pointed out the rows of neatly pruned fruit trees. "Tangerines, grapefruit, oranges. My stepdad makes marmalade for Valentine's Day."

"Of course he does." Cecil was a man of weirdly specific talents.

"So eat your cake." Diego winked. "You'll need your strength later."

If there was an extra little twinkle in his eye—if a stray but very visible bit of sentimentality got caught there—Healey wasn't about to mention it.

Healey's smile started somewhere behind his heart. It was slow to bloom, but when it finally burst, sheer happiness washed over him.

As a physicist, he calculated his joy had to be affecting everyone in a five-mile radius...

Healey forked up a bite and offered it to Diego first.

"You seem awful sure of things."

"I'm sure of myself." Diego positively set Healey on fire by lipping the cake off his fork. "Want to come along for the ride?"

Healey made Diego wait for his answer. Kissed him so he could share the rich, spicy chocolate flavor of his dessert while at the same time getting a little payback for the uncertain moments Diego'd put him through when they met. But then Diego's question had held just a little more apprehension than Healey liked. Did he not know how Healey felt by now? *Silly man.*

They'd have to work on that.

"Was that a yes?" Diego ground the words out.

"Nope." Healey cupped Diego's face between his palms. "It was a *hell, yes.*"

EXPLORE MORE OF BLUEWATER BAY

Starstruck
L.A. Witt

There's Something About Ari
L.B. Gregg

Hell on Wheels
Z.A. Maxfield

Lone Wolf
*Aleksandr Voinov and
L.A. Witt*

The Burnt Toast B&B
*Heidi Belleau and
Rachel Haimowitz*

Lights, Camera, Cupid!
A Valentine's Day collection

Wedding Favors
Anne Tenino

The Deep of the Sound
Amy Lane

When to Hold Them
G.B. Gordon

Rain Shadow
L.A. Witt

Stuck Landing
Lauren Gallagher

How the Cookie Crumbles
Jaime Samms

Selfie
Amy Lane

All the Wrong Places
Ann Gallagher

Bluewater Blues
G.B. Gordon

No Small Parts
Ally Blue

For a Good Time, Call . . .
Anne Tenino and E.J. Russell

Get a Grip
L.A. Witt

For more, visit:
riptidepublishing.com/titles/universe/bluewater-bay

Dear Reader,

Thank you for reading Z.A. Maxfield's *All Wheel Drive*!

We know your time is precious and you have many, many entertainment options, so it means a lot that you've chosen to spend your time reading. We really hope you enjoyed it.

We'd be honored if you'd consider posting a review—good or bad—on sites like **Amazon, Barnes & Noble, Kobo, Goodreads, Twitter, Facebook, Tumblr**, and your blog or website. We'd also be honored if you told your friends and family about this book. Word of mouth is a book's lifeblood!

For more information on upcoming releases, author interviews, blog tours, contests, giveaways, and more, please sign up for our weekly, spam-free newsletter and visit us around the web:

Newsletter: tinyurl.com/RiptideSignup
Twitter: twitter.com/RiptideBooks
Facebook: facebook.com/RiptidePublishing
Goodreads: tinyurl.com/RiptideOnGoodreads
Tumblr: riptidepublishing.tumblr.com

Thank you so much for Reading the Rainbow!

RiptidePublishing.com

ALSO BY Z.A. MAXFIELD

Hell on Wheels (a *Bluewater Bay* story)
Home the Hard Way
I'll Be There (in the *Lights! Camera! Cupid!* anthology)
Lost and Found
Crossing Borders
Drawn Together
Family Unit
ePistols At Dawn
The Pharaoh's Concubine
Rhapsody for Piano and Ghost
Gasp!
My Cowboy Heart
My Heartache Cowboy
My Cowboy Homecoming
My Cowboy Promises
My Cowboy Freedom

Blue Fire
Fugitive Color
Through the Years
Stirring Up
All Stirred Up
Grime and Punishment
Grime Doesn't Pay
Deep Desire
Deep Deception
Deep Deliverance
St. Nacho's
Physical Therapy
Jacob's Ladder
The Book Of Daniel
A Picture Perfect Christmas
I Heard Him Exclaim
Secret Light
What Child Is This?

ABOUT THE AUTHOR

Z.A. Maxfield started writing in 2007 on a dare from her children and never looked back.

Pathologically disorganized, and perennially optimistic, she writes as much as she can, reads as much as she dares, and enjoys her time with family and friends.

Three things reverberate throughout all her stories: Unconditional love, redemption, and the belief that miracles happen when we least expect them. If anyone asks her how a wife and mother of four can find time for a writing career, she'll answer, "It's amazing what you can accomplish if you give up housework."

Readers can visit ZAM at zamaxfield.com, Facebook, Twitter, or Tumblr.

Enjoy more stories like *All Wheel Drive* at RiptidePublishing.com!

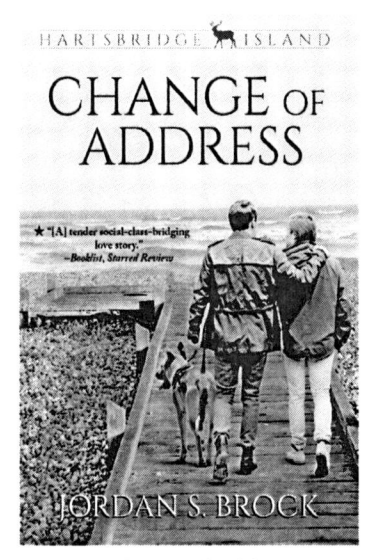

Change of Address
ISBN: 978-1-62649-464-0

Illumination
ISBN: 978-1-62649-051-2

Earn Bonus Bucks!

Earn 1 Bonus Buck for each dollar you spend. Find out how at RiptidePublishing.com/news/bonus-bucks.

Win Free Ebooks for a Year!

Pre-order coming soon titles directly through our site and you'll receive one entry into a drawing for a chance to win free books for a year! Get the details at RiptidePublishing.com/contests.

RIPTIDE PUBLISHING

CPSIA information can be obtained
at www.ICGtesting.com
Printed in the USA
LVOW07s1435091217
559215LV00003B/555/P